BEHOLD
THE
SINS

RACHEL SERRIN

Behold the Sins
Published by Serrin Press Copyright © 2021 by Rachel Serrin

ISBN Paperback: 9781736988022

ISBN Hardcover: 9781736988008

To those who, after all of the battles,
found a home within their mind.

Keep going. Keep breathing.
You are loved.

TABLE OF CONTENTS

Author's Note

The manifestation of this story in my brain was the equivalent of getting rammed by a semi-truck while rollerblading down a freeway. Painful. Disastrous. Life-changing. Monumental.

Although, that experience didn't actually happen to me. It's fiction. Just like this story. Everything you're about to read was ultimately my way of processing life, its issues, my religious background, romance, relationships, trauma, and the world we live in. The subconscious breeds creativity in a way none of us can truly perceive. I still continue to look back on the four years of writing these worlds with surprise and wonder.

Within these worlds, and in my mind, everyone is accepted and loved, but that doesn't mean there aren't severe exploitations that should not be addressed. Every issue in this book connects in one way, or another, to a real-world conflict that exists today. Conflicts that are not fiction, but are violations of basic human rights. Equality, love, recognition, compassion, and activism are necessary to heal the fractures brought upon by colonization, exploitation, ignorance, and ultimately, the sins we have committed as humanity. So, when you close this book, I beg of you to take a stand in any way, for those who remain oppressed, dismantled, and prejudiced.

With that being said, I am unfathomably grateful for your decision to read this book and your support of an independent author. Make sure to look in the mirror and say 'I love you' to yourself, name three things you're grateful for, and, of course, drink your water.

Trigger Warnings:
Abuse (Physical, Mental, Emotional, Verbal, Sexual)
Thoughts & Contemplation of Suicide
Death
Mental Illness
Cannibalism
Human Trafficking
Forced Prostitution
Sexual Content
Violence
Mentions of Genocide

CALESAL

The Wall

Emperor's Mansion

Arvalo's Tower

Jack Marin's Penthouse

NORTH

Platech Industries

Glide Train

Trollova Bridge

MID

The Aariva

FACTORY DISTRICT

Indira Apothecary   The Mondar Lion

Jenkins' Apartment

The Sins Screen   SOUTH

Southers Square

GOVERNMENT SECTOR

Trollova River

N

0   5
Miles

2022

PART I
THE FALL

1

The Party

The air always tasted horrible on Sins Eve.

As she had dealt with it for nineteen years, Violet thought she would be used to the choking dust that rose from the windstorms outside the walls, or the cracked skin on her lips where her breath wheezed from the drought in the air. The whole city of Calesal would feel it as the Sins drew near—less than a day away now. A reminder that if no bodies were sent into the portal at this time, every year, that if the bowl wasn't filled with blood, their walled world would succumb to the curse.

To death.

There wasn't enough water to quench the insistent thirst, so she resorted to shiva instead. Even in this club, the air cloyed the same as it did in the streets. Sweet, dusty, and thick. The liquor burned her throat as she leaned against the metal balcony and watched the thick crowd of Midians below. Bodies grinding, hazy smoke, the shouting voices and smiles of those untouched by the Sins. Plasmic lights danced above as the crowd did, tossing and morphing into neon shades of blue, purple, orange, pink, and red.

Violet sipped from the bottle she had swiped from the club's backroom stock, groaning again as she wheezed another breath. She hated it. Hated everything about the reminder of the game. Tomorrow seventy candidates will have their hands slashed. Tomorrow they will enter the Sky Arch for exile. Tomorrow—

tomorrow—everything about this world, their walled city, will be all but a memory.

She rolled her shoulders and tipped the bottle up.

Through the smoke, her eyes caught the blue-collared suspect below. For the past hour she had watched him schmooze with women, take shots at the bar, and wipe his nose an uncanny amount of times. Her target was the most boring man in all of existence, but as long as she watched and planned her opportunity, she could freely indulge without the prospect of Mai breathing down her neck during another job.

Blue-Collar smiled at a woman, clinked his glass with hers, and then continued on, until the maze of lights lost him from Violet's sight.

She sighed and leaned back, not caring.

Tonight she shouldn't have cared, but Mai needed a runner, and her incessant obsession with Violet had made Mai decide she was the one for the job.

Violet locked eyes with another one of Mai's runners on the balcony across. He blended with the shadows, and she just barely caught the warning shake of his head. *Tran? Toni? Tod?* She lifted the bottle to him, offering, but he went back to search for his own target.

Blue-Collar was back on the move, expression sobered as he headed for the door.

"Skiv." Violet rolled her eyes. "The safe exit is the other way."

Regardless, she said goodbye to her bottle with another long sip, placed it on the grate, and disappeared into the shadows of the rafters, down the ladder, and into the long service hallway bustling with workers.

She dodged trays with a bored look, but a smile curled as she caught Blue-Collar beelining for the service exit, a lit smoke between his pale lips. Underneath his shirt, there was a gardia mark tattooed on his upper arm—for which gang, she didn't know. There were five main gangs in the city, some under the City Commanders and other public figures, but that was Mai's assignment to figure it out. Well, now Violet's, since Mai couldn't be bothered to show up.

The job was typical. Find the target, identify the gardia mark, snatch a specified item to prove it, and drop it off to the leader.

Violet hadn't been able to say no and rip up the note of details like she'd wanted to. She needed to afford Meema's elderly home fee for the next month.

"I'll take that." She grabbed a tray of drinks, and hating the lack of movement this worker's uniform gave her, she winked at the surprised servant. "What table?"

He narrowed his eyes on her. "Forty-two."

"They need you in the private rooms, something about the host wanting a better bubbly krinder. He knows we are being cheap."

The man paled. "Really?"

"*Really*," said Violet, as her eyes caught Blue-Collar and the smoke that followed him. "They're pretty mad. Better run."

The servant's eyes watered, and he shoved past Violet in panic, nearly spilling a drink onto her.

"Rude," she muttered.

Blue-Collar looked back once, hand on the knob of the back door. Violet lifted the tray to hide her face. Through the warped glass, Blue-Collar exhaled sharply and exited. She followed him right out.

The sirens and muffled club music assaulted her. In the back alley, little light shined down amidst the trash and empty liquor bottles. A group of Midian men laughed in their crisp white shirts as they moved out of the alley and down the club street. One of them wiped at his nose.

She frowned.

When the door slammed, Blue-Collar sighed and leaned against the brick wall, blowing out smoke from his cig.

"You should really count the seconds it takes for you to walk through a door," Violet said as she angled the tray so the drinks spilled off and crashed to the ground.

He whirled on her. "What—?"

She slammed the tray into his face. Blood sprayed from his nose, the crunch telling her it was hard enough, and he slumped to the ground. She threw the tray to the side, letting it clatter amidst the vibrant sounds of Calesal's Sins Eve celebrations.

"Because if it doesn't slam seconds after you open it, that means someone followed you." She drew out her dagger and slashed at his right arm, parting the blue material. The red tattoo glared at her, a mess of snakes and arrows and roaring water, all encompassed in a circle.

A mark she had seen many times. A mark, if she hadn't been slightly inebriated, she might have reacted poorly to.

She plucked the silver watch from his wrist.

Blue-Collar was unconscious when she righted him up against the wall. She snatched the smoke from his hand and took a long drag. "Thank you for making my night easy, you skiv."

She pounded on the door until another servant poked his head out. She stepped right up, blocking the servant's vision of the unconscious man.

"What are you—?"

"I was having a light and the door shut on me." She shoved past the servant. "Thanks."

Unlike Blue-Collar, she shut the door behind her.

When she walked into the club, she straightened her long-sleeve, black server shirt. Her brown hair—high-ponytail braid, shaved underside for the incessantly sweaty city—swayed as she nodded to the thumping bass and passed between the onslaught of bodies. Smoke in her mouth, dodging every drunken patron, the blurring effects of shiva in her mind. She frowned, looking up to the metal rafters where her abandoned bottle would be.

But she straightened, dropped her butted smoke in a stray drink, and dove into the crowd.

She had a mission.

She grabbed a shiny bracelet there, another watch here, and then her eyes caught a massive, funny-looking ring on a long-ponytailed man. She knocked into his glass. It shattered to the floor.

He whirled on her.

"Oh skies! I'm so sorry!" She fussed with the stain on his shirt, yanking at the ring and slipping it into her pocket. "I'm so sorry I'm clumsy."

The man frowned at her apology. "Are you working?"

"I definitely just got fired." She smiled then darted into the crowd.

The clothes of the Midians surrounding her were always a bit of a shock. Dressy clothes bought for a simple night out, strong cologne, painted nails, and of course, the jewels.

The Mid—where this club was—acted as a barrier between the rich and skyrise-filled North, and the crumbling, drug and blood-stained streets of the South.

"Violet."

She blinked, almost thought she misheard her name within the loud room, but still she turned.

And Kole stood there.

An undignified groan left her. Of *course.*

Kole blinked down at her, deep brown, single-lid eyes flashing. His finger reached to brush her neck and she hastily jerked back away from his touch.

"What—why are you here? What is on your skin?" His pale skin gleamed with the hint of sweat, black hair gelled back.

She wiped at her neck, the tinge of red now staining her fingertip. *Oh. Blood.* "Just a pomegranate drink someone spilled on me."

"Oh," he said, stepping close amidst the grinding bodies. "But what are you doing here?"

"Nothing that concerns you." She tried to turn, but he pulled her back.

Her gut clenched at the contact, a shudder running through her. She yanked her arm out of his grip and he winced. "Sorry, I forgot—"

"You can't know I'm here," she said.

The light caught a slash of his cheekbone. Her eyes involuntarily dropped to his lips as he opened them. "Well, I was surprised to see you and you're wearing that. I'm fairly certain you don't work here..." He sighed. "I've been trying to reach you. You haven't been at your apartment—" She had been, she was just ignoring him. "—and I was thinking that our last night together didn't go so well—"

It *did*, but he just had feelings. Whereas she wouldn't know what feelings were if she choked on them like she choked on his—

He dipped his head in. "You can talk to me, you know. I do care about you, even if you don't want to hear it. But I do, and I just want you to feel alright given the Bloodswearing Ceremony tomorrow and what happened to your brother..." He trailed off as he caught her glare, wincing again. "I just want to make sure you're okay. Even if it is super strange that you're here."

Strange was Kole's innocent word. To any other Midian or Elite, her being here was not possible. She shouldn't have been let in. Only her little gardia job got her in the backdoor of this private party.

She expected her heart to lurch at his words, twist, feel something. But when Kole looked at her with those puppy dog eyes, nothing erupted in her chest. It was always the same. Numb. Pained. Nothing but that lingering grief.

Like he really did mean what he said and wanted to prove it to her, but all it ever did was truth-slap her with a cold reminder that she came from the harsh, poor part of the city and he stood on some platform high above her because of his parents. He didn't know her life—how a Souther lived. He didn't know how much distance was between them even if they had shared a bed.

Even if she did take his virginity.

She cringed at the thought and looked away. Meeting him months ago at one of these parties and agreeing to a fully paid dinner had been her downfall. *Damn* her mooching.

His hand brushed her skin, face yearning for her to suddenly spill all her deepest desires and throw herself in his arms.

She stepped back. "I have to go."

She did. She could feel Mai's hot anger permeating the room.

His face fell, but still nothing jabbed at her heart. It remained cold and empty, embracing that grief, sneering at anything else that attempted to slide in.

"Okay," he said, words lingering on his lips.

"You *promise* to leave and not follow me, right?" she asserted.

"The South doesn't bother me."

"You've hardly been there," she said, stepping away. "You don't need to lie to me. This is not the night for it." *It's not the night for feelings. Or getting tangled in the sheets.* "Promise me that once I'm through the door, you'll go right back to your friends and party on Sins Eve like you're supposed to. Okay?"

"Vi—"

"Promise me," she gritted out.

He finally sighed. "Fine. I promise."

"Good."

His expression flashed—hurt, concern, yearning. He leaned in, hesitated, and then continued with his motion, kissing her on the cheek before brushing past her and disappearing into the crowd.

His kiss burned like one of Calesal's hottest days. She refrained from rubbing it off.

Now, within that numbness, she felt guilt. It roiled through her stomach like nausea. She needed a bottle, needed something to swallow it down. Down, down, down, down...

A glimmer caught her eye. A golden ring with a huge ruby stacked into it. On a tall, lean, deliciously handsome, warm-brown-skinned man at that.

She slipped toward him. He threw his head back, dark curls glimmering in the light. Laughed. She grasped the ring—

He whirled like a blur, hand wrapping around her wrist. He lifted it and a look of surprise flashed over his face as she pinched the ring between her fingers.

His eyes met hers—a green so bright and startling that she nearly choked on her breath. Green like the forests painted on the walls of her old school. Green like the tufts of grass she collected and watched wither. Green like life—like the freedom she desperately craved and hated how it taunted.

She recognized the carved jaw and sinful eyes, but in the shock of it all, she couldn't put a name on her tongue.

The surprise on his face lasted long enough that one of his friends nudged him.

The man held a hand up, eyes dancing over her, studying her. He didn't so much as blink at the ring.

"You," he said, "have a death wish."

A body sidled up behind her and something sharp poked into her spine. She jostled forward, but a strong arm wrapped her waist and pinned her to the dagger.

"Just tell me when," was all the voice said.

The man tilted his head. "Ashan, you don't need to be so aggressive with my thief."

"I mistook you for someone else," blurted Violet. "Take it."

One of the man's friends reached for the ring, while other fingers enclosed her elbow.

The man rolled his eyes, annoyance in his voice. "If one of you touches her, you won't see the rising sun ever again. Ashan, no more murders tonight."

Faces paled. Violet trembled.

Ashan backed away from her. The others gave space, until it was only the man's hand gracing her wrist. His face slid into a charming, dimpled smile. He used his other hand to slide the ring on her finger. "Keep it. By tomorrow I will have no use for it."

He lightened his grip, but never let go.

Violet yanked her arm away and swiftly turned. But before she could take a step, that man's silky voice followed her. "Not the way I expected to meet you, Violet Sutton. But regardless..."

She reeled on him.

A knowing smile pulled at his lips. "I will tell your brother you say hello."

Before she could open her mouth or fling a fist into his beautiful face, Mai stomped up through the crowd and gave the man the most hateful, seething look.

The tension stifled. Mai death-glared the man, while the man promised something worse than death right back.

"We are going, *now*," Mai snarled, grabbing Violet's wrist so tight that Violet gasped.

Violet followed, unable to shape words. Stunned.

As Mai gripped her arm, she turned back to find the man watching her leave, hands in his pockets and a bittersweet look on his face, while his comrades gawked around him.

2

SNAPPED

MAI TURNED HEADS. Not because she was stunning. Or beautiful. Or pretty.

She *was* those things. At least Violet had thought so when she'd first met the daughter of Arvalo—the City Commander of Plastech—two years ago and shared her bed.

No, Mai turned heads because when her anger went unchecked, nearly everyone within a mile radius could feel the scalding rage radiating off her.

White skin, long, inky hair until mid-back, and wide-set, single-lid eyes that glared at each passerby down the busy street. Violet always wondered if Mai was just a plasbomb wrapped in flesh. But she'd seen Mai's blood. Heard her moans. A strange humanness that confused Violet because she was also certain that if she cracked an egg on Mai's skin, it would cook to a perfect sunny-side-up within minutes.

She never tried it. Mainly because she didn't like eggs.

The Midian club they'd darted out of lingered near the border of the South. As Mai powered down the street with Violet in tow, the buildings grew more ragged, the streets were littered with more garbage, and the air took on an opaque haze.

Violet didn't process much. The horns, the music, the loud chatter, the sirens, the alarms, and the blaring voices from plascreens all around were muffled. As if cloth wrapped her ears.

She stared blankly, her mind revolving around one thing and the man who'd said it.

I will tell your brother you say hello.

I will tell your brother you say hello.

I will tell your brother

You say

Hello.

The pain of Mai's grip became a minor release. As Mai found a seedy alley, pulled Violet in, and slammed her against the wall, it drew Violet out of her thoughts.

Her vision dotted. She was not unused to Mai's violent tendencies, but it still hurt.

"Did you do your job?" Mai snapped.

Violet's breath grew short. In and out. In and out. She couldn't feel it anymore. Was she even breathing? Oh—yes, there it was. But it hurt. Her chest hurt. Tightened. Skies, she couldn't breathe, couldn't—

A sharp pain stung across her cheek. Violet's head smacked to the side.

I will tell your brother you say hello.

A snarl ripped through Violet, and she lunged for Mai, shoving her into the opposite wall.

"Don't you *ever* touch me like that again," seethed Violet. Warm liquid dripped from her nose. She didn't bother wiping the blood. "My black eye from your last outrage just healed."

"Pity." Mai smirked at her. "I see why you wanted off. Little Violet having a panic attack because her brother went into the Sins two years ago? How sad. She must be so, so sad."

Violet shoved her away, something snapping within her. She was unused to anything but the grief and numbness, and this anger…well, Mai probably slapped it right to the front. Her hands trembled, and she clenched them. "Snakes, arrows, and water. Don't make me say it." She dug into her pocket and threw the watch at Mai's feet. "There you go. I'm done for the night."

She turned, walking back to the street—

Mai grabbed her, pressed her into the wall. "You fucked up tonight. Bad. Do you know that?"

"I didn't *kill* him," said Violet.

"What?" Mai's nostrils flared.

"What?"

Mai growled. "I'm so tired of you."

"That makes two of us," said Violet with the hint of a smile. "So let me go. Go back to your daddy and wallow." Violet groaned as Mai's nails dug into her shoulders like claws. But she enjoyed baiting the monster. "Oh wait, he ignores you and not your brothers. So you're stuck with—*ow*—people like me."

Mai's eyes alighted. "You don't know who that man was, do you?"

"The one you looked ready to disembowel?"

Fear flashed in Mai's eyes, followed by anger. Oh, that man terrified her. And if *Mai* was terrified, Violet should be digging her grave.

He knew her name. Gave her his *very* expensive ring. Taunted her about her brother and—

"You have been the bane of my existence ever since I met you," said Mai, drawing her face close to share breath with Violet. "I don't know if it is because you *want* someone to off you so you don't have to look at his silly name anymore on the Sins Screen, or because you're just annoying—"

"Probably that."

"But you ruined this mission. While you did the bare minimum, your sticky fingers got you noticed by *him*. And that means death—for all of us."

Violet laughed as blood dribbled onto her teeth. "Two birds, one stone then."

Mai shoved Violet away. "You think you can't be hurt because your brother is gone, don't you? You think I can't find a way to make you pay for royally fucking up back there? I will. And it will hurt."

"I don't care—"

A scream stripped through the air, pausing both women. Their heads snapped to the street, where people gazed down the road. Cars paused. Honked. Bikers yelled at pedestrians. Motorbikes revved. From the rows and rows of clubs that now had music screeching out came the sound of glass shattering and the unmistakable hiss of plasguns and clicks of boots.

"*Redders*," seethed Mai. "Someone probably slipped about you."

"You're so overdramatic." Violet scoffed. "I only slapped him with a tray."

"What?"

"What?"

Mai narrowed her eyes. "You are fucking dead. My father is going to kill you."

"Your father is too busy burying his dick into other women."

Redders—Red Empire Police—snapped orders through their coms. Mai shoved Violet against the wall as screams rose and more plasgun shots rang out. The slash of a plaswhip had Violet's skin heating. When that energy, that hot, burning plasma, actually melted skin…

The plasgun bullet scar on her shoulder tingled. But that wasn't from Redders wreaking havoc for their crime quotas. That was from gardia—the gangs of Calesal. The gardia infiltrated everywhere and were the reason why her brother was in another world.

Mai breathed through her anger, and Violet nearly snorted, wondering if Mai's father had signed her up for those meditation classes she'd slipped about once.

"I'm coming for you," Mai promised. "I'd kill you right now, but I don't want that *man* and *his* blood-lusting goons coming after my family if your body turns up on the shore of the Trollova River." Mai dragged a gentle finger down Violet's cheek. "I also want to make sure we have privacy and a lot of time together before I end you."

"You want to eat me out before you do?"

Mai pushed Violet and her sass away. "I'll see you tomorrow." She glanced back to the street and the screams that emitted from the Redder chaos as they poured into the bars in search of crimes. With one last sneer, Mai disappeared.

Once the woman left, Violet dropped her smile and slumped to the ground, uncaring of the Redders around her.

Mai didn't bother her. Punishment didn't scare her. It was all some ruse within the gardia. Mai made threats and Violet didn't blink at them anymore. She was convinced Mai suffered from short-term memory loss because the woman hardly followed up on anything—that or some other gardia member pissed her off more than Violet did.

Or Mai *did* have feelings for Violet, which would be strange, seeing as their romantic liaisons had ended months ago.

Violet wiped at her nose, regretting her name on the gardia papers to work as a runner for Mai. Now it was as if the rush of her job, or Mai's threats, were like a drug, pushing her to see just how far she could get to death before it took her.

The ache of losing Reed to the Sins stripped her raw. Her mind crawled among the broken glass of her childhood, shattered two years ago when Reed was sentenced.

She shared the same blue eyes as Reed, but he sported darker skin—most likely from their unknown father—compared to Violet's olive tone she inherited from their mother. But still, they did *look* like siblings. Same soft features, same annoyed glare, same pout. Now separated by entirely different worlds.

She stood up, wiped at her nose again, and slipped out onto the street, head ducked low as Redders bellowed at club-goers. She had to see her brother's name on that Sins Screen.

She had to know he was okay.

And that was the line she continued to straddle. She had always straddled.

The one between death and hope.

3

SPIRAL

SINS EVE WAS DIFFERENT IN the South. People drank. People drugged themselves. People stumbled along the roads from one bar to the next, shoving through doorways, hollering at their friends. It was the same, whether they were men or women or whatever they wanted to be.

The South took up a quarter of the city; a dense quarter smushed with at least a million people. Markets, bars, plasmechanics, restaurants, coffee shops, fruit stands, and more lined the wide main streets filled with potholes, while plasbikes and rusting cars wove through the crowds. This was the night most people left their homes and congregated together to either stare at the gaping four-story-tall Sins Screen at Southers' Square, or any other plascreen that rotated the remaining names of candidates.

Violet stood amidst the usual commotion, hands clenched at her side, head lifted to the blinding screen. It had taken her nearly two hours to trudge back to the middle of the South from the point she'd been at in the Mid. Her feet warmed her boots, sweat licked her temples. The stolen jewels lay in secret pockets, and the ruby ring snug against her breast. One she both wanted to stare at for hours or toss into the Trollova River.

But for now, she looked. Seven vertical panels graced the screen, one for each world. Sins unknown, order unknown, but most things could be guessed in how difficult the worlds were.

After only fifty years with tracker technology, most could predict when and how candidates managed to move on from one world to the next. When her brother finally popped into the long list of names in the sixth world, she had been ecstatic. It had only taken him a year, faster than most, but that meant her hope dwindled every day for the year he stayed planted there. She'd spent the night on a rooftop, solo, drinking shiva and smoking as she stared at the dark Aariva in the center of the city where the Bloodswearing ceremony was held. She'd sat in the exact spot where Reed and she normally watched from, reminiscing.

The crowd roared as another hand was cut. And then another. The sound shook her bones. One of the candidates was a man who grew up with her guardian—an older man thick with muscle and hands rubbed raw from leather handling. He was popular in the South, but he was caught in the nasty business of a drug trade and then sentenced to the Sins. Past the cheering of the crowd, Violet heard the wails of his wife.

She scowled toward the Aariva blocks away, the Souther crowd a blur between those dark pillars. One by one, as the blood dripped, each breath grew easier. Her eyes stopped burning from the dust winds, and the cracks in her lips lessened.

"Do you think you could ever do it?"

Reed knocked one of his legs with hers as they hung on the edge of the apartment building. "Well, you can't make it out, can you?"

Laughing erupted. His friends hung back by the chimney, lounging in the shaded spot while they shared swigs of shiva.

Violet ignored them. "No, but if you could…"

"You can't."

"Reed." She rolled her eyes. "It's just a question."

"It ain't a question to old Mr. Floyd!" Faroh called.

"Mr. Floyd had it coming," urged Quinn. "I always knew he was a shady skiv."

Violet scowled.

Reed kept his face neutral. "Sure," Reed finally said. "It might even be better than living in this shithole of a city."

"It is the only way out," she said.

"Could you do it, booger?" he asked with a crooked smile.

"Yes," Violet said stubbornly. She would never admit that she couldn't, even if the thought of never coming back to see Meema, to run the streets with Reed, to do the things that she liked, roiled a deep fear in her belly.

"And how would you?"

"I'd fight."

He scoffed. "You would fight all the rest going in? You don't even know what's in there. They would tear you up. They are street rats, like—"

"Like us?" Violet snapped. "It's not any better here with the wars."

"You aren't going in," Reed said sharply. "Now stop talking about it. Meema would have your head for those thoughts."

"She's off with Efan; she doesn't care where we are."

"If you think she doesn't care, then you really have a screw loose in that small booger brain of yours."

Her fingers crunched on the brick. "I think I could do it. And I think you could, too. We don't have too many people using us, and I think that is the point. To not be used by the Sins. So you can pass them."

He sighed deeply. "In the end, you don't know what's in there. So don't you think about it. If you ever end up in those worlds, I'll tear apart each one of them and bring you home. Don't you worry."

The warmth of the shiva halted her anxiety as she looked past the first five worlds to the sixth, dragged along the long list that met the edge of the screen, and landed at her brother's name.

Reed Sutton.

A gleaming green dot lay next to it, the same as the night before and the night before that. She exhaled in relief—or whatever false relief she was supposed to feel.

"There you are," came a familiar soft voice. A poke at Violet's left shoulder where the plasbullet had torn her skin years ago. "I was beginning to think I'd have to search rooftops for you when you weren't at your apartment."

Violet didn't move her gaze from Reed's name. "With how tonight went, there was a potential you'd have to search under fresh cement instead."

Jelan stepped in front of Violet, arms crossed. "That's not funny."

"I'm not trying to be funny," mumbled Violet.

"No, you're being depressive. Was the inferno worse tonight?"

Violet rubbed her cheek where Mai had slapped her. She'd wiped whatever blood leaked from her split lip in a stray window with a hissing cat before arriving. "Nothing abnormal. I just…got in trouble again."

She dropped her gaze to her friend, whose brilliant, yet tired, amber eyes zeroed in on Violet's mouth but said nothing.

The first thing Violet always noticed about Jelan was her soft face and stoic expression. It took a significant amount of surprise to move her, or to see some emotion that wasn't the quirk of her full lips or the narrowing of her wide-set eyes. Hints of ash and sweat dusted her deep brown skin—she'd just gotten off shift at her new plasmaintenance job.

"Did you even shower?" Violet teased.

"If I looked at my bed, I'd collapse into it and not wake for seventeen hours." Jelan shrugged, her long box braids brushing with the movement, followed by the clink of gilded beads woven at the ends. "And I wanted to see you…with tonight being all that it is."

"I'm fine," said Violet flatly. She nodded her head to the screen. "He's fine. Everything is wonderfully fine."

Jelan snorted and unfolded her arms. Her oversized overalls with scattered plasburns hung low on her shoulders. She nodded her head to the brightly lit convenience mart. "Drink, Miss Absolutely Fine?"

"Absolutely fine with me." Violet nudged Jelan's shoulder as they turned. "I'm also thinking… bad smut and making fun of my neighbor's late-night groans?"

"Sounds perfect," smiled Jelan, brushing a braid behind her back.

The second thing Violet always noticed about Jelan was her hands. Her delicate, burned hands of twisting dark skin from the tips of her fingers, to the thin concave of her wrist. As if in that accident she had as a child, she reached into the fire and cupped it.

After years of their friendship, Violet was used to it. But Jelan still slid her hands into the pockets of her overalls and nudged her back.

They beelined for the corner mart. The owner, a woman named Hoja, locked eyes with Violet through the window and lifted a bushy brow.

Violet smirked as she stepped in, Jelan on her heels. "Busy night, Hoja?"

"You look worse for wear, where have you been skivvin' off to?" Hoja placed her hands on her curvy hips, the wrinkles around her mouth deepening as she frowned.

"Around the Mid, but it hasn't been striking my fancy."

"Uh-huh." Her dark eyes flicked to Jelan. "Haven't seen you in a bit, J. What have you been up to?"

Violet took that as an opportunity to search the narrow shelves. Hoja slashed her a glare. While Violet stole from parties, she never stole from Souther marts—well, not all the time. Especially not from Hoja, who would flay her alive if her fingers found a pack of chewing gum.

"I got a job," said Jelan. "In Plastech. Well, nothing high-up or anything, but simple maintenance in the Factory District."

"Good for you, J. 'Bout time you put your skills to use after all the plaslights you fixed here. Pays well?"

Violet found the shiva rack and slid her finger along the shelf until she reached the cheapest bottle.

"Pays enough. Not too happy about the early-morning wake-up calls. Or the occasional plasburns. That shit hurts."

"Shut up, J, you love the morning," Violet called as she settled on a bottle.

"Hurry up, Sutton, or else I'm kicking you out."

Violet waltzed out of the shelves and to the counter. She placed the bottle on the small space amidst the towers of smokes and candies. "You have so little faith in me, Hoja."

"Maybe now you've been better, but I'd be a damn skiv not to remember your sticky fingers when you were a child." Hoja scanned the bottle and sighed at the poorly labeled glass. "This is your fourth this week, Sutton. What's wrong?"

Violet scowled and shoved the bottle into her back pocket, ignoring the question. "You got one of those smokes? The ones with the flavors?"

Hoja gave her a long look, flicking her eyes to Jelan, who settled against the doorframe, arms crossed.

Jelan shrugged. "It's all her. I have my issues."

"You ever get those breathing problems figured out?"

"After a few more paychecks, I'm hoping I can finally see a Mid doctor. The ones in the South… don't have the resources I need," said Jelan.

Hoja frowned but didn't press.

"Just one pack, please, dear lovely Hoja," urged Violet.

Sighing again, Hoja bent down to retrieve a pack and slid it to Violet. "I'm going to be forced to cut you off if you keep up like this."

"I appreciate your concern, but I'm *fine*," gritted Violet as she tried to maintain her smile. "Sins Eve is hard on a lot of people for obvious reasons."

"He was a good boy." Violet flinched. *Was.*

Hoja's lips tightened. "I'm sorry, I shouldn't have said—"

"It's fine," said Jelan as she walked up to grab the pack of smokes. She swung an arm over Violet's shoulders. "We'll have ourselves a night, and then it'll get easier."

Hoja nodded. "Fourteen marks."

Violet reached into her pocket to pull out a silver coin. Hoja took it and dropped six copper coins in return.

Before Violet could draw her arm back, Hoja gripped her wrist, stopping her. "Come 'round for dinner in the next couple of days.

Both of you. I lost my younger cousin to the Sins after Marin's stint…." Jelan winced at the name. Violet's blood burned beneath her skin. *Marin.* "So same year as your brother. I'll make a roast."

"I'll think about it." Violet shied from Hoja's touch and dipped underneath Jelan's arm. "Thanks, Hoja." She walked outside, drawing the shiva bottle and unscrewing the cap.

"Take care of her. She's spiraling." Hoja's voice flowed out. "She can't keep lookin' at his name. She needs to know he is gone."

"I'll try," was all Jelan said before she stepped out the door.

When they had walked far enough, back toward the dried fountain in the center of the square, did Jelan lean in, "She's just a mother. Don't let it get to you."

"I don't want pity," grumbled Violet. "Especially from a mother."

Jelan said nothing at that.

Violet caught her brother's name as they rounded the Sins Screen again and took a seat at the edge of the fountain. Same green light, same jump in her chest every time. But if she *didn't* look, just for a second, the dot next to his name might go red, and within a day, he'd be gone.

The thought sickened her.

Hope was for fools. Anyone from the South knew that.

It was a fool's hope to expect anyone to exit the Sins. No one had done it. Not in the five-hundred years the curse has been around.

Still, she would sit and watch for at least an hour before the alcohol burned through her veins and pushed her vision to a blurry mess. If one knew where to look, they would see the same figures paused among the commotions, faces uplifted to the screen and watching. She was never the only one.

"See, he's okay," Jelan said quietly. "The same as always."

She sighed. "That's the problem."

Jelan frowned slightly but didn't push it. She swiped the bottle from Violet and took a long sip.

Violet pulled out her pack of smokes and lighter while Jelan nursed the shiva bottle, observing the bodies that passed them.

The buildings around towered in mismatched stone and brick above their heads, plaslights of restaurants, clubs, and stores blinking in and out of rhythm. Loud music poured out of one club and fought the thumping bass of another. Tables and chairs smashed together as Southers hoarded them, throwing down cards, leaning over tall glasses of colored shiva, flicking the charred ends of their smokes onto the dirtied pavement below. Street cats chased each other through the maze of people, children then chasing the cats, and then dogs after the children. Parents hollered. Others drunkenly shouted back.

The life of the South continued.

"You have an extra one of those, sweetheart?"

Jelan's lips paused around the bottle as her gaze snagged behind Violet's shoulder.

"No," Violet said, not turning around.

Breath brushed her neck. "Come on. I thought you'd learned to share after all those times on that rooftop."

"Still dreaming about that, Faroh?" She twisted her head and blew smoke in his face. "Nothing else satisfying you other than the memory of my fifteen-year-old hands?"

Faroh frowned playfully. "How you wound me with your harsh words, little Vi—"

"Get lost."

"—but I always enjoyed them."

"Then enjoy them across the square."

He caught her gaze, and she scowled. Reed's old friend popped up now and then, taunted her, scratched at painful memories, and then proceeded to vanish. He was the person who got off on upsetting people, but she had been used to it for years, especially since *he* was the first to explore her body, to crest over her slight curves, and kiss unmarked skin.

Then he blabbed about it to her brother of all people.

She did enjoy seeing Faroh with a horrible black eye for weeks after that. What she hadn't enjoyed was Reed's disappointment in her.

"My friend? Violet, he is a piece of shit, how could you? How could you let someone like that...." Reed's hands shook as he ran them through his hair. "...take advantage of you?"

"I didn't know," she said with tears in her eyes.

"No, you didn't know any better." Reed's voice strained. "You never do. Do you like making bad decisions and feeling terrible after them? Do you do this for attention?"

"No," she breathed. "I believed him when he said—"

Reed was already making his way to the front door, opening it to the quiet street at curfew during the gardia wars. She stepped forward, protest in her throat, but Reed's hand silenced her.

"Don't. Believe. Anyone. Only me. Only Meema. That's it. Got it?"

She nodded as a tear slipped down her cheek.

"So believe me when I tell you this: I will always be on your side and stand with you through stupid decisions. I won't leave you. Not like mama. But right now, I'm going to go beat the shit out of him, and you're going to stay here, drink your tea, and go to bed early."

A sob choked out of her, but she nodded again.

"I'll be back," was all he said before the door slammed shut.

Faroh's mouth moved, but Violet's eyes found Reed's name yet again. Still blinking green. Still alive.

But still gone.

"Little Vi—"

Her arm shot out and shoved Faroh back. "Get *out* of my face."

Faroh stumbled back, but two thick hands caught him and hauled him up like a ragdoll.

"I'm going to kick you into the Trollova if you don't stop hounding girls in the square."

Garan Umbero, owner and manager of the popular bar in the square, shoved Faroh to the side, whose face betrayed every bit of offense. Garan's stern look matched his frightening size and the corded muscles that bulged beneath his deep brown skin.

Faroh opened his mouth, closed it, then opened again to blurt, "Sorry." He glowered at Violet, who flashed him the middle finger, and walked away.

Violet was fairly certain that Garan participated in an underground fighting ring by the way he not only handled his rowdy patrons, but also by the way he intimidated with just one look. At his glance this time, however, it was Jelan blushing in his presence. She'd climbed that tree quite a few times, and now only ever flushed around him.

Garan shot her a bright smile. "Jelan." His smile dropped slightly as he looked at Violet. "Sutton."

"You are a wonder, you know that?" Violet ignored Jelan's quizzical look. "It's been a long day of work, and I was really about to throw down with that skiv, but I already got in a fight earlier and didn't want to waste my energy. So you—perfect. Thank you." Violet slapped her hands on her thighs, feigning excitement. "And this girl—this *beautiful, amazing* girl just got a job in Plastech maintenance. And out of the South, too, leaving us skivs for better things and all that. Right, J?"

A scowl flashed across Jelan's face. "I'm not leaving anyone, nor the South. Not for a while, even if I wanted to."

Garan beamed. "You got the job?"

"Thanks to your contact," said Jelan. "I, uh…appreciate it."

"Well, you can show me appreciation by finally going out to dinner with me." Garan waved a hand toward his restaurant. "There's free food—"

Violet flashed a pointed look to Jelan, which she ignored.

"And drinks, of course. Sutton can—"

"I have to wash my windows that day, but thanks for the invite," said Violet. "I'm sure Jelan is super excited for that, though."

Jelan opened her mouth as if debating a denial before she said, "Okay. I'm off midweek."

"Then it's a date." Garan's gaze roamed. "I'm looking forward to it. Wear that…scent you always wear. The one that smells like vanilla." He dipped his head down. "I like it a lot."

A blush rose to Jelan's cheeks. "Okay."

Violet dragged a hit of her smoke, blowing toward the empty fountain. "She'll be there."

"Good." Garan turned to Violet, pointing over his shoulder. "I watch it every night, all night—no movement from him, but I'll let you know if something happens when you aren't around."

Violet's expression dropped. "Oh. I didn't know you did that."

"We Southers have to look out for each other," said Garan.

Violet didn't know if he was just saying that or being nice in general, just to get in Jelan's good graces. Her guard flashed up as her eyes roamed his face, looking for a lie, looking for something that told her it was a front to get closer to her friend, but Garan seemed genuinely concerned.

So she simply nodded, unsure of how to handle it.

Garan turned toward his bustling restaurant, ran a hand through his tight coils. He sighed deeply, "Sutton, there's a rumor that Mar—"

The Sins Screen emitted a loud ring—a shrill sound noting that someone had passed through a world. The music at various clubs screeched out. Chatter slowed, then stopped.

After the Bloodswearing Ceremony, it rang day and night. But when the passing of worlds slowed, it became a surprise to hear such a thing. Most settled into the fourth or sixth world, a lot died in the first and second. The third had the same names as always, and the fifth a handful.

All heads turned toward the Screen.

"Oh, my skies," breathed Jelan. "Someone made it to the seventh world."

A disturbing silence poured through the square. Violet whipped her head, hoping, praying that it was *his* name—

Darien Bones.

The sole name in the seventh panel. A bright red dot blinked next to him, and for a moment Violet could only hear the pounding of her heart, like his, probably. Was he running? Was he dying? But he made it to the seventh world, and the next would be home...

"Go!" Someone screamed at the screen. "Run! Run faster, you mutt!"

Another echoed the same cheer. Then another. Voices cried into the sickly air of Sins Eve, urging the lone candidate who blinked in the last panel. All around, some version of hope settled over the crowd and echoed in their voices. People slammed their drinks, gripped the arms of their neighbors, and screamed for this stranger—not a stranger. A fighter.

"Run! Run and come home!" A woman's voice shrieked with a broken sob. "Come home, my boy!"

Violet's gaze landed on the older woman leaning against a fruit cart. Her frail hands gripped the edge as she gaped at the screen, tears pouring. Two children clutched at her dress, worry, and confusion plastered on their expressions.

In unison, the South watched this man fight through the seventh.

And then, in unison, they watched his tracker blink red once more, then still.

Dead.

The older woman's despaired cry broke through the horrified silence as realization spread. Darien Bones. Dead in the seventh world. A world only a few had ever made it to and never lasted longer than a minute.

The woman—his mother, Violet presumed—screamed into the shaken air.

"I think those are his kids," muttered Jelan, eyes locked on the confused children at the woman's legs.

"He was a regular at my bar. Good man, but caught smuggling. His wife..." Garan took a steady breath. "...killed herself last year. She couldn't handle it anymore."

Violet's eyes burned, but some awful part of her was thankful. She despised herself for watching the woman wail into the air, some grateful beat in her heart that it wasn't Reed. But in the end, what did it mean for her brother? No one had ever survived the seventh—whatever existed in that world was not meant to be endured. Over and over, hope rose only to fall, the brethren of the South the sufferers for believing that such a curse, such a terrible way to die, could be stopped.

"I think I'm ready for another smoke," mumbled Violet. "Anyone want one?"

"I'll take one," said Garan with a solemn look. Jelan shook her head.

Violet reached to hand it to him, avoiding his pitiful gaze. His fingers clasped around the white wrap—

A blood-curdling scream ripped through the crowd and silenced it. Garan dropped the smoke. A hand pointed. Then another. Southers' Square erupted; new cries rang around, people stood out of their seats, glasses clattered to the ground, the volume rising, becoming overwhelming.

Violet was up and off the ledge, a scream in her throat, as she looked upon the plascreen at the sixth world where the list was almost endless....

Where half of the names had a red dot blinking next to them.

Danger.

Looming death.

A choked cry rose. Her heart tumbled away, unable to catch a rhythm.

Reed's name blinked along with them.

Then a solid red dot appeared, like a blazing ruby marking the last, final breath of their lives.

4

Bottom

No.

No no no no no no no.

Violet's knees met the pavement. Her lips moved. She didn't know what she was saying. The screams of the crowd sent a slither of cold down her spine. Hands were on her shoulders. Someone yelled her name.

"He's okay! Look! His mark is still blinking—"

"Sutton, get up. You have to go."

"Oh skies, Violet. The Redders. They're coming."

She blinked. Blinked again. Like the red dot next to Reed's name.

Tears spilled down her cheeks. Jelan leaned in close, lips on her ear, "Vi, we have to go!"

The sounds in the Southers' Square hit her like a punch to the gut. Screams filled the musty air. Glasses shattered. Whips lashed the ground. Plasguns blasted through windows. Bodies thumped the stone.

The unmistakable click of boots filled the air, matching the rapid beating of her heart.

"Go, Jelan, take her to Jenkins. You'll be safe there—" started Garan.

"No," mumbled Violet.

"I—what are they doing here? We've done nothing wrong!" Jelan stumbled back.

Garan grabbed her arm. "They're gathering, J. It is for control. Now go; take Sutton somewhere safe."

Reed's name continued to blink red, just like half of the sixth panel. The other half sported solid ruby dots next to their names. Death. That was what it meant. Their names would be erased from the board within a day, Darien Bones's just before them. Around her, Southers fell to their knees. A family huddled, wailing the name of a candidate.

"Vi! Dammit, she's out of it—Vi, where did you go?"

Garan yanked Violet's arm. She fell back into his hard chest. "You need to go, Sutton. Back to Jenkins. Anywhere. Go—*now!*"

The clicks of boots were everywhere. She finally blinked from the screen to find Jelan's terrified eyes. The rough texture of Jelan's hands gripped her bare shoulders, shaking her.

"Now!" Garan yelled as a group of Redders barreled toward his bar, and the patrons scattered. He gave a roar of anger, tackling one of the gray suits.

"Garan—no!" Jelan called.

"Go!" He yelled. "Get somewhere safe—"

A plastaser met his skin and Garan roared again, fighting it, but his body convulsed atop the Redder.

Violet couldn't breathe.

Couldn't breathe…couldn't breathe…couldn't breathe—

"Go," repeated Jelan with a breath. Her scarred hand wrapped Violet's wrist. Jelan yanked her through the throng. The crowd blurred. People ran, screaming as the gray-plated suits of helmeted Redders shoved past them. A man stumbled as a Redder tackled him, slapping a pair of glowing green plascuffs on his wrists. The man cried out, but the Redder only yanked him up and shoved him to a group of people.

Herded like cattle.

"*Garan,*" breathed Violet.

"He'll be okay," said Jelan, head whipping left and right. "He's good. He will be okay."

Violet blinked at her friend, unbelieving of those words.

Her broken breaths were the only things she could focus on. Her heartbeat in her ears snuffed out the screams, but the smell— there was a metallic tinge in the air. Blood.

She turned her head to catch the Sins Screen. Found her brother's name. The pain in her chest tightened so much she grabbed her shirt, clawed at her skin, as if to rip her heart out to stop it. A grief-filled moan escaped her. That pain she had been fighting for two years, raw as the day she shrieked his name, over and over, while he walked across that stage and sliced his hand.

When his blood poured into that bowl.

The nightmare, the memory she drowned out every night. It rushed back, clutched at her throat, whispered in her ear like a dark reminder that he would never come back. He was meant to die in the Sins, and she was meant to watch it.

He was in danger, serious enough danger that half of the candidates in the sixth world had died from it. Nothing like that had ever happened before. It must have been a massacre or some terrible natural disaster. And she could only watch.

The wind whipped through the square. A plasgun blasted into the stone of the fountain behind them. The crowd was so thick that Jelan could barely shove through one person before another barreled into their path. She redirected, her scarred hand tight on Violet's wrist, as she held her panic at bay and searched for a break in the chaos. Jelan paused, then jolted Violet again toward one of the five main streets that intersected the square like a star, where the number of Redders lessened, and lights dimmed along the pavement. Jelan huffed, wheezing a breath.

Her breathing problems.

That was enough to snap Violet out of it. She shoved her depression, her horrifying, numbing grief into her rusty metal box, snapped it shut, grabbed the key—

A plasbike revved by, followed by a beat-up car laying on the horn. Violet snapped her head to the window, and her knees wobbled in relief.

"Get in the skivvin' car!" Jenkins sang from the front seat, his boyfriend, bar-owner Holstar, in the passenger seat. Jenkins honked again as Southers sprinted about, diving away from the mass of Redders.

They dashed to it. Jelan opened the back door and slid in.

Violet had just shut the door when Jenkins gunned the car and swerved down the road. He passed other cars, plasbikes, cackling the whole way as his bug-like spectacles slid down his white-skinned nose. "You skivs, I heard about the reapings on the radio and knew you'd be here."

Holstar rubbed at his crooked nose. "We could have stayed in bed."

"Go," commanded Jelan, bracing her hands on the seats. "Get us out of here."

Jenkins hollered and pushed on the gas.

Violet exchanged an incredulous look with Jelan. It was no secret that Jenkins was weird and had deep ties to the gardia, and also no secret to Violet that he seemed to pop up at the rarest times, saving her from trouble. How he tracked her, how he even knew to be on the lookout for her, she'd never figured it out, and Jenkins hid that intelligence behind his bizarre personality. The know-it-all lunatic of the South, former mooch of Meema's dinners, and nosy in Violet's business most times by sending her ridiculous letters filled with ridiculous questions.

Hair cropped nearly to his scalp, pasty skin hanging on to thin bones, and fingers lined with rings that Reed suspected were either from Jenkins's consorts or kill list, he slashed her a big, bug-eyed look from the front seat. "You look like shit, young weed flower."

Violet's heart pounded too hard, too fast, to care about the stupid nickname he'd given her when they'd become neighbors nine years ago, around the time her mother had perished.

"I have to go back," breathed Violet. "I have to *see* him—"

"It's a mess there and all over the city. Redders didn't have enough candidates for this year's Sins, so they went to the streets to reap. It's all over the radio. There was also a riot planned on happening, rumor of assassinations at the ceremony tomorrow, so they needed to quell it. And you know what Redders do best...." Jenkins ran through a stoplight, oblivious to the honking cars. Jelan gaped out the window as Redders ran down the streets, corralling men and some women, lashing out plaswhips. "The city has gone to shit ever since Jack Marin was announced as a candidate."

"*What?*" gasped Violet.

"Jack Marin?" whispered Jelan.

"He was apprehended at one of his parties in the Mid. Everyone saw him go into the Redder motorcade, plascuffed and everything. They even gagged him. He was sentenced to the Sins for his crimes, so this city is about to be in a *lot* of shit."

"Skies, Vi, are you all right?"

Her skin grew clammy, stomach flipping.

Jack Marin. Reed. Jack Marin. Reed.

Reed defied the notorious City Commander of Trade and Commerce.

So Commander Jack Marin threw him in the Sins.

Holstar twisted in his seat, handing her a bucket. "I knew she would do this. We just had the seats cleaned."

"A third is dead in the sixth world, according to the last radio update," frowned Jenkins. "Coming to terms with Reed's inevitable demise might be good, Sutton. Jack Marin will do it if the Sins won't."

"*Jenkins!*" snapped Jelan.

Heat flashed through Violet, and bile crawled up her throat. She'd been trying not to think...to think that one day soon, or even months from now, his death was inevitable. But at the hands of Marin? Their story was in the news for months after Reed was bloodsworn and Marin was convicted of his crimes in the gardia wars, but not given a punishment.

Souther citizen, Reed Sutton, along with fifty other members, found guilty and sentenced to exile in the Sins for plasbombing a South school on behalf of Commander Marin's revealed gardia.

"My boy! My little boy! Not my boy!"

The croaked cry of Meema lingered in her ears, broken by the horn of a swerving car.

"—you had anyone go to the Sins? It's hard on anyone to watch that. You can't *not* watch it, either." Jelan defended her in the few times she raised her voice. "At least have some sympathy. And with Marin going in, it's not going to help when he's responsible for so much death and destruction in the city."

Violet yanked the bucket toward her face and buried it inside. Oh skies, it was coming up, she was going to…

She heaved into it. Bile only.

"I can't," she mumbled into the pail, "I can't—"

"It's okay, Vi. Just let it out."

"Only in the pail, please."

"I can't…"

"You wouldn't believe how many times I've seen her do this outside my bar. With her brother holding her hair back, slurring profanities at anyone who came near her." Holstar grubbed, wrinkling his nose as he looked back at her.

Tears slipped down her cheeks. "I can't keep doing this."

"Doing what?" Jelan asked.

"*This.*" She lowered the pail from her shattered expression.

Inside of her were floating tethers of all the things that kept her alive. This night had sliced through them all, and when she tried to grasp them, to tie them back together, they slipped through her fingers as if mocking her.

What do you have left, little Violet? What is left in your life that is worth fighting for?

Violet slowly set the pail down to the floor. Wiped her mouth. Jenkins's driving didn't help her nausea, but as the streetlights blurred in the city she both hated and loved, Violet tucked a matted lock of hair behind her ear.

What is left in your life that is worth fighting for?

"Take me to her," she mumbled.

Jenkins looked back at her, annoyed, for long enough that Holstar slapped his shoulder to have him pay attention to the road. "She's not going to give you what you need."

"*Take me to her,*" said Violet evenly.

"Meema?" asked Jelan.

"That or drop me over the wall. Can't your tattoo get you that?"

Tense silence slid into the car as Violet stared pointedly at Jenkins and Holstar.

Jenkins's hands were tight on the steering wheel. "No one can go outside of the wall. We don't even know if anything is out there, save for plasma mines and agriculture. Where would you go?"

The paintings of the forest she'd stared at in school popped in her head. "Somewhere to breathe."

"The gardia can't help you. At least…" trailed Holstar.

"Yours can't," clarified Jelan.

Jenkins rubbed at his arm. His amnesty from any persecution, except the Sins. That mark ushered many Southers to join the gangs ran by high Elites solely for its protection and importance, labeling one untouchable. Finding out who had a mark meant discovering the enemy's leadership, like the information Violet had given Mai today. Jenkins was an obscure leadership in a gardia, but he pulled Violet out of trouble—and out of handcuffs—before, so she kept her mouth shut about the tattoo.

"But the gardia *is* the city," said Violet. "It makes things move, both illegal and legal, and gives the South something to damn do. I don't care that Jack Marin has his own gardia, or that Arvalo dips his toe into it aside from his public duty, but they should be able to stop this all, right?"

"They are too busy fighting each other," Jelan mumbled. "None of the city commanders get along. Especially now that Marin is gone. He was some horrible glue the North and Mid loved, and he did a lot for this city. I'm sure they are mourning him as we speak." Jelan flicked a piece of dirt from underneath her nail. "Pity."

"Jack Marin comes with his faults, and his sentencing is dramatic. The commanders are all elitist shits who run their industries because old gangs took over the city so long ago, and the Empire was forced to power share." Jenkins swerved around another car. "At this point, the Empire is still responsible for the Sins because it is a dire circumstance to our tiny world. It was only ten years ago when a candidate fainted before the bowl, and they were late getting their blood—the drought got so bad because it was after sunset that a garment factory exploded.

"The Sins are archaic, weed flower. No city commander, Emperor, or gang is going to stop it. Not when the world will perish. They've tried to resist, but even your guardian could tell you that the Sins are clockwork. Blood must be given, or this world suffers."

Violet's eyes narrowed at the familiar roads, mouth a thin line.

"Weed flower," chuckled Jelan.

"We are cursed every summer solstice. It is when the Empire reminds us that ultimately, they have the power. They cage us in a wall and submit us to the curse. The cycle has gone on for nearly five-hundred years, but we've only known that those exiled are still alive based on the trackers for the last fifty."

"But no one has come out, so what's the point in continuing the suffering?" mumbled Violet.

"Because it is Southers who go in." Jenkins nodded to the North's skyscrapers in the distance. "Not them. Never them."

"Except their precious Jack Marin," Holstar said. .

At the mention of the name again, Violet's hands shook with rage. She wished, *wished* she could wrap them around the man's throat.

"It will be *fascinating* to see how he does on that screen," beamed Jenkins.

"The whole city hates him," said Jelan. "It's probably not enough of a punishment for what he did—destroying the South, rioting in the streets, those bodies on the bridge—skies, that one night where the plasma power grid zapped out. All that wasted food and more."

"And yet Elites still like him," said Holstar. "Why do you think that is?"

"He's a pretty boy with pretty words." Jenkins shoved his glasses up his nose. "Of course, they like him. All of the drugs and violence was an uprising—I'd imagine—against the Empire. The Elites want the Empire gone, but at the same time, it doesn't affect them. The gardia funnels money in from all situations, both illegal and legal."

"There were bodies on my street. I slept to gunshots every night," Violet snarled softly. "I don't care what it was for. He is the sky-damn reason my brother is even in the Sins."

It always hurt to say it out loud because her chest tightened, her head dizzied, and the hatred she felt for that name blurred her thoughts.

"It's no secret that Jack Marin still has a vendetta with Reed," murmured Holstar.

Not the way I expected to meet you, Violet Sutton.

Hands cupped her face. Amber eyes darted in her dazed vision.

But she could only focus on one last line, the last thing he had said to her in that silky voice of his.

I will tell your brother you say hello.

"It was him," she mumbled.

"Who? It was who? Vi, where did you go? What—you're as pale as a ghost."

Jenkins cackled in the background.

"It was him." Violet blinked, meeting Jelan's gaze. "I met him."

"Who?" She removed her hands.

She glanced at all of their eyes. "Jack Marin."

Jelan gasped. Holstar rolled his eyes.

Jenkins twisted in his seat. "He's pretty, isn't he?"

Anger rushed through her, the box brimming with all the emotion she turned her back on, ready to be let out. She had to channel it, find a way to deal with it. Something sparked, deep in her gut.

"We're here." Jenkins pulled up to the curb, nearly bumping into the car parked in front of the elderly home. He turned in his seat toward Violet. "She's not going to be able to help you."

Violet shoved open the car door, overrun with emotions, needing to find some peace, to get out because it was all boiling over, and she didn't want to burn herself with everything from the past two years.

She turned to Jelan. "I'll see you later."

Jelan frowned but nodded and held out her hand.

Without hesitation, Violet grasped it.

5

MEEMA

VIOLET SIGHED BACK INTO THE plush armchair. Bitten fingernails dug into the orange material, the same color as the petals on the ugly patterned wall. The radio sat on an end table, playing soft piano chords that Meema always loved. The cream rug was freshly vacuumed, the curtains on the window billowing softly in the arid wind. A clock ticked above the simple cot neatly made for her old guardian. Violet's eyes flicked to it, only to find the second hand had moved…a couple of seconds.

The night had quickly bled into the morning, and the morning slowly transitioned into the afternoon. She listened to the growing noises about the elderly home—the beep of a monitor, the groan of another patient, or the yell of a nurse when someone wasn't taking their assigned pills. Radios and plascreens alike blasted the news of Jack Marin's sentencing, along with those "rowdy southerners" caught the night before in various crimes. Arvalo's name was mentioned, and reporters gave congratulations to the City Commander, who worked with the Redders to bring justice to the crime-filled streets of the South.

Violet lolled her head to face Meema. Her guardian sat rigidly on the beige couch. Dark brown skin, gray eyes, matted black-gray hair, and in a simple shirt and pants the nurses had dressed her in. Meema had been a beauty back in the day, long before Violet was born. Now full of wrinkles, frown lines mostly, she retained a distant gaze caused by her memory illness.

The woman next to Violet had been married and divorced four times, all of her husbands perishing or disappearing by some accident. She denied any part in it, but Violet never missed the lack of tears on the harsh woman's face, or the hint of a curved lip whenever someone brought up one of the four men's names.

I played with them; they bought me whatever I wanted, complained when I didn't want children, and left for most of the day to work, leaving me in damned peace finally. That was it. That was what all the men were skivvin' good for.

But then you had us, Violet had said as a young child. *Me and Reed. We are your children. So you changed your mind about that.*

You two are the only children I will ever need, even though you drive me up the skyrises. Meema had pinched her cheek. *But I still love you, all the same.*

Love was a word Violet didn't hear often. Even when Violet was a child, Meema hardly said it until it was evident Violet needed the reminder. Otherwise, her love existed in her harsh words, commanding tones, her shrieks when Violet had chopped her hair off, or found a plastaser on the ground. This woman had molded Violet into the woman she was today, but scared the living shit out of her too. Or had, before her memory slipped through the gaps.

The hollow body whose eyes dipped from one floral pattern on the wall to the bed, then back, clutched the empty teacup with bony fingers. Her portly figure sagged into the couch, no determined ramrod spine, no hardened scowl.

"I think you're done with that." Violet sat up and plucked the cup out of her hands, placing it among the many water rings staining the coffee table before her. "Did you want another?"

Meema hummed a low tone.

"Okay, no more tea. Next time I'll—" Violet halted her words, gazed down to her hands. Her eyes burned. "I'll bring shiva next time. I promise."

Meema blinked. Tapped her fingers on her knees.

Violet settled back into the chair, a lump in her throat. The silence was peaceful, almost, and Violet usually came here for just that. A moment of peace, next to a woman who had raised her but now hardly remembered her. Sometimes she would lie in the chair and gaze at the ceiling until the deep oranges of the sunset drifted across. Other times, she stared numbly at Meema's hands, wishing maybe they would run through her hair again.

Now, a tear slipped down her cheek.

"I've messed up," she croaked softly, hugging her knees to her chest. "I don't know how long I can do this."

She didn't dare glance toward her old guardian. The tears were slow down her cheeks, and all she wanted was Meema to grab her face, tell her to snap out of it, tell her something—

"Mariana."

Her mother's name. Long dead. Not that Violet cared about that ghost of a woman. Meema ran through a couple of different memories, and thinking Violet was her mother was one of them.

She frowned but sat up, wiping her cheeks. "Yes?"

"Did Reed come back from school?" Gray eyes met hers.

"Yes, he did," said Violet.

"He loves that science class, but have him be careful with the teacher. She's got a rump on her, that skiv."

Violet hardly blinked. "I will tell him that."

"And that Violet," Meema frowned, wrinkles prominent. "Be careful with her."

Violet's interest perked. "Why? What has she done?"

"She punched that boy! She has too much of her father in her. You fail to give her any attention, so she rebels at school. I'm tired of picking her up with bruises on her face," Meema scoffed.

Her father hardly ever came up in conversation. "What about her father?"

"Ratchet old devil with his stupid leather coat. You were too obsessed with his love. His everything. But I remember when you brought him around... he had a smile to rival whatever gods created the skies." Meema's gaze hardened. "But your love wasn't enough for him to stay, except for his part in creating your kids."

Ouch. Violet's father was never in the picture. Before her mother died, Violet had heard of him only a handful of times. Her mother couldn't bear the loss, only mentioning his small quirks and how much Reed looked like him. Regardless, to Meema especially, he was a man her mother should never have fallen in love with. He was murdered, apparently, and Mariana carried his name to her grave.

"Violet is raking all trouble at school, and by her lonesome, at that. You brought her into the world, Mari. Now deal with it. She notices your distance from her. It troubles the girl. Don't give her a reason to hate you."

Too late, Violet thought. Her mother was a shadow to her. Violet was a mistake to the woman who birthed her. She was told it, had overheard it again and again. She was the mistake, while Reed was the golden child. Reed would get the love, and Violet would get a pity-filled glance like she would combust into flames at any moment.

Meema leaned over and tapped Violet's arm with her callused fingers. "The girl does not have to die. But with the way she keeps up in life, drawing attention, getting into trouble, she will. Love her, even though it is hard. You know the little shit needs it."

"Why does she have to die?" Violet asked, even though she had heard it before. Death loomed around her, and she was used to it.

Meema scowled. "Don't play dumb with me. I know your secret."

Now *that* was something she had never heard. "Tell me again what you know about my secret?"

But Meema's face blanked from her reigning scowl. Her eyes grew clearer as she turned to take Violet in on her lounge.

"Where in the skivvin' shit stains have you been?"

"Welcome back, Meema," Violet said. Ah, Corusgates, the memory illness depicted by the rapid switch from one time to another, buffered by long periods of numbness and incoherence. It was like a plaswhip on the brain to keep up with.

"Look at you! Got an ass, girl. Be careful with those boys—they act like they got forty hands and twelve dic—"

"Thanks." She rubbed at her temples. "I'm being careful, don't worry."

Emotion tore through. It had been months since her guardian had recognized her, and this seemed to be…present day. It helped her take a steady breath as tears pricked her eyes. "I have to tell you something, Meema."

"Are you pregnant?"

"What? No," Violet said. "I'm careful."

"Then what? Is your brother still alive?"

Her face ached for a response, and Violet hastily replied, "Yes. But—"

"Then tell me, girl! What world is he in now? Has anyone made it out? They keep me in this dumb fucking facility, and I tried to burn it down a while ago, but then you show up, and I ain't got the rest of my life—" she paused, face blanking again.

Violet lurched out of the chair to grab her hands. "No—no, stay with me, please. I want to tell you I love you. And I'm sorry. Please." Meema's face continued to blank. "*Please*—no, *no*, Meema!"

Meema took a second to gather her senses, confusion on her features, as she looked around the room, then back toward Violet. Her face settled, and she smiled. "I love you, too, little flower." She patted Violet's cheek. "Now go on. You don't want to be late for school."

Tears streamed down Violet's cheeks. "Of course."

Meema blinked at her, nose scrunching. "Well, what are you waiting for?"

"I am…" Violet swallowed her sob. "I am just going to miss you."

"Bah! You'll be back." She brushed Violet's hair back. "Just not with any bruises, okay?"

"Okay," Violet whispered. "I promise I'll come back."

"I'll make dinner when you get home. Peach stew, your favorite."

"Okay." Tears poured now, dripping onto Meema's hands. "I love you—"

"And if you find Reed out there, tell him to get his ass home," Meema snapped. "That boy needs to eat properly and remember he has a damn family. I don't care if you drag him down the street. Just *bring him home.*"

Violet dropped to her knees. She placed her tear-streaked face into her guardian's hands, clutching them.

"Oh, honey," Meema said. "Bad day?"

Violet could only nod into her hands, but Meema lifted her face so her gray eyes met her blue ones. "Whoever gives you a bad day, you tell 'em to fuck off. No matter what, you keep going, baby girl."

She broke. Her heart twisted. "Okay."

"You promise?"

"I promise."

"Good." She wiped her tears. "Now off you go. And bring your damned brother home!"

And in an instant, Meema's features began to blank, soften, distance. Violet clutched her hands harder, pressing her palms, kissing them as she let that emotion bubble up and release.

Long moments passed until an incessant honking of a horn called from the street. Violet had half a mind that Jenkins was out there, worrying about her. But she didn't want to go to him. She didn't—

"*Violet!*" shrieked a voice, muffled by the window. Mai's voice. "Come out of there this instant! You need to pay your fucking price!"

Ice crested her spine. No no no no no—

"You thought I'd forget about you?" Mai called. "Get out of there or I will burn this place to the ground!"

"Is that the landlord?" asked Meema. "I'll give him a piece of my skivvin' mind."

"It's not the landlord." Violet stopped her from getting up. "You stay. I'll take care of them."

Meema sneered in response. "He better not cut the power like he did last week."

"I'll castrate him if he does," said Violet.

Doors began to open in the hallway of the home, followed by gasps. Violet's heart slowed to a painful beat as Mai continued to scream out into the morning air.

Violet inhaled once. Salt from sweat. The lavender wash on Meema's clothes. The strawberry scent of her shampoo. She pressed her face once more into her guardian's hands, willing them to protect her.

But her guardian was gone and there was no one left to understand the pain of losing Reed. The desperation clawed at Violet to see him again, as she stared into the abyss of her mind and the grave Mai was digging for her.

Violet pried her face away. Lip trembling, she said, "I'll bring him home."

Meema's face pained before blanking again.

The blood-curdling howls that Violet had woken up to the morning of Reed's sentence would forever be etched in her brain. Meema loved Reed dearly, and that fateful morning, the pure agony within those grief-filled wails had shocked Violet before she'd even processed the loss. Violet had run down the stairs to find the door wide open, Meema kneeling on the street, screaming to the sky.

Why why why? Not my boy! Not my baby boy!

Violet placed a delicate kiss on her forehead and folded Jack Marin's ruby ring into her palm.

"I will bring him home. Just in time for dinner, okay?" Violet whispered.

Meema's thin brows drew together, confused.

Before it could hurt even more, Violet turned toward the window, brushing back the curtain. She gave one look back to her guardian, her only mother figure, as she stared stoically at Violet.

"I love you," Violet said. "And I will see you again. I promise."

And then she left, descending the side gutter with a slide of her bandana so her hands wouldn't burn, until Mai's cold eyes met hers, and the car door opened.

A threat Mai was clearly following up. The woman stepped close to Violet's face like when they breathed each other's air before a kiss. But now…now it was only a glower filled with promises of hurt.

Violet's heart thumped weakly.

"Where are we going?" Violet asked.

Mai brushed a strand of hair behind Violet's ear. Violet fought the urge to punch her as Mai crooned, "It's a holiday today, right?"

Violet held Mai's glare for a moment, daring even to lift her chin, which Mai snorted at.

"You're so beautiful when you're broken," Mai breathed. "I want to unravel all of it."

Is there anything left to break?

"You need to work on your poetry," deadpanned Violet as she turned and slid into the backseat. Mai scowled and took the front passenger.

Violet looked out the window as the driver veered through the streets of the Mid, to the archaic center of Calesal—the Aariva.

Her breaths ached, each one like needles pricking her throat. Of course, Mai wanted to bring her to the ceremony.

Of course, she wanted to rip off the bandage and laugh at a bleeding wound.

6

ʙLOODSWORN

THE LAST TIME VIOLET HAD been within the Aariva, she was held back by Reed's friends while she screamed for her brother as he walked across the stage, his gaze a thousand sorries she had never ended up hearing.

The body odor, the wind, and dust burning her eyes, the incessant sweat like second skin transported her to two years ago, but she shoved it down. This was a ruse, a scare. Mai had to be here anyway for her father, so she dragged Violet along to make her hurt.

The metal arena curved in an oval, towering black pillars sparked with red flames atop them. Between the pillars, rows of seats that had been empty for years were now packed with Elites and Midians. Banners with the insignia of the Empire of Veceras hung all around: two plaswhips crossed and a hawk soaring up in the middle, painted blood red and encased in a circle. Beyond the thousands of heads before them, a cream and black stage jutted out. On the lower of the three daises, a gleaming obsidian bowl beckoned like a black hole, two arches of the same obsidian material behind it.

The second dais held empire officials, mostly old and wrinkly men who'd never seen the sun, and a couple of scattered women who looked like they would rather be anywhere else. Upon the top dais, the chair for Emperor Neuven sat empty. Five other chairs surrounded his for the commanders of the city.

The wind whipped like a snake through the arena and carried the roar of the crowd. It was large enough to fit at least a fourth of the city but, judging from the infestation surrounding rooftops and the full balconies in the North, a distant blur, the biggest turnout of the Sins was upon them.

Two of Mai's guards flanked her as they rose in the elevator to the top of the stands. Violet felt very out of place—dried blood still on her face, stolen jewelry on her person, braid matted from the sweat at her back, and her obvious Souther clothes compared to the long dresses and pantsuits of the Elites.

They shuffled through the seats until one of the guards shoved her down. The area smelled of floral fragrance and cologne, and Violet wished she'd gagged enough to vomit on the guard.

"Enjoy the *show*," Mai sneered, then moved away to join her brothers nearer the stage.

Each guard took a seat beside her.

Violet could spot the Magister of the Sins, Domnus Quiope—a scrawny man dressed in polished leather and a long cape—step up to the podium near the bowl.

"*On this day, we recognize the five-hundred-and-twenty-first Bloodswearing Ceremony for the curse laid upon us,*" he announced, his rough voice drilling into the crowd. "*All that time ago, the skies brought forth the Sky Arches, an entrance and an exit to various worlds beyond, and between them, the bowl for those swearing themselves in to venture.*

"*The Bloodswearing Ceremony binds candidates to the game. It brings us together as a nation as we remember the feat of the Sins, in the hopes that one day, this curse that forces our citizens into the worlds—*"

"Skivvin' liar," a large woman spat. A group of Elite women turned from their seats, horrified.

If she hadn't been so terrified, Violet would have snorted.

"—*beyond. Lust. Pride. Gluttony. Envy. Wrath. Greed. Sloth. Seven worlds, each cursed with one of the deadly sins. It is known that if we do not continue to send candidates into the Sins, our world suffers disastrous consequences.*" Quiope raised his hands, motioning to the wind that whistled across the city, lashing at the banners. Elites and Midians in the stands cried as it grew louder. "*So every year, we gather on the summer solstice to pay our dues to this curse, and applaud the thousands of heartbeats remaining, and mourn the ones we lost before we could claim victory. I now call on our beloved emperor and the city commanders for their continuous work on their alliance to bring prosperity to our city.*"

Emperor Neuven appeared from the side of the vast stage, black leather ensemble tight around his protruding belly, while a silver diadem gleamed at his brow. His cape billowed behind him, followed by his consort; his third wife, four sons, and two daughters. All had different mothers except the two middle sons.

Quiope continued, looking down at a paper. "*The Sins work as such: each candidate will have their hand slashed and blood delivered into the bowl. They are then graced with twenty minutes and given their appropriate provisions before they step into the Entrance. Before their journey lies seven worlds of sin, and it is up to them and their redemption to fight the sin thrice in each world, as explained by the inscription above the Entrance Arch. With each win against a sin, the candidate will experience a burning sensation along their bloodsworn scar—which acts as their deep connection to the game and allows them the ability to travel between worlds. On the third win, the candidate will receive a key to be used in the plinth, the next portal, which will then transport them to the next world.*

"*All candidates' families will receive a generous payment each time a candidate passes through a world. The Empire strives to provide for those who give their sacrifice to break this curse.*"

Violet did receive those payments for the six times Reed passed through worlds, but those went straight to Meema's fees. They were not as generous as the Empire made them seem.

"*For over five-hundred years, our world has suffered and bowed to this unknown curse. We know the game must be played and sacrifices must be made. We hope that one of you will find your redemption and return with greatness for our city, empire, and world. Other countries don't know just how much we expend for this fight. They look to destroy our protective walls and bring war to our soil for continuing to send candidates. But we know—*"Quiope's hands lifted to the thrashing sky. "*We know that if we don't, this world will cease to exist. And it is bestowed upon our empire and city to make sure we persevere.*"

The stands roared, the floor cried out in opposition.

Quiope shoved his paper into his pocket and lifted his hand. "I will now read the prophecy to commence the Bloodswearing Ceremony."

He knelt before the obsidian bowl and dragged his hand within, smearing the dust that had gathered there.

"*Behold the sins.*
But beware the blood,
because beyond the war,
and beneath the stars
one shall rise
and another will fall.
By a blade of dawn
and the slash of dusk
the creator will perish
and return to dust.
Long ago, we had forgotten
what had doomed us all
but blood will rise
and awaken at its call."

Clouds drew toward the city. They blackened above, heads and faces lifted to the sky, gasping—

A streak of lightning cleaved the sky.

Before Quiope, the bowl began to smoke.

Violet always scoffed at the strange magic, but after Reed's sentencing, that smoke haunted her. Her chest grew tight as she stared, fully aware of the hold this curse had on their world. Lightning and droughts and earthquakes, like ten years ago, could not be manufactured. They simply couldn't, but she struggled to blindly believe that *this* needed to happen. That there was some otherworldly magic dooming them all, victimizing her neighbors and eventually her brother. All for this game and whoever rolled in the grave that created it.

"It is the time!" roared Quiope. "Bring out the candidates!"

The Southers roared in anger. The reaping at the square was not forgotten.

"Seventy, can you believe it?" someone near said. "They should send every Souther in if they could. It would stop the riots and, well, certainly help improve the city."

Violet jerked in her seat, ready to turn and throw a punch to the man behind her, but the guard shoved her shoulder forward.

"They are just excited to shove Marin in there—he gets what he deserves for siding with the gardia."

"How could you say such a thing?" an Elite woman gasped. "He is phenomenal. He did more good than you could ever know."

The other person brushed her off. "Get someone else to fawn over. Arvalo is good to send him there. The Sins are worse than death; he'll taste fear and then die soon enough."

Redders stood before the stage, hands on their plasguns as the Southers on the floor cried, spat in their faces, and shoved their hands. One Redder already had his whip out and flexed it against the ground.

"Skies, they act like animals," a woman near her said, placing her hand on her chest.

The guard next to her snorted.

"Why am I here?" Violet jerked her arm.

"Punish—"

"Breathing your awful body odor is punishment enough," snapped Violet. "Now, tell me why I'm here."

The other guard coughed a laugh while the one she interrupted reddened in the face. He turned to her, anger twisting his features. "Watch the candidates, Souther rat. Your friend is going in."

"Excuse me?" she snapped.

"*Watch*," he taunted.

Another crack of thunder shook the Aariva.

"Bring them out!"

"Forrest Kay!"

"Gerald Atonia!"

"Hung Danner!"

"Lov Zanser!"

They dragged candidate after candidate out, clothes hanging from thin and muscular bodies alike, all shades of skin tone and some with dark lines of tattoos. Some glanced at the setting sun searing in between the columns, eyes gaunt and hollow as if their life had been sucked dry. Clothes hung in shreds off some bodies; she suspected they had been dragged from the pit of the Empire's prison.

The first one, Forrest Kay, was shackled in chains head to toe, a yellow-toothed smirk on his face. The crowd roared angrily, and he simply laughed as he lumbered up to the bowl where Quiope was waiting with the bloodswearing blade.

A Redder hung Kay's right hand over the lip. The black blade sucked in all light as Quiope raised it and slashed. Kay hardly flinched, if not smiled more, as he watched his blood drip into the bowl.

Behind him, looming like dual moons outlined by obsidian, the two Sky Arches stood. Iridescent smoke shifted and curled within them.

There was a tug on her navel. The smoke wisped, the rainbow of colors like dancing ribbons. Her mouth parted, heartbeat loud in her ears. For a moment, she could hear something else—the pounding of metal, the guttural roar of a motor, a haughty cackle, and a thunderous crack of a whip.

When the smoke curled again in its dance, she stopped breathing.

A broad, hilly landscape. A dark sky with three moons shooting like an arrow. Firecrackers bursting with light. All behind the haze of the smoke, but there—

Violet blinked. Rubbed her eyes. Looked again. It was gone. The sounds, the image, gone, as if she had imagined it…

She probably had.

The Redders standing guard gave a wide berth to the otherworldly arches. If they walked through, if the smoke from those arches even touched someone, they'd turn into dust. She'd seen it once before, many years ago, when a fight had broken out before the candidates were sworn in.

That was also what happened if someone bloodsworn didn't enter the arches before the entire sunset. A janitor came out at some point to sweep up the remains.

It had fazed her before that Reed might be dead, and the trackers were fake. But after something like last night, and only in the sixth world? How would the Empire fabricate that? And why would they, when they sent Redders to reap Southers and throw them in as if they were cleaning stones from a gutter?

More and more names were called. Violet counted—eighteen, nineteen, twenty. As they moved across the stage, the clouds above softened, parted, and whitened from the growing storm. No rain would ever fall—that would be a blessing from the curse. A contradiction, Jenkins had put it.

"Jack Marin!"

Her head whipped to the stage as the entire crowd released a deafening cry.

The storm paused its retreat for the man strutting, handcuffed, between two pillars at the left of the stage. Lightning flashed as his eyes met the crowd. Screams were all she heard. Some of anger, hurt, others of love, adoration. They battled within the tepid air until they morphed into cries of…emotion. Attention. That was what Jack Marin was getting, and by the look of him, that was what he wanted.

Gasps rang out at his injuries. A yellowing bruise on his jawline, dried blood beneath his still-straight nose, heavy black from clotted blood underneath his left eye. He was still wearing the same all-black suit—now shredded along his torso and thighs, the material charred at the edges. By some advanced healing, the cuts were merely pink scars at this point, but dried blood still clung.

"Holy skies," said one female Elite. "How is he not dead?"

"Bummer," mumbled Violet, crossing her arms.

The Elite's friend scoffed. "He still looks hot."

Marin's eyes swept over the crowd as if he were disappointed it wasn't larger. A smile hung on his lips, a single dimple showing. Seven Redders flanked him, and when he reached the center stage, one of the other City Commanders held his hand up, stood, and descended the two platforms.

Quiope looked ready to throw himself off the stage with Marin's proximity. His face paled by two shades, and he situated himself behind another Redder while the other commander reached the podium.

Commander Arvalo was a pale, pointy-chinned, scowling, middle-aged man. One look at Marin, though, had an icy grin dragging on his face. But there was something about Arvalo that made her skin crawl—the lack of humanity behind his dark eyes. Mai certainly inherited her father's sneer.

"City Commander Jack Marin of Trade and Commerce," said Arvalo, his voice as sharp as his gaze. "On behalf of the Citadel of Calesal, I hereby sentence you to the Sins for your crimes on charges of treason against the Empire of Veceras, the Citadel of Calesal, your connection to the notorious gardia, and the murders of innocent people during the uprisings organized and acted on by you." Arvalo lifted his chin. "You have been found guilty, and you are now publicly stripped of your command to our city."

If Marin's look could kill Arvalo, he'd be a puddle of liquified bones.

The wind whipped, protesting the delay in the bloodswearing. Another streak of lightning flashed as Jack's curls swept to the side, crusted with blood at his temple. His jaw clenched, but he said nothing.

Arvalo stepped in front of him with haughty smugness. He nodded once, and two Redders ripped Marin's right shirtsleeve clean off, revealing the red tattoo of Marin's gardia on his upper arm.

Violet's jaw cracked as fury rushed through her.

The mark was too detailed to compare to her target last night, but she knew the crest of a wave and snakes within that red circle meant him. His gang. His war. His terror he brought upon the city for five years. For a long while, she was ashamed to hear the news that Reed had worked for him, but soon that shame simmered, and anger bubbled.

Manipulative, uncaring, sociopath. All things whispered about Jack Marin in the South. All things her brother was labeled when it was revealed Reed stood next to Marin for part of it.

The stands collectively released a horrific gasp at his tattoo. *Gardia? Gardia? How could he betray us to the gangs?*

One woman fainted a couple of rows in front.

Arvalo was handed a glowing device, smoke rising from the burning tip, and pressed it to Marin's gardia tattoo.

The crowd gasped as the horrible sound of burning skin filled the space, picked up by the microphone. Marin grunted but took it with a clenched jaw, those eyes startlingly clear, boring into Arvalo's so fiercely that Arvalo's smirk faltered for a second. There was a promise there, a promise of death and revenge, that he would return one day. Arvalo removed the device and handed it back to a Redder, a flash of disappointment to Marin's lackluster reaction.

When Arvalo retreated to his chair up at the highest dais, Marin released a long, steady breath. The skin where the tattoo had been was now gnarled with red-purple skin, blistering.

Quiope slashed Marin's hand. Blood poured into the bowl. The crowd roared. Lightning lit up the sky again. He watched it icily, and then, as if he felt her hot, burning gaze, his eyes flicked up.

Their eyes met. His lips twitched. Teasing her. She wanted to abandon everything to climb up on stage, take that scalding prong, and shove it straight into his face.

He gave her a look that said: *try me, I fucking dare you.*

And then he was walking across the stage, not giving her another glare, nodding toward the crowd as it bid its mixed farewell.

The storm slowed, lightning stopped. Fifty-five. Fifty-nine. Sixty-six.

"Jenji Opan!"

Violet's eyes roamed the remaining line as she fiddled with the giant, funny ring she'd stolen the night before her fingers had found Marin's ring.

It had buttons. She wondered if it would light up with plasma inside. She was itching to press it—

"Garan Umbero!"

Her head whipped to the stage.

He'll be okay, Jelan had said.

The hulking mass of Garan towered over his two Redder escorts. A fresh plasburn blistered at the back of his neck, followed by another that had torn a hole through his white shirt.

Violet's heart dropped in her chest. She swallowed her panicked sob as old screams banged around her mind:

Reed! No—not Reed! Please!

Take me…take me…take me.

Garan didn't tremble. Didn't balk as he stood over the bowl, and his hand was slashed. He didn't even fight. No one did.

Take me…take me…take me.

Tears burned her eyes.

He'll be okay.

The Souther crowd roared below. Hot anger, revenge, tension she wished she could join in on crackled like the sky above. Angry from the reaping, the number of people destined for the bowl who weren't criminals. Weren't like Jack Marin. People like Garan who only served their community and nothing more. People who didn't deserve to be exiled from their home.

But no matter if criminals littered the prisons. A reaping in the South would muzzle any of those who dared challenge the game. It was more than bending a knee to the curse—it was a way to force the knees of the citizens to the Empire's power over their lives.

"Stop them!" Quiope yelled from the podium. "No—keep the candidates coming! Scott Pollin!"

The storm returned due to the delay again. She closed her eyes, taking a deep breath, because this was the reaction when Reed was sentenced. But instead of others' screams, it was her. Her. Her. Her. Vocal cords shredding from the agony, tears blinding her eyes, shoulders aching as she was held back from running on that stage.

How she wished she'd fought for him. Done *something*.

Her heart picked up in a panic. She squeezed her eyes shut and attempted to drown out the crowd. She wanted to scream into the cursed air at how unfair it all was—how useless she was and would continue to be. She wanted to sprint. Fight. Light up like a flame and burn.

She white-knuckled the ring. One of the guards tightened his grip enough on her arm to have her gasp in pain. He dragged her closer so her hand, and the ring, was pressed into his bulging thigh.

"Sit still," he commanded.

Her thumb had found a notch. Curiously, she pressed it.

The luminous blue of the ring heated with plasma, bright sparks bursting from the center and burning through the guard's pants until they met his skin.

He convulsed next to her. Eyes rolled back into his head, skin reddening by the second as both plasmic heat and sharp plascution hit him. An Elite jumped out of the way behind them as the guard's head dropped back, and foam bubbled from his mouth.

Violet stared wide-eyed. "Woah."

"What the…" The other guard stood up, yanking her with him.

She flew with the momentum and aimed the ring straight into his neck.

He spasmed instantly, thick veins purpling at his neck and crawling along his jaw. His eyes rolled back.

He collapsed before her, head thunking on the back of his seat.

"Woah," she said again, looking toward the ring with the hint of a smile. "Finders keepers."

"Kole Akard!"

Her head snapped to the stage. Her peripheral vision blurred, ears limited to the dull pulse of her blood. Time slowed. Watch. Watch. Watch.

Your friend is going in.

Not Garan. Not even Jelan.

No. It was the innocent, kiss-on-the-cheek Kole. The puppy-in-love Kole.

And with the eyes of Mai on her back, Violet snapped.

She vaulted out of her seat to the cries of Elites around her. They dodged out of her way, but her mind was a frenzy, running, the only word in her head *no.*

No no no no no.

Not again.

Take me…take me…take me.

Because when her head whipped to that stage, she saw Reed. Saw his confusion, the defeat. She blinked. Back to Kole. He trembled on the stage, walking so slow—

And then she was running; along the back of chairs, stepping on the shoulders of a man, and lunging for the climbable pole at the end of the stands and closest to the stage.

"Oh no, you don't," snarled Mai, lunging across chairs for Violet.

Violet swung her fist, plastaser and all, and blasted Mai in the neck with the energy.

Mai dropped to the ground. Elites gasped, shrieked. Violet only growled, "Take your stupid daddy issues elsewhere."

Violet dove for a tall, gutter-like pole lining the stands. She wrapped her elbow around and plummeted.

The crowd gasped as she dropped. Fast.

But due to all of her time spent running from Redders, from her brother, from Meema's rages and strings of curses, sliding down poles and gutters was muscle memory.

The Souther crowd picked up its cries, pressing against the barricade holding them from the stage. Some jumped over, some tackled Redders. As she neared the ground, she leaped out for the edge of the stage, rolling onto her feet with ease.

Southers overtook the barricade and began to clamber on. Violet was running, sliding, not thinking, simply doing because she didn't want her life to fall apart. She didn't want to see another name on the screen.

She didn't want to be separated from her brother any longer.

She wanted hope. Family.

Blood.

"Settle this! Get her!" Quiope cried, but the Southers overran the stage, and the Redders were overwhelmed.

She sprinted toward Kole. He whirled on her, bruises on his cheek, confusion on his face.

"Violet?" he gasped. More Redders poured onto the stage, the clicks of their boots like the pounding of her pulse. "How are you—?"

"This might hurt."

"What—"

She shoved the plastaser on his exposed sternum and pressed the button. Kole spasmed, collapsing to the stage.

"Get her! Get someone! Now!" Quiope took a step toward her as if he would fight her off.

She snarled, and he dodged, dagger in his hand.

The sky flared above. The earth rumbled. The sun glowed in its final descent.

Violet had eyes for the glooming outline of the bowl filled nearly to the rim with blood. Waiting for one more.

Her navel tugged again.

Something snapped inside her. The bowl called. Her blood sang toward it, heating in a frenzy beneath her skin.

Come, child of the Sins. Give us your essence. Give us your life.

She lunged.

In a blur, she slammed the plastaser right into Quiope's hand and pressed. The bloodswearing blade fell. She caught it in her other hand, dropping the plastaser.

She stood before the bowl, dagger held aloft, as lightning and thunder cried above. The world was waiting for its last sacrifice.

Violet Sutton slashed her left hand. Blood poured into the bowl.

Stinging erupted.

"*No!*" Quiope screamed.

Her blood.

"*NO!*"

She watched it swirl in a daze.

Her blood. Her blood.

It churned. With the others. A mixture for the Sins.

A giant gong sounded above, below, within her. It shook her bones, her core, to the pounding heart within her chest. The blood of seventy candidates disappeared from the bowl. And then it seemed to sing.

For the first time in a long time, she felt as though she had done something right. Not for glory, not for fame, but because she was tired of the push and pull on these decrepit streets. She wanted out. She wanted life.

She wanted freedom.

And a chance.

A smile grew.

Wild and wicked.

She was going to see her brother again.

Plasma shocked the back of her neck. The smile faltered. Her limbs numbed and she fell forward, head careening into the bowl, knocking her into sweet, staticky darkness.

7

TRACKER

THE SEVEN DEADLY SINS WERE part of a childhood game throughout her life, especially for Southers. She grew up playing with the kids on her street in challenges of wrath, gluttony, lust, greed, envy, pride and sloth. Students studied the seven sins in Souther schools with disgruntled expressions from the teachers. Violet always remembered when the Midian principal had entered the room, and her teacher would strike up a big smile as she taught the depictions of gluttony.

"Over-consumption. That means not eating candy until your belly is going to burst, Mr. Silas. Gluttony establishes a terrible cycle of wasting food when we should be mindful of what we need and what we consume—"

The door slammed. The principal left.

The teacher's expression saddened. And Violet, always stuck in the front of the class because of her terrible focus, heard the next mumble,

"That also means not taking the kid's food for your family, hypocrite," the teacher grumbled to the closed door.

Regardless, they were just games. Words. Until an older brother's hand was slashed.

Wrath: Smash a plate against a wall and see how many pieces it breaks into, followed by one's loudest scream. For the older kids, it was fistfights.

Gluttony: *Do* see how many pieces of candy one can fit into your mouth.

Lust: Go into the closet with the other individual, and one closes their eyes until the other kisses them in the dark.

Greed: See how many marks one can steal from the local market.

Envy: A dare to prank the person one is jealous of.

Pride: Win at a sports game and receive the crown to wear for the rest of the week.

Sloth: See how long one can lie in bed before their bladder bursts. Points to those who pee the bed.

Also, like right now, lie limply while being dragged underneath an alcove within the Aariva. Unable to move. Unable to even pee her pants if she wanted to. The grip on her ankle numbed the feeling of her foot. Another arch passed above her. The hot linoleum of the stage gave way to shadow.

"Wake her," commanded a Redder through his com.

"She's already awake, sir."

"If she is to be a candidate—"

"She *is* a candidate," snarled a voice. Domnus Quiope's bulbous face appeared above her. "The bowl has accepted the offering. She must go through with the others." He met her gaze. "You might have just lost me my job with that stunt, girl."

Violet only croaked a breath, unable to laugh at the absurdity of what it did to *him*.

"Get her a female pack. I want the doctor in here with a plascution patch and the regular shots." Quiope sneered once more and then disappeared from her gaze.

"Sir," a group of Redders responded.

Whatever room she was in, it was bare. A closet for some basic privacy at the back of the Aariva. The crowd quieted through the stone, and the sweat had cooled on her skin. She could feel the blood leaking from her hand—a warm reminder of her act. Some chants started outside, and then gunshots fired into the air. The only movement she could make was a blink.

A moment later, two female faces looked down at her.

"Give her the plascution patch and check her vitals, Nina," instructed the sterner-looking one. She glanced at Violet. "My name is Dr. Evek. What is your name?"

A cool, tingly sensation blossomed from Violet's forearm. Violet jerked away as hands met her skin and tapped at her inner elbow.

The doctor brushed her hair back. "Shhh, it is all right. She is just going to take a blood sample, and we will do a quick check to make sure your vitals look good."

"Don't—" breathed Violet. "Don't touch me."

Another cool sensation to her palm.

"I'm going to have to touch you," said the doctor. "And you're going to let me."

"Don't touch me...." Violet's eyes lifted to the doctor's hand that petted her hair. "Like that."

"Oh." Dr. Evek frowned. "All right, then. I won't. What is your name?"

"Violet Sutton."

A pinch at her inner elbow.

"And why did you bloodswear yourself, Ms. Sutton?"

"I didn't want to hurt anymore," came Violet's broken whisper. "And I want to see my brother again."

"Is your brother in the game?"

A weak nod.

"Did you know that man you shocked?"

Another nod.

Dr. Evek frowned, deepening the lines around her mouth.

Violet's sensations slowly came back to her as the shock wore away. She wiggled her toes, scrunched her nose, and with a grunt, she peeled herself from the floor. The room whirled in her vision, and the nurse nudged Violet so she leaned against a wall. But Violet attempted to stand, swaying—

"Steady now. They shocked you pretty bad." Dr. Evek placed one of her palms over Violet's. "Nina, the vitals."

Nina handed her a plascreen tablet, one of the few Violet had ever seen, and Dr. Evek tapped away on it. A vial of her blood lay inserted into the top.

"Everything looks normal, save for standard deficiencies."

"For Southers?" blurted Violet, removing her hand.

Dr. Evek ignored her. "Did you eat at all in the last twenty-four hours?"

"Probably not."

"I will give you a shot that will help with nutrition before you go in, along with another. It is the normal protocol for female candidates to receive a birth control shot. At the moment, it only lasts a year, so be careful after."

Violet's gaze dropped to the healing patch on her left hand. The translucent bandage was rare and fast-healing, something nonexistent in the South. She clenched it. She knew she had made a deep cut out of desperation, but now it felt like it never happened.

All of it felt like it never happened.

"Fine," mumbled Violet.

She stared as Nina swabbed her upper arm and did the first shot.

"A boost of vitamins," clarified Dr. Evek as she handed over a silver bottle. "But drink this too. It is filled with protein and will keep you satisfied for a while."

Violet's mouth was too dry to even be worried about her next meal, but she drank the shake anyway.

Another pinch at her arm. "The birth control."

Again, Violet didn't meet the gaze of the other two women. Although Nina's more a scowl, pity lined their faces as they shuffled through their bags once more.

"And now for the tracker. You will need to hold still and relax for this one."

Violet glowered but didn't move as Nina unwrapped a thick syringe with a ridiculous needle.

"It goes above your clavicle—"

"Just get it over with," Violet said quickly.

Dr. Evek merely nodded and gripped Violet's jaw tightly. Nina's smooth hands wrapped the back of Violet's neck.

When the needle punctured, Violet's eyes watered at the momentary lack of breath. Her fists clenched.

"It's normal. Almost done," said Dr. Evek.

As she said that, the needle left, and Violet gasped for a breath. Nina pressed another healing patch at her neck.

The crowd still roared. Only ten minutes might have passed since Violet bloodswore herself, but in her disoriented state, Violet barely registered the darkening of the room. A knock sounded at the door, and a Redder's com broke through their sudden silence.

"Clothes for the candidate. Hurry up."

"Almost done." Dr. Evek called back before pulling Violet forward by the arm and muttering, "Quickly, Nina."

A smaller syringe and a colossal needle glinted in Nina's hand. Nina held Violet's arm taut, and the nurse had the needle in and out before she could blink.

"What—" Violet started.

"Listen to me very carefully." Dr. Evek's voice was barely above a whisper. "Clench your fist and tap three times to activate it. It takes only two seconds to reach your heart. It is a painless death."

A loud bang shook the door. "Hurry up, doctor!"

Dr. Evek didn't flinch. "You did a brave thing, saving that man. This world doesn't see much of that, but you proved that it could happen. That people can care, and maybe we can stop this curse once and for all. You do not deserve to befall whatever awaits you in those worlds."

"What is in my arm?" The pounding grew louder. The nurse hurried to pack away the items, wincing at each boom. "What awaits me? What are you talking about?"

"Seven worlds of sin. Seven worlds of other species, landscapes, and cultures, and still our people die. You don't deserve to die fighting a losing battle."

The image of her brother sprouted in her mind. Eyes open and unblinking. "*Our* people?" breathed Violet. The last of the doctor's words hit her. "You gave me a vial of death so I could off myself in the name of change?"

"If you did it within the first week, it would make a tremendous impact."

Violet's eyes snapped to meet the doctor's pleading look. Aghast, fury flashed into Violet so hard that her palms shook, and she scooted away. After being poked and prodded, given birth control so she didn't find the consequences after—Violet shook her head and seethed, "I am *not* your game."

Dr. Evek merely frowned and stood. "No one has exited the Sins for a reason, Sutton." She brushed her smock. "They are not supposed to."

Violet was shocked, nearly in tears, when the door banged open and a Redder clambered in. They threw a pile of black clothing at Violet. "Get changed."

"Good luck," Dr. Evek said.

Her arm throbbed, and she looked down. A small, thin rod of death indented the pink skin to the side of her wrist. A clench of the fist and three taps.

Now she was given death? All those drugs and shiva and daggers to her neck were laughing. She had walked along the edge of the tallest buildings in the city, and this...it was this easy?

A short, loud laugh bubbled out of her.

And it was all for a *show*?

Both the doctor and Redders looked back at Violet as she laughed again. And again.

"Crazy bitch," the Redder said.

The door slammed shut.

8

It's Cute

THE CLOTHES WERE SOME OF the finest Violet had ever worn.

A short-sleeve top made of black material molded to her skin, followed by tight dark pants with pockets that flexed when she lunged.

Didn't hurt that her ass looked good in them, also.

Simple calf-high socks, soft-soled leather boots, and a thick leather belt completed the outfit. She also had both a backpack and a tiny dark green pouch that she buckled around her hips.

The provisions were simple: two daggers, liquid hydration packets, bite-size nutrition bars, dried meat, a flint for fires, drops of purifying tablets, two bandanas, a collapsible sleeping bag, a simple brown sweater, a strange crunchy material for a jacket, and a leather body harness.

Violet stared at the harness for a long time before realizing she was supposed to put it on. It crisscrossed her chest and sported two side sheaths for her knives, which she filled.

Her food? It would last a week.

Her water? A week.

She dipped her gaze to the indent of the death vial and nearly wanted to laugh again. Looks like Calesal will be getting their show no matter what.

Her pessimistic outlook stopped there. She wasn't going to beat herself up for making such a desperate action to... *save Kole*, even though saving Kole had ten percent to do with it, and the other ninety was guilt.

Bring him home.

Meema's voice rang in her head. Reed was her reason; along with escaping this life that only dealt her bad hands she was gullible enough to pick up.

Whatever waited for her in the next world wouldn't have Reed haunting her at every corner. It wouldn't have Jelan, either, or Kole, for that matter. But Kole would be wrapped up in his parents' rich, loving arms, and Jelan...she would find her way. She would be okay.

"All changed, candidate?"

Violet didn't answer, and the Redder didn't care to hear one. He opened the door, helmet moving up and down to take in her appearance, and stepped aside to let her through. "Time for your journey."

Violet tightened the straps of her backpack and left the room.

Like she had suspected, she was behind the Aariva in a long, curved hallway made of tall pillars blanketed with banners of the Empire's sigil. The wind of the Sins had settled to a steady breeze, but lightning still marked the sky, brilliant against the last rays of the setting sun. Thunder cleaved in the distance.

The arches needed their candidates now.

As Violet numbly trudged behind two Redders, other doors opened along the wall she came out of. Candidates appeared, dressed similarly to her, some with haunted looks, some glaring at their bandaged, bloodsworn hand, and others with the hint of a smile on their face. Glances passed her way, but Violet kept her gaze on the back of the Redder's boot.

Jelan's soft face blossomed in her head. There was no disappointed expression—no, Jelan wouldn't give Violet that. Instead, she'd say: *Why? Why did you do it?*

"I'm sorry," whispered Violet to her friend. *I'm sorry you weren't enough. I'm sorry I didn't think of you. I'm sorry you will have to watch me now, a drink in your hand, and wonder about the dangers I will face.*

Do not worry, Vi, Jelan would say. *Be free of these walls and these screens. Go find your happiness. Bring your brother home.*

A tear slipped down Violet's cheek at that. She doubted the words would be kind, but Jelan would tell her to take her frantic decision and milk it for all it was worth.

And Meema…

My boy! My boy! My boy!

Would she become conscious soon and find her eyes on the screen, looking for Reed, as usual, only to see Violet's name there as well? Would she cry, break, as Violet did for Reed? Or would she chalk it up to Violet's chaotic nature for sentencing herself?

"Keep moving," a Redder snapped.

Violet hadn't realized she stopped her walking.

"If you ever end up in those worlds, I'll tear apart each one of them and bring you home. Don't you worry."

Violet lifted her gaze to the two Redder helmets staring back at her. Behind them, the last alcove of pillars led onto the stage where the Sky Arches stood, the swirling mist within an alien calling. Her bloodsworn mark seared as if sensing the proximity.

Violet took one step, then another.

"Going to save your brother, little Vi?" a deep voice rumbled.

She halted. Clenched her fists and ignored the slice of tension that ran through the back halls. Every click of a Redder boot stopped.

"Are you coming…" Quiope appeared from the stage, his words trailing as he glanced behind Violet's shoulder. He paled slightly and stepped behind a nearby Redder.

Violet lazily looked over her shoulder.

Jack Marin stood in the all-black glory of his candidate gear. She'd forgotten how tall he was, but it wasn't basic height that made him appear as intimidating as he did now. It was the calm iciness to his demeanor—an unbothered predator surrounded by easy prey. His lean stature gave way to no tension or fear, and there was even a slight smile on his lips. A dimple pinched his cheek.

His eyes flickered with a haunting expression, one she'd witnessed in far too many people who were on either the brink of happiness or crazy. Excited. Relieved.

"Mad I took the show from you, Marin?" she gritted out.

He seemed to ignore her question as his smile broadened. "It's cute."

"What is?"

He walked up to her, and four Redders appeared. Her gaze snagged on the two daggers at his side, but she knew Jack didn't need such weapons to deliver death. She'd heard the rumors, and glimpsed the bodies. She knew when Reed had come home pale and covered in blood one night, saying over and over.

He did it with his hands. Only his strong, beautiful hands.

Between the Redders, as unbothered as ever, he gazed down, that same flicker in his green eyes revealing a sense of awe. "The fire in you."

And then he brushed past her.

A gloved hand wrapped her arm and yanked. She spun toward the stage where candidates had lined up. The minute she stepped out, cries echoed from the floor. They reverberated toward the very back. Hands rose. Clapped.

The girl! She's going in!

"Why did you do it, Sutton?"

The broken voice of Garan snapped her head a couple of candidates to the front.

Garan continued, "Was it love? Did you just sell your fate for love?"

Violet avoided his gaze, instead finding Kole slumped against a pillar, dried blood along the side of his face. Two similar faces hovered around him—his mother with tears streaming down her face, his father an astonished expression.

Kole was crying too. "Violet... why?"

Something she couldn't place lingered within those words. His father bristled at the sharpness of Kole's *why*, and his mother downturned her eyes. Not the looks of nearly losing an innocent son to the Sins, but the look of a parent being in the wrong. Violet had seen that look in her mother's sharp face more times than she could count, and for a bright second, she regretted saving Kole, because a part of Kole looked like he might have been relieved if he separated from his guilty-looking parents.

"Sorry for shocking you," Violet said dryily, making sure her expression stayed bored. "Be happy, Kole."

When Violet turned back around, nearly half of the candidates had already entered the Arch. Jack Marin stepped up, turned to look once toward the city that both loved and feared him, and to the screams of the stands, he faced the Arch. Then stepped through.

His body was consumed by wisps of iridescent smoke until nothing but quiet whirls remained.

The candidates before her passed in without a word, faces solemn as they, too, looked back on the city once more.

She stepped forward and faced the Arch.

The wisps were the color of moonlight, twisting and glittering like a shimmered welcome into worlds unknown. Beyond that lay Reed. Beyond that lay freedom.

Like the bowl had, the Arch called to her, a deep, cool voice in her mind.

Welcome, child of the Sins.

Over her shoulder, she took one look back at the city that had bruised her, scarred her, and raised her.

Violet blinked back the wretched water in her eyes, turned toward the Arch, and stepped through it.

Warmth blossomed on her skin. Her bloodsworn mark tingled as the wisps engulfed her. A wicked smile split her face.

To the next adventure, indeed.

PART II
THE SINS

9

THE FIRST SIN

VIOLET SCREAMED THE ENTIRE TIME she fell. Warm darkness surrounded and claimed her breath. For a moment she was moving sideways, and then up, and finally, gravity locked on her bones, and she slammed straight into coarse, fluffy ground.

Sand. It sank into the folds of her clothes, scratched at her skin, crunched in her ears, slid out of her braid. Her ears screeched with a high-pitched sound. Blinding light watered her eyes. Disoriented, she gasped for a breath but only inhaled the hot grit. She clawed herself out of her pocket of sand, unable to see, unable to get a proper hold until she heaved herself up and scorching rays met her cheeks.

The air was harsh—not Sins Eve harsh, but thicker. Sweltering. The heat seared her skin; not humid, but dry. She blinked. Blinked again.

She had half a mind that she had ended up on the outskirts of Calesal, and the Sins were just some big joke. Her heart thundered in response—no, she was not in her world anymore. The knowingness of it slid along her skin, like fate wrapping its hands on her shoulders, tilting her chin up to the first world, the first sin, and saying *there, look at it.*

Is this the freedom you yearned for?

Her breaths were panicked. On hands and knees, Violet gaped before her.

"I've found the desert, Professor Doln," she mumbled, throat dry. "And you wouldn't skivvin' believe it."

The desert sprawled before her—endless mounds of curving dunes half as tall as skyscrapers and bright against the mammoth sun in the blue, cloudless sky. In the farthest distance, bleak, bare mountains jutted out. No birds. No life. No body of water. Just sand. Sand. And more sand.

In the dunes nearest her poked ruins. What might have been a small village was now consumed by the might of the wasteland. The tops of buildings met her toes; the hole of a window lay filled on a sandbank nearby. An abandoned temple of stone surrounded her immediate area. Columns poked out of the grain, etched with lines of twisted carvings until they halted two stories above her head. She squinted at the crested tops where a stone roof used to be. It hovered above her, looking unstable. The tallest thing in what might have been a beautiful village.

There was a stark similarity in the finite lines of the pillars, similar to the arches at the Aariva. Cool knowingness slid underneath her skin—that while this was clearly an archaic landscape of what might have existed hundreds of years ago, a connection lay between this formation and the smaller twins back in her city.

There was no way for her brain to wrap around the fact she was in a different world. She knew it. The world even knew it. *She* was alien here, and based on her surroundings, she held onto the desperate thought that there had to be another reason so many candidates perished in the first week that wasn't from hunger, dehydration, or the blazing dual suns above.

Two suns. *Skies.*

She stared at her hands as little streams of sand flowed along the bandage from her bloodsworn scar. She breathed in, and then out. She didn't want to move. She didn't know where to start.

It was hot, stupid, and miserable to be in this world. A part of her whined to go back...to curl under a blanket in her apartment and enjoy the stolen aircon. She wanted Jelan at her side as they clinked their shiva bottles and laughed. She wanted to share a smoke with Jenkins as he sat in a broken lawn chair that made him lopsided as he sprayed himself now and then with his hose.

Never in a million years did she think she would yearn for her life in Calesal, but—

"*Stop it*," she growled at herself. She chose this. She would learn to live with it.

At some point, her senses came back to her. She'd expected this world to smell barren, like hot rock—if that even had a particular smell. The sun beat and warmed the mounds, but it smelled like burnt rubber. Fuel. A nasty, oily scent that made her half gag.

The high-pitched screech echoed out of her ears, leaving the muffled quiet of the desert. Wind tumbled sand. And that was it. Not a soul in sight. Not a—

A shriek tore through the space, followed by the aggressive hum of an exhaust. Violet lurched to her feet, slipping on the unstable dunes, and whipped her head. The shriek sounded again, then another followed it. It bounced off, echoed all around. She covered her eyes from the blaring sun, but nothing was there.

Violet touched the handles of her daggers, her knowledge basic on how to use them. She'd practiced throwing them in her old backyard, and that was it.

She took her time sliding down the mound, but eventually, her ass met the grain, and she skated the rest of the way, burying her boots. Her face twisted in irritation. "Great."

Something latched onto that irritation and yanked. She snarled at her boots—

The sound that came out of her was so shocking that she halted. Took a breath.

The fury faded.

Please no, please no, not this one, she begged in her thoughts.

Another scream tore through the air, this one deeper.

Dunes poured before her, high enough that she had to lift her head. The mountains peaked in the distance, and beyond the crescent arc of the closest mound, shadows moved back and forth.

Violet took one step forward. Paused.

The South taught her to be wary of danger. Be observant, keep your head down. Self-preservation told her to go toward any living thing. The desert provided no hope for survival, and where people—aliens, breathing things—lived, she would too.

But they were screaming.

Huffing a deep breath, Violet stomped across the sand, slipping when it became too deep. She dropped to her hands as the dune rose, crawling up and up while the screams continued. The sun blistered her skin, her breath became labored, and her hands burned at each grip. By the time she neared the top, Violet was on her elbows, holding onto the nearly vertical rise for dear life. She peeked over the edge, and her breathing stopped entirely when she beheld what was snarling before her.

Oh, she was *definitely* not in her world anymore.

A clearing of desert, more ruins, and a very alien scene.

Lean, muscled, and skinned-looking dogs whimpered far below. Three of them. One barked, pawed at the ground, fissured brown skin absorbing the light.

Two candidates lay bound and gagged on their stomachs, surrounded by five dwarfish, beefy-muscled males with reddish skin and wiry, vermilion hair. They hollered warring cries into the air, talking to each other in strange, echoing sounds, while two of them cracked long leather whips against the ground. She winced with each crack.

"Ooyee!" One cried out, a jagged scar piercing his cheek and lining down to his neck.

The others tilted their heads to the sky and echoed the cry. A hunting party.

So no, maybe her self-preservation would not succeed by following the nearest living thing.

A candidate, one she didn't recognize, spat out his gag and said, "*What are you?*"

They all but danced around him, jumping, hollering, celebrating. Tight leathers wrapped their corded muscles, stitched like second skin and clinging with few straps. Metal glistened in the light each time they moved. There were at least four curved, sharp knives bound to each one.

"We are Droans!" the scarred one cried. "Bah hah! Arafat, two in one. How did we get so lucky?"

Droans. She blinked.

The one who must be Arafat, a stoic Droan with a black vest of leather, hissed at the barking dogs, turned to the scarred one, and lifted his chin. "We must continue. There will be more!"

Another Droan cracked his whip and walked up to shove the gag back into the candidate's mouth. "More appear by Tetro," he said in a hoarse, crackling voice. "We always get lucky there, too."

Violet blinked again in surprise. They spoke *her* language…and she could more or less understand them. That was not something she gave thought to—any species she imagined would be in here she didn't give thought to. To her, it was a game of completing the Sins, but it seemed this particular species *also* saw the Sins as a game.

She ducked behind the lip of the dune as the scarred Droan turned its head.

"Isolo—start the bikes! *Hargra* be gone!" the one called Arafat said. The dogs—*hargra*—barked in anticipation and tore off across the sand in the direction of the mountains.

That was the destination. The mountains. She squinted toward the blurred horizon. Tetro—was that the mountain?

A Droan—the one called Isolo—swung his stout legs over the hunk of welded metal bits considered *bikes* and kicked at a bar. The bike sputtered to life, plumes of red smoke bursting from the back. The long tassels from Isolo's headband fluttered upward in a stream of air.

And then the bike *rose.*

Violet's jaw slacked open. She scurried up a hair's breadth more as Isolo hopped off and started the other bike.

The loud clamor sounded out their conversation. They turned to each other, yelled something, pointed at the candidates. One wrapped his whip along his arms, effortlessly twirling it and locking it around his hip.

One Droan paraded to the quiet candidate and lifted him with ease. The candidate squirmed in his grip before he was strapped on the back of a bike. The same Droan turned back to the other candidate…

But the second candidate ran. He made it all of ten feet before a whip whistled through the air and wrapped around his ankle, splatting him into the sand. The scarred Droan jerked on the whip and the candidate flew back toward them.

Baffled by the Droan's strength, Violet sucked in a breath.

The poorly attempted escape ticked off the leader—Arafat—as his chest puffed in his black vest and he fisted four-fingered hands. Isolo swiped at his headband tassels and yelled at Arafat, who grew redder by the second. He bounded over toward a large boulder.

"Steady, Arafat!" Isolo cried over the roar of the bikes. "We must find more before the Honkav clan! We must win the rings this year! For our Bastov glory!"

But Arafat opened his arms out as far as they could go, gripped the boulder, and lifted.

Violet's heart beat wildly in her ears. She couldn't believe what she was seeing. The boulder…it was at least four times the size of him. And yet, he only grunted in bored exertion.

The other Droans strapped the last candidate on the bike and watched, some with arms crossed, others sharing the anger that thundered through Arafat. They stomped the ground. Violet could have sworn the dune shook beneath her.

In the wildest of displays she had ever seen, Arafat roared, launching the large rock as if it were a lime.

Her heart thrashed.

Violet wondered if Reed was really going to be worth this.

The boulder arced more than forty feet and smashed into a temple column with an earth-shaking crack. Debris exploded, rumbled down the sandy hill, tiny rocks cascading near her perch. The Droans cheered gutturally. Whips lashed at the ground in wild excitement.

At the same moment they screamed, a painful lash hit her ankle and pulled. Violet bit her yelp. She twisted to meet the face of a female Droan. Four other Droans, both male and female, glared up from their motorbikes packed with candidates on the ground.

"Look at you." The female Droan leaned down. Arafat's roar filled the background. "Burning now from the suns. Shouldn't you know to run, female candidate? Bastov shits lost a good one with you—"

The dune began to shake. The woman Droan snarled and tugged on the whip at Violet's ankle, but Violet was already flying backward as sand gave way. The female Droan yanked with her. Violet tumbled over and over, her pack slamming into her side and sand buffeting into her vision. She scrambled for a grip but only slid and slid and slid until she spun along leveled ground and coughed out half of the desert.

The female Droan reacted fast, lunging for the end of the whip and yanking Violet toward her.

"No!" Violet screamed as the woman reached for a large needle at her baldric. "Stop!"

But the female Droan whipped the needle at Violet. No—behind her. The needle sliced her cheek, blood dripped down. But it continued on.

And hit one of the opposing male Droans in the thigh. One that had been running toward them, another needle in his hand. The weapon dropped. Bright red blood spurted as he fell to his knees.

The rest of the Droans whirled around. Whips lashed out. More needles made an appearance.

"Crava," snarled Arafat, a promise of death in his tone.

Caught in a battle, one phrase screamed in Violet's head.

The Sin of Wrath.

10

Pact

THE RUGGED APPEARANCE OF THE Droans enhanced Wrath. As if over time, their skin gnarled into permanent frowns, their red hair matched the same feeling of burning vehemence, and their beady eyes snagged only on what triggered them most.

A beat of silence passed where the only sound was her hammering pulse and the hot wind surging across the sand.

Isolo, headband and all, stepped away from the bikes as his eyes flicked from Arafat, to Crava—the female Droan—and to Violet. Observing. Unsure of what to do. A vein at his neck pulsed, and his four-fingered hands drifted toward his needles.

Arafat's anger hadn't subsided from throwing the boulder, and this situation ignited more wrath, which had Isolo opening his mouth, "Crava, you step onto our hunting grounds. Leave now."

"I find her first, Isolo," hissed Crava. Violet tried to scramble up, but Crava tightened the pull of the whip, which made Violet's hands slip out beneath her. "She is my catch."

"Crava!" a voice called from behind the dune. Moments later, hoverbikes revved up and over the newly shaped mound and shot toward their companion. Most of the candidates collected and strapped to the back of the other gang's bikes were unconscious, but some, gagged and bound, stared wide-eyed at the scene. Violet did not recognize any face.

Would Garan be nearby? Would these strangely strong Droans be able to take him down? It seemed like a good plan for Violet to team up with the bar owner, but that hope was fickle in her current situation.

"Females are prized," started Arafat. "We claimed this land for our hunting on Drop Day. No other clan may hunt on it."

"I did not hunt, Arafat. Calm yourself." Crava shrugged. "I saw the female and decided to take her."

Arafat's whole body shook. "You lie."

"Do not let the sin cloud your mind," called an opposing Droan. "We saw the female, we took her. Fair is fair. She will fight for our clan in the rings."

Fight? Rings? Were the candidates caught in a war and forced to fight? That would explain why a chunk always died. Now she *really* wanted to find Garan because she would not win against a candidate, or most definitely a Droan. Violet was flattered that they prized females, but she was close to raising her hand and admitting that she would be the worst choice out of the whole lot.

She had half a mind to blurt about Jack Marin so that damned man would get the angry Droanian search party, and she'd be free to fight the sin.

"*I* am the leader," Arafat snapped, bulbous nose crimson. "You do not make the calls when you have broken the rules—"

Crava snapped back, "You will kill all tributes with your anger. We will take the female, and then you can continue your hunt."

"We are allowed a chance to fight for the female," called the scarred one.

Isolo nodded. "Yes, Runon. The rings are the battle for our Bastov clan's power over Tetro, which you have held for long and brought more war in our lands, but here, in the sands, we battle for our fighters." His hand drew out a needle. "We will fight for the female."

Again, flattered, but Violet was too busy wiggling her toes and flexing her ankle to thank them for the compliment. Her eyes darted to the idle hoverbike with the strapped candidate.

The scarred one—Runon—unwrapped his whip from his belt. He glanced once toward another Droan. Violet noticed they looked extremely alike. Twins. Both had curling muddy hair, deep wrinkled skin and round, protruding chins. The other one, with no scar, carefully watched his brother as he pulled a strap to tighten the last candidate of their initial catch.

Before Crava could react, both Runon and Isolo lashed out. Crava took a needle to the arm, then another to her hand, which had her dropping the whip. Crava's comrades lurched off their bikes and into action, needles sputtering from their baldrics. The two groups collided in a contest of meaty fists, groaning leathers, and spit.

Runon advanced on Violet. The crack of a whip flashed in her vision, but she had freed her foot and swung to the side. The whip splintered the ground where her knee had been.

Violet jumped to her feet and bolted for the idle bike. Runon let out a cry and raced for her. Furious shrieks followed her, along with the metallic tinge of blood. Her legs ate up the distance compared to the Droans, so by the time her hands met the worn handlebars of the bike, they were only halfway.

She panicked. Up close, the bike was merely an assortment of metal that floated. No buttons, no pedal.

"Oh skies," she seethed and smacked the handlebar.

Her right wrist slid back on the accelerator, and she volleyed forward.

"Get it! Get it!" Isolo cried. "No—get on the bike!"

Another was screaming—Arafat—but was drowned out with the roar of the engine. Violet cranked the accelerator as much as it would go and would have flown off had she not been gripping the seat with her thighs for dear life. Her braid slapped her back, and the candidate at her rear shrieked as the bike roared up the steep incline of a sand dune, peeked over, and dove back down.

In the direction of the mountains.

Getting away from these Droans was the only thing on her mind. She could take the candidate's boot and hide for a couple of days before moving. Perhaps she will best Wrath and get the key in that time. The mountains seemed the safest. Water, old candidates, nicer Droans, or even a cave—*something* had to be there.

Sand buffeted her eyes. Burned. She yelped as they hurtled down, the candidate screaming along with her, bike lurching and sputtering so much she was sure it would nosedive into the ground and fling her off. They descended, reached leveled ground, and a flat desert expanded in front of her.

When her vision cleared, she spotted a sprawling village at the base of the mountain.

She pumped the bike straight for it. She could get lost in a city. Burrow in some abandoned alleyway and disguise herself as a taller Droan until she figured out how to best Wrath.

Her eyes teared up from the harshness of the wind, and she frantically searched for something to cover them—something to help because, skies, they were *burning*.

Her head twisted back, and she groaned in relief, but it was short-lasting as the rest of the hoverbikes summited the dune and chased her. All five male Droans of the one clan, plus the poor candidate strapped to the back, were crammed onto the lengthy saddle. One circled his whip in the air, over and over.

The other clan followed closely behind.

A loud groan snagged her attention. Her eyes snapped down to the candidate on her bike.

He flailed his arm at her, pleading incoherent words through his gag. When she furrowed her brows, he screamed.

"Shut up!" cried Violet.

He screamed again. Yanked his gag out and yelled, "Stop the bike, you crazy bitch!"

Fury struck like lightning. Her vision reddened, blurred, and her hands trembled on the bars.

Anger poured into her like shiva. She drank it. Let it fill her and fuel her.

Hurt him, commanded a chilling voice in her mind.

She faltered, but it was just enough to let the foreign darkness, the voice, intrude.

The command flooded through her. Gripped her bones, held her nerves, and took control.

With one hand still on the accelerator and rage in her mind, Violet watched her fingers jerk loose the straps binding him to the bike. Borderline blind, she untwisted the knots, crying in frustration when one got stuck. He flinched away from her, and that pissed her off more.

She slapped him. And then continued untying.

"No!" he screamed. "No! Stop—what are you doing!"

His words flew over her head.

Hurt him, the voice said again.

She obeyed.

He began to scramble as the binds loosened. She unsheathed a dagger and his eyes bugged wide. "*No.*"

She sliced through the last of the ties, and the candidate flew off the bike.

The darkness danced within her. She reveled in watching him slam into the ground, and a snarl ripped through her as the voice said: *That's not enough. He's not hurt enough.*

She whipped the bike around, her vision dotting black.

Frustration boiled through her. The darkness pressed forward and controlled her movements while her consciousness slammed its fist against the sinful cage.

She was going to rip him apart, throw him across the desert, pummel him, kill—

"No," she gasped. Her hand released the accelerator.

Make him suffer.

A blur whipped by. Halted. Figures hopped off and yelled.

But she was stuck in her head. No, she didn't want to kill. Did she?

She slowed as her mind fought off the intruder. Her head dizzied. Her eyes watered. When did the dagger get in her hand? She inhaled deeply—

A whip cracked and wrapped around her wrist. She flew off the bike and slammed into the sand. Her shoulder jolted with pain.

Short legs were in her vision.

"Breathe, you monger," said a harsh voice.

She couldn't. Her chest was so tight. The red in her vision snarled at the distraction. She craved blood and destruction. She wanted to burn in all the anger that had built up in her life—

"Breathe." Something poked her arm. "Fight it."

"Don't *touch me*," she growled, baring her teeth.

"Wrap it up and bring it, Isolo! Runon, get the bike!"

"Breathe."

Her chest opened and air flowed through it.

Fury wish-washed beneath her skin. Her muscles clenched and unclenched.

She rolled to her side and coughed, fighting off the intruder in her head. The sane part shooed it out and slammed the door to her mind shut.

Her palm seared. She gasped and grabbed it, for a moment thinking she'd find a dagger through it. She tore the bandage off and stared at the angry bloodsworn mark. It pained her like she'd slashed it, but no blood showed.

Isolo kneeled in front of her, watching. "You will not pass through this world if you cannot fight it," he muttered, as if he didn't want the others to hear.

Crava arrived with her clan, whips out. "You—"

"We caught her, Crava," said Isolo. "You know the rules. Now go."

Crava studied the situation, looked back to the candidates strapped to her bikes, and then huffed, "You will lose again, Isolo, if you help them. Just like how you lost your mate." She swung a leg onto her bike and the clan zoomed off.

Violet sat up, feeling as though she'd been run over by forty cars after facing Wrath. She stumbled to her feet, disoriented. Took a step back. She needed to run, get lost in the city—

A whip cracked. She flinched back as the other three Droans herded her. Arafat tossed the two other candidates before Isolo. "Make. The. Pact."

Isolo's look was challenging. Arafat was clearly the leader, which boggled Violet because he was the one with less self-control than all of them. But some leaders needed anger in order to command.

Isolo turned to her, spitting into his hand. "Shake on it."

"What?" she said.

"Make a pact. All of the humans do. It protects you from the city's Wrath."

"I am calling bullshit on that," she said.

Arafat growled.

"Do it," Isolo said, low.

"No."

Arafat nudged awake one of the candidates, bent before him with a crescent blade flashing, spat into his gnarled hand, and said, "Make a pact and I won't kill you."

The candidate balked at him.

"Swear you won't leave the city unless you have won the rings." Arafat sliced through the restraints. "Spit in your hand and shake."

Arms free, the candidate did as told, spitting into his hand and shaking Arafat's.

Runon's scar was scoured with sand as he stepped up to the other candidate, who did the same with a low moan, a large bump growing on his eye.

Isolo turned to her. "Make the pact, swear you will win the rings, and then you can leave the city."

"What are the rings?"

"Make the pact," urged Isolo, looking back at Arafat.

That look was one she'd seen before. When a child closed the door on her face underneath the intense stare of a parent, instructing them not to play with Violet. When Reed glanced at his strange new friend one night she begged him to come home, and then sighed, turning away. A look that frightened. A look to defeat.

But this was a game.

And she needed to play it.

"I win one fight in one ring, and then I get to leave the city," she said, spitting into her hand. "One fight. One ring. One win. Then you give me supplies and a bike and no harm comes to me after. No more pacts. No more bargains. Also, whatever time during the rings you give me information, food, and a weapon."

Isolo's beady eyes widened slightly, but an impressed look passed his face.

Runon scoffed and rolled his whip up. "Do it. I want to drink my *varnatha* after today."

Isolo exchanged a look with Arafat.

But Arafat spat in his hand, shoved past Isolo, and shook Violet's. He sneered. "You are not leaving."

"Fuck that."

Violet shoved her booted foot into his chest and pushed him to the ground. She turned, ran back toward the desert, wanting no part in a stupid spit game. Her knees wobbled under the exhaustion of Wrath, but she pushed, running like she had the streets of Calesal. Running for her life.

The Droans hollered behind her, but there was no stomping, no crack of whips. She turned her head—

Her body slammed into an invisible wall. Pain…pain…pain. The world flipped as she collapsed onto her back.

She groaned and twisted into her side, a part of her surprised she had still not broken any bones. Maybe it was all the times she had slipped off fire escapes and smashed into the ledges below, or the schoolyard fights she'd had with kids who picked on her.

She crawled to her feet, swaying. Her head pounded like a brick had landed on it.

Violet ran forward until that invisible barrier stopped her again. She almost didn't believe it. How could a spit pact, a bond, stop her from leaving?

"No. No, no, no, no, *NO!*"

She pounded on it, then at another point, then another. The invisible wall was solid. She shoved her dagger into it and the blade went through, but her hand stopped. Her body stopped.

"Fight in the rings." Arafat sneered.

She turned. Looked at her hand. "What did you do?"

"*We* did nothing," Runon spoke.

She slammed her hand again, meeting that invisible barrier. "What. Did. You. *Do?*"

Wrath crawled into her throat, tightening it, reddening her vision. She took a deep inhale. Settling it.

But it lingered in the back of her mind, ready to strike like a whip.

Isolo didn't meet her gaze. "You are bound to fight in the ring. One ring. For our clan, so we may get control over the city, and then you may leave."

"What? So you can enjoy watching me get pummeled by you guys?"

Runon scoffed. "You fight the other candidates of the other clans. Not Droans. But females are strongest of the pack, so you will win."

Violet's expression turned incredulous.

"You think you could ever leave?" he taunted. "Pact on piss, spit, blood…it binds. There is no escape. You must act out the pact, or you will remain in this city. Forever. Unless you win the rings."

"*I want to go.*" Violet clenched her shaking hands.

Their whips flashed out. Arafat gestured to the expanse, black eyes glittering. "Then go."

She screamed in frustration, "Break the pact or I will kill you all."

Her skin burned to touch. She couldn't see beyond the haze and the feeling that had her wanting to stab, stab, stab…the feeling of their bones…the blood. All that blood.

"You can fight for your freedom in the rings."

Whips lashed around her wrists, her ankles, until she collapsed to her knees. Wrath hissed within her, but it slithered to a dark corner of her mind.

Another time we will kill them, the voice said. *For now, we let the anger build.*

Arafat drew her boot out of his bag. "Put it on."

She snarled, Wrath clanging within her, but their grips were steel on her binds, letting up enough for Violet to kick out her foot and jam on her boot.

Runon huffed a laugh and tossed her a pair of goggles. "Don't forget next time."

11

LEATHER

THE CITY OF TETRO SEEMED to be formed from metal structures that had been dumped from the trash. Every spare piece of metal, every rip of fabric, every bolt, *nothing* was ever wasted and had built this city from the ground up. Fabric blew in the desert wind, crisscrossing in faded colors as hanging tapestries above the streets and alleys. The ground was sturdy, dried mud with darker prints following the foot traffic of Droans. Homes were fused of metal and mud, built on top of each other. Some structures towered, others lay squat, and then there were the ones that climbed up the side of the mountainous expanse.

During the short ride from the edge of her breakdown, Runon had grabbed her multiple times, four-fingered fist bunched in her shirt, and hauled her back onto the bike. Wrath whined within her, cracking its whip in retaliation so much that she snapped her teeth, attempting to bite off his finger when he tried to touch her again.

He only cackled.

When they arrived on the outskirts of the city, he shoved her off the bike, muttering something about pulling her teeth out.

The Droans ditched the hoverbikes in a parking area filled with hundreds of them. Arafat—less red-faced now—glared at her as he wrapped a tan scarf around his balding head. His beady eyes flicked to Isolo, who returned the heavy look.

The Droans wrapped a faded purple scarf around her head and neck, leaving space for her mouth, nose, and eyes. She noticed, as she spotted more and more of the squat, muscular people, that this was common to do beneath the beating sun. Her scalp was thankful for it.

Two giant, columned gates marked the entrance to the rowdy city, lined with guards in dented metal helmets. Two of the Droans, Bahro—Runon's twin—and Ifan, slung the candidate men over their shoulders. The one was still knocked out, but not dead, from shoving him off the bike.

Even though the sin had caught her, she didn't regret it. One step closer to Reed, but it terrified her to think of how easy it might have been to kill. Runon kept close enough to her that one wrong move, one attempt to escape, she knew his whip would lash out and have her choking in front of the myriad of Droans.

In this world, every lick of the air tasted like fury, irritation. Even the sweat on her brows had her fighting the beckon of the sin, and she was used to that back in Calesal. Wrath was evident in every bit of this city—the angry welding job of homes, the loud, screeching sounds of metal slamming into metal as they passed greasy workshops, the harsh crack of their language, and even the foul, petrol smell that had followed her since she arrived.

Arafat skirted through the crowd. As they turned one way and then another, every street looked the same. Bustling, crowded, filled with harsh, interesting language. Her own tongue trickled here and there, and while she wasn't complaining, she wondered why they ever bothered to learn it.

The females scared Violet the most, and they apparently scared the Droan males too. Crava had been a child compared to the females. Many hosted scars along their gnarled skin, beady eyes following every movement in the crowd. Scarves of different colors wrapped around their heads, like Violet's, but some were torn, and some had stains that looked an awful lot like blood. They carried curved knives and long, crooked needles, and everyone had leathers.

Whips were a sacred piece. Violet passed numerous shops where they not only pounded metal, shaping and curving it into weapons, but also worked leather. Long lines of leathers were draped outside to dry, while inside, they were molded. Families stood around one shop, and a young Droan boy, half her height and with more hair than her consort combined, excitedly stood on his feet to peer as the maker wove the fresh leather whip.

Runon turned to check on her, then followed her gaze. "Droanian leathers. Only ever earned."

Surprised he made conversation, she asked, "At what age?"

"The whip and knives are blessed at eight years, some younger, if they train to fight in the rings."

"*At eight?*" she balked, shuddering. When she was eight, she was still flicking her boogers into Reed's sodas, not handling knives.

"We are Wrath," he mumbled. "Fighting is our blood."

She didn't want to ask if that was *because* of the sin or if that had always been their culture. Either way, the thought of their entire tradition crushed around a sin had her throat tightening.

"And then if you fight in the rings?"

Isolo mentioned something about her going there. Another shudder.

"If you kill a Droan from another clan in the rings you take his leathers for yourself. Add it to your collection. You wear it, always."

That information was enlightening. As she passed by more Droans, she noticed how some had single-colored leathers of red, light brown, or black, and how some had leathers of different colors sliding up their arms, over their ankles and legs, and even pieces stitched to make an entirely new whip itself.

Some—she counted—*one, two, three... ten, fourteen...twenty-five.* They passed her as though she were nothing, sauntering by as they wore twenty-five other leathers of faded colors. Twenty-five deaths.

And those with deaths were given nods, or a wide berth, as they walked through.

She also noticed most of them were females.

"If you have a lot of leathers," she asked Runon. "Like *a lot*. What does that mean?"

He shrugged. "A lot have died."

She glared.

He smirked, scars twisting on his face. "You rise, top of your family. Or the top of your clan. But that is only two times a year, or if the sin takes hold and a fight needs to happen between clans. The killing done in the rings, or the Panthon."

"The Panthon…" she repeated. "Care to explain?"

"No."

Her expression hardened, but it wiped off her face as two Droans barreled into their group line. They rolled in a blur and careened into a metal pole holding up tapestries. It split with a heavy crack, falling onto the two fighting bodies. They paid no mind, nor expressed any sort of pain. He *had* to have hit that with his head. A fist rose and slammed into the round nose of the other Droan. He growled, the sound terrifying and animalistic. She gawked as the other grabbed a glass, cracked it on the ground, and shoved it straight into the head of the Droan atop him. Blood spat out, but still they continued to fight, unfazed.

"Honkav scum," snarled the Droan. The other swung his fist again.

Everyone else sidestepped the brawl, until a female Droan stomped over—a barmaid— and separated the two fighters with astonishing ease. Her face reddened with anger, she sucked on her hanging tooth, yelled an explosion of curse words, righted the pole, and stalked back to the bar across the street.

"There are three clans in the city," muttered Runon. "Honkav, Bastov, and Lirav. We had been at peace before the curse, but many died, and cities ruined since it started. Now we fight in the rings for power."

"You can't…have screaming matches?" asked Violet.

"We are Droans. We are made to fight and build and conquer." Runon spat on the ground. "Even then, you cannot argue with anger. None will win. The only one who wins against the sin is the one who still breathes."

Violet's face was a mix of shock, fear, and awe.

Runon fixed her headscarf, and a full smile almost graced his face as he watched her expression. "Not a place for a human, bah!"

Isolo hissed at him from ahead.

Bahro whispered something to Runon, yet Runon shrugged, and she caught the end: "*no matter.*"

Violet's legs were ready to collapse on her by the time they reached a giant complex of dried mud and metal four stories high, ridged with steps up to the rooftop and manned by Droans. They dragged her through the yawning gates, and she nearly soiled herself at the sight.

The dust and mold smell made it hard to breathe as she looked on. Rows and rows of *pens*—fences and mud cages, each stuffed with captured candidates. Most were knocked unconscious, curled in their cages, while some stirred and peered up to look at the new arrivals. There was a heightened animosity—Violet was sure, surprisingly, that she was being treated better than the rest of them. Most were from her group—fresh blood and cuts, aching burns from leather around wrists. But there were others...candidates who never made it out of the sin.

There was no haunted look in their eyes like she suspected. No desperate call to be let go so they could move on. These candidates were bulky— muscled with scars and burns as if they'd seen fight after fight. One man smiled at her, missing teeth and all, a crazed glint in his eye.

Beyond the cages, through open windows and cloth curtains, sat the rings. Droans wrestled in them, torsos bare, pinning one another down and huffing with exertion. One flung another straight into the metal barriers with a thunderous crack. But the Droan got back up, shook his head, ignored the blood running from his back, and charged his opponent. A referee lashed his whip and the Droans separated, sneering at each other.

"Guess they needed to battle it out," muttered Runon.

"Between the clans?" asked Violet.

"Yes. If there is an argument, they fight in the rings with an overseer so no deaths happen. But two times a year there are battles to the death, and that is when one can win their leathers," clarified Isolo.

She paused. "And us?"

"If we win the most candidate rings, we govern the city," said Isolo. "The Honkav clan has turned the city to favor them instead of all. Too many people have to leave because buildings have been bombed or fights are too bad. They want the city for themselves...."

"And this city is all we have left," finished Runon.

She halted. Stared between the two Droans and breathed, "This is the last of it? The last of your people?"

"There are others in the mountains, near the springs, but only small villages." Arafat closed in. "You want to leave, yes? Then you fight for our clan and win."

Bahro and Ifan dropped the two candidates off in the same cage. In fact, most candidates were doubled or tripled up. She snapped her gaze around, meeting some familiar faces—no friends, but ones she recognized. She didn't spot Garan.

The Droans placed her in a single cage. No roommates, thankfully. Closer to the rings, private, fortified from the other candidates.

And without another word, they locked it.

12

Jack Marin

The minute night fell and her body was more energized after lying in her tiny closet space for a holding cell, she said screw Arafat and his unending fury. Screw listening to the moans of the candidates and the whines that this wasn't what they expected.

The Droans left her with her bag and knife, not caring that she could surprise them with an attack.

But that made it all the more obvious that a knife probably wouldn't do much damage to a Droan.

The small Droanian guard in the quiet night beneath torchlight told her that they weren't worried about candidates leaving. It was the entire reason for the pact. A smart choice on their part. A wandering candidate would draw eyes, and Violet supposed that despite their clan wars, the wrath against the candidates was stronger.

Violet shimmied her knife into the padlocked grate of the cage. A pang slashed her heart—Reed had taught her this. *Soon.* Just two more times against the sin. One ring.

Then six more worlds.

As the padlock clicked softly and the cage door swung open, that strangled hope pushed her forward.

She tiptoed through the labyrinth of cages, dodged a very drunk Droan, and slipped out a side entrance as another Droan left.

Before her sprawled the mazes of streets with looming homes, ignited in an odd sort of beauty by firelight. Mud archways passed over smaller streets, followed by bridges and twists of more roads. The chaotic markets she'd seen during the day had been taken down, now just empty stalls and bare posts. One cloth, forgotten, hung from a dark window and Violet grabbed it, wrapping her head and shoulders.

Now…where to?

Making herself scarce was not unusual. She'd escaped the wrath of Meema many times in her life. But what then? Find Arafat and kill him? She'd never killed anyone before, and even though the Droans were alien to her, it didn't make taking a life any easier.

The cry of a crowd drew her attention. Somewhere to the east. A party. Her gaze flicked to the rooftops…perhaps she could find some leverage to get her out of the pact. Something she could actually do.

Like stealing a watch.

Her fingers found the notches in the walls, and with a heavy grunt, she hauled herself over the lip of a rooftop and silently met the ground. Carpets splayed before her along with low, empty tables, cushions for seats, half-eaten dinner plates, and fully drunken bottles of—she lifted one to sniff it, gagged—some petrol that would funnel through a plasbike.

So, of course, she took a sip.

The burn was similar to shiva and a warmth spread over her. One more sip, and Violet plugged the bottle and put it in her backpack.

Her stomach growled. She reached for the spread of dishes, choosing one that looked like flattened bread. Sniffed it. Shrugged. Took a bite.

A spice assaulted her senses. She chewed through the garlic-like substance and, with curiosity, took the bread and dipped it in a brown chunky-looking soup. Then ate it.

She moaned at the taste. This was nothing she'd ever had before. In Calesal it was noodles and seafood and plates of meat and lots of sweets. This was spicy, but the good kind of hot that melted into the mouth. She grabbed more of the not-bread, dipped it into the not-soup, and indulged.

Not a soul sat on the rooftop, so she enjoyed herself. She glanced up to the sky, glimpsed the plethora of stars that looked like Calesal had vomited its plaslights, and for the first time, she knew what freedom felt like. No wall—except a spit pact, which she would take care of—and no hovering Mai or worried Jelan. Just her, the stars, some damned good food, and—

"Who knew the little one would find the way to the food."

Violet burst up from her seat, but two hands grabbed her shoulders and pushed her back down. Hot breath met her neck as the unfamiliar voice said, "Looks delicious."

The cool metal of a dagger slid against the skin at her collarbone.

Two other figures sat across the table from her. One with a scar along his jaw reached for a handful of food and dropped it in his mouth.

"Damn, the short ones can cook," he said.

The other, a bony muscular type, cocked his head at her. "And there's dessert."

Violet flared her nostrils. "Go to Lust for a show."

"I don't need Lust to take care of my needs," he said. "The name's Wick. And yours?"

"Dessert, apparently," she growled.

She'd dealt with roaming hands, grody men, and filthy words her whole life, but there was a fear here—this wasn't her territory; she didn't know the barman or the bouncer at a club.

The dagger pressed into her skin. "She's got a mouth."

"All Souther women talk like that, it's why I don't prefer them," said Wick.

Her eyes drifted to the top of his palm. Her pulse picked up because there lay a sentencing mark, a twisted burn one received when they are sent to the bowels of Calesal's prisons.

Wick caught her gaze and smiled. "Murder. Rape. As I said, I preferred the Midian women, but we don't get those in the game.

I saw you sacrifice yourself and thought, oh skies, they *do* want me to have some fun during my exile."

The dagger pressed harder. Chills crawled down her back.

There was a burn in her eyes, but Violet wouldn't dare cry. He'd love it, embrace it, and they would laugh at her pain.

Violet adjusted herself, letting the blade prick her skin. But it was enough to sneak her right hand to the hilt of her left dagger.

"Hold on." Wick leaned his elbows on the table. "I think I recognize you. Wait—*yeah*. You're Sutton's little sister." He snorted. "You had that mother who lost her mind. She was a pretty lady, your mother, too bad I never had a taste. *And* she has two kids in the Sins as well. You must be a dead wit like her."

"And your mom must've dropped you down the stairs with how ugly you turned out," Violet exhaled sharply. "That or screwed a donkey."

"*Bitch*," Wick growled. "I'm going to shove that mouth full of—"

A blade crashed into Wick's neck. Blood splashed over the table, on Violet's face.

Wick clawed at his neck, wide-eyed, paling by the second as he touched the pointed end sticking out one side and the hilt on the other. He gurgled, opening his mouth as more blood sputtered out. By the time his eyes searched the rooftop, he had careened forward and smacked into the table. Dead.

Violet was yanked up by the hair. Metal dug into her neck and a terrified gasp escaped. The man behind her snarled, "If you come any closer, I'll slit her throat—"

She jammed her dagger into the man's side and pulled it out. He jerked behind her. With one large push, he fell off the rooftop and hit the ground with a thunk.

A warbled scream had Violet whirling back to the bloody scene.

Jack Marin stood over the dead body of the last man. Ice panged her stomach and she took a fearful step back. The bloody dagger in his hand, the fury-filled glimmer in those eyes.

He took a deep breath. A pause later, he lifted his bloodsworn hand and clenched it.

"I didn't mean to make such a mess," he muttered with a frown.

Violet took another step back.

His eyes flicked to her. Trapped her within that piercing gaze.

She could feel Wick's blood slipping down her face. Her nerves replayed the squelch of the dagger going into that man's stomach. She ached to look down to the ground, to hope he wasn't dead, because that would mean...

Jack rolled his eyes. "They were going to hurt you. You acted in defense."

"Is he—" She stepped over to the rooftop.

"Don't look," commanded Jack.

She paused. Turning her back on the commander *would* be worse than glancing at her first kill.

"I thought we could talk," he said.

"In what world would you think I'd want to converse with you?"

"This one." He shrugged and looked at the rooftops around. "Maybe the next if you warm up to me."

She flashed him an incredulous look.

Jack bent and wiped his blade on the clothes of the fallen. "Why'd you do it?"

"Do what?"

"Sacrifice yourself for your little privileged lover."

"I didn't—" She shook her head. "He wasn't—it wasn't like that."

"You were just desperate to see your brother again."

Wrath woke in her mind, a snake ready to strike. "Don't you talk about him. Don't you act like you know me, either."

"I have a whole file on you back in Calesal, of course I know a lot about you." He lifted a finger. "Friend of Jelan Gregory, plasmechanic, lives in the dormitory compound on Fifth Street." Another finger. "You frequent Frank's Noodles Bar every Thursday. Well, used to, now." Another finger. "The pawn shop. Hallfor, the owner, gets a very unique picture of you every time you come in to sell since he's the only one who won't blab about you. Oh, and then there are your visits to the square around midnight and—"

"So Jenkins tells all this to you?" She swallowed against the tightness in her throat. "Is this why he always knows where I am?"

"He's responsible, or was responsible for keeping an eye on you, but there wasn't much to your life, to be honest. You've been rather boring."

Boring. Skies, she wished she had a smoke. A drink. Her fingers twitched, as if to reach for one and Jack's eyes caught the movement.

He swung his backpack around and unzipped it. When he pulled his hand out, two smokes and a lighter lay between his fingers. "Two minutes."

The thought of an inhale, the relief it would give her, had her taking a step forward. Her eyes caught the bandage of where the burn mark of his gardia tattoo lay, and she stopped.

"I'm good," she said, even though her mouth watered.

"I gave you my ring. That cost money. You should be nicer to me and at least give me a conversation."

"I threw your ring into the river."

"Lovely," he mused. "I don't think I've ever had a proper look at you, now that you're all grown up. Even though he's a little darker, you look remarkably like Reed—"

"Don't say his name," she gritted. "Not after what you did."

"And what did I do, little Violet?"

"Don't say that, either." She clenched her fist. Reed called her that. *Little* flower. *Little* booger. *Little* Violet.

"Oh, sorry, I forgot another thing I know." He put the smokes away and her throat whined. "I know that you screwed up your whole life by making a scene on the stage and sentencing yourself to the Sins. For *love.*" He rolled his eyes. "Reed will not be happy to see you, by the way."

"Stop it," snarled Violet. Wrath tightened the grip on her dagger. She fought it back.

Not yet. Not yet.

"Jack, she is just intolerable. Jack, she is driving me crazy. Jack, Jack, Jack…But you need to protect her, Jack, only you can. Skies, and then that night happened. I spent so long thinking Reed was in love with me with all that he begged me to do." A beat of silence. A huff of laughter. "It's funny because that might be true. I mean, he did go into the Sins for me, after all."

Her vision blackened. She held still. "Do you enjoy taunting me? Does this pet your stupid ego?"

"A little bit." He smiled, a dimple appearing. "You got this little flame in you and I'm curious to see how much it can burn. Just like all those buildings that burned because Reed ordered it that fateful last night. The whole reason we are all in this shit, anyway. Because of *his* decisions."

Her heart beat into her throat. The floor swayed under her feet.

"I can tell you all the ways I'm able to kill your traitorous brother to make you hate me even more. Then maybe you'll stop being stupid enough to wander an alien city, and instead fight me like you want to."

She tried to breathe, but it was so tight. She couldn't—

Look at how he treats you. You hate him. Show him how much you hate him.

Red flooded her vision. The city fires, the dark night around her, blurred.

"There you are." Jack's gaze was on her. "Did that hit a nerve?"

The rope on Wrath pulled taut. Snapped. She lunged at him.

Jack casually twisted out of the way, grabbed the back of her shirt, and hauled her up. "Is that all you got?"

She swiped the dagger. He grasped her wrist, halting the blade. Her other fist slammed into his nose.

Pain flared at her knuckles, but it was blanketed by her fury. Jack stumbled back in surprise, nose bloodied, lips twitching. "Oh, come on, you can do better than that."

Kill him. You want him to hurt. He *caused your pain.* He *ripped your brother from you.* He *is responsible for tearing your family apart.*

But *he* is saying all these things.

Don't. Believe. Anyone. Only Me. Only Meema. Got it?

Suddenly it was not Jack she saw anymore, but Reed. Freckled and surprised, he blinked down at her. "You really hate me that much?"

"Of course, I hate you for what you did," she snarled. "I *hate* you for leaving me! I hate you for breaking me. I hate you for going to him and ruining our family. I—"

Her body slammed into something hard. Pain lashed down her spine. A grip on her throat. A muffled, echoing voice telling her to stop. To get out of it. To fight it.

Her head throbbed. Wetness slid down her cheeks.

"*Breathe*, Violet," a familiar voice growled. "My skies, or else I am going to kill *you* and be done with this nonsense."

Her vision slowly returned with a painful inhale. Wrath was a frenzy inside of her, feeding on her pain.

"Fight it," the voice said again. "Fight *back*. For once in your damned life."

Why that voice was telling her to fight, she didn't know.

In her mind, she turned to that invader and pushed at it. Punched it. Fought it until it was past the doors to her sanity.

Green eyes stared down at her. Her shoulders groaned against a door. Annoyance graced Jack's face.

There were cuts on his arms. Small, hardly bleeding, but there. Embarrassment traded places with the Sin.

She pushed Jack away. Her bloodsworn mark seared her hand. *Two times now.*

He didn't seem to notice it. He was breathing hard, fighting something within himself. She was half afraid he would erupt at her, and *that* would be deadly.

He took a steady inhale, a flushed exhale, and lifted his gaze to her.

But she was running across the rooftops, desperate for a moment.

Jack didn't follow her.

Her flighty escape was fueled by relentless panic. She climbed down to the ground. Night markets sprawled, filled with bodies of Droans that, with her scarf, she could blend in with.

Screw that skiv, Jack Marin. He was an abomination. Her hate tore through her, and she slowed, just for a second, as that tickle of Wrath jerked her arm and made her want to turn around.

No, her sane mind said. Keep going. Lose him.

She pulled the scarf tighter around her head as other Droans did. They yelled at each other, laughed in high cackles, snapped barters on more…interesting items. Long swords, crescent knives, black whips going for prices in a language she couldn't read. Her heart hammered. She knew the South of Calesal like the back of her hand, but here? Skies, she was already lost.

But there was a chaotic adventure here. Things just like Calesal. Doors wide open in the cool night, Droans packing into bars, slamming glasses that looked like the new alcohol in her backpack.

She weaved through the crowd, being mindful not to push others. Beady eyes flicked her way, but she kept her head down.

Her fingers found a scarf at a Droan woman's hip. She slid it on, changing her disguise, as she ducked onto another busy street and lost herself in the madness.

Just as she positioned it over her lips, a four-fingered hand grabbed her and pulled her into a tiny alley.

"You want to die, candidate?"

Isolo peered at her, annoyance on his face. Runon was next to him, along with Bahro, his twin.

"Someone is already trying to kill me," she muttered. "Tall guy, green eyes, handsome, but it is all a ploy—he is actually interested in Droans—"

Runon handed her a rag and motioned to his face. Wick's blood. She hurriedly wiped it.

Isolo shoved her shoulder back into the wall. "We will not take care of your enemy."

"Then what *are* you good for?" she asked, still looking out of the alley. "I'm not going back to those cages. Not right now."

Isolo followed her gaze, huffed. Runon and Bahro huffed back.

After a long moment, Isolo nodded down the other end of the alley, where another busy street gathered.

Runon chuckled. "She can't handle *varnatha*."

Violet pulled the bottle from her backpack. "This?"

Runon gaped.

"Good, right?" said Bahro.

Isolo huffed an answer.

Violet put the bottle away as they turned onto the street and weaved through the crowd. Her Droan cadre was relatively...calm, compared to the reaction she imagined she'd get if she were spotted escaping. But technically, as evident, there wasn't an *escape* when there was a spit pact. So Violet followed them, in awe of the wild, Droanian night. Because they would, at least, give her protection against Jack Marin.

Isolo found a packed bar with tables spilling out. Female Droans shot back giant glasses of *varnatha* and males hovered around them, urging them along. Whips wrapped thighs, Droans wrestled on the ground. They laughed, despite the overcoming sin that twitched jaws and forehead veins. It was almost unbelievable they could enjoy themselves.

Isolo, Runon, and Bahro were unbothered by her presence for the most part. If she had to continually come in contact with humans who used their world as a game, then she would be pissing herself in wrath day in and day out.

Perhaps they did that and realized it was pointless because candidates would still be sentenced, noosed by the curse on Veceras.

So everyone was cursed, one way or another.

Isolo found an empty table and plopped down, followed by the twins. Violet hesitated.

"Sit," said Isolo.

"We will see how well you handle your *varnatha*," said Bahro.

She sat across from them, left with ample room.

Isolo hailed a barman who brought over a tray of filled glasses, followed by two bowls of the soupy mixture she'd seen on the rooftop and the same flattened bread. The second it was on the table, all three of them dove in.

They used their fingers, wiping them on their pants when necessary. No napkin, no utensils, no plates or….

Violet shrugged. "What is that?"

Mouth full, Bahro said, "Usual dinner. *Bruznak,* in our tongue. Pan, beans, and greens. Have some."

"Like this." Next to her, Runon grabbed a flatbread and pinched it to create a spoon. He placed it in her hand and motioned to the vegetable slop.

Remembering how good it tasted, Violet did as he said. It was sloppy eating as it dripped onto her fingers and chin before she managed to shove it into her mouth. She didn't hold back her satisfied groan. "It's good."

The rooftop food had different spices. This was both sweet and tangy, paired greatly with the soft, warm bread. She licked her fingers, not caring how dirty they were.

Runon grinned broadly, misshapen teeth glinting in the wick light. "Bruznak is normal. Tagha and Fyrgi are better. For when girl and boy become bigger."

"Birthdays," Violet clarified, eyeing them carefully before reaching for more. "We have the same in my city. We celebrate with cake."

She explained further at the three Droans' confused faces until they nodded in understanding. They did not have sugar here. Pity.

It was different seeing a Droan relaxed. She had expected…well, she hadn't thought about it much before entering, but she didn't expect to *enjoy* spending time with an alien species. Yet as she filled her belly, Runon and Bahro laughed at jokes told between the others, and Isolo re-wrapped his whip, taking great care with his hands, and she realized that…they were as human—no, as *live*—as her.

Runon grabbed a glass and passed it to Bahro. Bahro took a long, heavy sip.

And Runon slapped him right across the face.

Violet flinched, tension rising back in her, but the two Droans howled into the night and laughed. Tables around them howled back, followed by drinks and more slapping. One female Droan decked her partner so hard that they flew straight into the bar wall.

Bahro then passed it to Iso, Iso drank, and Bahro slapped him on the cheek, a loud crack resounding. They laughed again.

Isolo passed the bottle to Violet. "Human's turn."

Her eyes bugged. "I think I'm good."

"Bah! It is how we end the night before Shavov!"

"Shavov?"

"Night drums," said Bahro. "Before the rings."

A shiver ran down her spine, thinking of Arafat and how he'd shit fury out of his ass if he saw her here.

"I'll drink but no slap," she said.

Isolo shook his head. "It makes it better, the slap."

With half a mind they might get angry and throw her to a female Droan if she refused, Violet swiped the glass, lugged back a deep, burning shot of liquor, coughed as it seized up her taste buds, and pinched her eyes shut.

The slap came swiftly on her cheek, but it wasn't as hard as the cracks made it sound. It certainly knocked her to the side of the table. She shook her head, eyeing Runon, a small smile on her face. "Your turn!"

Runon took his fill and Violet lightly hit his face. He balked. "Harder!"

"Really?"

"Yes—"

Violet careened her hand across his cheek, palm stinging from the impact. But Runon took one look at her, one that made her think she was indeed about to be thrown into the street, and then he cackled into the air. "So soft!"

"*That* was soft?" she said, bewildered.

"You need practice," Isolo chuckled. "Droanian women hit men across the bars. Or through walls."

"Henra did that to Iso—" Bahro started, but his face fell. "*Adiva*, Iso."

Iso only nodded, suddenly more somber.

Violet sat back. "Who is Henra?"

Runon and Bahro exchanged glances, saddened by the name.

"My mate," Iso finally said. "Killed by a human two years past."

"Oh," Violet's mood sank. "I'm sorry to hear that."

"*Adiva*," Runon corrected her. "Means, 'I am greatly sorry.'"

Violet turned to Iso and said, sincerely, "*Adiva*, Iso. May she be embraced by the Skies."

Iso took his leather-wrapped hand and fisted it against his chest. His heart. Nodding once to her, he grabbed his glass and drank deeply. The slaps only went for the first round, thankfully.

"Now watch," Bahro motioned to her, pointing to the mountain.

As the three gleaming moons peeked over the outlined mountain and lit the city of Tetro, blasts of firecrackers roared upward. Against the dark sky, they burst in colors of red, orange, and yellow, twisting and turning in different lines.

Runon, Bahro, and Iso stood, along with the rest of the bar, the street, and howled into the sky.

Around the city, more howls came, until it seemed alive with the primal sound. Violet, a little dizzy from the alcohol, watched, a small smile gracing her face.

The drums started and the Droans danced, and in the end, still with stiff shoulders, Violet nodded to the beat with them.

A taste of freedom on her lips.

13

The Best Walk Ever
JELAN

"**Time's up! Clock out, everyone!**" the supervisor called through the warehouse. Immediately, the welding of new fixtures, the steady hum and pungent burning of plasma, ceased.

The rising sun burst through the large factory windows. Rays of orange gleamed on the long industrial assembly belts, the bilateral inspection tables, and the black shipping trucks that would deliver the bottled sodas all over the city.

The steady clang, the low buzz, all stopped at the announcement. The stench of the burning energy—tangy and sharp—was doused when the factory doors opened to let in the fresh air. The freshest air Calesal had every time after the Sins.

Jelan sighed as she lifted her mask and wiped the sweat from her upper lip. She carefully removed the testing wires for the new plasbulb and flicked the off switch on the hand-sized generator. Tools to the canvas belt slung around her hips, unfinished bulbs to the cushioned packing boxes, and generators back in the cart.

She checked it all one last time.

Supervisor Callonuth watched her with a steady gaze as he handed off the week's pay to each passing mechanic. "You finished up, Gregory?"

"Yes, sir." She placed her generator on the cart as another mechanic rolled by with it.

"Good job today, Murian," Callonuth said to another worker, handing over a thick envelope. "See you tomorrow."

Callonuth's short stature did not lessen his superiority or the critical gaze of every worker under him. He turned to her. "I see you improving. Fifty-two bulbs today. This factory will be upgraded by the end of the month with that work. Good job." He handed her the white envelope, and when Jelan grasped it, she had to rein in her disappointment.

"Thank you," she said quietly, brushing past him.

She frowned. Her week's pay was clearly less than the guy's in front of her, even though she *knew* her plasbulb goal was the best for today.

No matter what he praised her for, it didn't add to her paycheck. And maybe that was the whole reason for his words—that he was supplementing her low pay somehow.

But that didn't pay her rent. Nor get her any closer to a doctor appointment in the Mid for her lungs.

Jelan was very aware she was the only female on this Plastech team. It didn't bother her too much while working—the men left her alone and she was able to focus on her work. She kept her head down, but she did notice the glances her way, the eyes that trailed over her body and disregarded her flawless work. As long as they let her be, she would ignore the lack of respect.

But constantly bettering them might give her too much attention. Their egos were fragile enough, threatened by her mere presence.

She dropped her kit off in the mechanic's van and turned hastily onto a wide street between the rows of buildings in the Factory District. The factory workers trudged past her for the start of shift, coffees in hand, smokes burning at their lips, while she was looking forward to her bed and minute-ready pancakes. With tiny chocolates. Yes, that would be *her* reward for putting in more effort.

Jelan scanned her worker's pass at the Glide train stop. There was still some disbelief that she was allowed on. Well, not that she was *allowed* on, but that she could now afford to use the city train with her job's travel benefits. The Glide wove through all the winding streets of the Mid, on high rails between the skyrises of the North, and in only a few select areas in the South. The nearest stop to her shared home was still a fifteen-block walk farther, but she was counting her blessings. Little by little.

It was a forty-minute ride until the train stopped paving its path through part of the Mid, screeching to a halt a few blocks into the South. Jelan spent most of it fighting sleep. The hours were long, her bed was not comfortable, her room not dark enough for her liking, and yesterday her roommate had decided that it was a good time to re-organize her drawers.

To keep her mind active, she liked to change her walk home. Sometimes it was through the metal-wielding alleys where bright sparks burned her gaze, but she still looked on, fascinated by the handiwork and wondering if one day she'd be able to do such a thing, plasma energy included.

Today she didn't want to be around anymore sparks. She needed to relax, so she took a few extra turns down a residential street. Early morning risers smoked on their balconies high above. Liquid splashed on the street in front of her, and when Jelan looked up, a man was shaking out his mug.

"Watch ya' head!" he yelled and then slammed his door.

Jelan wrinkled her nose, sidestepped the puddle, and continued.

When she reached a corner bakery she favored, her mouth was already watering. She handed over her money for a cup of coffee with cream and a warm chocolate scone. The scone was gone by the time the door shut behind her.

She could just go home, but her legs took her elsewhere. One, two, three blocks and the sharp algae smell of the Trollova River greeted her. She passed the large boardwalk, dodging morning runners or night drinkers, and stepped onto the pebbled shore. Murky water lapped, along with trash, and to her right, the gleaming Trollova Bridge loomed in the distance. Across the curving river sat the Government Sector, the buildings a mix of marble and metal, pristine in the morning light. A place few would ever venture, solely reserved for high-achievement individuals or, if one had an army to make it across the heavily manned bridge, could challenge the Emperor to the throne.

The rafters were clean, but she remembered the blood that spattered. The bodies that used to hang there years ago.

Treasonous bodies.

Jelan sipped her coffee and turned. The beach was quiet at this time of day, and it calmed her nerves after the hiss and scalding heat of the night's work. She'd walk for a mile or two, reset her mind, and draw her plasma sketches until her lids could not be forced open any longer.

She reached a mishmash of reeds and continued on the small path through. Anything to get away from people who were people watching her, judging her and her work, paying her low checks with barely enough to cover a doctor's appointment. The ache in her lungs had only become worse since Violet—

Jelan paused. The ache blossomed across her whole chest. She sighed deeply.

Heartbreak. Her closest friend gone to the Sins. Last Jelan had seen, Violet was still alive, that blinking green dot next to her name. Perhaps Jelan should check once more, even though she glimpsed over at the plascreen before her shift last night.

She wanted to hate her friend for doing such a thing, but only sadness came over her, enhanced by being in Violet's exact shoes with her brother. Violet would watch, would mourn, and Jelan would comfort her. Day in and day out, but even after two years it never got better, and Jelan knew she wasn't the one to help in the situation. Now Jelan was left staring at that wretched screen, rooting for her friend and Garan.

No matter that Jelan never developed feelings for Garan, the fact that his name blinked above Violet's didn't fail to bring horror to the condition, if not denial. It happened so fast that night…

She rubbed at her eyes and the burn in them. All yesterday she wept until Jenkins dragged her to check that plascreen for Violet's name. Jelan had been asleep throughout the whole ordeal…and she hated herself for it. Now Violet's *for love* actions were plastered on the news, and while Jelan's ache was raw, she'd managed a croaking laugh when Jenkins explained the situation.

"Shit," she muttered.

Jenkins had invited her over for dinner. Tonight. Jelan continued her walk, pondering over the best way to decline, eyes darting over the reeds as if they might give her answers.

Her gaze snagged on a protruding thing nestled within the grass and haphazardly covered by mud and stone. She stopped again.

It looked like a hand.

She was just too tired, too sad, too *everything*, but still she bent down and—

"Shit!" She reared back, dropping her coffee cup. It spilled open and poured through the gravel, a tiny flood following the rivulets between stalks, and then along an arm, the curve of a shoulder, the sick twist of a neck.

Jelan stopped breathing.

A body lay in the marsh.

The blue-black skin was covered in mangled burns and Jelan would know those from anywhere. The same that scarred her hands, but this person—this body—was covered in it. Plasburns.

Only an explosion could do such a thing. But where? Here on the shore of the Trollova? No such thing would exist, and there was no equipment in sight—

A crunch of a boot had her whirling, her braids slapping her back. Four shadowy figures moved down the shore and entered the marsh. Jelan's heart pounded so fiercely she struggled to keep her breath. She took a step back. One figure pointed her way. The com of a radio reached her—but they weren't Redders.

She ducked into the shoots, grimacing as it brought her closer to the body. Maybe she should signal them, tell them that it was here and that she only just witnessed it. Her thoughts muddled and she crouched a step back, then another.

The hiss of a radio—*"Secure the area. I want the body brought back to me in thirty. Don't let this get out."*

"Yes, sir," one figure said.

Definitely not Redders.

Only one word slammed into her head. *Gardia.* Gang business.

Jelan moved away as fast as she could, keeping her head below sight. She didn't spare one glance at the body.

Rest in peace, I guess.

When the reeds ended, Jelan looked back once to spy on the figures' heads, but they had stopped approximately where the body was. She raced back toward the boardwalk, head down, lungs throbbing, until she scanned herself into her building, unlocked her door, and collapsed into bed. The contorted, burned body replayed in her mind, over and over, but Jelan squeezed her eyes shut.

She never saw it. She had taken a nice walk down the shore, raced home to use the bathroom and that was that.

Jelan slept for a long, but restless, five hours. Her dreams flittered with Violet shaving Jelan's head, Jelan yelling at her that she had to go back into the Sins, and then Garan popping out a baby with bright red nails. By the time Jelan woke, her sheets were twisted around her middle, damp with sweat, and fingers wrapped her braids. She loosed a relieved breath that her hair remained.

Her roommate, Eliza, was thankfully out most of the day, so there was no one bursting in and out of the room, chomping her gum loudly, and disturbing her sleep.

The four-story dormitory home was always filled with sounds. A cackle of laughter, a scream of fright, the heady moans of sex, a drop of a book, or the consistent beep of the main door as it opened and closed. The toilet would flush every fifteen minutes, and the stove burner would gasp on every thirty.

It was only when her mind caught up with her that she remembered the—

Nope. No body. Only a calm, serene, delightful walk this morning. That was it.

She distracted herself and glanced up to the peeling wall covered with sketches upon sketches of her plasmic designs.

One caught her eye, as it always did. The design would collapse onto any wrist like a thick-plated bracelet, but when waved at a certain motion, or tapped—she hadn't decided yet—a shield would erupt.

The difficulty would be in controlling the substance and keeping it to a grid that neutralized it to only a certain diameter, or else one tap would explode the hot energy into all directions and most likely kill the user. Or severely burn them.

That particular design would require more thinking.

The mattress creaked as she stood, stretched the consistent ache in her back, and checked the clock.

She scowled. Jenkins' it was. She needed a distraction after today, and perhaps he'd let it slip about the men and what they were doing there—

No. No men. No body. Only the best walk of her entire life.

She padded over to the shared closet and fished out something easy to wear. She stole a dollop of Eliza's lip balm—she knew the skiv was stealing her body moisturizer—patted her braids down to satisfy the itch and slicked her baby hairs along her hairline.

In the small mirror plastered to the wall, Jelan turned her head to the side, then the other, eyes searching for something out of place, a flaw that was never there.

Violet never—

Jelan clenched her fist. The quiet she normally liked roared loud in her ears. The gap of her friend's presence grew larger. Violet *this*, Violet *that*. She both missed and cursed the damned girl for leaving her like this. She wished she could tell Violet about her fantastic stroll.

Damn bitch.

If only Jelan had been a better friend.

Be kind to yourself, her father's voice rang in her ears, the deep huskiness that would send her to sleep every night with his wild storytelling. *You're always thinking, always planning. The moment is not so bad to live in, is it?*

Her throat tightened. Tears pricked her eyes. As the South was full of alarms and voices and bangs and slams, that dull roar grew. Her heart hammered faster, and her nostrils flared.

Her father. Her skies-damned father was now wasting away in an apartment deep at the bottom of the South, where the last of the streets meet the South Wall. She hadn't seen him in so long... not since he'd asked her for more money.

She gazed down.

Gnarled hands looked back at her. She unclenched her hands.

The scars twisted and turned, making her fingertips, her palms, unrecognizable. Violet once said Jelan would be able to get away with any crime because her hands lacked prints.

She'd also said that they looked like flaming shooting stars crisscrossing over her skin.

A slight smirk grew on her lips. Vi had drunkenly flipped straight into the Square's dried fountain after that.

She put on her shoes, grabbed her bag, her house key, and a handful of bills, then checked the mirror once more, smoothed over her eyebrows, and headed downstairs.

She stepped out of her building, and her heart lodged in her throat.

Two guards stood before her, a big black car idle on the street behind them.

One nodded his head. "Jelan Gregory."

She took a step back.

The same guard stepped forward. "There is someone here who wants to meet you."

Ice crested her spine. She stiffened, and her mind immediately went to the body. They know, and they think *she* did it. But there was no way...how *would* they know?

No. No. She was just being paranoid. Violet probably had lingering business.

"I'm good, thanks." Another step back.

His mouth thinned. "It's not a question."

"Whatever *she* did has nothing to do with me. I don't know anything." She had already observed their clothing—obscure Souther clothes that looked too clean, sleeves rolled up revealing the hint of a gardia tattoo on the arm. Purposefully done. But she couldn't tell what gardia they were from.

Two plasguns at their hips, an earpiece, fingers laden with rings, and the stance of men who knew how to rip her throat out within a heartbeat.

"Sutton's dealings have been…dealt with. This is something that has to do with you. And your safety."

"I feel rather unsafe at the moment."

"We are instructed not to touch you. But the boss requires a conversation that does not have to do with her."

"I'm leaving," she said bluntly and turned. "I have work."

Another guard stepped up the stoop to her building.

"I don't know anything," she said, hating how her voice wavered.

"He just wants to talk."

"Who is *he?*"

The guard remained silent.

"Please move," she whispered.

The faint sizzle of a voice and the guard raised his hand to his ear, listening as someone spoke within. He huffed an answer and stepped aside.

Jelan ran for the main street and farther down before her lungs tightened and forced her to slow. Breathe. Anxiety and asthma did not mix well. She clutched at her throat and willed air to come into it, but it hurt—skies, it hurt when it got this bad.

Eventually, she managed to fix her breathing. Without another look back, she darted away.

"Two guards, you said?"

Jelan rubbed her temples as Jenkins set her drink onto his dining room table in his hoarder house.

She dragged her eyes from the nude male painting and turned to the spectacled man. Her boots stuffed into one of Jenkins's many mismatched carpets that he loved collecting. Papers and plasma lines ran the walls of his navy-cabinet kitchen.

"Their boss wanted to speak with me." She grabbed the drink and brought the pink concoction to her lips. "I figured it had been because of her...*job.*"

Jenkins waved his drink. "She dipped into quite a few things she probably shouldn't have, but what Sutton did, while slightly illegal, wouldn't have mattered anymore since she entered."

"I don't know your ties to your...business, but if you can leave my name out of it and tell whoever this is to go away, that would be great."

Jenkins grinned. "If they want to talk to you, they will."

"Stop being so cryptic," mumbled Jelan. "Who do you work for, Jenkins? Which gardia?"

"You just want me to say it aloud," said Jenkins. "You little tease. Can't you wrap your head around the fact that most people serve the one and the only?"

"Well, I don't want to serve the one and only," her voice rose, and she cringed at it. She never got angry. Bury the emotion, to let it simmer, and then snuff it out. Everything about this feeling was foreign to her. "I'm fine with where I am. I miss the shit out of my friend, but I know how to move on, be okay—"

"It's bigger than that." He pushed up his spectacles. His button nose wrinkled, bug-like gray eyes blinking rapidly. "Them reaching out to you. It has to do with...." He trailed. Cringing.

"What?" she pressed.

Not the body. Please not the body.

But the look on Jenkins's face had her heart dropping. Fast.

"What?" she asked again, voice softening.

"Have you talked to your brother recently?"

Jelan scoffed at the unexpected question. "Not in three years."

Jenkins—all-knowing Jenkins—let his eyes flash to her hands and then back to her face. "Word has spread in the Underground that there's been a promotion within Arvalo's gardia. Not only that, but there has been an influx of Plastechs abandoning their jobs for some odd work in the gardia. Arvalo's gardia, specifically. The Commander of Plastech Industries himself."

"I don't care about Arvalo's gardia or the illegality of it. All gardia dealings are illegal enough, so losing Plastech to that doesn't surprise me. What does this have to do with my brother?"

Jenkins sighed and leaned against the wall. Paper crumpled underneath his back.

"Do you know what your brother does, Jelan?"

"Last time I spoke to him, he was gambling away his life."

"Well, you'll be pleased to hear that he has moved from gambling coins and drugs, to Plastech."

She blanched. "What?"

"Almost like women trafficked to the North for pleasure. But Ahmad Gregory is a name that slipped who recruited these workers. In the last twenty-four hours, ten bodies were discovered dead, lapping at the trash shores of the Trollova River." Jenkins pushed his glasses up again. "The alive one was covered in plasburns— from human testing—"

She shook her head in disbelief.

The body. The plasburns.

Human testing.

Jenkins turned to one of the many stacks of newspapers shoved against the narrow hallway. He grabbed the first one and threw it to Jelan.

She caught it, unfolded it, and read.

Renowned Plastech Engineer, Dr. Fona Gravein, dead after an explosion at PlasIndustries.

The article went on to state that new development had surged through the business. They were working on a new model for plasguns to retain more heat in order to fire faster bullets.

"Allegedly," said Jenkins.

The experiment went wrong. The neutralizing table for the chaotic energy fractured underneath the strain, and it exploded.

"Plasguns have been developed for nearly a hundred-and-twenty years," he clarified. "It's bizarre to think that a simple update would destroy an entire floor. Fifteen people dead—and that's a low number because that explosion happened at three in the morning after the Bloodswearing Ceremony."

"An under-the-table sort of thing," murmured Jelan.

"At the end of the article, they say they are already taking applicants to fill the positions." Jenkins gave her a knowing look. "Applicants? For a head engineer in Plastech through a newspaper service? They are desperate. On top of that, within an *hour* of Jack Marin going into the Sins, confidential plans were stolen from the Government Sector."

"Is that coincidental?"

"No. Arvalo hates Marin, particularly because Marin was so good at predicting his moves—except at the end of the gardia wars, that is. Part of Marin's job was, more or less, keeping Arvalo in line. Now with pretty boy Jack gone, Arvalo can make moves. It's causing a ruckus among the other City Commanders."

The answer was there, bright as a hot day, but Jelan reeled with the information and breathed, "How do you know all of this?"

"Because he joins me for weekly dinners and spritzers, and because he is my head communications liaison with all dealings in the South Sector."

She whipped toward the smooth voice and nearly peed herself right then.

The man leaned against the doorframe from the living room. His warm brown skin was smooth beneath his crisp shirt and simple breeches. Narrowed brown eyes, expressionless face, shaven jaw. "Jelan Gregory. Plasmaintenance. Sister to Ahmad Gregory. Daughter to Vaughn Gregory." His lips twitched. "Friend to Violet Sutton."

She took a step back.

Jenkins cackled. "You do know how to make an entrance, Lucien."

"You look like him," she whispered.

"Yes, I imagine I would resemble my brother." He smiled slightly. He didn't strike her as a person who smiled a lot.

"Jack Marin."

"The one and only." He walked over to her and extended his hand. "I'm lesser known, though, and I prefer it that way. My name is Lucien. Lucien Marin."

"What do you want with me?" Again, she cursed the lack of bare *will* in her voice. That was the kind of voice stomped over and taken advantage of. She needed to practice in the mirror at some point.

"I want to talk; about your work, your ideas, the body that your coffee cup was found next to this morning." He drew a plastic bag out of his small pack and showed her scrawled name on the discarded cup. "And mostly if you want to join the Marin Empire as a plasmic engineer."

She blanched. "What?"

"I am here to offer you a position within the gardia, because I want you on our side." His eyes gleamed. "There is a war brewing within the city, Jelan Gregory, and I need your help to stop it."

14

THE IRIS

DAYS PASSED AND THE WARRING rings echoed over Tetro. Candidates were dragged from the cages. Some twitched with sin and went willingly, while others clung to the bars of their cage, refusing to leave.

There was a large arena where it all happened. Through the veiled curtains separating the cages and the rings, Violet glimpsed the blood splatters as one punch led to another, as teeth soared and the last gasps of breath left. She was not the only candidate to ask for one ring in the spit pact; a handful were escorted out of the rings after winning, covered in blood, given full backpacks and leave of the city.

Tallies were kept for each clan, and while Violet couldn't read the language, Arafat's frustration told her their clan wasn't winning. Still, the crowd cheered and banged on the metal rafters. They enjoyed the blood.

Probably because it wasn't their own.

She watched it all. Whatever elation she felt from the other night had faded into hopelessness. Isolo didn't show his face, Runon's smile as he collected the food trays began to fade, and Arafat stomped by her cage loudly, ruining her sleep. Their hang the other night was nothing more than a memory, and it would stay that way. It hadn't made them friends. It hadn't made them want to revoke the spit pact and let her leave.

She never knew what homesickness felt like. No one in Calesal did. But now, as she curled and let the world of Wrath dance around her, she wished she was in her tiny bed, Jelan reading at her feet, and…

She opened her eyes.

And what?

Was that all?

The entire time, the capsule of death pulsed in her wrist. She stared and stared at that tiny pink indent. Clench her fist, tap three times.

Within, she was a blank canvas staring up at the clay ceiling, watching as dust fell when a candidate was tackled, or when the Droans wrestled during intermissions. She listened and felt the reverberations within the arena, the cries of the candidates, the cackling laughter. The crowd roared. She tilted her head and glimpsed the bright blue sky. Not her sky. Not her home. Not her world.

A blank canvas. She scoffed. What would she paint on it? What color was in her life?

Twice she'd beaten the sin. Once more, and according to the Empire, she would have the key.

Something other than fury powered through her, pushing her to sit up and scowl at the fresh tray of food Runon had dropped off in the morning. With a steady hand, she pulled it over and devoured every bite.

Two bloodied candidates, one lifeless, the other groaning, were dragged out of the ring. The crowd cried for the next round.

She ate her next bite.

Fight back. For once in your life.

One ring. That was all she had to do. One life and her freedom was granted. She'd technically already taken one, but Jack's words about defense made it easier to handle. This…could she make *this* situation a defense?

The latch to her cage slid with a groan and keys jiggled, twisting the handle. The door swung open.

She looked up.

Isolo's beady eyes took in the space before landing on her. He huffed deeply as she raised another bite of bread to her mouth.

"Is this the day that I die?" she asked evenly.

"Only if you want it to be," he replied.

"That's not very comforting."

He huffed again. "It is our life, our world. The people are angry and tired. Droans have died from this sin for many years. We are exhausted from it."

"Is that your usual excuse for how many candidates die?"

He ignored her. "You're eating."

"Do you care?"

Isolo wrinkled his nose, watched as she ate another bit of bread—nothing like what she had when drinking with their small cadre. It was bland, old, and Isolo's face proved it.

"So if I kill Arafat, will my pact be revoked?"

His face remained neutral. "Yes."

"So then there's only one death today."

"You'd be mad to kill a Droan." He fingered one of his crescent blades.

"But if I do I get those cool hand leathers, don't I?"

He scoffed and looked down at his own wrappings.

"Whose leathers are those?" she asked, even though she already garnered the answer.

"My mate," he said. "Henra. The candidate who killed her escaped after. He did not deserve her *konath*."

"Her what?"

"Her hope."

Silence passed between them.

Violet put her bread down. "You have been kind to me, even though you didn't need to. Why?"

"Wrath is a selfish anger," said Isolo, looking back at the rings. "It is from the hurt within. The scars that mark your heart, and the ones you have not dealt with. But no matter how many fights you take, neither opponent wins." He turned back to her. "Only Wrath. Only the Sin wins. If you give in to it."

She thinned her lips.

"And then, when it wins, you stand surrounded by blood. Destruction. Because you could not handle it yourself, so you let the hurt burn you, and everything around you, down."

The white scars crawling along Iso's arms drew her attention. She glimpsed his leathers and the remarkable colors gracing it.

"Did you fight after you lost her?" she asked.

"Yes," he said. "And it never brought her back."

She looked away from his intense gaze.

The Droans didn't make the candidates fight because they were full of rage. The rage engulfed them because it took everything away from *them*. So what did they need to get their freedom back?

The same thing she needed.

A key.

Iso followed her thoughts, nodding once, and then dropping his voice. "Do not let them have it."

He straightened, stepped to the side of the cage, and glared as Arafat strolled up, face already twisted into a sneer. "It is your turn."

"One ring," she reminded, standing.

At his taunting smile, Violet had made her decision.

She was going to paint the whole damned canvas red.

She was going to the Panthon.

They blindfolded her. At the sound of a roaring crowd, fear curled in her gut. They tied her hands with leathers and shoved her forward with a pole. She stumbled. Droans cackled, spat at the ground, and angry snarls of wrath followed her like the sun against her back.

The light vanished. She inhaled dust. Coughed it out. The crowd's screams deafened, drilling into her head. She swallowed the lump in her throat and willed her legs to move.

One life.

And then freedom.

She shouldn't have climbed that dune, shouldn't have made that stupid pact that kept her here. The failure of it all tightened her chest.

There was no room for selflessness in this sin. The emotion erupted because it needed an outlet. To explode. It was harsh, defensive, like some terrified, caged animal that both fiercely hated and feared its captors. She remembered her tantrums when she was a child, how they would build up before spilling over the lip of the pot, and she had no choice but to scream and let it all out.

The grinding of metal signaled a gate lifting. Her pack was taken and tossed to the side.

"You can keep the knives," said a Droan.

The pole pushed her out. There was quiet for a moment as she was led and pressed against a wall. Her hands were untied, but something metal shifted over her ankles, holding her in place.

Violet tugged her blindfold down.

Bright sun rays shined down onto the dirt floor of an expansive crescent arena. Up and up, fused ridges of metal angrily towered above her head, ridges that created seating, which thousands of Droans now crowded. One half of the wall was carved into the mountain that stood over Tetro—and not just a rocky wall, but a hangar—like the giant doors of factories or the yawning columns of the Aariva. Nearly as tall as a four-story building, plated with metal.

A gasp reached her ears, and she looked toward her left, where other candidates were chained to the floor.

"Garan," she breathed. "Garan!"

"Sutton?" He pulled his blindfold off. With wide eyes, his face twisted from confusion to horror. He caught her gaze and opened his mouth—

A drum beat, starting low, rumbling, then growing louder and louder, matching her heartbeat. More blindfolds fell. Forty or so candidates squinted at the bright Panthon, some bruised from previous fights, others without a mark.

And then a group of Droans piled out, including Arafat. Three leaders each wore a different colored leather headband.

One spoke first. "*Harah-kinash!*" He pointed to them. "Welcome, candidates of the Sins. You are the players in our life, and every year, we ask you to play *our* game."

Arafat stepped up. "One ring, one win, and whoever stands at the end may leave the city."

"*Fuck*," she muttered.

"Was this your doing?"

She whipped her head to the right. Jack Marin frowned at the metal holding his ankles.

"I was trying to be smart," she snapped.

"This defeats the purpose." His gaze skipped over the other candidates. "How will they continue to use us to fight their battles if we all just kill ourselves?"

Because it wasn't *all* about their power. They'd tallied up and had candidates fight, but more than anything, they wanted the same thing everyone locked to the arena wanted.

The key to the next world. In that, the Droans can escape this sin and the destruction of their world. Violet's mind boggled at how it worked—wouldn't a kill conform to wrath? Or was the only battle that mattered inside the head?

The capsule in her wrist pulsed in response. Her wrath progressed the more she was wronged by others—Reed, Jack, even the one candidate that called her a bitch. So she had to fight that. But if she received the key here, they would take it.

And she hated the fact Arafat outsmarted her, because she was delighted in herself that she managed to get one of those hoverbikes in the pact too.

Now that was off the cards.

"Ugh," Jack whined. "I fancy something more than pathetic slaughtering. It gets old after a while."

She shot him a look. He rolled his eyes.

"Maybe not all of you have to die! Bah!" called one Droan. "We will see who stands tall and strong. We will see who wins against the Sin. Fighting, rage, fury—you will face Wrath. Will it be a bigger opponent than each of you?"

Arafat lifted his hand. Weapons were thrown to the ground from the stands. Spears, swords, daggers, hatches, axes, whips. Arafat grinned at her.

That darkness awoke. Perhaps later she could figure out besting Wrath a third time. As it purred within her, hissing and yearning to lash out, she had half a thought to let it. Let it unleash on the one person who's wronged her this whole world.

Arafat grinned more.

"Skies," said Jack, looking at her. "Just stay out of my way. They're all going to come after me, anyway."

"How do you know that?"

"Because in their minds, you would be used for other things." Darkness crawled over his features, hardening his jaw. "Or at least, that's what others were saying throughout the night."

Wrath lashed within her, wanting to be released.

"Easy now," said Jack. "You just sit pretty, and I'll take care of them."

"Skiv."

A smile. "I know."

A roaring drumbeat sounded.

"Begin!"

The metal bars at their ankles opened. Violet hesitated, but the other candidates didn't. Some lunged and slid and grabbed the nearest weapon. They turned on their fellow candidates and within moments, blood shined.

Jack swaggered to where a sword lay. A candidate howled his name and charged him. With ease, Jack drew the weapon, arched his body, and severed the candidate's arm. He twisted around, pulled their head back, and sliced their throat. The body hit the ground, but Jack was indifferent. He smirked at the sword and then proceeded to pick up two daggers, more interested in a scavenger hunt of the best weapons than those who charged him.

Across the arena, one candidate looked at her with wide eyes as a spear went through his skull. It impaled him into the far wall.

Violet panicked, Wrath thrashing within her, an animal wanting a release. She bit it down, pinned it, held on to it because *that* was how she would get killed. She was no match for the howls and cries of fury around the Panthon. So she stayed, planted by the wall, watching as Jack butted the hilt of his sword into one of his attackers, caving their eye.

A foul-smelling weight tackled her to the ground. Her shoulder lit with pain. She twisted, snarling as she lost her grip of wrath.

The crooked yellow teeth of a candidate gleamed. "Your brother got mine sentenced to the Sins. An eye for an eye, right?"

"My brother didn't do *shit!*" Violet swung a fist, unable to reach her daggers.

The candidate cackled. "Then why was he sentenced with mine?"

"Maybe you should go ask your own brother!"

"He's *dead.*"

The rage roared in the candidate. It licked at his face, reddened his eyes, his pupils so dilated they were entirely black. His thick fingers wrapped around her neck, squeezing hard. Air gone, her eyes bugged.

She clawed at his face, catching his eye and raking her nail into it. Wet warmth slid down her fingertips. The man let out a guttural howl, but his grip did not relent. His ire took him over, dragging him into a depth so deep that he was set on killing her.

Spots dotted her vision. She couldn't inhale. She pressed her nail farther into his eye, but he didn't budge. Didn't seem to feel it. Her nerves inflamed, her chest burned. She tried to gasp, tried to breathe—

With a wicked squelch, a dagger went through the man's neck. He convulsed. Blood splashed on her shirt. She pried his fingers off, shoving him to the side and watching as he twitched, eyes rolling back, until he fell limp.

Dead.

She dry heaved, her next inhale painful as she sucked air into her lungs.

"Get up, Sutton."

A warm hand yanked her to her feet, and Garan, covered in blood, handed her a machete. "Be useful. We can survive this."

He whirled as another candidate lunged for him. His brute strength poured into his sword as he lobbed the candidate's head off.

Candidates littered the ground, weapons tossed aside when the others preferred hands, teeth, and nails. A woman candidate shoved a machete into the chest of another, and with a war cry, chopped off another's hand.

Wrath roared, demanding death. Destruction. Chaos. But Violet was useless here. So undeniably useless…She held the machete, unsure of how to use it or of what to do. She didn't want to kill. Wrath whined within her at that, but her eyes flicked to the stands to find Arafat, his smile beaming.

She turned. "Garan—"

He stood there, hulking mass and all. Bodies littered his feet, but horror winked in his kind eyes. The world slowed as her gaze drifted down. A sword poked from his chest. He blinked at it. "Sutton," he breathed as blood dribbled out of his mouth.

The giant of a man collapsed to the ground. He twitched and then steadied, eyes unblinking.

A tattooed candidate smiled, a prison mark atop his hand. "Pity, I did like his bar."

He drew out a dagger and turned to her.

Her blood roared, searing her skin, and she snarled.

Wrath unleashed.

Red stained her vision. She was on fire. She lunged with a strangled scream, waving the machete in front of her. An animal. She swung, he narrowly dodged but the blade sliced his arm. He waved his dagger. It slashed her hip, but she didn't feel pain. She arced the blade again and caught the man's hand, cutting it clean off. The hand went flying, his dagger along with it.

Surprise streaked across his face. A garbled cry left his throat. His bloodied stump spurted crimson and more blood splashed on her, but she reveled in it.

Loved it.

Now finish him, said the voice.

She kicked out at his chest. He collapsed onto his back. She raised the machete.

Something, a notion, flickered inside of her, but Wrath pulled its strings taut—

Breathe, the rational part instructed.

She met the man's eyes through her blackened vision.

Kill him, urged the voice.

Breathe, the other pleaded.

The red swarmed. Blood. Blood. Blood. There was so much blood, and it was all for a game. She brought the blade down.

Breathe!

She slammed the machete next to the man's head. It embedded into the ground. She faltered, blinked, wiping the sweat and blood from her face.

"What—" he started.

But Wrath was screaming in her head. *Don't you want to kill him! Hurt him! He killed Garan! Make him suffer. Watch him die—*

"Shut up!" she cried. "I won't! I won't! *I won't!*"

Violet took a rigid inhale, throat still burning, and a long, deep exhale.

Her bloodsworn palm seared and Wrath vanished with a whine. A hand grabbed her shoulder—

A flash of light. Violet swung her open hand, caught something that blinked into the air, and smacked it across the figure's face with as much power as she could muster.

Jack.

He stumbled back, clutching his cheek. Shocked. Surprised. His gaze flicked to what lay in her hand.

She gaped at it, too.

Her palm wrapped cool, smooth metal—a thin silver cylinder the size of her forearm. It gleamed, shimmered in the burning sun. Twin lines of a darker metal twisted at each end, and in the middle a dim light shined like the glow of the moon.

"What is that?" Jack asked, bewildered.

Sudden silence tensed the arena. Droans opened the gates and moved from the stands. Whips lashed out and Jack flinched at each whack. Pale. He squeezed his eyes shut and recoiled as one whip came close to them, shaking his head.

A red mark sliced his cheek where she had hit him. But her .gaze continued upward past the lip of the arena and toward a brilliant beacon beyond the mountainous horizon. Miles and miles away.

The same color of the moonlight in the cylinder.

In her hand, she held the key.

In the sky sparkled the portal. Or a beacon to it.

Around the arena, candidates leveled her up, eyes shifting from her face to the object. She clutched it tightly, noticing how not one of them glanced at the blazing light in the background. Could they not see it? Was it only her? No head gazed up, and that beacon shined so brightly it was like one of the suns itself.

A horn blew. The clan leaders stepped out of the main gate, including Arafat and the rest of his group. The smile on Arafat's face was sinister. One of proud recognition. Behind him, Iso looked pale against the tan stone. He had a white-knuckle grip on the hilt of his dagger.

All around, the Droanian guards smacked whips at the candidates until they were herded back against the wall. Jack's expression soured. He fingered the scar on his neck, but did not move.

"She is given the Iris!" one of the many Droans howled. "The Iris! The key!"

She brought the Iris closer to her body. Jack angled himself to defend, eyes zeroed in on every whip. He clutched his blade.

"Thrice you beat Wrath," Arafat said. He held his hand out. "Give it to me."

"Remove the pact," she said.

"Bah! Arafat, dispose of it and take the Iris," another Droan snapped.

Jack stilled. His defensiveness almost warped wrath back into her veins.

She took a step toward the open gate. "Let me go."

Arafat turned to Isolo and whispered harshly into his ear. Iso paled even further, looking at Arafat in bewilderment. "*No.*"

But Arafat shoved him forward. Violet widened her stance, but it was Iso. The Isolo who slapped her after drinking their liquor. The one who helped her the first time she felled wrath, and the one who had lost his wife. He would not...

"You should learn, Iso, that you cannot care about them," growled Arafat. "They do not care about us."

Runon frowned.

An unreadable expression passed Iso's face as he met her eyes. Slowly, he walked toward her and began unwrapping the leathers at his wrists.

She shoved the Iris into the waistband of her pants and prepared for attack.

But when Iso stood before her, looking up, a moment of clarity passed along his gnarled features. In his black eyes, she saw a decision made, and her heart sank.

"Give me your hands."

"I will not fight you," Violet stood her ground. "I will not die, but I will not fight you. Tell them—allow them to let me go. I need to find my brother—"

"Your hands," Iso snarled.

Behind him, Arafat's eyes widened, as did those of the rest of the Droan cavalry. They watched in silent confusion as Violet extended her hands and Iso began wrapping his leathers gently around her wrists, her palms, over her bloodsworn scar, and between her fingers. The leather was smooth, worn, and slightly damp from sweat. When he finished wrapping, he held her hands briefly before unsheathing his dagger.

Violet fell to her knees. The Iris pressed harshly into her back. "Iso, no—please don't do this."

"Pacts are sacred with Droans. Spits can be many, but ones made of blood override it. Blood is more binding, as you would know."

Face somber, he stepped forward. His hand twitched.

Violet's mouth widened.

"No—" Jack started, but a whip flung out from the Droans and wrapped around his leg. He gurgled a cry and reacted so belligerently from the leather around his leg, she was sure he was going to pop it out of its socket.

Iso met her eyes and raised the dagger.

"You betray our clan!"

A glint of metal flashed through the air and collided into Iso's back. Iso gaped as blood sputtered from his mouth.

Only the sin wins.

In the background, Arafat smirked, flexing his hand. Wrath oozed from him.

"No!" she cried, lurching for Isolo as he collapsed onto his knees.

Whips rolled out. Eyes turned to her. The Iris at her back.

A rumble shook the earth.

And the giant door before the mountain opened.

15

BLOODBOND

THE DROANS IN THE ARENA sprang up in cries of rage.

The Sin thickened the air, making it hard to breathe, enveloping everyone while Violet grasped Iso's shoulders, aware of how Wrath tickled her skin but never invaded.

Arafat was assaulted by other Droans, his burning ire reddening his skin further. A whip lashed out and wrapped his body, arms tight to his sides, and he fell. They yelled, screamed. The crowd was disgusted. She replayed the scene in her mind, understanding how horrible it looked.

A Droan killed with his back turned.

Tears never reached her eyes.

The earth pounded as that hangar opened. Candidates ran toward the gates. Weapons were picked up. Clashed. But she could only look down.

Iso's beady eyes stared at the sky, and his skin...it grew colder by the second. Still, she did not cry. Only confused—*Why? Why? Why?*

A hand grasped her arm, and she whirled to find Jack before her, face hard with an emotion she couldn't place.

"Let me go!" she cried as he tried to drag her away.

"It's time to leave," he said.

"I don't want to go anywhere with you!"

"*Violet,*" snapped Jack. He grasped her jaw, turned her head toward the monstrous machines. War machines. Bathed in black, shadows in the bright light, some with arms and legs and a Droan plopped in a command seat. Other machines were on all fours or had large treads that ate the ground.

"It's time to go."

And then he yanked her toward the gate, groaning as the Droans scrambled to close it.

The imprint of the Iris was still on Jack's cheek as he raced for the gate, dragging her with him. With one final look, Violet turned back to view Iso's body.

The scene burned a memory into her head. A gasp of pain left her.

Garan's blood pooled like a giant halo around his body, Iso's not far away. Together, their blood mixed, both dead expressions staring at one another. Two species of two different worlds, lifeless, of the same colored blood beneath it all. Victims of violence.

Runon, Bahro, and Ifan gathered around Iso.

The lid on her emotions lifted. Peeked out unto the world.

She shut it quickly.

Runon watched her sprint across the arena with a saddened face. He gave her a single nod goodbye. And brought a fist to his chest.

Jack's grip tightened further. "Prepare to slide."

He jerked her forward. She picked up her pace, diving for the space between the thick prongs of the gate and the ground. The rocky earth cut up her skin. She grit her teeth as she slid under. She bounced up, twisted to see Jack dive under, narrowly dodging the flash of a whip. He dove for two discarded candidates' backpacks and ducked under the last of the prongs to meet her. The gate slid shut and the cavalry of Droans within clambered to open it back up.

"Keep going!" He shoved a bag at her, breaking into a sprint.

There was so much happening that the Droans barely blinked at them, and when they did react to the two escaping candidates, their movements were too slow.

The Panthon led straight into the thick market streets of Tetro. Droans converged, eyes looking up toward the rising monster machines as more and more exited the hangar beneath the mountain. They groaned, shook the earth with each step, and Violet barely caught up with Jack as he turned into a tiny alley and shoved through.

"Do not let go of that key!" he commanded.

She glowered. "I can shove it up your ass to keep it safe, where all the other sticks are!"

An angered laugh emitted.

They reached the end of the alley and turned onto the next market street, filled to the brim with stalls and tables spilling out from eateries. Droans dodged out of the way, only to stand and yell, or in worse cases, chase them. But although they bested humans in strength, they lacked speed. Their short legs carried them slowly, while Jack and Violet's ate up the sandy streets, agile through the posts, tables, and billowing fabrics in the markets.

"Make a left! I know where we are! Hoverbikes on the right!"

Jack shot to the left down a small alley, having to turn his body so he could fit. Violet was right on his tail. They made it out, and before them lay the mass of parked hoverbikes.

A Droan was starting one up, but Jack shoved him off before the Droan could even glance. Jack swung his leg over it, and Violet hopped on.

"Sorry!" she called as Jack figured out the accelerator and gunned it.

They zoomed down the road—a straight shot toward the edge of the city. Red fumes billowed behind them. Violet had to squint against the dusty wind. She found goggles clipped to the side of the bike and strapped one pair on her head and then Jack's.

He powered through the last blocks and they shot out of the yawning gates of Tetro.

The bright beacon gleamed ahead. A smile stretched on her face; she could leave this chaotic place and go to the next—

A horrified gasp left her. "Slow down! The pact will stop us from leaving."

Jack turned his head. "So what do you propose to do to solve it?"

The spot where she'd sprinted toward days ago, only to meet the invisible barrier, loomed ahead. Her heart tumbled within her chest, before Isolo's words clicked.

As awful an idea as it was, Violet unwrapped Iso's leathers from her right hand, yanked the bloodied dagger out of Jack's belt and slashed her palm. "A bloodbond. Iso—" Her chest tightened, but she shook her head. "It overrides it."

"It sounds a lot more binding than a spit pact."

"I swear, Jack Marin, by my hand, proxy, accident, that I…" she gulped, but accepted the truth. "Will not kill you."

He slowed the bike and twisted fully to face her. His dark curls danced in the wind, eyes wide as he stared at her through the ridiculous goggles. *Surprised. Shocked.* She was sure that expression was rare on his face.

The sting on her palm heightened as the harsh wind bit into the wound. His eyes dipped to her hand, then back up, and she could have sworn a look of relief flashed across before he took the blade from her and slashed his palm.

"And I swear to you, Violet Sutton, by my hand, proxy, or accident, that I will not kill you, even if you are the most stubborn, annoying person I've ever met."

A scowl. She almost considered drawing her hand back, but Jack's bloody palm met hers and warmth spread along her arm while a flash of light burst from the contact. They both stared at their connected palms.

"Skivvin' magic," she cursed.

"The universe is a lot weirder outside of the walls," he muttered.

When she pulled away, the cut was already stitching back together.

Jack spared her a quick look, then wasted no time turning back and gunning the accelerator. "Let's hope this works, little Violet, because we have company."

They drew closer and closer to where she had collided with the barrier.

And they flew right past.

A smile split on her face. Jack turned to look at her, and the smile dropped. He grinned, "Are you holding on?"

"No, I was thinking I'd rather be dragged."

A length of leather slapped her in the face. "Suit yourself. If you could use most of the rope so I don't have to hear you, that would be great. Actually, I might have a gag somewhere."

She wrapped the leather around her hand, aching to shove him off like she did the other candidate.

Jack merely chuckled at her silence and gunned it harder. "I'm told I blow people away. So grab on."

She bit her yelp and clutched at the sides of the bike rather than his waist.

Jack looked back past her shoulder, something in line with fear on his face. She twisted her head, followed his gaze. To her horror, those monstrous machines stomped, rolled, and trampled through the city and out onto the beginning of the desert expanse.

An army of Droans clambered for their hoverbikes, numerous balls of red fumes curling into the air all at once, and powered forward. Whips hung in the air, and she could hear the war cries as they echoed from one to another.

The Iris warmed against her side. She looked back to the beacon, sure Jack could not see it, and pointed him in that general direction. It was miles away, and as they raced the Droanian army at their back, Violet's stomach twisted as lingering revulsion for Jack Marin and self-preservation battled within her.

He was the sole reason she was even out of the city and breathing. Yet while the wrath didn't invade her again, it still dangled its noose, glancing to Jack Marin's neck and back to her.

❀❀❀

Jack thrust the accelerator as far it could go. The bike shook beneath, protesting the speed. Still, it flung them across the desert in a blur of sand and scouring air.

The Droanian army bellowed a distance behind, on the horizon. Specks of red fumes cloyed into the air like markers of approaching death and blood and fury.

Violet hastily turned to the front, eyes rising to the beacon, now much larger. Her palms clammed at the anticipation of making it—could it really be the next world? She wondered if there would be a hunting party waiting for candidates as they arrived.

Probably worse. She could not fathom what was beyond that beacon. Wrath smashed through the glass walls and left it in fine, dusted sand.

But hope pressed her forward, had her stretching her neck over Jack's shoulder to watch. Five worlds until Reed. Only five.

Jack drove them forward under Violet's instructions. She fought with herself to deter him away, or just punch him off the bike and leave him to the Droans' wrath. But her first priority was distance between themselves and the mob, and as much as she wanted to leave Jack behind, it was not her top concern. If they slowed, if they even swerved to a different direction, that army would be on their asses before she could say *skiv off*.

The sun dipped in the sky, counting the seconds. Perhaps the darkness of the desert would be better? But with the advanced technologies she glimpsed on those machines, she doubted they would be useless without lights. Or not even spotlights—maybe they could *see* in the dark.

"Keep going," was all she said, still refusing to grip his body at the speed they were going.

"Are you going to tell me what we are headed for?"

"No."

"Violet."

"Oh, don't *Violet* me," she fussed.

"Fine, *asshole*." She rolled her eyes. "Can you give me a bit more navigation than 'keep going'?"

She let silence eat up the space as the bike ate up the distance, before she said, "No."

"You know, while I can't kill you, I can take—"

The bike sputtered dark red flames. It slowed down drastically, lurching back and forth. Violet had no choice but to grip Jack to steady herself as her head slammed into his back and Jack's body careened forward. The bike swerved in a last-ditch effort, Jack twisting the throttle desperately, but then it gave a loud, resounding groan before it plopped straight into the sand and stalled.

"Damn," Jack muttered. He turned to look back—

Violet was already gone, booking it toward the beacon. The Iris dug into her back. Her pack bounced on it. Jack called out a string of curses and pounded after her.

"Violet! Get the *fuck* back here!"

"No!" she growled.

"You are not leaving me!"

"Why shouldn't I?"

"I gave you a bloodbond!"

"That doesn't mean *shit*," she scoffed.

"Means a lot to me," he grubbed.

"Is this just to use me, huh? You have a big grand plan to have things to fall back on so I'd owe you? Hm, Jack?" She grit through her teeth. "When were you planning on disposing of me to take the Iris for yourself?"

He rolled his eyes. "Soon."

"Fine, then." She swung around and flung her fist out, but he caught it. She brought her knee up, but he evaded that too.

He pushed her back, a frustrated snarl emitting between his straight teeth. "Stop it. I'm not being serious. I'm just making sure I come with."

"Screw that." She sprinted toward the beacon, less than a mile away.

She made it about four steps before his hand grasped her ankle and dragged her back. "Give me the key, Violet! I need the collateral!"

Violet lurched face-forward to the ground. She took the impact on her shoulder. She kicked at him until she landed a hit on his brow bone. Jack flinched back.

"And why in the world would I do that?" She hurried to stand and turned back toward the beacon, calling behind, "Were you dropped as a kid? On the head? Multiple times?"

Jack pushed up on his feet. "I want it—" He swiped at her, she ducked, and he swiped again. "To ensure that I will be *coming*."

She shimmied out of his reach and yelled, "*No!*"

"Get back here."

She stomped away. "No!"

"You are not leaving."

"Yes. I. Am."

"Viol—"

"No! Go screw a Droan for all I care. You aren't using me!"

"Can you shut up for one damn sec—"

"*No.*"

Jack furiously ran a hand through his hair and looked up. "Skies, grant me the *fucking* patience."

She ripped him a middle finger from behind and hurried toward the light.

Heavy footsteps caught up to her quickly. "Get back here."

"No!" She dodged to the left.

"I swear to the skies—"

"Swear all you want!"

"You are not..." He missed her again as she spun. "...Going away."

"Skiv off, dickwad!"

"You and your damn mouth." He lunged for her, missing again.

"You and your damn *attitude*."

He scoffed. "My attitude? You—" He reached. "*Violet.*"

"No!"

And then she didn't hear his answer. She continued her sprint, heart thrashing at the exertion, but curiosity bit her in the ass and the silence had her turning—

Her gut leadened.

Jack gazed at her. Eyes dilated black.

Wrath.

"Now I'm really going to hurt you," he said, an icy edge to his voice. So unlike her fire, Jack's wrath was riddled with a callous deadliness.

Fear slowed her down as she blinked at his prowling figure, those eyes boring into hers with a promise of pain. The very man created from the rumors that the South feared. He always came across as aloof, as cunning and gritty, but to see him *actually* angry…

His body jerked as if he were fighting it, but he shook his head and those black eyes were back on her. "Your brother deserved his place in the Sins for what he did to me and the city."

She faltered, backing up a step and then another, willing her legs to *move*. But pride roared in her chest. "You want to go there finally? You *ruined* my life! His life! You put him in the game because you couldn't handle the fact that you lost the gardia wars."

Wrath-Jack snarled and picked up his pace. She twisted around, knowing she shouldn't have baited the dangerous creature he was, but she couldn't help it.

"I was saving the city!" he called as he chased her. "You all painted me as awful—"

"You *are* awful!"

"I'm going to rip that tongue from your mouth." His steps pounded the ground. "You're all talk. You think your brother wasn't awful too? You think he was a gracious older brother—Yes, *yes,* he ruined me and now I have to fight to find him. When I do, when I get my hands on him—"

"Shut up!" she cried, tears burning her eyes, because memories flashed.

Reed teasing her, taunting her, belittling her because he had that power. He would stand up for her in an instant, but he could tear her back down a second later. And *oh*, how she tried to avoid thinking about those instances they eventually grew out of, but how they did bruise her within, making her think that Reed's words justified her worth.

But he would never ruin a city. He would *never* do what Jack was claiming. Jack Marin was the monster.

"When I catch you, I'm going to rip you apart!" he snarled.

"I'd like to see you try!"

"I *hate* you!"

Her legs frantically pumped, his presence close behind. He snarled and then shushed himself, fighting the sin, then mumbling some angered things about family, a man named Lucien, another called Avan, a woman named Lily, and then her brother again—Reed. Reed. Reed.

The ground shook, knocking her off balance. She flew forward and caught herself before she ate sand.

That was when she truly felt it. Sand rose and fell. Her whole body was vibrating. When she turned, Jack's brown, sweaty face paled as he battled within himself. He shoved his hand into his hair, pulled at it. "Stop it, stop it. No, they hurt me. *Stop it.*"

She took one glance at the sight behind them and thought she might soil herself. This—*this* was not what she signed up for. It was more than some angry Droans on bikes. It was…it was…

Beyond a giant cloud of chaotic dust, monsters roared, up and up, rising along the horizon as the sun blurred them in its bleak haze. Mishmashes of metal, the machines were a couple of miles away at least, but gaining fast. Every rumble shook her bones. Violet took one fearful step back, rooted in her place. Beyond the hulking war machines, hoverbikes groaned and sputtered red fumes.

An arm on the nearest machine raised. At the center of its fist, a bright orange light glowed….and glowed…and glowed until it was a blinding white. It shot out with a deafening roar, the sound hitting Violet's ears seconds after the blast flew high into the sky and plowed into the mountain beside them.

Jack's eyes flashed back to her, black as the depths of his soul. She scurried up as he lunged at her, flinging his dagger out.

It scraped her arm and she whirled away, throwing all of her energy into running for the beacon.

Skies, she was dealing with *too* much right now.

The ground jolted. She hardly kept her balance.

The duo ran across the flattening earth. Her legs pumped as another machine roared into the air, and a blasted fireball met the ground behind them.

She didn't bother navigating Jack toward the beacon—he was following her anyway. She cried over the dulling clashes of machinery, the angry noise of the hoverbikes—and the loud, shrieking hollers of the Droans riding them.

Another blast. Heat seared her skin as smaller fireballs descended on them. She zig-zagged her running, holding tightly to the Iris, focusing on the gleaming silver table that appeared.

She dared one look back at the Droan army and wished she hadn't. They would be upon them in minutes. Droans on top of one of the towering machines, so big it winked out the sun. Another shot fired, close enough to deafen her with its sharp ringing. Violet threw the last of her energy to sprint toward the silver table—the same color as the Iris.

Wind whipped. Sand pinched her skin and she squinted ahead through those stupid goggles. The Iris grew warm in her hand, vibrating at the proximity to the portal.

Thirty feet. The shadows of the machines covered their bodies.

Twenty feet. A whip cracked in the air.

She swallowed. Heat pressed. A blast roared, singeing the tips of her hair. A ball hit next to her and she cried as pain blistered her knuckles and arm.

"Violet! Get back here!" Jack cried.

She turned toward him at the table with a ferocious glare. She noticed his eyes clearing up, green peeking through.

She held her hand out. Jack ran forward, grabbed it—

She drew him close and said, "I fucking hate you, too."

Then she kicked him in the chest.

He flew back toward the ground. He wheezed for breath, eyes bugging wide before he lurched up.

To his roar of anger, she turned and shoved the damned Iris into the insert. It clicked in.

She met Jack's wide eyes as her body flared with light. Her ears rang—a loud, shrieking noise that gave every instinct to cover them. She held on in desperation. The heat burned her skin, and a bright, blinding light swallowed the world of Wrath around her.

16

THE SECOND SIN

THROUGH THE BRIGHT LIGHT, THE absence of sound, the warm and cold feeling of passing between worlds, the only thing Violet knew was that she was screaming. Again.

Gravity jolted her straight into bare, chilly ground.

She was disoriented from her senses. It was as if the transition singed every feeling and reset it. Even her thoughts parried, then disappeared, as she tried to grasp herself. Her heart palpitated in her chest.

Thump. Thump thump. Thump. Thump thump thump…

Did she die and then come back to life?

Breath was the first to come back to her. The fresh, crisp air hollowed every sense to that breath. Her lungs filled with the sweet, watery taste of it, and she gulped it down as if it might be both her first and her last. Tears pricked at her eyes at the pure *relief* it gave to be away from the heat.

She half expected this world to be inside an air conditioner.

On top of the air, she tasted metal. She realized that must be blood from the ache on her tongue. Warmth pooled in her mouth until she had half a mind to move her muscles and spit it out.

She smelled—oh skies, she hardly had names for the smells. There was earth, as if she had been shoved straight into the lumberyard in the factory district in Calesal. Wood—lots of wood and it was *fresh*, as if…as if…

Her fingers clenched the ground. Leaves crunched. She shuddered, bringing herself up to her knees. The wind blew against her cheeks, cooling them from the heat of Wrath. Her clothes sizzled slightly.

She tore the hoverbike goggles off her head.

She peeled her eyelids open and let them adjust. Fine bark and needle-like leaves stuck out between her fingers, against her burnt skin and swollen knuckles. Dirt lined the cracks in her nails, the small hairs of her arms, and the scars left from drunken nights.

Sunlight puckered through towering shadows over her head. She was reluctant to look up. It was another world—another sin. Look up. Look up.

A grief-filled gasp slid out of her mouth from her chest.

Everything that happened in Wrath flashed; the angry pull of whips, the smell of leather, the warmth of fresh blood, Isolo's barren gaze, Garan's death, Jack's murderous pursuit, and the singe of heat in those last few moments.

Her mind lingered on Jack.

She'd left him there.

By the time she'd winked out from Wrath, those machines would have been on him, destroying him. And she…she…

She was responsible for that. Right?

Bringing her burned, leather-wrapped hands up to her face, Violet scrubbed at her skin, mixed emotions battling within her. Blood still covered her; dark stains on her black shirt. Her hair was sticky with it.

None of that bothered her. She left Jack Marin in Wrath to succumb to death. Would the streets cheer? Cry?

While she wasn't as experienced in ruining lives like he was, she did get some satisfaction in what she had done to him. Even if he was…

Dead.

Good, the emotionless part said. *Your life will be a thousand times easier.*

She agreed.

So Violet took a sweet, jittery inhale and looked up at the new sin before her.

A clearing, a meadow, a forest, a mountain. In that order.

Her heart leaped with joy.

Trees climbed high into a faint blue-purple sky. There was a mix of needled canopy and thick, plump bushes with red, star-shaped leaves. The height of four-story buildings or more, the trees dominated the rich forest as far as she could see, thick roots embedded into the ground and crawling down the gently sloping hill farther and farther until it all blurred together. The earthy, woodsy smell along with something else—she raised the needles to her nose and sniffed—it was that. Whatever the needle-looking things were called. And it was fresh—no stink from the shredding of wood or dirt mixed with piss. Pure, relentless nature unbound and flourishing before her.

The sky shifted with lazy clouds, drifting against the curious purple. Her eyes roamed the birds that chirped in the treetops or the bigger ones soaring with graceful purpose. She followed a gray-black-beaked bird with tanned wings that must have spread to her full height until her breath caught in her throat and the bird was forgotten.

A plateau extended out twenty feet in front of her. She checked her limbs, thankful nothing was broken from that horrendous fall, and scurried up. She all but staggered past the yawning gap in the forest onto a bed of rock mixed with green moss and peeking blue flowers. The rock extended outward and then dropped like a lurch in her stomach. The height was nothing she was afraid of, but the view that expanded before her made her palms clammy. This sin must be beauty because she was going to let it wrap its fist around her soul and take her.

Mountains.

Massive, rigid alps jutted into the sky like hands reaching for the heavens above. They touched in white-capped points—*snow*, she realized, and her heart danced in her chest. Dark gray rock let loose in boulders and cliffs while waterfalls and streams sluiced down the mountainsides. There were so *many* of those majestic rises extending into the distance, farther than she could see, until the farthest were all but shadows.

The mountain she was on bowed toward its twin, another monstrous peak at the other side of the valley. They acknowledged each other, firm in their grip on the earth but separated by a misty, rushing river curving between.

She cocked her head at the other side of the far twin. Something dark shrouded behind it. The side that faced her was laden with rocks and snow but barren of any life, *any* green that elated her soul. Cliffs trailed down the edge until they met the mere hill that sat next to it. Beyond that hill—a blur in her eyes—blackened land stretched out, with distant puffs of smoke.

Something made her hesitate. This was the exact thing that happened in Wrath—a place that clearly looked inhabited, but a feeling that she shouldn't go.

At the same time, this world was lush and inviting. Was that ruined portion, probably seven miles away, the sin?

Violet's pack was light against her back, a stark reminder that whatever she had might not last for very long. But there was plenty of water around; that much she knew and wasn't worried about. Food, however.

Was she supposed to hunt? She didn't have a plasgun or even one of those arrow things she'd read about in books. Only a short dagger that meant she'd have to all but be on top of her prey…and then what? Skin it—

She cringed.

Maybe there were fish in the streams… She huffed in frustration. Was she going to go around stabbing the water until she got lucky?

The reality of her situation diminished the allure of her world. Beating the sin was one thing, but surviving the elements was another. If she were caught again, would she be fed for long enough to win the sin and move on?

"Skies, this is shit, I tell you—" She shut her mouth quickly, looking around at her surroundings. The Droans had been waiting for her when she entered the Sins. She listened but could only hear the steady rush of water, the chirping of birds, and the cooing wind between the trees. No odd footsteps. No cracks of whips. No Jack taunting at her.

There was loneliness. It weighed on her shoulders but loosened her chest. She carefully watched the nature around her, but as far as she could tell, there was no one. Only her.

She pressed her boot on a bed of needles and stomped. They would make for quiet feet and easy sneak attacks…but the crunchy red leaves that periodically drifted to the forest floor would not. Being alone was not a burden, but the lack of noise—or people—set her on edge. There was nothing this serene in Calesal. For so long, in the citadel, she thought she would be happy to trek alone, exploring the world outside of the wall, away from her pathetic life in the South. She had sat on rooftops that peeked over the city's divide and watched the forests beyond for hours. Surrounded by the putrid, burning smells and incessant honks of cars and sirens, she had sat there *hoping* there could be a time when she left it all behind. That was her idea of freedom. Now she was standing in it, and she didn't know what to feel.

The Sin? There was nothing tugging on her gut. Nothing made her feel on edge or stressed or…anything. What was left? Envy, Pride, Sloth, Gluttony, Greed, Lust.

Too many; damn.

It was definitely not Lust; she was sure of that. In the back of her mind, Lust was the one she worried about—that, or Greed.

No, this world was neither of those two. Sloth? It was serene and peaceful here, and the absence of people made her wonder if they were lazily hanging from trees closer to the river. But the ruined, dark land beyond the mountain told her *that* was not the work of Sloth.

"Envy, Pride or Gluttony, then," she mumbled, biting her lip. It was the best she could decipher. She wasn't particularly jealous of anything yet…definitely not, because no other person was around her, and she hadn't eaten anything to test if it was Gluttony.

Pride…she had no idea what to expect for that. Fame? Riches? She despised the Elites for what they flaunted and boasted. No, it was not Pride. It couldn't be. There was nothing to be prideful about here.

Violet strapped her pack tighter to her spine. One bright sun shined down and curved toward the barren mountain opposite her.

Her head still ached from her fall, and thinking about all this was not helping. She needed to move, understand the sin, beat it thrice, get the next Iris, and shove the damned thing into the table with the light. The faster she got through these worlds, the closer she was to the sixth. To Reed.

Violet huffed and set her sights across the valley toward that blackened land.

Green surrounded her as she began her trek. Her ears pricked at every sound, and she stopped, turning only to find a small, fuzzy animal munching on a plant or birds escaping into the trees. The quiet would take some getting used to. Alone, small in this new world, a semblance of freedom embraced her.

On her way, Violet collected all kinds of leaves—bright, beautiful green—and shoved them into her pockets like treasures to stow within her heart.

She just hoped she'd live long enough to show them to Reed.

17

MONDAR LION
JELAN

JELAN HAD BEEN TOO OVERWHELMED with all of the information and stomped right out of the house.

"She's not going to want to stay for dinner now."

"She'll come back around."

"When you are ready, you can find me here tomorrow night."

And then Lucien had handed her a slip of paper with an address to a club in the Mid. The Mondar Lion.

She beelined straight home. Pretended like none of the day had ever happened. When her late shift came around, she trudged over and buried her mind into the intricate work of plasbulbs.

The following morning near the end of her shift, as she was melding another wire to a new plasbulb in a garment factory, a yell shook the working silence.

"—indisposed?" Supervisor Callonuth cried into his radio. A static of a voice spoke back to him. "He's missed his last two shifts and I'm down on my numbers. Well, where is he? What in the skies happened?"

As the voice on the other side spoke, Callonuth paled. His eyes drifted to his workers, and Jelan looked down to her bulb, pretending to be swamped by her work.

"Send his family my best," said Callonuth, this time with a lower voice. "Yes—yes, all right."

Her heart beat rapidly in her ears and all she could think was:
Normal. Normal. I just want normal. This is all one big dream and I'm about to wake up.

When the clock ran out and she returned her gear, Callonuth had his usual scowl on his face, and said nothing else.

Jelan went straight to the first bar she glimpsed the minute she arrived back in the South.

It was still so early in the morning that most bars were open. Patrons slopped drunkenly in their seats, bartenders wiped vomit off the tables, and Jelan ignored it all as she took her seat and ordered a shot of the strongest shiva they had.

She shot it back and slammed the empty glass on the bar. Her eyes caught the pixelated plascreen above as it switched from table sports to a skating list of names in each world. She motioned for another shot, and when she brought it to her lips, Jelan choked.

Garan Umbero.

Red dot. Unblinking.

Dead.

"No," she breathed. "No no no no no."

Her eyes darted to find Violet's name, but it wasn't there.

Through her coughing fit, the shiva burning her throat, the list moved to the second world, and Violet's name appeared along with the few older candidates still there.

"Holy shit."

Jelan slapped payment on the table and hurried out of the bar. She needed to see the big screen. Needed to know that it was just a televised mistake.

Not Garan. Not Garan.

A mix of desperation and elation coursed through her as she powered down the streets. The markets were opening up, doors flung out and propped by crates, the smell of bread and coffee and oil in the air. Jelan controlled her breathing, but she had to slow as her breaths became too short. She pushed through it, even when tightness clawed at her chest.

The Sins Screen loomed in front of her; bright, boastful, and per usual when something interesting happened, heads turned and fingers pointed.

She shoved past a group of huddled women done with their night out and stumbled before the fountain.

"No," she breathed.

Garan's name was still there. Bright red dot and all.

Skies, her chest ached. She rubbed at it, taking deep, long breaths until the pain slightly diminished.

A wail turned Jelan's head. Umbero's bar still glowed from the night, and before the front doors amidst the empty tables and chairs, a young woman kneeled.

"Kaisha, Garan's sister. She took over the bar when he was sentenced."

She whipped around. Jenkins lounged on the lip of the fountain, right where Violet and she had been that fateful night. He lifted a bottle. "Cheers to Violet."

He poured a bit out. "Condolences to Garan."

"How can you be so crass?" She clenched her fists. "Do the Sins mean nothing to you?"

"It certainly is easier to watch them die on a screen." He sipped his bottle, never answering a question fully. "Saves money when you don't have to bury a body, too."

The wails of Garan's sister flooded the square. Jenkins winked at Jelan, and she had half a mind to push him into the fountain.

"She was the first one to make it to the second world, by the way." He nodded to the screen.

Jelan turned.

Violet Sutton.

A bright green dot lingered next to her name. Jelan's heart swelled. "When?"

"A little after midnight. I have an alert on her for any movements or changes to her tracker. It blared and nearly scared the skiv out of Ms. Kush the cat. She was hissing for the next hour," he said. "Do you see who is there now, though? It's *very* interesting."

Jelan's brows furrowed as she scanned the second world again. "It's the usual list of names—Oh. *Oh.*"

"Jack skivvin' Marin," he cackled. "He went in nearly right after her. But his tracker was flashing red for a while before it finally settled, hm, maybe two hours ago? It makes me think they fought. But the young weed didn't manage to kill him."

"She's not a killer and you know that," she said, glancing down to where Jenkins's gardia tattoo would be. "Your amnesty would be in jeopardy if he died."

He smiled. "Amnesty for *life*. No matter if he is dead or alive or in the fucking Sins, scarred one."

She shoved her hands into her pockets, scowling.

"Are you going to see him tonight?" he asked, changing the subject.

"One of my co-workers went missing," she mumbled.

He tapped his arm. "You siding with him will grant you safety."

"I don't want—need safety. I just want to live normally."

"Do you tell yourself that to sleep better?" Jenkins leaned forward, dropping his voice. "Or are you just afraid of your potential if you broke some rules?"

"Working with...*him* is not just breaking the rules."

"You may go back to work tomorrow and find three more co-workers gone, maybe find their bodies on the shore during your next calming walk. Do you think your brother will protect you from all of this?"

Jelan's silence was enough of an answer.

"I'd be very interested to meet a person who didn't step on others to reach their success in this city." Jenkins pushed his glasses up. "What a rare soul that would be."

"Is there a way?" asked Jelan.

A shrug. "Lucien will divulge what you need to know once you meet him."

Once she met him. No choice given.

Great.

Jenkins turned to her. "Does your brother know about your new job, Jelan?"

"Like I said, I haven't spoken to him in three years."

"Keep it that way." He waved his hand, dismissing her. "Go—meet with him. Tonight at the club."

"And if I refuse?"

"Then he will offer you protection. Money."

"Until I accept, that is."

Jenkins grinned. "Welcome to the business, darling. Enjoy tonight."

The dismissiveness had Jelan wanting to scream. Frustration built within her. She wanted to throttle her brother. Yell at him. Cry to the world.

Tone it down, her mother's voice filled her head. *Put that anger away in a box and lock it. People don't want to see that. Reserve yourself.*

Jelan inhaled sharply. Clenched her burnt fists.

Am I muzzled enough for you now, Mother?

❈❈❈

The minute Jelan got back to her room, she took down every single drawing and stashed them away. Her anger over her brother, the entire situation of losing Garan unfairly, muddled the fear she should be feeling. People in her line of work were going missing, were bribed or outright kidnapped for whatever Arvalo was concocting.

And when they failed, they ended up dead.

She didn't understand the fatal part of it. Most engineers were bound to fail. That was how the best inventions evolved. They failed numerous times, tried again until finally, it all clicked, and the product worked.

The desperation behind the story was tangible.

Arvalo had the city in his hands now that Jack Marin was out of the picture. He had blueprints to a mysterious weapon that would allow him leverage over whatever he desired—control, domination via the empire which still maintained it—and he was abusing Plastech to get him those results.

And her brother was intertwined within it, working for him, after a similar plasmic explosion had blown their family apart.

There was a ghostly burn on her hands. As if she were reaching again, into that fire, screaming for her mother and younger brother all those years ago. Dead now. It was Ahmad who pulled Jelan out, their father who managed to wrench the window open on the outdated apartment building and toss two kids twelve feet to the pavement.

Did their history, their tragedy, mean nothing to Ahmad?

Their father drank himself silly to forget that night. He'd saved them, only to abandon them. Fourteen-year-old Jelan and sixteen-year-old Ahmad. Her brother had raised her for three years, only to fall into gambling and vanish from her life. They had a giant falling out at the end, and Jelan, twenty years old now, still could not forgive Ahmad.

It was why Jelan couldn't blame Violet for tumbling into a depression and then going after her brother. What transpired between Jelan and Ahmad's relationship during those three years— the dependency, the family that was found—Violet had hung on to that her entire life. To have it ripped away was suffocating, drowning, burning.

Ahmad certainly made it easy for Jelan to despise him. They had screamed at each other, but at that point Jelan was screaming at the drugs muddling him, not her brother.

Jelan loosed a deep sigh and sank into her bed with a creak. She wanted a normal life. She wanted to work *normally*, grow old normally, love normally, live normally.

She rubbed at her eyes.

Right?

But now, there was fear looming over her head. Did her other co-workers know about the danger of being associated with Plastech? There were thousands of them in the city—was Arvalo going to go through them all one by one until someone managed to get it right and provide him his threat?

Her heart picked up its beat. She glanced to her hands.

Hands that built and molded, burned and bled.

Not normal hands.

The speaker buzzed. Someone was at the door downstairs. Eliza was away at her job, so…someone was here for her.

Her gut flipped. Did Ahmad finally find out about her? Was he about to hand her over to his boss?

Another buzz. Another buzz.

Jelan huffed, grabbed her dagger and slid it into her belt, and headed downstairs.

When she opened the door, a strange man with dark hair and not-Souther clothes was fidgeting with his fingers, looking up and down the street.

"Can I help you?" she said, wary.

The man turned. His single-lid, angular eyes flashed at her, deep brown darting from the door she exited, then back to the street.

"Are you Jelan Gregory?" His voice was nervous.

"Are you where you're supposed to be?" she quipped.

He looked up to the building, then the call panel on the side. "I'm looking for Jelan Gregory."

"And?"

"Well, Jelan Gregory—"

"Stop saying my name like that," she snapped. Her confusion and anger still wafted within her. She buried it. "It's weird. I'm Jelan. Do I know you?"

"Kole Akard."

Her gaze widened. She made sure she had her key for the building on her before stepping out and letting the door shut. She nodded to the wide stoop.

Kole stepped onto it. Jelan looked him up and down—simple button shirt, tan trousers, clean. Mid-level clean.

Violet hadn't mentioned much about him except that she had an endeavor she wasn't sure about anymore. Seeing him in person,

watching him look nervously about the South, very obviously out
of place, Jelan was frankly surprised Violet even spoke to him, let
alone slept with him.

And saved his ass from the Sins.

Violet had been desperate for something other than the spiral
she was living. Kole would have been different, but in the end, she
would have broken him, as it was clear she already had.

"What do you want?" She crossed her arms. She didn't want this
interruption in the day. She wanted to take her sleeping draught
and save her energy for the inevitable conversation she would have
with Lucien Marin later.

Kole smiled sheepishly. "You Souther women are so…"

Jelan narrowed her eyes. "No, go on. Finish it."

"Interesting," he said quickly. "Very interesting. It's why I—"

"Fell in love with her?" Jelan reined in her emotions. She was
still so angry—*so angry*—because of Ahmad.

Kole looked away in resignation. "I—it wasn't like that."

"What do you need from me? A way to feel closer to Violet? To
mourn her?"

Tone it down.

But skies, she wanted to burst into flames.

Still, Jelan took a deep breath in and out, taming it, not because
she'd been emotionally wrung like a rag when she was a child, but
because the look on Kole's innocent, ignorant face told her that he
did not deserve it. He did not know any better.

"I'm sorry," said Jelan, calming herself with another breath. "I
just got some bad news. Now is not a good time. Come back later."

She turned. Her hand reached the handle—

"Do you want to get drinks sometime?" Kole said behind her.

She glanced back at him.

"Just because, well—I've been struggling ever since she went
in. Saved me, and all that. And I really need a friend. Not like the
ones in the Mid or North, but someone who…" Kole shook his
head, eyes dropping to his feet. "I figured I would ask. Because I
do miss her—or what I imagined was her. I'm not affected by this

in my world, but you all are, and I was hoping if there were a way for that loss to get better, it would be here, because it hurts." He looked up to her again, pleading. "It really hurts."

Jelan almost wanted to wrinkle her nose at the confession. The pliable softness about him read as vulnerable to her. Weak.

"You get over the grief," she said. "Time will heal."

"I know that, but that's not what I'm—"

"If you're looking for a hug, a pat on the back, some comfort, you won't find it here." She gave him a pointed stare. "Go back to your world, Kole."

His gaze was pleading. "Just one drink. I don't bite. Not like—"

She lifted her hand. "Please don't mention those things about my friend. I've heard it all already."

"Really?"

"She fucks and tells." Jelan looked him up and down again. He was hot, that was for sure. But clean—too clean.

"Great," he huffed a laugh. "Besides the minute by minute you probably got of my bedroom skills, I mean no harm. Or intrusion. I only want to get a drink—I'll pay."

She perked up at that. "Oh?"

He smiled. "She did the same thing too. When I mentioned I'd pay for dinner."

He had a nice smile. A very nice smile. Not that Jelan was interested. Violet and she had a pact that none of their conquests would ever overlap. It usually didn't happen due to Jelan only preferring men and Violet leaning toward women as of late, other than Kole. But once said conquest had been spoken about, it was off limits.

Still, he had a nice smile. She could admire that.

"If you include dinner in that, I'll agree," bargained Jelan.

"Deal. This week?"

"Sure, I'm free…." Jelan paused. After tonight and the rest of the news, she didn't know where she stood with her safety and job. "The weekend? Saturday?"

"I'll pick you up then," he smiled. His nervousness fell off him, and a bit of charm poked through. "At eight. There's a good place in the Mid."

"Okay." Jelan stepped up and reached for the doorknob. "And Kole?"

He was back on the sidewalk, a car with a driver idling behind him. He lifted a dark brow. "Yeah?"

"Just so you are aware, if you get sentenced to the Sins again, I'm not saving you."

Fear flashed before a smile graced it again. He seemed to relax, almost, even though it had been only a week since the incident.

"Duly noted."

❀❀❀

"Dancers go through the back door."

Jelan reined in every flinch of movement as the tall, narrowed-eyed bouncer looked down at her. The twin scars on his neck were like lines of shadows against the flickering red lights outside the Mondar Lion.

Everything in her body wanted to turn right around and stomp back to the safety of her dormitory. This whole *meeting Lucien Marin because Plastech employees were being kidnapped or dying in a secret project for Arvalo's reign of terror* was ridiculous, and standing outside the Midian club in her Souther leathers, canvas pants, and boots with plasma burns on them made her feel even more ridiculous.

"I'm here to meet—"

The bouncer jerked his thumb to the dark alley. "Through the back."

Midians groaned in the long line as the jazz music pulsated out of the four-story club. Through Jelan's eavesdropping, there apparently was a well-known jazz band on the schedule for tonight.

"But I'm—"

"In the back—"

"She's with me."

The bouncer paled, whirled around. Everyone in the line bristled, quieting their complaints.

Lucien Marin stepped out of the tall alcove of the entrance, dressed similarly to when she'd met him in Jenkins' hoarder apartment. Simple white shirt, fitted black pants. But this time his sleeves were rolled on his brown skin, showing the gardia mark above his elbow. His territory, then.

"She's with—?"

"With me. Now if you want to harass or question any other perfectly eligible attendees, then you can turn those questions to the street as you look for another job." Lucien's gaze was hard. Unquestioning. Silent commands that ran through the Marin brothers.

It definitely had Jelan wondering how much worse the reaction would be if it were Jack.

"I'm sorry, sir." The bouncer bowed. Turned to Jelan. "Go right in."

"You can apologize to her, too, for wasting her time."

The bouncer's eyes widened. "Oh—my deepest apologies."

Well, that's one way to make a man lose his pride, thought Jelan as she brushed past the bouncer and followed Lucien through the entrance.

Inside the club, the wooden walls were swathed with thick red drapes. Low-lit chandeliers hung above gambling tables strewn about the center, whereas private booths pressed against the wall, velvet curtains ready to hide parties from wandering eyes.

Lucien waltzed past the crisp-suited servers who gave a wide berth to him, and questioning looks to Jelan. He nodded to the dancers dressed in jeweled corsets and stockings, even greeting some by name.

So he owned the club. And made use of its amenities.

Lucien walked up to a dark curtain with two guards, who parted it for him and then Jelan. When the flap closed behind them and muffled the testing blows of a saxophone as the band prepared to play, Jelan asked, "Why here?"

"I like this place." Lucien slid into one side of the crimson-cushioned booth.

Jelan didn't know how to respond to that, so she took her seat across from him, back straight.

"Drink?" he asked.

She didn't see a waiter, but he chuckled at her lifted brow.

He slid a compartment back from the table and a touchpad glowed. "So no one interrupts us."

"Or eavesdrops," said Jelan.

"Or that," said Lucien. "What do you like?"

She stared down at the touchpad as he scrolled through lists and lists of drinks. She wrung her hands under the table, unable to answer. She only knew one type of alcohol, and that was shiva. This was not the kind of place to drink shiva.

"How about I surprise you?"

She nodded.

He pushed a button, and it glowed green. He pressed one for his own.

Within a minute, one of the guards slid their glasses through the curtain and returned to his position. Lucien smirked as Jelan stared at the dark cherry concoction before her.

She poked the colorful umbrella decorating the top of it. "This doesn't fit with the whole dark, gambling, drug vibe."

"Four floors up is the drug room. If you want the drug vibe."

"What?" she blinked at him.

"They're crafting some dust that can increase serotonin in the brain by a very non-pharmaceutical amount."

Jelan cupped her glass and watched him.

He was completely serious.

"Why am I here?" she asked. She still couldn't comprehend the situation.

"I want to hire you," he said. "As my personal Plastech engineer. The Marin Empire doesn't run plasmic industries—that's Arvalo's realm—and based on what Jenkins has told you—"

"Skies, you guys are fast," she breathed.

Lucien smirked, continuing, "Based on what Jenkins has told you, Arvalo is running through plastechs like water. When they fail, they die. I need to know what they are trying to build and what secret plot Arvalo is up to, and I need an engineer who *can* build it—"

She thought of the exploded floor. "Absolutely not."

"—and create something to counteract it."

"Oh," she said, taking a long sip of her drink before continuing, "I'm just one person, and I only have two months' experience in Plastech…" Jelan almost wanted to laugh at the absurdity of it. "What—like *why* me? Other than the stupid shit my brother is in."

"Arvalo has a roster of every Plastech engineer since that is his industry. The city can continue to hire maintenance workers, but they can't afford to keep losing creators. Engineers. That's what he's after, and I need to be on top of it. Starting with you."

"But I'm not an engineer," she said quietly. Even though it had been her dream.

He lifted his hip to reach his pocket and then pulled out a familiar piece of paper. He unfolded and slid it across the table.

She stared at the drawing. *Her* drawing.

Of the plashield.

"You invaded my room?" she said quietly.

"Actually, no. This is what we found when we emptied Sutton's apartment."

Jelan's mouth thinned. She remembered that night—she and Violet lying in her bed while Jelan scribbled blueprints and Violet devoured some smutty romance she'd stolen from the neighbor. Then after all of their drinks, Jelan had misplaced her drawing, barely remembering she'd done it.

The one stuck on her wall was the second rendering.

"Where did you find it?"

"In a book called *The Dark Prince and His Conquest.*" Lucien's eyes sparkled. "I peeked at the summary. Sounds like an enthralling read. I might have to get a copy of it myself." He leaned back and drew his dark liquor glass to his mouth. "Your drawing was actually stuffed in a particularly fascinating excerpt. Heavily underlined, I might add. Something about two men bending the woman over and finding use for multiple holes."

Jelan didn't react. It didn't surprise her that Violet was reading that, no. It more surprised her that Violet used a revered plashield drawing as a bookmark for her filthy books.

"We want this." Lucien tapped the drawing. "This can counteract it. And it is unlike anything I've ever seen."

"I have a hard time believing that," she deadpanned.

His lips parted, and he cocked his head at her, before shaking it. "You need to give yourself credit for your intelligence. This detailed of a sketch from someone who didn't even go to plastrade school is beyond even the top engineers in the city."

She stared at him, waiting for the bait. The lie. The indication that his admiration was merely a way to get her to sign the skivvin' contract and tie her life away to the dirty world of the gardia. But Lucien's gaze, while sharp, glimmered with pureness. He was not a man to compliment, nor a man to charm or swoon. That was what his brother was for.

Lucien was cold hard facts. Logical. Realistic. He only said what he meant.

And *that* she could relate to. As much as she hated it.

"You will be paid exceptionally well, given new living quarters and everything you might need to make this…" He tapped the drawing again. "A reality. Once completed, you can have full pay for the rest of your life and continue to build new mechanics as much as you want, or tell us all to fuck off and never speak to you again."

She smiled into her drink, then wiped it off her face before he got any ideas that she was comfortable around him. "What's the catch, then?"

"These living quarters will be at Jack Marin's penthouse."

She almost spat out her drink. "At his *penthouse*? Why? Why not just send me to some lab?"

He twisted his glass, as if he had thought this through over and over again, and couldn't find a better option. "Your brother *will* find your name as a Plastech engineer. He will put two and two together, and then your life will be in danger. The safest place is the penthouse—only a select few people have ever entered or are allowed to enter. The North is exceptionally big, and Jack has multiple penthouses, but this one is unknown and under an entirely different name. It is well protected."

Jelan looked down at her drink, then her hands. "I don't have a choice, do I?"

"I'm trying to give you a good choice," he said. "To lay it all on the table—believe me, all of what has been said is top secret—and to allow you to trust me that this work is bigger than any of us." He leaned forward. "We need you, Jelan. We need this. Because I don't want another war—but Arvalo will stop at nothing to bring this country to its knees."

She couldn't wrap her head around it, but there was a warmth in her gut. Not the cold, ugly feeling she would get when she walked down the wrong alley or found herself alone on the street. No, this was a feeling that told her, *Yes, take it. Because you can build your dreams with your bare hands.*

And beyond this praise that she could potentially save the city and stop Arvalo, which again, was so over her head, she couldn't resist the excitement bubbling in her chest to finally pursue her sketches.

Finally *doing* instead of dreaming.

She flicked her gaze to meet Lucien's semi-pleading one. "I expect paychecks."

"Three thousand."

"A month?" She blinked, unable to fathom that amount in coin. That was…Midian coin. Not buy a penthouse coin, but rent a comfortable apartment in lower-Mid coin.

"A week."

Her eyes bugged. "A *week?*"

He smiled at her.

Her heart thundered in her chest. Was this really happening? This wasn't some fever dream she was going to wake from? She had the urge to rub her eyes. She couldn't care less about her Souther clothing, her anything.

Her lips twitched into a smile and she didn't hide it. "So when do I start?"

Lucien raised his glass, smirking.

"Tomorrow."

18

GWEN

IT TOOK NEARLY THE REST of the day to reach the river. Fear kept her at the edge where tall reeds met moss, and moss met multicolored stone before dipping into the clear water underneath.

Violet didn't know how to swim. And she was afraid her inability would be her death, regardless of the sin. Only Elites learned in their elaborate swimming pools atop their penthouses. The river seemed to mock her for the fact the biggest body of water she had ever been in was a bath.

Nearby, black, lithe-legged creatures with brown-gold horns drank. She watched, judging whether they were a predator, but the nearest one lifted its head, regarded her, and lowered back down to drink as if she were nothing but a rodent.

Violet continued her trek, looking for a way to cross the river. Her wish was granted in a spot where the current leveled to rocks, just shallow enough to reach her knees. Freezing water sloshed her pants and soaked her boots. She used a lone branch to maintain her balance as she crossed.

It took hours to climb the slope on the other side of the river. She noticed the wildlife thinned out, and so did the trees. There was less foliage—less vegetation—less everything. Goosebumps prickled her arms, and she guided her hand to the hilt of her dagger. Her boots crunched more loudly than they usually did. She froze.

Burnt debris littered the ground, as if the earth had been set afire and left to sizzle to death. Nothing like the rolling bumps of green on the other side of the valley. The pinnacle of the hill still blocked her view, but her gut told her *this* was the ruined part she was looking for. It also told her to turn around and run far, far away. Make a home on the other side of the valley, forget about this ravaged land, and move on.

She took a fearful step for Reed, and then another, until she plowed up the destroyed hill and beheld the sight before her.

The reek hit her first. The stench made her gag. It smelled of burnt skin and feces—worse than the piss streets of the South. She thought *that* smell was bad, but this—this she could taste on her tongue, and she wanted to scrape every bit of it out. Bile grew in her mouth.

The mountain—half of it decimated from this viewpoint—towered over miles and miles of land dark like death. Black dirt and the rubble of nature lay on the earth. Beyond the first mile she could see, people milled about. Her heart throbbed against her chest, fear clamming her palms, as she looked on to what *seemed* like people standing or sitting between tall, chained fences with barbed wiring at the top. But they were simply there, huddled together, churned in the dark mud.

She blinked. Rubbed her eyes. The people were *green*. No, she was seeing things. She was too far away.

And in the middle of it all, spouting dark fumes from a large smokestack, a glimmering metal factory rose like a palace in giant contrast to the darkness surrounding it. Numerous homes lingered beneath it, and a stone-like wall separated them from the fences of people beyond it.

White-skinned people on the backs of muscled, four-legged animals patrolled the edge of the fence.

They were cages. The patrols jammed the steel of their swords against the fences, and the sound screeched to her spot. The captives, almost naked, recoiled, holding on to each other. Beyond, a line of prisoners was chained and moved further into the sprawling complex, led by another patrol.

Violet took one terrified step back, and then another. It looked like—

Something whistled. An arrow pierced the ground next to her boot. Violet ducked, turning toward the forest. Another arrow shot to her side, narrowly missing her hand. She pushed herself up, hesitated. The shooter was coming *from* the woods, and like skiv she was going to run to the camp—

Another arrow flew by, the wind of it on her cheek. She dodged and ran toward another forest area, slipping down the ashen hill until she reached the first break of trees. Another arrow caught the tail of her braid and embedded itself into a trunk.

She jerked into the tree by force. She desperately clawed at the arrow—a handmade yet sharp thing of wood and rock, serrated at the end. She yanked her braid, tearing some of the hair out with it. A small force slammed her to the ground. Dirt sprayed. Violet lost her breath as the warm body on top of her silently pinned her hips down and pressed cold metal to her throat.

"That was a stupid, *stupid* thing for you to do, *agia*," a hoarse voice seethed.

Violet found her breath, her vision, and looked up.

A dark-green-skinned wrinkled woman with hard black eyes stared at her like death incarnate. She was shorter than Violet, but muscles bulged underneath her mismatch of muted clothes and the faded, thick scarves that wrapped her shoulders and neck. The wind shifted strands of white-gray hair, cold features marked with red mud, all hooded in a brown cloak.

Violet was so surprised by the ambush that her throat seized up. She gaped, keenly aware of the metal a breath away from breaking the skin at her neck.

The old female regarded her with disgust, frowning, lines etched deep into her face—so like Meema's.

"Dumb shit going to the *Farm*," the woman spat the word like it was from the bowels of hell. Her accent was lilted with coarseness from her throat. "You want to be cut up and eaten?"

That jolted her. "What?"

A reproachful look. "You saw the cages. You saw the Inaj. You want to be one of them?"

"I—I didn't know." The blade pressed farther. "No—no. I don't want to be one of them."

"The *Crale*," she snarled. "Would *delight* in a candidate like you, huh? Ready to offer yourself up on a plate?"

"The Crale?"

"Don't you know this, dumb *agia!* " Her features twisted in unrelenting ire. Was this Wrath again?

Her confused, fearful face must have given the female an answer because she shifted atop her and hilted the blade in a quick movement. Agile and swift, she stood up, reached for the arrow embedded into the tree, and yanked it out. "A new candidate. It is time, then."

Not a question. The female stalked back out onto the hill. Violet stood, removing a twig from her hair, and watched as the female gathered the rest of the arrows, keeping her head down and hidden within her hood. She shoved the arrows into the handmade bag slung across her back, and retrieved a bow hidden beneath a pile of leaves in the forest.

"Why did you shoot at me?" Violet asked.

The woman turned to her, settling the bow across her chest. "Because you were stupid."

"I realize that, yes. So, thank you. But…why bother to help me?"

A long silence. Violet felt naked as the woman studied her, up and down, not missing a single detail with those big, judging eyes. "Because I have seen too many fall into their clutches. And few ever survive the Farm."

"What is that? The Farm? Wait—where are you going?"

"Move on from the Farm, *agia*. Go to the next world. There is nothing for you here."

"Why do you say that? What Sin is this?" Violet followed her, careful with her steps, noticing how the female made no noise in her cloth-wrapped boots. "Will you stop—I'll follow you anyway. So answer me!"

"If you follow me, I will kill you, hm?" No turn of the head. "How about that?"

Violet's brows crunched. "I'll kill you first, then."

A cackle. "I'd like to see that—"

Violet's dagger embedded into the tree right where the female had been a breath before. No flinching, no nothing from the small figure.

The dagger rang against the wood in the short silence.

The female paused her stalking, turned back, and gave Violet another long study, glancing once to the dagger in the bark. Her eyes made a decision, and Violet now regretted showing off.

But the female merely ripped it out in one stroke, a hint of surprise on her face as she threw it at Violet's feet. An acknowledgment. "Come, then, candidate."

When Violet opened her mouth, the woman beat her to it— "My name is Gwen, I am of the Inaj, of the people who are hunted and devoured by the Crale." A twisted, wrinkly, and angered smile. "Welcome to Gluttony."

19

SPARK

VIOLET'S SKIN GREW CLAMMY, SALIVA pooled in her mouth, and she vomited onto the forest floor.

Gwen made no move to help her. She stood in her spot as Violet leaned on a tree, skin both hot and cold, wiping her mouth of spit and bile.

It was a long, tense moment before Violet straightened, kicked leaves over her sort-of-vomit, and met Gwen's unreadable gaze. "You said—skies—you said *I* would end up on their plate?"

"Why not? Candidates are a delicacy."

"A delicacy…" Violet trailed. She couldn't bear to look at her body. She would see…meat? *No.* Her stomach flipped again but she swallowed it down. "Is that really what is back there? The fences, the cages…. There are so many. I thought Gluttony was supposed to be overeating or consuming so much that it was a bunch of overweight people. I didn't—they didn't—oh skies—"

"Come." Gwen nodded her head toward the other side of the valley. The untouched, vibrant one. What had happened in this world to create such horror? Violet wanted to know, but she was afraid of vomiting again. Oh skies, she wanted out. Out. Out. *Out* of this damned world.

So many questions spilled into her mind, but they all circled back to the Farm. Gwen noticed and snapped her dagger on a tree—a turquoise-bladed thing with a dark, obsidian hilt. "Distance helps, *agia.*"

The warrior woman turned and stalked a pathway. That was all that mattered to Violet as she checked her dagger and followed.

They crossed back over the river, the same shallow part Violet had waded hours ago. Gwen marched with fervor, thin legs carrying her as if she knew every rock and ball of moss on the ground. Violet stared at her two boots the entire way, until her panting and the sweat on her brow made her look up and see they were underneath the Good Mountain. Farther away. The shaking had finally died down in her hands, the goosebumps gone from her skin.

They covered miles. Water streamed down the cracks, a calming sound. She never wanted to go back. How did Reed get through this?

Gwen paused at a cliff, looking up once, then back at Violet.

"You have leaves in your pockets," she said plainly.

Violet looked down at her stuffed pants. She glanced back up. "So?"

Gwen cocked her head, then looked past her. No one followed, but the suspicion was there. Gwen seemed to be a loner, and while self-preservation told her not to trust anyone, Violet was partially desperate for a bath with all the dried blood caked on her clothes. When she turned, Gwen icily stared at the mountain hiding the Farm.

"We call it the Srax Peak. In our language, *srax* means a 'beauty that hides the dark'." Her gaze reminded Violet of Jack's when he was deciding whether or not to murder something. A predator weighing a prey—or another predator.

"Fitting," Violet muttered. She looked above their heads. "And this one?"

"Its sister, Follin Peak."

"Follin and Srax…" Violet pulled on the straps to her pack.

Silence passed. Gwen studied her, and Violet's guard flashed up. Trusting her could lead to her death. Gwen might be Inaj, but…

Violet's hand hovered near her dagger. "I will kill you before you use me as bait to barter your people back. I'm not falling for that."

"Hah! You? For all the Inaj?" Gwen bared her teeth, flashing large, sharp canines. "There are thousands there. Tens of thousands. The Farm is for most of the planet…as small as the this earth is. A little candidate, no matter that you are a rare human woman, might fetch a hundred Inaj." Gwen thought, then continued, "There will always be more candidates."

"Okay, great, so it's settled. There's nothing I can do." Relief flooded through her. She might not have to deal with the Farm at all—but the thought was followed by an insatiable guilty feeling, which she hastily pushed away and shoved into a box she never wanted to open. "So how do I get to the next Sin?"

Gwen shook her head. "We are all but a game."

"Yes." Violet stood her ground. "You *are* a game. And I'm sorry for that, but I'm here to find my brother and then leave in some kind of peace. I haven't felt the Gluttony as I did in Wrath. I've eaten but have not wanted to eat more. What is it? How do I complete it?"

"How about—"

"I'm *not* making any more bargains." She motioned to the burns on her hands. "That was shit in the last world. Tell me how to get out of *this one*."

Gwen studied her carefully, and Violet tried to maintain her temper. She would feel guilty for leaving them behind, but what could she do? There were tens of thousands of Inaj set for slaughter to be *consumed* by the Crale. Were the Crale the people patrolling? The shiny factory at the center flipped her stomach. Was that where—?

Violet shook her head. This was not her issue, not her cause, and not her care.

And she didn't need Gwen…Violet recognized the lie straight after she thought it. She couldn't hunt or live off the land—so if

Gluttony was the Sin, how in the skivvin' hell was she supposed to best it if she failed to eat?

"Ugh!" Violet ripped off her pack and threw it against the rock. She fisted her fingers, burn scabs tightening on her knuckles. "I just want to find my damned brother, who, skies above, never should have gotten into this mess in the first place! That's it! That's all I want!" She turned toward Gwen. "Is that too much to ask?"

Gwen had sat down on the ground, one knee bent and her arm thrown over it.

"Enjoying the show?" Violet clenched her jaw. But at the Inaj's calmness, she managed to take a long breath and settle herself.

Skies, why was it so damn hard to be selfish *now*?

And then it hit her.

"I—" She unclenched her fists. "I'm being fooled."

"By who?" Gwen now ran her turquoise dagger underneath her fingernails.

"My world." Violet settled herself on the ground, back to a boulder. She sighed. "All they ever said was that it *was* a game. That's what my people believe. I only ever wondered what the Sins would do to a candidate." She glanced at Gwen. "Not what the Sins would do to the world it has cursed for over five-hundred years. I never thought of the worlds, and well—how could I imagine such a thing? But it was for redemption…for glory, fame, to break the curse. Seven worlds, seven Sins…."

Gwen spoke quietly, "We are not less than you."

Violet should be stabbed for ever acknowledging such a thing. "No, you're not."

"Your brother, where is he?"

"Whatever the sixth world is—do you know?"

Gwen shook her head. "The only ones who travel the worlds are candidates…." She took a shuddering breath. "And the Worldbreaker."

"The Worldbreaker?" Violet gazed at the old scars on Gwen's hands. Most of her long tunic covered her skin, but the visible scars were stark in the day's dwindling light. She had a sickening feeling she knew where they were from, and the looming presence of Srax Mountain grew stronger.

Gwen's face paled as she thought—or remembered. This woman, a warrior from what Violet judged, *feared* whoever this Worldbreaker was, even when something like the Farm lingered so close.

The Inaj took a long, deep sigh. "He is the one who rules the Sins. He oversees all the worlds. He has visited Sagitta—Gluttony—many times, but not recently...." Her eyes grew distant. "I saw him once. A pale, scarred man. Unlike anything I have ever witnessed in my long years. And he has ruled longer than that."

Violet's eyes widened. "How old are you?"

"I have seen two Strasser's comets in my life." A pause. "So over seventy years."

"And this man—"

"My grandfather knew of him, and his father, too. The Worldbreaker does not know age. He is considered the devil to the Inaj, and a blessing to the Crale. We call him *af daxlo*—the one who rules death."

Bumps rose on Violet's arm. It was common knowledge that someone had created the Sins, but that would have been over five-hundred years ago. For the Worldbreaker to have been known by generations, it could mean—

Cold sweat licked down her back. "And you know what he looks like...how?"

Gwen gave her a reserved look and stood. "We must move before the sun sets."

"Are you going to answer me?" Violet demanded.

"Maybe...eventually. If I decide I like you. But I want to make it your decision when I tell you this—I will explain how to best Gluttony and move on to the next world. I have seen many years of candidates, and some never venture to the Farm—but you must venture to the towns. Gluttony is in the food, the water, the alcohol, and the land. But not this land. It originates where the

Crale populates, and it grows from there. On your own, you will not succeed. Surrounded by others and their constant temptations, *then* you can complete your trials and move on to the next Sin."

An icy look. "Your decisions are yours, but it will pave your actions for the rest of your life. It is how the land works—the earth knows what is happening to it, all of the horrors beyond the Srax, and it blackens its land in response. It *responds* to something it cannot ignore." Gwen shifted the bow across her chest, gaze hard. Unyielding. "It shows more about your character, your level of respect to the land and the life it has given you, to turn your back on a horror you have witnessed. In your eyes, *agia*, I can see that you have spent your life running from problems because you are afraid to face them. Why are you running to your brother instead of running toward a life of your own?"

"You don't get to ask such things of me," Violet snarled softly. "You don't know me. Do not condescend to me for my decisions."

Unaffected by her rising ire, Gwen strolled forward, close enough until Violet could see the wrinkles around her forest-green frown lines and the hairs of her unruly brows.

Within that hood, a glimmer sparked, flashing against the sun at their backs. A silver coil threaded and punctured the skin at her ear. A tag.

"You wanted to show me you were made of something by throwing that dagger." She jabbed a harsh finger at the center of Violet's chest. "Was that to scare me into *thinking* or *believing* you were worth the threat you posed?"

Violet shoved her finger away. "And what have you done? Hm? Why are you *here* while your people are *there*?"

Fury raged in Gwen's face, and Violet backed up a step, sense heightening to her dagger and to every movement the Inaj made.

Violet continued, "Don't act like you know my life—*don't* treat me like I don't have a heart when I cannot help your people. I saw what was there; the men, the weapons, the hopelessness of it. Of course, I care! But I'm here to find my brother—"

"And what will he give you, *agia*?"

Violet's cheeks reddened. "He is my family! You miss yours? Are they in the Farm? Well, my brother is in the skies-damned sixth world and he has been there for a year, suffering probably, and unable to come out. I am his sister, I have a duty to my family, and he is my freedom—" Violet cursed herself, but the words... they were spilling amidst her anger. Things she had never thought of, fumbling out like sewage in a gutter. "He is my freedom and deserves better than what was given to him. He needs me...."

"Or do you need him?" Gwen pushed. "You are afraid of life, *agia*—"

A lifted chin. "My name is Violet."

"You are afraid of life. You put your desires on your brother, thinking he is your answer. You say to yourself 'once I have this, once I am with my brother, once I do this, *then* my life will be better. *Then* I can live.' The earth does not wait for bigger streams to water its land. The birds do not wait for bigger worms to feed their nests. The skies do not wait for the perfect day to storm. The world does not wait for you, and neither does life." Gwen spread her arms out, motioning to the ambiance around them. At that moment, as if she beckoned it, the wind grew stronger, rushing through the trees. Leaves fluttered off branches and danced around them. Some animal howled into the air, and birds frenzied above. The sun winked in and out behind passing clouds, and after it all, Gwen's mouth curved. "You will die waiting, Violet the candidate. Unless you decide to live a life of your own."

The wind brushed her fury, tickling her skin, shaking hair from her braid. It cooled and calmed her, and Gwen's words struck deep within her heart. Her gut twisted in response—a burrowing flock of butterflies fighting for release within.

Shame burned her ears. To think of the two years she had spent drinking and numbing Reed's absence, she lost her life. The spark, whatever fire ebbed and flowed within her, had all but sputtered out. Jack had prodded it once or twice, but in the end, she was a depressed fool who put her happiness on something else.

And not herself.

She didn't know exactly what Gwen was asking of her, but it could be a sign of the skies—that she was blindly going down the wrong path, and whatever she was meant to do in the world was something else. She would find her brother, but...

Tears pricked her eyes. "Why are you saying all of this?"

"Because there is a fire in you, *agia*. It is in your eyes. It wants to burn. But you have to light it and see for yourself what you are capable of. We all have it. Some small, some large. Many choose to ignore it—and I pity them." Gwen stroked her chin. "I see my younger self in you. After all these years, I still look back and see I could have done so much more. But chains held me and I failed to see my potential."

Violet glanced at Gwen's silver coil meshed with her ear, and knew that the chains might have been literal. She stayed silent.

Gwen turned her back, the light growing darker by the second. "There is a train that cuts through the mountains. Cross the river and pass Srax Peak on the forested side, and you will find the beginning of it. It will take you to the towns laden with Crale. There you will find the food and other things to best Gluttony. Know that it will not be easy."

Without a look, Gwen hiked up the rest of the hill and disappeared around a boulder.

A choice. Leave and beat Gluttony, or follow the warrior-woman who saw Violet for who she was—broken and hopeless. Find Reed or take a detour to find her life. But as the world grew dark, and she was wary of whoever the Crale were and what they did to the Inaj, Violet straightened her pack, and set off after Gwen.

Her scowl softened.

20

PLATES

AT THE BACKSIDE OF FOLLIN Peak, Gwen's home was tucked into a plateau half-surrounded by boulders and against a fissure. It faced an expanse of mountains that continued into the distance. Night had bloomed by the time Violet stepped through the threshold of two boulders.

Patches of grass dotted the stone beneath her boots. Wildflowers peeked up through cracks, petals closed for the night.

It was the perfect home—or hideaway—for a single person. Impossible to see from the ground, the cottage meshed expertly with the land *as* it grew, and not thwarting growth like the skyrises in Calesal did. Moss dotted the sides, and wood was rounded into logs and pressed with dried mud. There was even a few feet of porch where a rocking chair sat. Long, serrated spears, more bows, and too many arrows all lay against the home.

A sharp crack drew Violet's gaze from the hut and to Gwen, who squatted before a now-blazing hearth. She retreated and slammed the hut door, curtains billowing from the glass window.

Violet lingered, eyes roaming everywhere…from the beautiful, dark forest beneath the cliff, to the well-made home, to the toilet fashioned some ways away and under the protection of a curving boulder, and even to the garden that sprouted at the far side of the house, near the stream. Some things were a bit disconcertingly modern to see in the middle of nature, but if there were towns nearby, it probably wouldn't take much to steal from them.

Before Violet could wonder more if she was to follow or not, the door opened with a creak, and Gwen poked her head out. "Make yourself useful and watch the fire." The door slammed shut again.

Not unused to the attitude, having had Meema as her guardian for most of her life, Violet dropped her pack at the front of the stoop and sauntered over to sit on the ground before the fire. It warmed her cold fingers, and soon enough she was taking off her boots and stretching her legs before the flame, stoking it with a stick now and then.

Gwen kicked the door out with a tray in hand. She placed it on the ground before the fire, picked up an iron grate, and locked it on two hooks embedded into the rock. She grabbed two slabs of meat and laid them neatly across. Juices dripped, meat sizzling.

Violet's stomach rumbled, and Gwen looked at her, a thin smile on her face. "Hungry?"

"A bit," said Violet. "What kind of meat is...*that*?"

"Dorelk—beasts that roam the highlands. This one was an elder in the pack and the slowest. No fight needed."

"Is that a good thing?"

"Good for my belly."

Violet's brows lifted. "How big of a beast?"

"Three times the size of you, human."

"So ten times the size of you."

Their gazes met. Gwen's black eyes pierced, but it wasn't intimidating it was...grateful, almost.

"How long have you lived here?" asked Violet, glancing at the cottage.

Gwen tossed some thick greens the size of a fist onto the grate. "Longer than you have been alive, *agia*."

"And on your own?"

"At this house? Yes." She unrolled thin strips of bread on the tray and flipped the meat. She wrapped up the bread with the meat and vegetable and took a big chomp out of it, sighing as she did. "Dorelk. A very good thing."

Violet was quick to follow. She bit into her food and just about moaned at the taste. Rich, juicy and so simple compared to the massive amounts of spices and sugar in her world. The meat was smoky, the greens crunchy, and the bread soft, warmed by the cooked food. She decided she liked dorelk.

Cleanup was easy. Before long, Gwen put out the fire. Violet's skin protested. It was colder up in the mountains, and with her simple jacket, the Empire had not equipped her for it.

Gwen turned the small wooden knob and the cottage door yawned open, revealing the cozy inside lit by a soft fire.

Violet shivered but remained outside. Gwen did not judge her for it.

"It would be a waste to kill you," she said.

"Lovely," muttered Violet.

Gwen stepped into the cottage and came back out with a huge, serrated blade. She turned the hilt to Violet. "If you want to surround yourself with weapons while you sleep, fine. I'm too tired to dispose of a body."

Violet grasped the handle and almost buckled at the weight of it.

Gwen snorted and held the door open.

Violet stepped in, but Gwen snapped at her quickly to take her boots off by the door. A grass mat—rung with leftover dried mud—welcomed the first step. Violet placed her boots next to it.

Next to Gwen's.

It was…her perfect kind of home. Simple and comfortable. A plush couch made with colorful fabrics lay facing the fireplace on the western wall. In the back was a makeshift kitchen—as much as one could have without appliances. Pipes must run from the nearby stream as a faucet sat soundly above a clay basin. Wooden counters, worn or spiked with holes from cutting knives, wrapped part of the kitchen.

A door sat by the back that led to the outside. Must be where the garden was.

A straw and grass rug covered most of the floor, dyed different colors and very used. To the right, wooden bars had been jammed into the eastern wall to create a sort of staircase up to a small loft, where a simple mattress and a couple of blankets sat, not-so-neatly folded.

"I like it." She walked in, inspecting the kitchen, in awe at the difference a home like this posed to her city, or even Wrath. The ability to all live the same, even if by different means, was... uncanny. Her way of life in Calesal was *much* more chaotic than this peaceful sanctuary. "I've never seen anything like this, actually."

The only light was a small lamp from the upper loft and the hearth. It warmed Violet's skin. Slowly, her eyelids grew heavy and she turned back toward—

The front wall above the main door bulged out like a beacon. Her eyes snapped open, like a shot of coffee straight into her veins.

Carvings, papers, and writings of all kinds spread over the entire wall, from ceiling to floor, and littered around the gaping centerpiece—a giant, ever-growing map of what Violet could only assume was the section of Gluttony she was in.

She took a step forward, jaw dropping.

Everything was meticulously labeled, even parts of what looked to be the Farm behind a rudimentary drawing of Srax Mountain. However, the Farm stopped at one point. The cages, the roads, the factory, but after that—a small town to the north, another to the south, then nothing. Notes filled the vacant spots, scribbles of questions written, yet unanswered. Some in her language, others in Inaj. But the parts that were detailed about the Farm were... *exceptionally* detailed. Names wrapped in little boxes. Giant lights lined the roads. Rotation arrows of guards and the paths they took. One building stood out in particular—*Candidate House*.

A deep, cold sweat slithered down her back. "You did all of this?"

Gwen took a seat on the edge of the couch. Slowly she raised her hands and brushed the hood of her cloak back. The coil in her ear sparkled in the firelight. She sat, solemn, and wrung her hands together before sighing. She removed her cloak.

Violet held the gasp in her throat. She refrained from any movements in her surprise…and disgust at what lay on Gwen's skin. Only in a short-sleeve tunic, the Inaj showed signs of age, yet was as muscular as Violet had suspected. But what lay in patches *on* her skin—she had never seen before.

Gruesome, blue-gray tinted metal worked as bandages along her green forearms, sporadically climbing up to her shoulders. They were stitched in, and Gwen's skin bulged around them, as if it wanted to reject the chaotic metal.

"You were one of them," whispered Violet. "You were in the Farm."

But Gwen stated that *no one* made it out. Yet she did. She was the exception.

"My village was raided by the Crale in the night after I received my first moon cycle." Gwen's voice was hoarse, cold. Her eyes drifted away to memory as her hands gently stroked the edges of the metal. "My whole tribe—more than two hundred of us— gone. The elders were slain, the young taken away to grow up under the Crale. My mother died trying to fight them off. They called her death a 'waste of food.' Bah, what do they know about that?" Slowly, she rolled her shoulders and raised her chin.

Her story was tragic, but she would not cower before its trauma. Violet wondered if this was her first time telling it.

"I was in the Farm for breeding purposes for fifteen years. Depending on your age, they either hold you for breeding, send you straight to slaughter, or put you in a cage to fatten you up. I reached my peak the year I managed to escape. I birthed fourteen children during my time there."

Violet's breath had left her.

"All babies are taken straight from the mother, so there is no attachment made. After the fifth, it became easier to part with them. They would test my skin—my *meat*—" she caressed the plates. "And then covered them with this metal to make sure I was healthy and edible to their standards. Fifteen years, *agia*." She finally met her eyes. "To think of all those Inaj still in there, living the life I had lived…it makes me wonder why the land gave me luck to leave."

"How…" Violet had to place a hand on her stomach. The nausea was strong, and saliva coiled in her mouth. "How did you escape?"

"One of the guards took a favor to me," Gwen rolled her eyes. "Dumb *conjua*. Bored and young. They are the easiest to manipulate. But some Inaj try too hard, and guards are trained on cues to see who is working to escape. I had to learn, to watch when one failed, and when another worked. One night I had a chance. He had told me about his home, how to get there, and in the end gave me information for routes and roads out of there. Away from the mines."

"Mines?"

"Explosives in the ground. You step on one—boom. They surround every camp. It is what *you* would have stepped on if you had walked down that hill."

"Ah," said Violet. "That would have blown."

Gwen scowled at her. "It has been a long, long time since that night. I had drawn my map in the ground over and over. I could still draw it now." She motioned to the wall. "And I did. There is a path toward the north of Srax, meant as an escape route for the ruling family—the Stradinths. Royal *conjuas*, they are. But that night was a holiday for the Crale, so they were preoccupied. The guard had let me out to see the festivities and I killed him. We were alone at that point. He had wanted to take advantage of me. I put his clothes on and dragged him right to the barrier of the mines. Sawed off his arm and threw it as far as I could. Rolled his body right after. Then ran toward the mark of a pathway. No body, no idea of a missing Inaj. I hid in the mountains for two days to watch the response to it. No one searched for me, so I made my way across the river toward Follin. It took a year to find and build this home, even more to search old villages and nearby towns for furniture and supplies. Now, here I am. And that is my story."

"So what is your plan now? After all these years?" Violet shuffled on her feet, unease rising.

Gwen looked at the wall. "I feel I have done all that I can in mapping it out, knowing exactly how it works, but it has been a long time, and I fear things have changed. I will admit I am lost, *agia*. I do not know what to do." She sighed. "I chose to be an outcast to my people and the tribes surrounding because this world twists the mind. They want their land back and to free their people, but there are so many Crale now and they blacken our land so it is impossible unless someone from the inside starts the fire. They—the Crale—need to understand that each one of them, whether they like it or not, participates in our agony."

Gwen's pain hit her like a punch in the stomach. Not nausea, but heartbreak rose and twisted for all those still trapped at the Farm, hopeless within their cages. It was *nothing* like the walls of Calesal trapping her freedom—this—*this* was life lived and exploited simply for the benefit of another person. And that was the most awful life Violet could ever think of.

Was that not what Calesal was built upon? All those who work beneath the Elites who do nothing but benefit from it? Wrath didn't seem so…exploitative.

"I'm sorry this has happened to you," she mumbled.

And she was to move on and leave it behind? It was easier when she was ignorant—but was that better?

Suddenly, the girl who lived in Calesal seemed further away. She was different. Molded. That girl, that younger version, would leave in the middle of the night from Gwen's home, look for the villages, and move on. But now, was that the kind of person she wanted to be?

"You are welcome to stay the night. If you still want to leave…." Gwen stood, gathering up her cloak, and headed to the stairs up to the loft. She turned, fixing a stern gaze. "I will not stop you."

"Wait." Gwen paused on the steps and Violet turned. "I—" But she didn't know what she was going to say. It tore her apart to be helpless in this situation, and tore her even more that her instincts *were* to run. To hide. But the moment she sliced her hand over that damned bowl, it was the moment *that* part of her died. So Violet swallowed whatever fear coiled at her throat, and lifted her chin, "And if I decide to stay? Even for a bit?"

Gwen watched her, studied her, on that ladder. The firelight shadowed her green wrinkles, the plates along her skin and the gray hairs wisping about her face. "If I wake and you are still here, I will teach you how to fight and how to burn."

After setting the daggers down, Violet picked up the patchwork blanket and wrapped it tight around her shoulders. As she lay on the couch, facing the flame, she knew sleep would not come easy, even after Gwen baring her story. But for the first time in a while, there was no fear, no worry, no wondering about the next, or yearning for the future.

Reed could wait. If only for a few days.

There was only here, only now. As those thoughts eddied within her mind, her eyes drifted shut, and darkness claimed her.

21

New Beginning

JELAN

WHEN THE LAST OF JELAN'S three bags dropped to the sidewalk outside of a North skyrise, her cheeks flushed with regret.

This was not her life.

This was not her home.

This was temporary.

It was a job, and that was that. But she didn't belong here, and that felt uncomfortably evident as she looked up and down the street to the restaurants spilling onto the sidewalks, filled with Elites holding large glasses of krinder, chatting and laughing, and then up to the gleaming buildings of decadent balconies and swimming pools.

The clean streets were unlike anything Jelan had ever seen. There wasn't a single reason she ever needed to visit the North, and so she had never been. In her twenty years of life, she'd only ever stared at the skyrises in the distance, wondering if life was more forgiving with money and a penthouse and status.

Shame burned her as she looked toward her threadbare bags. The driver gave her a small smile. He filed back into the car and drove off.

Just a week ago she'd been ignorant.

And now, she wondered if keeping her head down would have been the easier route.

Tone it down.

Her mother's bittersweet voice clambered within Jelan's mind. All of what she had learned was to keep her head down. Dream of realism, not fathomless possibilities. *This* opportunity was the fathomless possibility that her mother worried would be their downfall, because Jelan's father had those same dreams with his consistent inventions on scraps of metal.

And look where that got their family.

As Jelan gathered her bags and walked up to the reception door, the smooth guest card pass gripped between her fingers, she made a note that maybe it was time to pay her father another visit.

Eventually. Not today. But eventually.

She prepared to shoulder the door, but a gloved guard opened it for her. Dark eyes narrowed. "Are you where you're supposed to be?"

Jelan internally sighed at the repeat from yesterday. She dropped a bag and flashed the card.

The guard balked, shifting from the card and then back to her. Then again. As if she had counterfeited the entire thing for entrance.

A long silence passed before Jelan finally muttered, "I'm moving in with Donra Felps."

"Moving in?"

"So you will be seeing a lot of me." If she was let out of the penthouse, that was.

The guard huffed toward the reception desk. "They will need your identification."

"Fine," said Jelan as she picked up her bags and lugged them to the desk.

Her paperwork consisted of little information. Lucien had explained that it wasn't necessary, and as long as it was filed under 'Donra Felps' then reception knew not to ask questions.

Once the paperwork was confirmed, Jelan piled into the clean elevator, another guard following her. Soft music played above as Jelan stared pointedly at her warped reflection in the gilded doors, the man silent beside her. Up and up the light ticked on the number of floors. Sixteen. Twenty-seven. Thirty-three.

It dinged at forty-one.

The guard nodded to four *more* guards at the penthouse entrance. They took her bags, no expression shifting, and beckoned her forward through a pristine marble archway, and then into a three-story, open-air foyer.

Her mouth fell open. Eyes widened. Heart pounded.

The marble, stone and wood onslaught of the penthouse—a palace, more like—turned out to be homier than she had imagined. But still, it exuded a richness that Jelan couldn't comprehend. A giant staircase curved to her left, leading to the landings above, hallways that disappeared and, based on the width of the building, probably went on and on and on. Plush carpet met her dirty work boots. Paintings danced with color. There was a freshness to the potted plants atop mahogany tables or stashed in corners. And then, above all of that, a fountain pattered softly, the water curving into a river before a dais that led into a sitting room stacked with shelves of books and glass tables.

More hallways extended beyond the stairs, while the right, including the sitting room, featured wide rooms for dining, reading, cooking in the bustling kitchen filled with servants, and then the entrance to a sprawling veranda that overlooked the city.

The Mid *and* South of the city, she realized.

Jelan was very aware of how most Elites clambered for balconies facing the wall and the pastures beyond. She was surprised— because Jack Marin could have definitely afforded the alternative— to see that the view stayed on the citadel, watching it.

As if, against all the rumors, he truly did want to improve it.

"Jelan."

Lucien exited from the hallway beneath the stairs in his typical button-up shirt and slacks. His face was shaved, his hair slicked back. Clean. Respectful. A bit of ink dotted his forefinger. He was left-handed. And he also must have been working.

"I'm happy to see you arrived here all right. Would you like a drink?"

She cleared her throat. "I'm—I'm okay."

Lucien motioned to the guards and they set her stuff down at the stairs. She swallowed.

"Come, let us sit and relax for a moment. I apologize I wasn't able to get you myself. Work has been…stressful." He flashed her a tight smile. "That shouldn't be an excuse for my manners, but—"

"I didn't mind," she swallowed.

"Good." He gestured to the sitting room. "I'll have the servants bring refreshments, should you change your mind."

She silenced her steps as much as she could within the peaceful home. Her beads clinked each other, and Jelan had the urge to… do something with her hair. With her clothes. To shower again, even though she had spent nearly an hour in the shared bathroom at her dormitory scrubbing her skin, the dips between her toes.

Just as they walked in, the elevator door dinged open, and Jelan instinctively took a step back into a corner. Lucien flashed her a raised brow. She ignored it.

"Lucie!" a saccharine voice sang.

"Lucie?" Jelan said.

"If you ever call me that I'll behead you," he grumbled.

Jelan's lips twitched.

Heels clipped on the marble flooring in the main foyer and a plump, brown-skinned woman with soft curls of dark hair turned into the sitting room.

She stopped as she took in Lucien, then Jelan, and her already beaming smile grew wider. "Oh! I didn't think I would be meeting you so soon!"

"Meeting me?" Jelan muttered.

Lucien shrugged. "Tivra." He smiled warmly and opened his arms.

As the woman paraded toward his embrace, Jelan noticed her unmistakably pregnant belly.

Jelan placed her hands behind her back, so when Tivra turned to her, a hug was not on the cards. Tivra merely smiled and held out her palm. "Tivra Zaman, very good friend of the Marin brothers."

"Jelan." She reluctantly shook hands as Tivra looked down to the scarred mess. But her smile grew wider, if that were possible, and she grasped Jelan's hand in between her own.

"Tivra is a very…touchy-feely person," said Lucien. "Jelan is not."

"I'll be more mindful of that next time." Tivra's brown eyes crinkled warmly.

Lucien walked over to the mirrored glass table and poured three bubbling drinks, dropping orange slices in them. "How much longer until you can share a glass of krinder with us?"

"Twelve weeks. But we will have to celebrate that when Jack is back." She accepted the glass and Jelan tentatively took hers.

She sipped on the fruity carbonation while Lucien and Tivra looked at her, a smile on Lucien's lips.

"What?" replied Jelan, blushing.

"Cheers." He lifted his glass. "To a healthy baby."

"And your damned brother returning back in one piece." Tivra sipped and placed her other hand on her stomach. "Now you will have to take over godfather duties," she said to Lucien.

"Jack is still a better option, but of course, I'll—"

"Jack is the godfather?" Jelan blurted.

Tivra's smile was back. "Well, of course. I mean, he has helped out so much." She rubbed her belly again.

Jelan's eyes nearly popped out of her head. "Is that *his* baby?"

Tivra blanched at her before bursting into laughter. Lucien chuckled into his glass.

"*Skies*, no," Tivra giggled. "My wife would castrate him if he even tried."

"Wife?" Jelan's brows furrowed, feeling embarrassed even asking.

"There are procedures to create a fertilized egg without needing the...act," said Lucien. "So, no, Jack only helped fund their bills and hired the best fertility doctor for them."

"As in, there was no need for Jack's *thing*," said Tivra, shivering. "However, he has already made a wonderful godfather." She turned to Lucien. "Did I tell you he had a custom crib made for the nursery? On top of the room his designer is working on. Honestly, it was *too* much. This baby will be spoiled by him. He's already had all these flowers sent to me every week, wishing me luck and well wishes."

"You will be in for a treat when the baby comes." Lucien smiled knowingly.

Tivra beamed at him.

"Well, I don't want to bother you. I have to talk to Henry about the baby shower ideas. Is he here?"

"Upstairs," said Lucien.

"Great." Tivra turned to Jelan. "It was so very nice to meet you. You are obviously invited to the shower if you are interested, but...I understand if you aren't."

"Thank you," mumbled Jelan.

"I'm looking forward to it." Lucien pulled Tivra into a hug. "He sends his wishes, and something else is on the way. But you will find that out later."

Tivra patted Lucien's cheek. "We all miss him, but he will be back. We know it."

They said their goodbyes and Tivra strutted out of the room, already calling for whoever Henry was. A squeal sounded through the penthouse, telling Jelan they must have found each other.

Lucien turned to her, and Jelan's cheeks burned. "I know this is all different..."

"Did you plan on having her come here to get me to stay?" Jelan asked the obvious question.

Lucien's eyes widened. "What? No. I did not. Tivra is welcome here anytime. She is one of the few who are welcome here without notice, actually. It is a safe place." He sighed and stepped forward.

"Know that you are welcome here, not as a guest, but as a friend. You can pick whatever room you like—even Jack's. I know he wouldn't care. But just so you're aware, we have made arrangements to bring Violet's guardian here—"

"What?"

"—and to get her the proper treatment for her memory illness. When Reed left, and Violet turned eighteen, the care went to her. However, since they are both gone, Reed had left a notarized document stating that the care for Coco Mathan would be left in Jack Marin's name if something happened to Violet."

"And now that Jack left…."

"I'm merely fulfilling his wishes," said Lucien. "Legally, we couldn't do much with Violet responsible for her, and the girl wouldn't have taken it very well if her guardian up and left and suddenly posted a new address at Jack Marin's penthouse, would she?"

Violet would have burst into flames from anger. Lucien smiled at Jelan's expression.

"Meema will be fine here?" asked Jelan, knowing the answer. Tivra had given her all the answers, actually.

"She will, hopefully, be fully recovered by the time the two get back. I know it."

"Both of you talked as if they were just on holiday."

"A redeeming holiday, sure." Lucien sipped his drink. "If there is one thing you need to know about my brother, Jelan, it is that he *always* finds a way out of situations. Always. A thousand backup plans are running in his head, and because of a contract, I am willing to bet a lot of money he will drag that girl right out of the exit with him. I just don't know when it will be."

Casual silence passed while Jelan took in Lucien's words. There was a comfort in knowing Jack would, more or less, take care of Violet and make sure she came back in one piece.

"So I can pick my own room?" asked Jelan.

Lucien's face brightened. "Of course. Whatever one you like."

He gave her a tour throughout the place. Sweet-smiling servants welcomed her as they fluttered in and out of the rooms. Lucien addressed them by name, asking about their families, home life, and more. Jelan watched him carefully, but the man was warmly regarded by the staff here. It boggled her.

He showed her Jack's personal art gallery, the expansive office with one wall an entire window of the city, the various common rooms with plush couches and glass tables, a two-level library, a training room in which Jelan admired the swords and daggers and plasguns, and then on the top floor Lucien showed her the bedrooms.

The minute she stepped into the second, she breathed, "This one."

It was freshly decorated in a muted purple and gray, easy colors on the eyes. There was a fireplace against the wall stocked with more art and shelves holding trailing plants. The bed was the biggest she had ever seen. A bathroom stood adjacent to the room with a tub big enough for five people, the porcelain sunken into the ground against a window with yet another view of the sprawling city.

The servants that had been following them with her bags neatly placed them at the foot of the bed. Lucien didn't even blink at her meager possessions, even though her heart raced for him to see such a thing.

"We can get you more, go shopping, whatever you need—"

"I don't care about all of that," she said quickly. "Thank you, for all of this."

"There are a couple more things…." Lucien took a small bag from a servant and pulled a box out. "I have this for you. It will help with your breathing. We will arrange a specialist to come once a week to work with you on exercises and so on. Training if you need it, meditation, whatever you prefer." Lucien handed her the black package. Jelan took it warily, narrowing her eyes.

She carefully slid her fingers beneath the paper until it unfolded in front of her. A medical box stamped with an outlined bird soaring toward the half-moon and three stars.

"Where is this from?" she asked.

"A contact who likes his logos." Lucien shrugged. "Open it."

She did. Inside was an inhaler and a couple of bottles of medicine to go along with it. Jelan had never been able to afford it. "I didn't do anything for this...."

"You don't have to do anything for it. Consider it my gift. You deserve to breathe freely, Jelan. Like I said, there will be a specialist who can come in and work with you on breathing techniques."

She turned away quickly, facing the window as she held relief in a box. Emotions drew up from a small part of her. She did not want Lucien to see her break. Her eyes welled for just a moment, but she tilted her chin up, let the tears dry quickly before shutting the box and putting it on the bed. "And the other things?"

A smile. "Let me show you."

Lucien led her back to the first floor. They passed down numerous hallways—hallways that would be *hers* to explore.

They stopped before a simple white door and Lucien turned flashed her another knowing smile. He pressed down on the handle. Flung it open.

And before her was a room filled with Plastech gear, mechanic tables, tools, instruments, twisting spheres filled with the colorful energy, and a mediator grid meant for testing the limits of the energy.

Lucien stepped aside to let her wander in, her mouth falling open. "You can have anything you need. This lab is entirely yours. So now you can get started on that plashield."

Tears burned in her eyes. She didn't cry—she *never* cried. Now, she wanted to fall to her knees and ask the skies whatever she had done to deserve this.

But Jelan only turned, lips curling into a smile, and said, "Perhaps that shield, then."

22

THE FIRST HUNT

"YOUR FOUNDATION IS IN YOUR stance, your legs—" Gwen tapped the spear, her chosen weapon for their first lesson, against Violet's calves. "—move you where you want to go. For women, the power is in the lower body. We birth children, and we can do it again, over and over, and our body recovers from it. Men excel in the upper body, but that only stops before the brain."

Violet snorted. "Very true."

Gwen twirled around her, tapping the spear against Violet's abdomen. "All of your power, though, comes from here. No matter if you punch, kick, shoot an arrow, it all comes from your stomach. Build this muscle, and everything else will follow."

Violet nodded, spreading her stance and raising her hands. "You have taught this before, haven't you?"

"I was the best warrior in my tribe," Gwen said proudly, readying her own stance.

"Well, don't go easy on me, then."

"Of course."

And Gwen attacked.

She was a blur as she moved, agile in the rocky meadow they trained on, miles away from the cottage. Violet dodged the spear, ducking every other breath to avoid its savage hit. Gwen did not hold back during their whole training session, which had started at dawn. They ran first—up hills, down hills, buckling knees and finding proper footing. That came the easiest to Violet.

The technique today was defensive. Gwen attacked and identified Violet's weak spots, and they worked from there. Violet was more prone to running away or fighting blindly, so there were *a lot* of weak spots. Sweat dripped from her brow, but it was cool, refreshing, so unlike Wrath and Calesal, where it felt as if she were being boiled alive. She blocked the spear with her arm, wincing at the impact, but used Gwen's momentum to trip her. The Inaj careened toward the ground and caught herself with her hands, spear already taken by Violet.

Violet twirled the thing, but suddenly she was thrown back, a force knocking her to the ground. The spear clattered out of her hand and a knife rested at her throat. "There's usually another weapon, *agia*. Just because you took the first one doesn't mean it is over."

"Noted," Violet coughed.

Gwen drew herself up and stalked away to grab the spear. "You're learning fast. I thought you would be more stubborn."

"I thought I would, too." Violet shrugged, swigging water from her canteen. "But if the Crale know how to fight and are trained for it, I want to be."

A solemn look flashed over Gwen's face, but it was gone in an instant. She looked toward the sun. "We must hunt. For food."

Stunned, Violet said, "What? Now?"

"Last night was my last remaining dorelk. Don't worry, it will be easy." Gwen shouldered her pack. "Let's go."

Without much to protest, Violet grabbed her pack and followed.

Gwen led her across the fields in the direction of the cottage, but soon they turned north, Follin at their backs. They hiked through a thick forest of what Violet finally found out were *pine* trees. Pine needles littered the ground, with pinecones as well. Gwen cackled at her confusion. Two miles later, they reached a peaceful pasture filled with buttery sunlight, wispy grasses, and big, bulbous flowers of all colors.

And in the middle stood the beasts.

Gwen yanked her behind a rock as Violet stood there, dumbfounded by the animals. They were the size of two or three refrigerators, with long, curved horns and hooves the width of cooking pans. Rich hair glossed in the sun, different colors from a dark, endless black to a sunny, bright brown. With giant bellies and chomping teeth, the animals grazed quietly a hundred feet away, unaware of the two other species preparing for a kill.

"How do we know which one to choose?" Violet whispered. She watched an ear twitch and longhaired tail swish on a near beast.

"Pakik are usually calm creatures. They roam the hills in search of sweetgrass." Gwen ran her finger through the fuzzy pasture. "Not much of a mind, besides self-preservation, as most of us have it, but they are emotional. They care deeply for their young. Separation from mother and calf can take three years at most. The elders can live to twenty, maybe thirty years before they collapse one day and pass on to the hills. Before the Crale set their sight on the Inaj, those farms were filled with pakik—so many of them reared to be food on their table. It left nothing for my ancestors. Dorelk was another one."

Violet watched as one pakik lifted its large head toward the sun, and its thick lids shuttered closed as it basked.

"Those animals lasted two years if they lived at the Farm. My ancestors worked to protect the creatures that could not defend themselves against the Crale, and in the end, the Inaj proved to be a better hunt anyway."

"How long ago was that? Do you know?"

A moment of thought. "The Crale have been consuming the land since the Sin began. But they did not hunt the Inaj until I was a child. We had millions of people spread across this land, and it was ours, rightfully so, until the curse of the Sin pressed the Crale closer and closer."

"Did your people experience the Sin, then? Before the Crale?"

"From what I witnessed, it affects those who have the most access to food. Towns, cities where food is shipped in large quantities. We Inaj only take what is necessary and nothing more. The Crale waste and leave behind their mess to continue to another. The Crale are intelligent, though—do not doubt them. Higher families have assigned servants to stop them from consuming too much. There is a…line to be crossed with Gluttony, when you cannot go back."

"As there was with Wrath," Violet mumbled. "And so the families listen to the servants?"

Gwen watched the pakik from around the rock, no rush in hunting, but plans ran behind her eyes. She was patient. "Those servants who have the job are subject to potential death if they are not careful."

"You've seen it."

"Many times," she said. "For some, it takes many servants to bring a Crale back to reality once they go too far. Some servants are not strong enough, though."

"I'm guessing they don't volunteer for that position."

"It is usually an Inaj, or a mix of Crale and Inaj."

"Do the Crale eat…"

"No," Gwen interrupted, and Violet was glad for it. "Crale never devour anything with Crale blood, no matter how small. It is the only rule. To the Crale, the Inaj are inferiors. Animals, and only that."

"But with the Sin, you both speak the same language now—my language. Shouldn't that mean something? That you are the same instead of different?"

"I'm sure in your city, *agia*, you all speak the same language, but is there hatred still?" Gwen unstrapped her bow and pulled out an arrow. Violet said nothing, so Gwen murmured, "I thought so."

Before Violet's thoughts and memories of Calesal carried her away, Gwen snapped, "We need to hunt. Watch and learn."

Gwen was gone in a blur, bounding up to a large and rather gray-haired pakik. Her steps were quiet, as if barely touching the ground. With one pull of the arrow, it whooshed silently through the wind, finding a mark straight into its eye.

The pakik groaned and slumped. A clean shot. Violet stared, dumbfounded, as Gwen took quick steps back down the hill until she reached the rock again and slid next to Violet.

The herd bristled. Heads lifted from the grass, some still munching as they beheld their brethren's demise. A giant buck roared into the air and the herd pounded the earth in the opposite direction, matching the roars of the giant. A warning and a mourning.

"With pakik, you cannot linger long after the kill if the herd is still there or they will charge you and impale you with their horns. Again, not intelligent, but emotional."

"Have you seen that before?"

"Lived it. It is not fun." Gwen watched the herd gallop off, their hooves booming on the ground, and they disappeared into the trees where flocks of birds rose up. She shot out again, legs fast. "Come!"

Violet's eyes widened, and she almost hesitated, but Gwen gave her a quick look that told her she would not be eating tonight if she did not follow. They sprinted to the fallen pakik. Up close, it was a hairy mess, but its big, dark eyes were wide, one sloshed and replaced with Gwen's arrow.

"*Ahna ki lonefan el hals nos gonfla lara.*" Gwen kneeled before the beast, closed her eyes and repeated it thrice with her hands embedded into the fur on its head. She pet it, muttering after, "*Inah fa. Inah fa. Inah fa.*" She ripped out the arrow in one clean sweep and placed it in its holder at her back. "We must work quickly, *agia*. Take out the wraps in my pack."

Violet did as she was told. Large waxy paper, made of pressed grass, bark, and other things, stuck to her hand, but she carefully laid it out on the ground.

Gwen removed her knife and moved around to the belly. She drew quick, long strokes underneath the neck, down to the hipbones, and up along the inner thighs. She was an expert in her movements, cutting and skinning. It was…different. Hard to watch when Calesal sheltered the residents from the outside farms, or butchers managed it in the back of their shops. But she knew the production was nothing like this—in the middle of the highlands, surrounded by nature, *working* for her food.

Blood spilled onto the sweetgrass. It was methodical, and Violet studied every flick of Gwen's hand, the careful precision with which she made her cuts.

The guts spilled and Violet's stomach roiled. As they fell, Gwen, hands bloodied, passed Violet certain pieces to wrap. Violet held her breath as she did so carefully, the smell raw, metallic, and stiff. It took a bit of mouth breathing to continue through the chunks of meat being handed to her as Gwen worked away, but after a good while, Gwen had carved most of the beast, and all that was left was the skeleton and hide.

Violet was busy shoving packets upon packets of fresh meat into their bags when Gwen said, "You did well, *agia*."

"Compared to what?" Violet asked as she accidentally got a whiff of a rather bloody steak and wrapped it quickly.

"Some children from my village developed sensitive emotions to animals, and it was difficult for their first kill. But alas, it is the lesson of life, and we must eat somehow if we want to survive." Gwen stood and began to carve the skin from its back. "In Inaj, we do not waste the given body of any being. The guts will be left for the birds and wolves, and the bones left for critters to build their homes. We will take what is needed, but we make sure we do not waste." Gwen snapped some bones and pulled out a ribbon from her jacket. She wrapped them up tightly, like logs, and attached them to her pack. "The hide is heavy. So you will be carrying it."

Violet scowled but accepted the folded hide without a word.

"More training," Gwen said.

Gwen flipped her bloodied knife around and used the hilt to press into Violet's cheek, forcing her to face the carcass she'd been avoiding. "Look at it. Remember it. And thank it. '*Inah fa*' is how we give thanks in Inaji."

Suddenly, tears were slipping down Violet's face as she beheld it.

"Stop that," said Gwen harshly. "It is life. This is not the Farm, but we need to eat. We need to provide for ourselves so we can live. It is in the hills now, gone to the endless wild and abundance of nature. We will honor it by living, thanking it for what it has given us."

Gwen removed her blade and pocketed it. She heaved her pack onto her shoulders and turned to Violet once more. "Say it. Say thank you."

Another tear slipped as Violet knelt before the carcass and whispered an honor, "*Inah fa*."

And in some answer back, the wind shifted and whispered—
Fa Hanif.

❋❋❋

Violet picked at her food, unable to stomach anything after today. It had been difficult to abandon the carcass in the fields, but as soon as they dipped into the treeline, black birds flocked to it as if they had been waiting for their absence. Yet after that, it had been even more difficult to carry the heavy weight of it all for miles to the hut. Gwen had a cool storage dug into the rock where she stored the meat. She had laid out the hide in front of the cottage, which Violet now stared at.

Gwen took a big chomp, pulling the strip of fatty meat with her teeth. Mouth full, she said, "If you don't eat, then its death would have been for nothing."

"It felt...wrong," she mumbled.

"Of course it does the first time," said Gwen as she chewed.

"But we need to eat with the mindset that we are not at the top. We need to survive just like the wolves, pakik, dorelk, and more. Even the Crale need to survive, but they choose a vile method to do so, and that is what makes the difference." She pointed a fatty piece. "It is about our choices. I decided to kill this pakik for my nourishment, but I know only one will last me for a very long time. So I do not need to go out and kill another."

Violet stared at her plate.

"A wolf does not think about what its food thinks. It knows it has to eat," Gwen said. "But it knows only one pakik will feed it. It will leave the rest of the herd once it is satisfied. The opposite is the sin of the Crale. We are intelligent enough to have a choice, unlike a wolf, which only needs to choose the easiest target for its meal. It is our choices that preserve or shift the balance of the world. Do I want to shoot for the calf suckling its mother because it does not yet know how to defend itself? Or do I want to go for the testy elder, who has lived a long life with its herd, nearing the end? The elder will be bigger and will satisfy my needs for longer than a young calf, but if the hunt goes wrong, it means a bigger risk. There are millions of choices we have within a day, and it is what you choose to do each second that sets the tone of this land and your life."

"I suppose," Violet mumbled. She picked up the meat with her fingers, still warm from the fire. It was charred and juicy. Before she overthought it, she took a small bite.

Gwen smiled at her and shoved her shoulders. "Do not be hard on yourself, *agia*. You only have bad thoughts because you saw the kill for the first time. Never before have you seen your food slaughtered before you. It takes time to understand the balance of things. But I will be here to teach you."

23

AGIA

OVER THE NEXT TWO MONTHS, Gwen did just that.

Violet woke on her own at dawn and jogged through the forests, across the rocky terrain of the cliffs. When she came back, Gwen was sipping her tea and made Violet practice movements to build her muscle.

They scaled the treetops, balancing on them in an effort to hone her mind to her body, as well as the world around them, and then climbed to the tallest of branches where a hawk's nest lay, stealing an egg or two. One day a hawk *did* catch Violet with her hand in the nest, and Violet nearly toppled out of the tree. When she managed to climb back to the ground, Gwen only cackled at her bloody, pecked hands.

The next time she stole eggs, Violet left berries in its nest as a thanks.

They walked meadows and plains, past large herds of more pakik and the dorelk, which was the antlered animal she had seen her first day by the water. She learned how to wield a dagger and the spots to kill. She took up the bow and arrow, and with practice, managed to bring down a bird.

She bathed in the stream near the cottage. She carved fresh wooden arrows with bone tips from the pakik, and even fashioned her own cloak for the cold nights from its hide.

In training, Violet eventually moved on to the offensive. She practiced every day, even when Gwen wanted to sit and smoke a leafy pipe on her stoop. "Be calculating *and* aggressive. Not one or the other."

Violet lunged at the rock before her, sliding as Gwen had once done between her legs, and popping up the other side to jab the blade into the air, where the spine of her attacker might be.

The dark sky loomed above them. Swirling, thick gray clouds danced, and a bolt of light slashed across the sky, followed by the loud crack of two mountains hitting together. Rain poured.

Violet lowered her dagger and tilted her head up. Droplets caught her lashes, doused her hair, and refreshed her skin. A bright, shining smile split her face, and a laugh bubbled out of her. She paused, whipping her head to Gwen.

Gwen beamed at her. "Rain, *agia*."

"I've never...." Violet lifted her hand so the droplets fell between her fingers. "I've never seen rain before."

"Soon the snows will come, but for now, come inside before you catch a chill."

❀❀❀

She had not been looking forward to this moment.

Shooting down a bird from the sky was one thing. There was distance, and frankly, when that one hawk pecked the shit out of her hand, Violet had no qualms about taking down one of its brethren.

But when it came to hunting the slower-moving animals, something in Violet's mouth soured.

Behind the outcropping of a small boulder, she squatted with her bow in hand, arrow notched, the feather at the end tickling her fingers in the brisk wind. It had turned colder with the consistent storms, and she was looking forward to curling up by the hearth after the trek it took just to find this herd.

Gwen was hiding in the trees, her green skin an excellent camouflage—and something Violet was partially jealous of because she stuck out sorely.

Violet narrowed her left eye, catching a lone pakik straying farther from the herd. She'd nimbly followed it as it grazed, hiding behind rocks when it ruffled or turned its head. Now that she was close enough, she needed a clean shot straight through that eye.

She exhaled. Drew the arrow back with a groan and released it.

The arrow missed the eyes, but shot cleanly through its temple. The pakik was dead before its body slumped to the ground.

Like last time, the herd twisted its attention to the dead pakik, released a cry both of mourning and warning, and scampered away across the meadow.

"I expected better," said Gwen from behind.

Violet whirled on the woman. "I thought it was fine—" Her eyes drifted behind the Inaj's shoulder. "Gwen?"

Gwen turned her head sharply. For the first time ever, the Inaj looked shocked.

Far across the other half of the clearing, faces peeked out between trees. Green faces—some lighter in color, others darker. Their wide eyes blinked at them, tight cloaks hiding most of their skin from the cold.

"Stay back, *agia*." There was a waver to Gwen's voice.

A male stepped out, furs wrapped around his neck. He was the exact shade of green as the moss hugging the edge of the river.

His eyes flashed furiously as they landed on Violet.

He said something in Inaj, and Gwen promptly responded, motioning to the dead pakik behind her. The male's eyes narrowed, darting from Gwen to Violet, but never once glancing toward the pakik.

Violet's hand tightened on her bow, ready to reach for an arrow at her back. The tension choked the breath out of her. The other Inaj within the tree line had no weapons out.

Before any altercation began, Gwen snarled something sassy in Inaj. The male wrinkled his nose, but nodded his people off. They disappeared.

At Violet's confused gaze, Gwen said, "Pakik is running low with the coming winter. They are not used to others hunting on their lands. We ventured very far from home, so I imagine they haven't seen anyone else in a long while."

Gwen swept past her to the dead pakik, muttering something about wanting bones for new weapons, and Violet had no choice but to follow.

Weeks passed from that instance, the cold making Violet yearn for hot Calesal days again. They would sit by the hearth at night after long days of training—but since the run-in with the Inaj tribe, Gwen had been looking at the map more and more, sometimes adding writing here and there, while Violet sipped her tea and watched in silence.

Every night, Violet spent time staring up at the map, memorizing it all, wondering when Gwen would mention an idea, something that they could do.

One night, Gwen finally had Violet relaxed enough to brush her hair and twist it into braids, talking about how her mother had done the same for her. Violet's shoulders stiffened at that. Gwen merely tugged her hair again and said, "I've noticed from the first day that you did not have a mother. You do not act like someone who does. Why is that?"

Violet resisted pulling away. Gwen was testing her. *Testing* her so that it might not be used against her.

"I had one, but she wasn't a mother," said Violet.

"Is that why you recoil when something brushes your skin that you are not aware of?"

"How observant." Violet played with the tufts of carpet between her crossed legs. "No, I just don't like people touching me…affectionately."

"Touch is important."

Memories flashed; Reed and she under the covers in Meema's bed, pretending they were in another world within their fort. They'd bounce words off each other to make stories in the way children do, before she would lunge at Reed when he teased her and tickled him. And he would hug her, if just for a moment, before they flinched at gunshots from the wars.

"I'm fine without it," said Violet.

Gwen jerked her by her braid. Violet hadn't even realized she'd been leaning away.

"Your mother never touched you, then. That will do something to a child."

"My mother was a ghost for all of my life. She didn't want anything to do with me, and in the end, I wanted nothing to do with her."

"Why do you think that was?"

"Because I was a mistake," blurted Violet. Her eyes widened as she remembered.

"She was a mistake!" Her mother cried from the kitchen. "She wasn't even supposed to be born! And now I have to watch her grow up? I have to watch her live, only to die?"

"There is no taking back your stupidity for falling in love with that man who was only going to leave you. Who I don't even believe exists." Meema's voice bit the walls of the house, and Violet had halted at the door because of it.

"Of course, he exists! I have two forms of proof for that. Did you know Reed likes peppermint? He loves to take a big whiff of it before he drinks his tea. Just like his father—"

"She does that, too, Mariana!"

Her mother fell silent.

Meema continued, "She is here, and you ignore her. No, you give all that attention to her brother. Reed reminds you so much of their father, and when your other child pops out only to look like you, you are disappointed. You don't love her—you never allowed yourself to, and look what it has done to the child! Look at how she despises you!"

"She was a mistake," sobbed her mother. "She was a mistake."

"The only mistake I see is you not loving her like a mother should."

Her mother had scoffed and exited the kitchen, and young Violet had met that glassy stare, those blue eyes she'd also inherited, and stiffened at the door. Moments passed when they looked at each other, and Violet had hoped her mother would apologize for saying such things. Would drop to her knees and wrap her arms around her. Violet would have forgiven her then, as her sensitive heart always would.

But her mother merely wiped her tears, fixed her unruly bun, and disappeared up the stairs without another glance.

It was Meema who exited the kitchen at the slam of the door and found Violet hugging her knees, tears staining her cheeks, and picked her up, whispering funny stories in her ear until Violet forgot all about what she heard.

Violet hurriedly brushed away a tear.

"A mistake?" breathed Gwen.

Violet drew away, stood, and her braid unfurled before Gwen could have fastened it. "I'm not interested in talking about it."

"Best to talk—"

"I know it's good to talk, but there is nothing to *talk about.*" Violet whirled. "She never cared for me. Only my brother, and then my brother would pass that on to me because he pitied me. *He* was my family. Meema, too, but she was only around when she noticed how thin my mother got during those years. So then she took care of us. My brother and me." She furiously wiped at another tear. "I don't care about my mother. She is dead and it was for the better, because at the end, she just became another mouth to feed."

Gwen watched, silent as grief poured out of Violet. She had buried every mother issue so deep, and now it was crawling out of the ground, out of her mouth in pain-filled sobs when she remembered how her mother flinched away from her, shut the door on her face, despised her and blamed Violet for being born.

Violet clutched at the center of her chest. "I hated her so much. She wouldn't even touch me, only looked at me like death loomed over my head, waiting for someone to come to the home and steal

me away. Like I was too much of a burden to ever love. I know—"
A shaky inhale. "I know I was not an easy child, but…but…."

"You didn't deserve it," finished Gwen.

Something in her chest cracked and Violet fell to her knees. The
tears spilled and spilled, hot on her skin. "I deserved to be held. I
deserved to have my tears wiped and my cuts bandaged and not to
be looked at like I should have never been there in the first place.
I—I—" Her voice quieted. "I deserved to be loved."

Gwen's face softened, but her eyes flashed fiercely. She stood,
walked over to Violet, and searched her eyes for permission.

Violet nodded just once.

Gwen's coarse fingers brushed her cheeks, wiping her tears away
until she cradled Violet's head and let her cry into her scarred
palm.

"You are loved, *agia*," Gwen murmured into her hair. "So very
loved."

And when they went to bed that night, Violet slept soundly.

Until Gwen woke her with a start.

A dagger in her hand.

24

RIO

THERE WAS A CANDIDATE CHAINED to a boulder at the base of Follin Mountain.

He'd been screaming all night.

Gwen said it was a trap.

Only these things circled Violet's mind as the sun crept over the mountain and daylight became a spotlight. Since the time Gwen had woken her, they'd been taking turns inching to the edge of the plateau, peering down where Violet could glimpse the mop of greasy brown hair and an extremely terrified man in scraps of clothing.

"He's from the Farm," said Gwen, pointing to the silver ear tag that glimmered. "One of the candidates they hold for special occasions. By now, the Farm would know there are more candidates, and they will try to catch them. Perhaps one of your brethren said you were here."

"He's all bones." Violet frowned. "Why would they bring a candidate out here?"

"Because you would have sympathy for one of your people." Gwen leaned close to the ground, eyes darting through the forest below. "They will let him die."

"How do they know I'm here?"

"The Inaj."

"I—what?" Violet whipped her head. "You weren't talking about the pakik with that tribe, were you?"

"I was afraid of this happening if we ventured too far into other tribal lands."

"Afraid of what? Of them…of them turning me over?"

"Yes. To help the Inaj at the Farm."

"You said it didn't matter."

"Might have lied."

"How many?" Violet swallowed, throat constricting.

"A thousand Inaj." Gwen scoffed. "But the Crale would find a way out of it. Tribes who don't know how the Crale works will be bluffed into turning information about candidates over when they start showing up, and receive little in return."

Violet blinked at her, ire on her tongue. "A thousand? Why *didn't* you turn me over?"

"I am one person. Where am I supposed to take a thousand traumatized Inaj? How will I feed them? How will I rid them of their nightmares? How will I ensure that the Crale won't come after them again when we are still vulnerable?" Gwen shook her head. "At this point, there is no trickling the Inaj out. The Farm needs to be destroyed entirely."

The candidate below cried out again, every now and then interrupting their conversations: "Help! *Help!*"

"I should shoot him and put him out of misery."

Gwen began crawling back to the hut, but Violet grabbed her plated arm.

"No—he's innocent."

"You don't know that," snapped Gwen.

"Oh skies, help me! I hate this, I hate this—I can see you in the trees! Why did you put me here? Skivvin' skies, help! Help me!"

Violet wrinkled her nose. Some kind of candidate he was.

"There are wolves out here! They'll eat me—but it's not like you could hah! No—no stop!"

An arrow shot out and bounced off the boulder. Blood trickled from the man's ear.

"They will keep him screaming until you come running—or until someone falls into their trap."

"My name is Rio Gaverra and I have six sisters and I just want to go home, skivvin' dammit! I'm tired of this stupid shit! Help me! Please, skies, I'd take my little sister pissing all over my dinner for the rest of my life than this!"

Most of the candidates from her year had already gone into Gluttony, but according to Gwen, the drop spots were usually closer to the towns and purposefully built there so the Crale could pick up candidates one by one before they'd even had time to blink.

This candidate did not seem like the hardened criminals who usually went in. She wondered if he was even from her year at all.

"So when do we do something?" Violet asked. At Gwen's hard gaze, she rolled her eyes. "We have to do something. We are not just shooting him."

Gwen crawled back toward the cabin, hidden and unseeable from the ground where Crale guard roamed. "We attack at night."

Violet's lips twitched as she peered back down. Her body stilled because the candidate, nearly a hundred feet below—Rio—looked up, met her gaze, blinked at her with big, doe-brown eyes—and then continued his tirade about his family without sparing her another glance.

So at least he wouldn't rat them out.

❋❋❋

When night fell and only the moon stood overhead, Violet and Gwen made their way down the mountain.

They watched the shadows of the Crale men—the hunters, as Gwen called them—stand rigidly in scattered spots while facing Rio. Their dark clothing blended them within the forest, just as Violet and Gwen's did.

Rio had stopped his yelling when the sun went down. Violet

could hear his teeth chatter behind a pine trunk. She lingered nearest the first guard, dagger warm in her hand.

Gwen turned to her, barely visible with her camouflage skin and dark hood. Her eyes shined with anticipated mischief. "Do not falter, *agia*. The land is watching you."

Violet reached out for Gwen's hand at the last moment, squeezing it, familiar with her leathery skin and the brush of metal plates. Gwen squeezed back, climbed up the tree, leaped through the branches like a wraith, then drew an arrow.

The first shot was quiet in the still night.

Violet bounded over the mossy parts, the landscape drilled into her head, until she reached the hunter before he fell. She buckled her knees under his dead weight, lowering him to the ground gently so no sound emitted. Gwen's arrow stuck out of his eye. Dead before he'd even blinked.

The wind moved through the forest, and Violet glimpsed Gwen's shadow as she leapt to the next tree. Branches creaked and so did her bow. The arrow whistled through the air, embedded into the head of the next hunter, and Violet caught his weight.

They couldn't get a final count with their perch on the cliff, but Gwen guessed eight hunters lingered in the woods.

The next one went just as smoothly. Something gnawed at Violet's gut at how *smoothly* it had gone. Gwen must have thought the same as she took her time leaping to the next branch. Was Rio not the trap? But why in the world would they sacrifice Crale for the alternate trap?

The chatter of Rio's teeth shook up the silence.

Gwen signaled with a perfect mimicked *coo* of a bird. Violet pressed her back against the tree, steadying her breath, as one hunter sauntered by her.

"Vikter? Any sign?"

The hunter moved past Violet's hiding spot. To her growing panic, she realized Vikter must be among the dead.

"Vikter?"

The hunter paused, dropped his head to search the ground. Violet was already moving toward him, dagger raised—

An arrow flew and hit the hunter in the throat. Gurgling erupted, and Violet dove to catch him before his body slammed on a bed of dried branches. She lowered him to the ground, cupped her hand over his mouth while he choked on his blood, until he slowly stopped convulsing and died in her arms.

She wrinkled her nose and wiped her hands on his dark tunic.

"What was that?" said another hunter.

Four left. It was better odds than eight.

She was already behind another tree, thankful for the training Gwen transferred to nighttime. Gwen had actually shot arrows while Violet hid from her.

The hunter who spoke cracked branches as he walked. His breath was ragged—scared. Suspicious.

Panic flooded her. She could feel Gwen's eyes, watching her movements, waiting for the next opportunity to shoot him down.

"Who's out there?"

"Do you see someone, Chani?"

"I heard something..." The hunter nearest her said. "I—" He spotted the glimmering pool of blood and stumbled back. "They're here! Send for the princess!"

The princess?

An arrow volleyed through the air and slammed itself in the hunter's mouth. Violet didn't bother catching him.

Now was the second part of the plan, should things have gone this way.

She was stationed to be on the ground because no matter what they did to her, they wanted her alive, and that was her leverage.

Violet pushed herself away from the tree as the three other hunters sent warring cries into the crisp air. To add to her panic, a handful of cries returned. Once the signal was received, bows— thick things with dangerous bolts of metal called crossbows— raised and swept the area in honed skill.

She sprinted through the trees. They whirled as she stepped on a branch purposely, and when they hurried to check it out, she was long gone. She lumbered from one patch of moss to the next, the fluffy stuff illuminated by the moon, before her boots hit the clearing where the candidate was. The whistle of an arrow and a gurgled cry told her Gwen had found another mark.

Rio's big eyes snapped to her when she exited the tree line. He trembled against the stone, opening his mouth—

"Do *not* say a word," she hissed as she reached him. "Or else I will kill you."

He took one look at her, relief mixing with fear, and nodded.

Violet pulled the twisted metal Gwen had fashioned, memorizing how the chain and locks worked at the Farm, and began her work at one of the manacles. When her fingers brushed his skin, she nearly gasped at how cold he was. The first manacle dropped, and Violet caught it with the top of her boot, lowering it gently to the rock beneath so the sound was minimal.

"Thank you," Rio breathed.

"Skiv," she said.

He sagged in relief. "Fucking skies, *thank you*."

She worked on the other one, churning the pick inside until it clicked open, and Rio buckled into her arms. She caught him, helped him stand. "Can you walk?"

"Yeah, yeah, just give me a second." His knees cracked as he stood. "Did they say 'princess'?" She nodded, and his rich brown face paled by four shades, voice dropping to a whisper. "You have to leave—you have to *go*. Now."

Violet whistled into the air to signal Gwen that it was time to make herself scarce, then grabbed Rio's arm and—

"Duck!" he shouted, colliding with her and bringing her to the ground. A thick metal bolt blasted into the rock above their heads, followed by a saccharine voice.

"Ugh! I missed! Give me the next one."

"She's *here*." Rio's hands trembled as he rolled off Violet. "Go—go!"

They clambered up and raced for the edge of the forest line. Another bolt whistled past them and embedded into a nearby tree with a crack.

Run—as far and as fast as you can—Gwen had told her when Violet would unchain Rio. *Don't stop running until you are sure no one has followed you, and then run some more until your legs give out.*

All those morning runs had prepared her for this—*she* was prepared for this, but Rio was already huffing.

"Oh! Come back! I thought we should have some fun!"

Rio winced at the voice. Fear. He feared that woman.

"Come on," whispered Violet. "We have to keep going."

"I haven't eaten in two days," he said through shallow breaths. "Just so you know."

"Well, if you want to eat again, you need to run."

Another bolt flew past them, followed by a blur of a hunter. "Found them!"

Skies, this second group was fast.

Violet grabbed Rio's arm and changed direction, hurtling them to a grove of thicket and bushes. She threw him in and followed, biting her wince at the thorns scraping her face.

As they quieted their breaths and watched one hunter sprint past, she ran the escape routes through her head—the Crale would not know the territory as well as Gwen or Violet did, but they *were* hunters. Nighttime was her real advantage. She wondered if finding the hidden path back to the cottage was a smarter idea. It was more fortified to defend—only one entrance and one exit—but if they did find the cottage, which would be inevitable, they could eventually starve them all out.

But with the pakik she'd just hunted, that would take at least a month, even with Rio as another mouth to feed.

"Who are you?" Rio breathed as one hunter ran away, whirled his head around, and changed directions to look for them.

A warring cry sounded—the woman.

"Violet," she breathed back.

"We won't find them in the dark. We'd—" A gurgle of a cry and the thump of a body.

"Ugh! There's one in the trees!"

"They said she was with one of *them*."

Violet's heart panicked. No—*Gwen*. She should be keeping quiet, not shooting. *Go away. Hide. Don't fight.*

"Aha! I see you!"

They both stilled within the thicket. Violet's heartbeat flooded her ears.

She caught sight of the clearing where Rio had been chained. A hand brushed her arm. Gripped it. Rio stared, fear in his eyes.

Time stilled to each and every breath. Within that clearing, two hooded hunters dragged a limp figure and threw them on the ground.

Instinct had Violet lunging, but Rio wrapped his arms around her and pulled her body tight against his. "You can't."

She struggled, tried to move, but he pleaded in her ear, "*You can't.*"

Horror washed through her as another figure with cornsilk hair walked out of the tree line. The Crale woman pushed her hood back and her impossibly pale white, stale-bread skin gleamed in the moonlight, igniting the evil smile that curved on her face.

"You're not the girl I'm looking for." She sneered as Gwen flipped herself around. Deep dark lines of blood ran along Gwen's face. The bolt of an arrow stuck out of her thigh.

Violet squirmed again in Rio's grasp, but he held tight.

Gwen spat a string of curses in Inaji and the Crale woman's face twisted into a snarl. She stomped over to the Inaj and kicked her in the stomach. Gwen buckled underneath the impact but recovered quickly.

"Fucking scum of the earth," the woman, the princess, said. "You're not even worth a place on my plate."

Gwen growled, "Five Crale down by one Inaj—does that hurt you, Kiane?"

Red flared in her vision. Violet recognized the name—the *princess* of the Stradinths. She'd never heard Gwen mention her as a princess before, only as a *conjua*.

Kiane unsheathed a long, pointed sword and slashed it against Gwen's thigh. Violet jerked forward, a cry escaping her lips. Rio slammed a hand over her mouth.

Gwen didn't wail at the wound, only watched as Kiane raised the sword and dragged her finger along the blood there. She stuck the digit in her mouth. Sucked. "*Disgusting.* No wonder I like the younger ones."

The sword came down on Gwen's other thigh, spraying blood. Another wicked slice, followed by the gruff laughs of the hunters. Kiane sliced and sliced and sliced at Gwen until Violet's vision was blurred with tears, a gaping hole being torn in her chest.

A slice at Gwen's face threw back her hood, and Kiane paused, eyes catching the glimmer of the Farm tag. Her face twisted in unrefined anger. "An escapee? Well, now I'll let your death be slow."

The sickening sounds of the sword meeting skin, the spray of blood, had Violet sobbing in Rio's hand. She wanted to run out of the brush and defend Gwen, wanted to take that sword and stab it through Kiane's body over and over again, wanted to burn everything about the Farm to the ground.

She didn't know that it would end like this. That her sliver of home, her peace, would fall to its knees at such a vile, horrendous thing.

Rio was shushing in her ear, his grip on her mouth never releasing, even as tears poured out of her eyes and snot blew out of her nose at each sob. He held her close, whispering murmurs of nothing to drag her attention to the brush they sat in.

"That'll do it," said Kiane as she bent down to wipe her blade on Gwen's cloak. "You can suffer in your little land, your little world, while you know I'm hunting for your human friend. I'm going to enjoy her very, very much." She turned to the hunters. "*Find the humans.*"

The hunters disappeared into the forest. Violet barely breathed as one ran close to their hiding place. Her wide eyes watched as Kiane lingered, cocked her head again at Gwen, who trembled and moaned on the ground, and she raised the sword again, slashing deep along Gwen's stomach.

Violet's heartbreaking cry was snuffed by a whip of the wind, the crackle of tree branches, and Rio's hand.

Kiane lifted her head to the forest. "Oh, look, your land is calling you. Go to your stupid hills, or whatever you pathetic animals believe in."

And then Kiane sheathed her sword and sauntered into the forest, a high, sickening laugh following her.

Violet trembled in Rio's grasp, but he did not relent. They waited until Kiane's voice was a mere blip on the wind, and then longer for anyone who lingered. Violet's senses stayed honed to Gwen's limp body, until after what felt like an hour, Rio released her mouth and let her go.

Violet lunged out of the thicket and sprinted to Gwen.

"Gwen," she whispered, biting on a sob. "Oh skies."

Her clothes were tatters, her silver coil stained red, and her beautiful hair matted with dirt. All across her deep green skin, slashes of Kiane's sword danced with oozing blood. Gwen's dark eyes flicked to Violet, and more blood sputtered out of her mouth as she tried to open it.

"No—no, don't talk. I'll help you. I just have to put pressure on the wounds. I—I—" Her throat watered with another sob. Her tears dripped onto Gwen's mutilated skin. "Hold on for me, okay? You're going to be all right."

Rio lingered at the edge of the forest, looking around wildly before hurrying over. He took in Gwen's state and let out a deep gasp, "*Skies.*"

"Help her," Violet breathed. She looked up to Rio as more blood leaked and dripped into the ground. Gwen was pale, so very pale. "Do *something*. I—I—oh, why did you have to fight them? Come on, you can't leave me. You can't, you can't, you can't—"

"Violet," Rio whispered, falling to his knees.

Gwen's eyes slowly met hers. A tear slipped and flowed down her temple. She croaked, "*Agia.*"

"Yes, yes, that is me. *Agia.*" Tears poured down Violet's cheeks.

"*Agia, ne pokes rai.*" Gwen rubbed a thumb on Violet's cheek, wiping the tears.

"What—what does that mean?"

"Let me go," Rio whispered. "She said, 'Daughter, let me go.'"

Violet turned to her. "Daughter?"

"Always." Gwen gave a small smile.

Violet grasped for Gwen's hand, slick with her blood. "You've been calling me daughter—the whole time?" She choked. "Not insulting me?"

Gwen wheezed, "*Conjua.*"

Rio winced. "Nasty word. No real translation, but 'mothercunt' might be close."

"There it is," laughed Violet between her sobs. "You *conjua*, stay with me. Then you can call me that all you want."

"*Ne pokes rai.*" Gwen struggled for another breath.

Violet trembled. "No, I can't—I can't do that. You know I can't do that."

The wind answered her. *Time. Time. Time.* Rio's saddened eyes met hers. A slight nod tore a new gash in Violet's heart. It squeezed and squeezed, and she was sure her chest was going to compress, break—

"Win," Gwen said. "Win, *agia.*"

"I can't let you go," Violet sobbed. "I can't do that to you. Please, don't make me do that."

Gwen nodded.

Rio shifted so he kneeled at Gwen's head. He smoothed her hair back, gently, like he might have spent many nights brushing his younger siblings. "She will suffer for longer if you don't. You know what she is asking of you."

"No—we can cauterize her wounds. I can light a fire and heat a blade—"

"Violet."

"There's alcohol or some disinfectant…somewhere. Or I can make some. Then we can let her rest. She just needs rest—"

"Violet."

"And then it will all be okay—" She sobbed into Gwen's hand, turned her head, kissed it, that memory of Gwen kneeling with her, telling her she was loved. Wiping her tears like a mother would, teaching her how to find her own life, how to fight, how to *be* on her own and without another. This beautiful, strong Inaj who saved her from horror, risked her own life to protect her, and *loved* her.

"I can't—" She scrunched her face in anguish. "I love you. I can't do that."

Gwen regarded her, desperation on her mauled face. "Do not let them…take me."

Do not let the Farm be the death of me, after all this time.

"No, no, *no*—"

"Agia," Gwen said. *"Rai nosiera."*

"Save me," Rio translated. The moonlight shined within the tears lining his eyes.

She shook her head, but as she looked into Gwen's hazy eyes, she knew she could not deny Gwen's dying wish. So, gripping her hand, Violet removed the blue blade from Gwen's side and brought it up. The rising moonlight gleamed against it. She keeled over, bringing her head to Gwen's chest, and then rose so her lips met Gwen's forehead. "I love you."

"A rai, agia," Gwen muttered.

In the only bit of Inaj that Violet knew, she whispered, *"Ahna ki lonefan el hals nos gonfla lara."* She brushed Gwen's cheek. "May you find the hills you have been looking for."

The phrase Gwen had whispered to the pakik and every life taken in this world. A peaceful goodbye.

And with that, Violet buried her face into Gwen's neck and shoved the dagger into the center of the Inaj's chest.

Gwen's chest rose once more, fell, and did not rise again.

"Inah fa," breathed Violet.

In the world—Gwen's world—the earth stilled, kneeling toward the lost soldier of its land. The wind brushed Violet's hair, cool air drying the waterworks. The stars twinkled above in their final goodbye, and the peaceful life she lived amidst the darkness across the valley—the sweet, safe home Violet had found here in

this world—left.
　　Gwen returned to the hills.

25

THE FARM

As Violet breathed into Gwen's cooling neck, a slow set of claps sounded behind her.

"That was beautiful," that sickly sweet voice drawled. "Truly moving."

Violet's eyes were puffy from her tears. They seeped down her cheeks, still splattering on Gwen's body. A cool rage watered and hardened over her grief as she lifted her head and turned to Kiane emerging from the tree line.

The sky lightened as the sun rose in the east. Her eyes adjusted, flicking to the figures that followed Kiane. More hunters. Crossbows raised, pointed at her and Rio trembling at Gwen's head.

And then behind the hunters, Inaj strapped head to toe with weapons, some riding on dorelk, looked down at her, and at Gwen, with somber expressions. The man Gwen had had the altercation with in Inaj stepped forward, brilliant green skin soft along his hard face.

"You were not supposed to kill the Inaj," he said with a heavy accent.

Kiane scoffed. "She got in the way. You will get your trade for the candidate tomorrow."

"Tomorrow?" the man balked. "We want—"

"You'll get your damned people," she snapped. Waved her hand. "A thousand for the girl; children and younger ones like you said. They are being rounded up at the moment."

The Inaj man scowled but said nothing back.

Rio let out a defeated sigh and slipped his hands over Gwen's eyes, shutting them. In the light, Violet noticed the hollowness of his face, the dirt marking his slightly crooked nose, along his high cheekbones, and his unruly curls matted with blood. They shared a look—they hardly knew each other, but that look coursed strength through Violet's body. Southers. Born from dirt, die in dirt.

But they always went down with a fight.

The hunters slowly advanced on them, blocking out exits, and Violet wished she'd had time to bury Gwen.

"Get up," snarled Kiane. "You aren't escaping this time. And you—" Her eyes flicked to Rio. "I'll deal with you later."

Violet ignored her and turned to Gwen. Her body chilled to the temperature of the crisp, dewy morning. No birds chirped overhead, no sounds that usually awakened her to a calm morning in the mountains. The land Gwen protected and loved so fiercely bowed its head, mourned her, and then whispered to Violet.

Protect us.

Violet grasped Gwen's turquoise dagger and pulled it from her chest.

She stood. Gripped the hilt. A calm fury honed her senses to Kiane's light footsteps.

"If you try anything—"

Violet whirled and threw the dagger straight at the Crale.

Kiane barely managed to fling herself out of the way. The dagger caught her arm. A great slash of black blood sprayed.

Kiane's face twisted to that of an enraged animal. "*Bitch.*"

"*Conjua,*" Violet spat back and lunged for her.

Her body hit Kiane's with full-forced rage. Anger. Grief. Hurt. It spilled out of her as they rolled and clawed at each other, tears still bursting in Violet's eyes.

"I'm going to kill you." Violet pulled at her hair, snarling.

Kiane jammed her knee up, knocking Violet in the gut and halting her breath. Violet bit down on the tightness as her hand drew back and punched Kiane's pretty little face.

"Enough!"

Hands were at her arms, yanking her off. Violet was a frenzy of escaping emotions. No thoughts eddied within her as she snarled and cried, the grief of Gwen's death building so much that she didn't know how to handle it.

Kiane stumbled up, face ferocious. "I'm going to enjoy killing you like I did your scum friend."

"Don't you talk about her!" Violet screamed. Two hunters struggled to hold her back. The cool edge of a dagger pressed into her neck as her hands were bound with rope. "Don't you fucking say shit about her!"

Black blood dribbled out of Kiane's mouth, her nose, at the claw marks from Violet's fingernails. "Gag her. I don't want to hear her damned voice again."

Her hair was yanked back, and Violet cried at the stinging pain along her scalp.

"Bury her!" snarled Violet toward the lingering Inaj camouflaged in the trees. "Bury her at her cottage. Bury her within the walls! Look at it! Look at it!"

A cloth wrapped her mouth, snuffing her words.

"Much better." Kiane wiped her face with a rag handed from a hunter. "Gag the other one, too."

Rio did not put up a fight. His entire being was defeated, and Violet was overwhelmed with guilt for not helping him more. For perhaps not fighting them off, or barricading themselves in the cottage or... or...

Tears soaked her gag. The hunters shoved her forward.

Just yesterday, they were staring at the map, thinking, plotting, wondering if perhaps it could all be saved.

And now, it was just her.

Only her.

As it always was.

❈ ❈ ❈

The journey passed in a blur of soaking boots while crossing the river, being shoved into a metal car on a churning train, piled into the bed of a truck, and watching, bleary-eyed, as Kiane adoringly played with Gwen's dagger.

The train continued on once they got off. Gwen had mentioned the lines and lines of towns filling the valley of the mountains until the coast, all land stolen by the Crale.

By the time they reached the town, most of the day had passed.

The town was unremarkable. Stone streets, overgrown ivy climbing up the buildings, cars weaving through, but mostly foot traffic filled with the pallid, plump, and white faces of the Crale. Violet had thought her skin was lighter than most in Calesal, more olive-toned and tolerant of the sun, but the Crale looked as though they had had the life sucked out of them, as if one sun ray might burn them alive.

One thing she noticed was the dirtiness. Peels and half-eaten fruits dumped onto the streets, water thrown out the back of eateries, half-drunk bottles of what must be alcohol scattered along the sidewalks. *This* was Gluttony—they consumed what they could and discarded it when they lost interest. Taking, churning, wasting.

It did remind her of Calesal. Dumpsters behind Mid buildings filled with food that was still edible, along with perfectly fine soda bottles. She and Reed used to scoff and bitch on rooftops about the Elites they glimpsed, which wasn't often, and how they would sip their drinks only once and never touch them again. Because they could afford it.

After being silenced with the gag and bound, Violet only watched. Didn't react. Her energy pulled and pushed within her, a chaotic river dammed by her pride in holding it together. Fortified by Gwen after all these months.

She just wondered when the dam would break.

Not yet. Not yet. Not yet.

It was a long dirt road to the Farm, and on either side of that were squares and squares of endless cages. The Inaj within them, dressed in tatters and with sunken eyes, stared at the two candidates. Rio trembled and hyperventilated. He passed out, only to be shoved by a hunter to go through the motions of fear again.

Violet didn't waver her gaze. She watched. Looked. Made eye contact with each who turned their head. Green of all shades gazed at the truck, from the young pale shade of a child to the mossy green of an adult.

She smelled the hopelessness. It was so tangible, so bleak. The cages bore nothing more than a roof with a bench, four posts for shelter, a waterspout, a hole in the ground for a toilet, and a trough piled high with grain and other food.

Spotlights towered along the road, manned by guards. They walked along the high bridges that crisscrossed over the cages, holding those damned crossbows. Now that she was in the Farm, even farther beyond the caged pastures of Inaj, there were fields laden with giant, bulky machinery.

"Ahnsa," said Kiane. "The best oil to exist. Doesn't go bad, powers everything, and roasts a nice hunk of meat."

Violet huffed into her gag.

Rio leaned into her, his skin laden with goosebumps. Fear coiled in Violet's gut. From all of what Gwen told her, this was hell on earth, and she was destined to be in the belly of it. Maybe literally. It roiled her gut, and she breathed through the gag, taming the bile that pooled in her mouth.

The royal house proudly stood within its own walls, blocking out the cages and surrounded by a garden that must also block out the smells. The giant steel buildings of the factory lingered some way behind it. Her bones iced as she looked upon the wafting smoke and the fuel-like smell emitting.

The truck rolled to a stop and the hunters yanked them off.

Violet screamed a volley of curses their way, but they were muffled against the gag.

They dragged them through the heavily manned gates. The gardens were well kept and clean, unlike the towns, and Violet suspected that had to do with the Inaj servants. Big wooden doors were pulled open by Inaj. Servants milled about; some dressed finely, others more simply. But they walked with heads down, clearly serving a duty.

Rio didn't fight back. He paled as he took in the stone hallway draped with petrol sconces and the concave ceiling with wrought iron chandeliers. The fumes made her eyes water. His face flashed with recognition, despair, all kinds of grief, and Violet had to shove down that guilt again. *He* was used to find *her*. By the Crale. Her guilt for it all would not help their situation.

There was little to help. She was trying not to think about how this might be her last night…ever.

They were led into a wide room; flanking doors, subliminal art, and the occasional chair against the wood-paneled walls. A foyer. A standing room. Something of the sorts. A strong floral fragrance accosted them, and she wondered why they bothered to try to hide the rancidness of the Farm. Why they even built their estate in the *middle* of it. For as scary as the Crale were, perhaps the noose of Gluttony made them lose brain cells.

She was thrown to the ground, enough to send her sliding. Rio slammed down next to her. He groaned and flipped himself onto his stomach, chin pressed into the cool floor. His eyes flashed between fear and bravery. Violet tried to hold on to the latter, but her gut was sinking fast.

Servants filed in to fill spots along the walls, heads bowed. Hunters laden with crossbows darted to the corners.

The right door creaked open, and two men silently walked through. One was stout and round, face wrapped by a pasty beard and black hair pulled into a knot at his neck. His dark eyes landed on them, lighting up at Rio, and then narrowing at her. Violet sneered.

The other was younger and, despite the raw ego rolling off him, he was easier on the eyes. Blond hair, pale skin, sharp eyebrows, and a gaze that judged every breathing thing. Hands behind his back, he strode in, and Violet thought his walk looked oddly familiar.

"Caught you back, again, didn't we?" the round man snarled. "Foul-mouthed Southern rat."

"Now, now, Lark, I know your kind isn't keen on the lowers of your city." The younger one's head tilted, his voice smooth. Everything about him was *smooth*. Violet hated it.

Lark scoffed, "Rats from the South, that's what they are, Kowai."

She spat a curse within her gag. Belly down, she attempted to roll, but a boot pressed into her back and she choked for a breath.

"Stay still," growled the hunter who handled her.

She spat another curse.

"Feisty." Lark smiled. "Those always taste the best."

Another traitor from her city. Lark glared at her greedily and she wanted to bite that look right off his face. That look—so known to the women of the South as they walked down the street and received it multiple times a day.

She assumed he was a *Southern rat* himself but wanted to embrace a new role in a new world. A solid guess would be that he had worked in the metal-welding factories judging by the tiny cuts and burns on his hands, the twisted flesh along his neck—and also the goggle marks rung by his temples as permanent reminders of his work.

He would be easy to break.

The other—Kowai—would not be. A native Crale, impossibly white and fit, he studied her carefully, and when their eyes met, he smiled.

Then licked his lips.

Violet swallowed her bile back down.

Kiane sighed dramatically as she stomped by. Siblings.

Kowai looked his sister up and down and then back at her beaten face. "Who did that to you?"

With blazing eyes, Kiane's gaze flicked to Violet. He followed. He snorted.

The doors opened to the front, and out stepped a group of older men—old enough to be her father—with white skin, pale hair like Kowai, and dressed in robes and leathers. She tried not to look at the leathers too long. They gathered at the front, one man standing out above the rest; fair, cropped hair, dark eyes and a tall, burly stature. She noticed the belly on him, bulging against his hammered belt.

Rio swore on the floor.

"My drink," he said, voice a rasp of knives on wood.

One of the Inaj servants at the wall picked up a glass goblet of red liquid and brought it over.

Violet stared at the red liquid. It was…too dark to be wine. Too thick. The floor seemed to sway and the room turned. The boot at her back twisted into her spine, a voice in her ear, "No fainting."

The main man regarded her carefully and inclined his head. But it wasn't in acknowledgment, it was a sign—for the bows in the room clicked and pointed at her.

"This the girl? The human girl?" he asked.

"Yes, Master Stradinth."

The head of the royal family. He carried an aura of extreme importance, but also one of cool indifference. He was curious about her by the way he tilted his head and took in her body. That was *not* the same look that Lark gave her.

"I have been searching for you for a long while. You are quite elusive—but it didn't take long for the Inaj to cooperate and let me in on your whereabouts." He sipped the glass and licked the red from his lips. "I am saddened to hear the Inaj woman was deemed unfit for production. I always hate to see a loss."

Kiane's sadistic smile grew.

Violet growled into her gag.

"And the girl has a temper," he continued and then laughed. "You cared for the woman, didn't you? Why?"

Rio moaned and shared a look with her. He shook his head.

Stay calm. Don't answer.

"You did wonderfully, darling—" Stradinth turned to Kiane, eyes roaming over her injuries. "What happened?"

"The bitch happened when I killed her *precious friend.*" Kiane brushed her hair over her shoulder. "I'll have it fixed up in time for the holidays. And I have many plans for her, too."

"We are grateful to have two more candidates—pure delicacies—for Hospurin in a week, aren't we?" Murmurs agreed with him. "We have one person to celebrate for his marvelous plan in catching the human woman."

She continued to meet Rio's gaze and found comfort within it. *Breathe. Breathe. Breathe.*

"Call him in," Stradinth said. A servant left, head bowed, and went through a door.

It was silent for a moment.

Careful steps sauntered—soft-soled boots, familiar. The dread rose, and out walked, in contrast to the white skin of the other men, Jack Marin.

Surprise stopped her breathing. If she thought being captured by a people-eating farm was bad, *this* was worse.

Because *skies*, the last time she saw him, she had deliberately left him to the wrath of the Droans. She did that. To a commander of the city. Regret raced through her, wishing she had gotten on his good side so perhaps he could save her…

But Stradinth said *his plan.* Jack's plan? To capture her?

Was that the skies' way of throwing her actions back in her face?

Dressed in pants, black knee-high boots, and a dark shirt, Jack's face was unreadable. He had shaved the beard on his jawline, and his hair was tucked back behind his ears. He regarded the room with familiar interest, but there was a coolness to his face, a sharp look that reminded her just *why* Calesal was and would remain scared of him.

"Master Stradinth." Jack bowed slightly. "I hope your ride into the fields went well."

"Splendid, thank you," said Stradinth. "Next time, you will be sure to join me. I do hope you are feeling less ill."

"Much better after a day of rest." He smirked. "The gardens do look lovely this time of year. I enjoyed them very much."

Ill? Jack didn't look ill. He looked perfectly put together. The role he was curating in front of this family, in this world, was different. He needed to act respectful, hold his alluring command by a thread to maintain his pride. However, she knew him—knew what he looked like when he unraveled before wrath, his unbothered face when he had slit another's throat, and when a lie was deliberately said for her to catch.

Without a single glance, he was telling her that this family was already wrapped around his finger.

The moment Jack had entered, Kiane's eternal scowl smoothed to a beaming expression. She sidled over to him, glancing up. "It was an awfully good time catching them."

Jack looked down to her. Smiled. *Smiled*, before his brows drew together. His hand raised to cradle her face, brushing over her bruised nose and red scratches. Concern laced his voice. "What happened to you? Are you all right?"

Kiane kissed his cheek. "The girl put up a fight, but I'm fine."

Violet's heart thundered in her chest as Jack's gaze slid to her. The green in them shifted, but only for a moment. "Did she now?"

"I'd killed her friend," giggled Kiane. "She snapped, just a bit."

Jack's brow raised, but his eyes never wavered from Violet. Burning, burning, burning into her, searching her face, dipping to her gag, slithering along the rest of her body as if he were marking any injuries.

"She weeded herself out, for the most part." Kiane rested her head on Jack's shoulder.

"I do recall you mentioning she had blonde hair and brown eyes, however," Kowai said. "It is curious you forgot, isn't it?"

"I must have been so taken by your sister's features that I forgot all else," said Jack. "A mistake. But it wouldn't have been hard to find a girl with a bloodsworn scar on her hand, now would it?"

Kowai glared. "I suppose so."

She bit into her gag. These two had tension. Skies, she could choke on it. By the way Rio's eyes darted, he had noticed it too.

"She is a delicacy, Kiane. She will be perfect for Hospurin," Stradinth said calmly.

Kiane lifted her chin. "I want her tongue removed before, though, because she said some awful things to me."

"Now, Kiane, her tongue might be the best part." Kowai smirked.

Jack's eyes sparkled at Violet as if he was wondering just *what* Violet had said to Kiane.

"No. Plenty of food surrounds us." Stradinth brushed his shirt. "We must not give in to the Sin, for it will overtake us."

Kiane pouted and turned to whisper in Jack's ear, her hand rubbing along his chest.

Violet's stomach leadened. If they avoided it…what did the Sin exactly look like?

"Take them to the candidates' cages. Be sure they eat and are hydrated. We want only the best for our family before the holidays," said Stradinth.

The hunter hauled her up.

Another guard lifted Rio—

"Wait! Father!" Kiane called, and Violet wouldn't have minded being deaf if it meant not hearing the Crale speak again.

Stradinth halted and turned toward his daughter.

"Please, Father, I want to get reacquainted after all the time we spent apart. We almost lost him." She flashed a smile up, wrapping her hand into Jack's.

Rio's eyes bugged.

"I promise I won't bite." Kiane smiled, walking forward to drag her finger along Rio's cheek. "Just like all of the other times we spent together."

Rio squirmed and muffled a cry. All of his remaining confidence waned and broke. His knees buckled as the guard hauled him forward.

Violet started, yelling within her gag, hoping that Kiane would decide to take her and leave Rio alone. The hunter yanked her against his chest, but she managed to twist her hands enough so her fingernails clawed into his skin. He yelped. Violet whirled, shouldered the hunter back—

Two more were on her and grasped her by the elbows, pulling hard enough that tears burned her eyes at the pain.

"Stop being a nuisance!" Kiane strutted over and slapped Violet across the cheek, grabbed her by the chin, and sneered, "You will get your turn. Don't you worry."

Jack frowned. An indifferent frown. *Skiv*. Violet's cheek burned from the impact.

"Take the human to the cellar. Kiane wants time to play with him," Stradinth said. A hunter yanked Rio down the hallway. Rio shared one look back, one horrified, fearful look with Violet, before the guard shoved him through the door to the left and slammed it shut.

"The rest of you—"

"If I may interrupt, Master." Jack's smooth voice garnered the attention of the room. Violet's cheek throbbed harder. "I have enjoyed my time here and the wonders you have given me at the expense of your family. Obviously, this was a discussion for another time, but I would like to prove my loyalty to your daughter and your name by escorting this...*thing*...myself." His gaze danced with Violet's.

Stradinth gave Jack a long look over, but with another glance to Kiane, who beamed at Jack's request, he nodded and clapped Jack on the shoulder. "You will make a fine Crale. Take her to the candidates' cages. Punish her if she bites." He pulled Jack close. "I look forward to you joining us at our table soon."

Jack's eyes crinkled as he smiled. It looked genuine. Some involuntary reaction occurred in her...her throat tightened, and the ground swayed underneath her feet. To see him look at a vile monster like *that*—

This was Jack's domain. Maybe not the cannibalism of this Farm, but feeding off the power of others and rising to the top to create his perfect little throne—yes, this was his niche and what he was good at. So of course, that smile was real. Of course, he wanted to step up and prove not only to them, but also to her that he was the predator and everyone else in the world was simply prey.

"I look forward to the day too." Jack shook the Crale's hand with vigor. "So very much."

"Be back soon!" Kiane called.

The hunters handed Violet off, and Jack's grip was tight around her upper arm. He turned her toward a side door.

She was about to soil herself. She didn't know whether that, or vomit, would happen first. This was it. Her horror had been at bay, but now she could feel it rising with the anticipation of seeing, up close, how this operation worked. Every thought left her as Jack pushed the door open, dragged her through the perfect garden, and walked past the guarded wall of the estate.

Jack squeezed her arm as the gate shut. He looked down at her, a curl falling from his head, and as she met his eyes, his emotions unraveled. Everything he kept tight and taut loosened at the sight of her. His disgusting smile dropped, along with the dimples, and he grit through his teeth, "Ready, darling?"

26

Fracture

WHILE JACK DEATH-GRIPPED HER ARM and dragged her down the muddy, spotlighted road toward a barn-like building, Violet partially regretted ever making a bloodbond with him.

Having him outright kill her would be a thousand times better than whatever punishment he wanted to inflict.

She'd heard of the bodies along the bridge in Calesal, carved with his initials. She'd seen her dead neighbor with a bullet hole in his head and the *JM* along his hand. She *knew* what happened when he needed retribution. Her brother was proof of that.

As if he listened to her thoughts, his grip hardened, and Violet hissed at it.

He didn't spare her a look.

His gaze was forward, jaw so tight she thought it might crack. He was very, very angry.

And skies, the last time she saw him full of fury, she had kicked him away with a giant *I fucking hate you, too.*

Oh, she was so, so dead. Or as close to dead as their bloodbond would let her be.

A part of her feared him, cowered away from the closeness, and even the icy silence that exuded from him. That part might have been pure self-preservation, and she hung on to it, because it had failed her when Gwen...

She almost stopped walking at the pang within her heart. Fresh, bare, new, vulnerable, raw, deep…tears pricked her eyes. No, *skies*, no, she would not cry in front of him. Not give him a way to hurt her even more, shove a nail into her chest when it was already bloody and raw. He would do it. Of course, he would do it.

The barn loomed two stories tall and relatively close to the estate. Jack turned a corner. She was dragged after him, the only sound his short breaths and the stumbling squelch of her boots in the mud.

The spotlights dimmed as they walked away. Darkness swallowed.

She blinked—

He slammed her into the side of the barn. The force shook the metal wall, a crack ringing in her ears as her head flew back and pounded it. His fingertips dug into her shoulders, and he drew her head back to face his. He ripped the gag off her mouth.

Those eyes burned through her, filled with battling emotions.

She swallowed, the back of her head pained. "Miss me?"

"Have I ever told you how incredibly stupid you are?" he seethed. "Do you need me to tell you, again, how much you fucked up? Hm? Is that something you want to hear?"

"No, go on, tell me," she said.

He fumbled with his anger, but there was no wrath to lure him down. Instead, he searched her eyes and she thought for a second that he might kiss her. Something between relief and loathing lingered in his gaze. He leaned close.

She leaned back, cringing.

But he…inhaled. *Smelled* her. And then breathed out. "I can't."

"Sounds like your plan worked," she said, voice low. "So, what are you going to do to me?"

Surprisingly, he didn't react. In fact, he took a heady breath and lessened the pressure of his fingers. "I don't know why they kept saying that. I only suggested that they work with the Inaj tribe to catch you. They were so adamant about setting a trap against the tribe and taking all those people and…"

"You'd rather they have me."

"Not really," he said. "But I know you're not going to believe me."

"So they took Rio and set a trap."

"Rio? The candidate?" He sighed. "Violet, I didn't think you'd actually go *save* him."

"Why wouldn't I?"

"Why *would* you?" He blinked at her. "In what world does anyone from the South do something that doesn't benefit them in one way or another? You submitted yourself to the Sins because you wanted your brother, and because you didn't want the guilt of that guy going in for you. So, *why* would I think you'd actually save someone and risk getting in trouble in the process?"

"Because of *her*," she snarled softly.

"Who? The…" He groaned, shook his head. "Kiane said something about killing your friend? Is that where you've been all this time?"

"Get off me," she snarled, hating how her hands were still behind her back.

He didn't back off. Instead, he pressed forward, lips brushing her ear. "I thought you would be out of this rotten world by now, but—"

"But I made a friend," she hissed. "And now she's dead and your stupid skivvin' girlfriend killed her."

A deep sigh escaped him. He opened his mouth—

His head picked up and turned toward a crunch of leaves. Quickly, Jack dragged her down the shady side of the house, farther away from the spotlights, until he found another hidden niche against the barn.

"I'm sorry," he mumbled. "About your friend."

"Like you give a flying shit," she said.

He scowled. "You have to listen to me. You cannot pull *anything* here. Violet, I'm serious. *Nothing*. Just sit tight. Act pretty. They will hold you for longer if you are more…edible. Fatten you up, although it certainly looks like you've been eating well." His eyes dipped and then met her face again. "Candidates are a delicacy."

"I'll be the worst delicacy of their lives," she seethed.

"Easy." Jack grabbed her chin. "None of that. Keep your head down."

"Why in the world do you care?"

"As much of a pain as you are, I don't want to see you dead."

"That's rich."

"Cut the attitude."

"Or what?" snapped Violet. "They'll cut me up on a plate?"

"*Violet*—"

"But for Jack, the self-preservation runs strong. You'll step on anyone to keep yourself alive." She jerked her chin out of his hand, ignoring how his eyes blazed in restrained anger. "You fuck that girl and whisper little things to keep yourself on her good side and off the dinner table?"

"Now I really want to snap your neck."

"Do it," she taunted. "I dare you."

He shook his head, as if shaking out the image. Iciness raged from him. Before her, he stood taller, shoulders back, face hard with stone-cold rage. Wild eyes bore into hers and his voice was calculating and dark—Commander Marin. "I have and will always do whatever I can to survive. You do not know me. You do not *know* where I came from. I will fuck, kill, maim, torture whomever if it means surviving, because there was a time in my life where I didn't think I would see the next day. Or the one after that. For *seven* years. Do not test me, Violet Sutton. You will regret it."

She thinned her mouth. Her eyes dipped down.

And that was when she noticed, peeking beneath his rolled sleeve, the twists of burns along his left forearm, as if he had raised it as a shield against an inferno.

In a different world.

Jack followed her gaze. His jaw clenched. "Hurt like a bitch, if you're wondering."

"I'm not," she said.

"I deserved it." His fingers dragged over the ridged skin. "I guess, for trying to kill you."

"We had a bloodbond, so you wouldn't have succeeded."

"For the other times," he said, lips twitching at his joke.

The steady movement of boots snapped their heads toward the lighted road. Violet caught the interested gaze of Inaj peering through the fence at them, then as their eyes flicked to Jack, far enough away to not be able to hear them…but to have seen…

Jack grabbed her arm and dragged her around the corner of the barn and a bar-locked door.

He shoved the bar aside and let it creak open.

A lump rose to her throat as Jack pushed her inside, found a cage among the most-empty ones not filled with sleeping candidates, unlocked one, and threw her in it. She stumbled, catching herself against the wooden back wall, and turned as he slammed the cage door. He leaned forward, knuckles white as he looked around her cell, then to her. His eyes blazed so bright she thought they might catch fire.

His voice dropped to a harsh whisper. "If you want to live, keep your head down. Do as they say. Do not act out because I cannot save you if you do."

"Do you really want to?" she murmured.

"A little." He looked her up and down. "Just a little."

She slowly walked up to the bars, drawing close to his face. "Do something, Jack Marin." Her eyes burned as the emotions poured within her again. "She did not die for this." Her throat constricted. "I did not kill her for this."

"Violet."

But she was already looking down, at her hands, her arms still covered in Gwen's blood, and a distraught sob cracked through her chest. She could still smell the Inaj, fire and pine and something wonderfully pure. And the cold of her skin, the brightness of her eyes, the last rise of her chest.

Violet reached a crimson hand to her heart and clutched at her shirt. She doubled over as a pang, so raw and painful, ripped through her.

Gwen. Gwen. Gwen.

Anguish pulled at her, cradled her face, and she leaned into it. Cried. Sobbed. Wallowed and screamed.

Tears spilled. The numbness called her, opening its arms into its familiar embrace, but for the *first* time, she turned away and felt everything as a raw eruption.

"Violet—"

"Go away!" she cried with a snarl and lunged for his face. Jack recoiled back out of her hand's reach. A flash of surprise hit him. But skies, she did not care. Not at all as she cried and screamed for Gwen. For Gwen. For Gwen. She was gone, and she wasn't coming back. To whatever lands…and Violet had been the one to kill her.

Now surrounded, helpless and hopeless, by the suffering Inaj, the people Gwen wanted to see free in her lifetime, Violet collapsed into herself. The darkness shifted and she was swallowed into a familiar well of despair. Tears, pain, blood, death, and all.

The little capsule in her wrist pulsed in response.

At some point, the traitor candidate—Lark—stalked in, followed by Rio, who limped behind, eyes heavy and head lolling. Three scratches marked his face, as if claws had raked down in an angry slash. They dropped him in the cage across from hers. Once the cage was shut, Rio curled away, shivering. Lark turned to Violet. The guards behind stepped up, holding a box out.

"Let's have a look at that pretty ear, shall we?" Lark unlocked her cage and entered. The silver of the coil flashed and she flinched back, pressed against the wall. Fear roared. Lark grabbed her and shoved her into a kneeling position.

"No—please, *no*," she gasped. He pulled her hair back. Her right ear was cleaned. "No—no!"

"Hold still, and it will hurt less."

"Skiv!" she cried. He clenched her face, stilling her. Her eyes darted and they caught Jack leaning against the door to the candidate house, features solemn.

Cold metal met her ear and punctured. She cried out. It echoed throughout the house. Red-hot pain flared in her ear and the world grew dizzy. She could smell the tang of her blood. Then they twisted it.

The floor swayed and Lark held her upright. The pain was too much. She forgot how to breathe. Tears streamed down her cheeks. She moaned as Lark clenched her jaw, and the coil gave one final twist into her ear. It was on fire; she was sure they had lit it on fire.

"There, now you're our property."

Eventually all that pain burst like firecrackers and then snuffed out. She felt her knees hit the ground, her body collapsing after that, and the slow murmurs of Rio lulled her to sleep.

❋❋❋

"*Violet.*"

She moaned, her cheek pressed against cold stone.

"Violet."

She blinked her eyes open. They adjusted. Found Rio leaning on the floor with her in the cage across.

"Okay, I just had to make sure you were alive. You sleep like the dead."

Her ear pulsed hotly, and she reached up—

"No, don't touch it. I know it hurts, but you really don't want to be treated for infection here."

"What time is it?" she whispered.

"Almost the morning." He frowned and scratched his finger on the ground. "Are you feeling okay? Dizzy? Nauseous? You should eat. You haven't eaten."

"What are you? A doctor?"

"Actually, a sort-of nurse," he said softly. "I practiced medicine under my father in the South. Until, well…until I was sent in."

The room blurred as she lifted her head and groaned at the sudden rush of black in her vision.

Rio clicked his tongue. "You came up too fast."

"Where's the water?"

"To your left."

"I—what—"

"Other left."

"I can hardly *see*, Rio."

"Relax; it'll go away."

"I know what a head rush is," she snapped. When her vision cleared, she reached for the pail of water and drank heavily.

"But not your directions." He smirked.

She wiped her mouth as water dripped down. "So, a nurse from the South? How'd you get sentenced?"

He winced. "Caught stealing. I—well, my father died and left my family without much because of his infirmary in the South. I tried to manage it, but I didn't know everything he did… so I had to steal from dumpsters, the markets, and all kinds of things. I have six siblings, so…" He shrugged. "I didn't really have a choice. My mother had to raise everyone since my father wasn't there anymore. I'm the eldest and, well, one morning I was caught by a Redder, and the next thing I was slashing my hand. That was a year ago, I think. I'm not very stealthy."

She dipped her hands into the pail and rubbed at her face. "Probably weren't very good at tricks gambling in Lovita's either."

His smile beamed like the sun. "No, but I could out-drink anyone."

"You're as skinny as a stick."

"It's the reason I'm still here. Don't have much meat on my bones, so they can't eat me. They don't really know what to do with me."

"So they used you as bait…" She pressed her fingers into her eyes, heart twisting.

"I'm sorry about your friend," he said softly.

"I'm sorry you have been trapped here for so long," she mumbled back.

"I've got the Iris like four times, but they do searches and take it away. I didn't know you could get the Iris multiple times, but I guess it resets. However, the magic works. I'm not sure, but the candidates here, all of them are new and from your year and…why are you staring at me like that?"

She looked at him, *really* looked at him, and a steadiness passed. He could have let her go within that thicket, let her run and rat herself out and used it as a distraction for his own escape. But he didn't. He held her, if not soothed her, while Gwen was…Gwen was…

He cupped his hand as if there were a glass in it, and held it up, a small smile on his face. "We must pour one out like Southers do."

Her chest tightened. "Yes, we must." Violet followed his lead and cupped her hand too.

"To Gwen—a skiv done dirty. A skiv gone too soon." He shared a look with Violet. "And a skiv loved by those who matter. Once a skiv…."

"Always a skiv," she finished. "May she rise to the skies, and the heavens beyond."

They both dumped their imaginary cups and pretended to sip the rest. And even while they sat within the cages, within the Farm Gwen had escaped from, blossoming warmth filled her chest.

Hope. Or a version of it.

"Thank you," she whispered. "For being there."

"I think I wouldn't have made it far if I ran, and, well, the punishment would be less if I stayed." Those big eyes blinked back fear. "She's awful. I'm glad you beat her up. I've never really seen someone stand up to her. Not even *him*." Rio shuddered.

"Jack?"

"You guys on a first-name basis?" he paled. "Do you—?"

"No, I don't work for him. It's complicated. He…well, he and my brother have some bad blood."

Rio took a second to think, his finger drawing odd shapes on the stone. His head perked, and then he was staring at Violet. "Skies, it takes a minute, but wow…I knew he had a sister, but I guess I didn't expect you to look…well, to be fair, you don't look that great now, but it is okay. I just—you're paler than him."

Rio crossed his legs, shoved his hands under his thighs to warm them. "I definitely remember that news. What was it? Reed Sutton overthrows Jack Marin's gardia and ends up getting three buildings blown up in the process? Skies, and now Marin is in the Sins and *here*."

Violet opened her mouth, but Rio continued, unaware— "I had met your brother before, actually. He had come into the infirmary with a nasty slice on his arm and needed it stitched up. Dropped some bills on the counter and left before we could even bandage it."

That must have been during the time Reed worked for Jack. She saw so little of her brother during those three years, and it was likely one of the numerous wounds he'd taken. She would find his bloodied clothes in the laundry, buried at the bottom so no one would ask questions.

"I came to find him," she breathed.

Rio nodded, and didn't press. The comfort she felt with him, the unsaid easiness that passed between them, settled her.

She relaxed her shoulders, unclenched her jaw. "How did you get through Wrath?"

"I'm not a very angry person, so it took me a while," he said. "I—well, I kind of just ended up screaming so much for help that they just kicked me out of the city due to annoyance. So, being loud works to an advantage…sometimes. Until I was stepping on all these branches and the hunters for the Farm found me. But the Inaj, they're nice. They sometimes stick the pregnant ones in the cells here and the women liked to braid my hair and teach me words."

Her lips twitched. "That's lovely."

"It was…I hope they're okay. I really do."

"You seem like too good a person to be in here." She frowned. "They all do."

He rocked forward, then back, as if he couldn't handle stillness or quiet. "You should eat."

Violet gave him a look and he sheepishly smiled, but she turned toward a small trough in the cell that had been filled with grain and bread. Hunger ravaged her and she dove in a hand, pulled out a hulking piece of lumpy bread and bit.

Rio lunged forward. "Wait, no—small bites!"

But the minute she'd bitten into it, a wad as big as her fist, a sensation of both starvation and pleasure poured into her mouth, her saliva.

"No—"

Her hand was in the trough. Skies, this was good. Great. She wanted more. Needed more and there was so *much* food in there. She piled it into her mouth, hardly noticing the protest of her stomach, the burn of so much at once going down her throat. She ate and ate, a hungering ache growing within that she needed to satisfy, needed to sate.

"Violet, stop! You need to eat small bites or else—"

She turned and growled at him. *Growled.*

He'll stop you. Continue. Taste it. It tastes amazing. Go to the next. You want more. What else tastes good? What else do you crave?

It burned and burned and wouldn't go away. Her mouth filled with saliva and she dove into the trough again, pleasure and pain mixing in a way to fill that hunger, that dying need.

Far away, a gate creaked and something slammed into her face. Her neck was grabbed and she jolted up.

The pale green face of a young Inaj woman looked down at her. "You need to be more careful."

The pain of the slap had slithered away the sin.

Her scar burned.

The Inaj blinked at her. Violet blinked back, then looked down at her hands covered in saliva and grain, then the bread spilled all over the floor.

"Navee, she's learning," said Rio. "You can let her go."

Navee released her throat. Her brown hair was twisted into a bun at the base of her neck. Servant clothes hung loosely off her. She was barely at the edge of puberty.

Shame burned Violet's cheeks as she shoved herself away from the trough and rid her hands of the food.

"Small bites," Navee said. "Or else it gets you."

"This didn't happen in the mountains," said Violet, looking at her hands, wiping her mouth. Shock and embarrassment flooded through her. "Gwen said the food is different."

"It's processed," confirmed Rio. "There are factories all over the place that produce it in mass quantities. It's like…something similar to sugar in our world, but stronger. It's supposed to be different and make you want more."

Navee bent before Violet and drew out a rag that smelled of shiva. "I need to clean your ear."

Violet stared at her face, searching for suspicious action, before she nodded and turned her head. She bit down on her hiss as the alcohol stung. Navee murmured sympathies.

"Do you work in the estate?" Violet asked the Inaj when she dipped the rag into a small container at her belt.

"Most young Inaj do," she said.

"Is there a way to burn it to the ground?"

"*Violet*," warned Rio.

Navee, to Violet's surprise, shrugged. "The fumes they harvest for the overlord can be…flammable."

"Overlord? Stradinth?"

"No, the bigger guy." Rio pressed his face against the iron and whispered, "One who rules over the Stradinths. According to the older Inaj, he hasn't been around in a long time, but they produce stuff for him in the fields nearby."

"You're not supposed to tell people I told you that, Rio," snapped Navee in her light, not-very-intimidating voice.

"And he hasn't stopped this place?" she dared ask.

Navee scoffed. "He doesn't care what they do here. As long as they produce his oil."

"Is this the Worldbreaker?" asked Violet.

Rio and Navee both stilled at the name.

Navee's hand trembled on her ear. "This discussion ends now."

"But—"

"You can't say that name here." Rio's eyes darted around. Even a few candidates had picked their heads up at the name, delusional from their sleep. "Navee knows best."

"That I do. Now, all done." The Inaj righted herself. She shoved the rag in her pocket and turned—

"Wait." Violet stood hastily. "Are you going back to the estate? Can you give a message?"

Navee gawked at her. "To *who?*"

"Kiane's plaything," said Violet. "The pretty one with an ego the size of a mountain."

Navee blinked. "Jack. Oh—I do like him."

"I don't," said Violet. "But tell him I like my food burned."

Confusion flashed over Navee's face, before it settled, and she nodded. She shut the cage, locked it, and left without another word.

"Small *bites*," reminded Rio.

28

SKIES

THE DAYS IN THE CELL passed by slowly. Violet had managed to scrape away enough wood with her fingernail to create a small hole in the wall. Through it, she could see the long stone fence before the royal estate, flowering trees poking above, and the guards operating the gate.

Unfortunately, that also gave her a viewpoint on the sprawling line of chained Inaj filing into the factory.

Every day, around dawn, when the sun peeked through the cracks of the wood, she heard the screams. Rio would always press his hands to his ears, blocking them out, and she—she would rest her eye at the hole to glimpse Inaj in chains, muscled and lean, heads hung low as the guards on four-legged steeds led them down a path that twisted and careened, ashen and dark, into the open factory door.

The faces of the Inaj were unreadable, if not blank with emotion. Some tears were shed, some trembled as the line moved, or when guards lashed out, and some bit back in restrained anger, fighting against the self-preservation that boiled to keep any being alive.

When they entered the shining metal factory, the wide doors a blur in the distance, screams erupted, only to be cut off.

Rio said it was *ada*. A poison. Given when they entered. Meant to shred the inedible insides of a body, including the vocal cords, and paralyze the victim's limbs.

So she watched them assemble at dawn. Watched the pregnant Inaj take their daily walks lined by guards, the servants whisper to each other until they were under the gaze of a hunter.

Perhaps in the end, they didn't feel it—at least that was what Violet told herself. She nibbled on whatever food they dumped into her trough, but for the most part was content with her rumbling stomach. Her hands took an entire day to stop shaking from the effects of Gluttony, and her saliva was sweet, weird to taste, wanting more, until it became dry enough that no amount of water could quench it.

Like Wrath, there was a heavy hangover with the sin. But with Wrath she needed to sleep off its effects. Gluttony was like coming down from a drug. Even if she had the smallest dose, she sweated it out as rain poured and cold raised goosebumps on her skin. The withdrawal made it hard to avoid the food; so hard she was left staring at that stupid capsule in her wrist.

Her concept of time was limited to the change of sunlight through her little peephole. Rio would mumble his guesses, and Violet would glance out, letting him know if he was right or not.

The few times she saw Jack swirled some dark feeling in her stomach.

He would lead Kiane by the hand and sweep her around in a dance before he bent to kiss her. He...he truly did seem to like her, and she him. The way she looked at him, with absurd infatuation—maybe it was a boost for his ego, or maybe it was a game for him, as so many things were. Jack did his part and courted her, his motions even more prominent under the guards' gazes. She hated to see it, but still, she watched.

She didn't know how she was *supposed* to feel about him. Was it tolerance? A sense of camaraderie that she felt with Rio and the other candidates? That they were in this together? From the same home? The same origins?

But she couldn't feel that. He was on the other side of the wall playing the role of the handsome, charming man he was so good at.

And they were waiting…wasting away until the Crale holiday called Hospurin. When they were doomed to walk through those factory doors for their insides to slop into soup.

In the end, Violet hoped that their ties to Calesal prevailed over his need for pride and self-preservation. That perhaps, with his power and his calculating mind, he might save them. Her. Rio.

Maybe even all of them.

The delusion behind her thought stopped the hope altogether. When had Jack Marin ever proved he did something for others? He had dropped her brother into the Sins to buy himself time.

But she couldn't believe that Jack would want to stay here. At the hip of Kiane. *Here. Eating—*

"What do you see?" muttered Rio. "Let me guess…" He counted his fingers. "Close to sunset, right?"

Violet looked through the hole. "Just about."

Rio scratched a line on his side of the wall. "That's fourteen for me and two for you. You're not very good at clock stuff."

She snorted.

"What I would give for a smoke right now," sighed Rio.

"My left tit," a grousing voice called from another cage. Bonner.

"Reasonable, since yours are bigger than mine," said Violet.

"Or a glass of shiva," another candidate called. "Skivvin' dammit. Would at least make waiting for death better."

Violet blinked back a burning in her eyes. Jelan was so far away—all of it was so far away. Unreachable. She missed hanging from rooftops and drowning their worries in alcohol; the way Jelan's face glowed when she laughed, the clink of her beads, the ruggedness of her hands. Her friend would be watching her tracker and the green dot next to it, wondering what Violet was doing in the second world for so long when other candidates had already moved on. Wondering *what* the hold-up was.

Violet leaned her head back on the wall. "I'd kill for pomegranates. And shiva. And a smoke. I'd kill for it all."

"Kill all you want. You won't get it again," said a brown-haired Souther with tattoos and dirt caked on his face.

"Okay, you lousy, depressive sport," said Rio to the candidate. "Go rock yourself to sleep with those thoughts. We don't want them."

Still, numbness clenched at her with those words. Because as much as she missed Jelan, she was terrified that she would never see her again. Never laugh with her. Never hug her. Violet rubbed at her eyes while that capsule pulsed. Hope was a thin string, frayed and ready to snap, and she was grasping it with her pinky.

The lock to the door jolted with a creak. It swung open, revealing the four hunters and Kowai beyond it. The setting sun shined off his pale hair.

She held her breath, stepping back from the cage door. She and Rio exchanged a terrified look. He shook his head and pressed against the wall as if it could swallow him.

Kowai's eyes swept the barn, passing over Rio and Violet. "Not them."

He stepped in with his hands behind his back.

Her throat was closing, and she kept glancing back to Rio, then to the other candidates terrified in the cages.

"That one," said Kowai, eyes on the candidate Rio had just snapped at.

Violet sagged against the wall as the hunters rushed past her and Rio's cages to the furthest one. The candidate shot up into a sitting position, face paling fifteen shades. His eyes darted from one hunter to another, as if he were sizing them up, debating which one he should take first.

Violet had seen fear on even the most vicious Souther men. But when death stared one down, a death that was *known* and already had a play-by-play through the minds of those sentenced, it was a different kind of fear that passed through them. Her blood iced underneath her skin. Her eyes burned. She wanted to look away—skies, she should look away, but they stayed glued to the hunters as two raised their crossbows, one opened the cage, and one stepped in.

"No—no!" The candidate stood and jerked as the hunter advanced on him. "I'm not going!"

"Gag him," commanded Kowai.

Two hunters advanced, pressed the candidate into the wall. In a frenzy, like an animal writhing for its life, he lashed out. One fist careened into a face, and then he swung the other, but the hunters anticipated that. An arrow shot and jammed into his shoulder. Another into his chest.

The candidate cried out in pain.

Violet's stomach roiled. She gripped it, willing her bile to stay down.

Animals. That's all they were—no matter the conversations, no matter the blazing life within their eyes. It was so unlike the graceful way Gwen had taught her to hunt—to thank the creatures for their life. There was no bow of the head, no murmured gratitude and a prayer sent to the hills for safe passage.

This was brutal. Blood seeped from his wounds. The hunters flipped the candidate around and chained his hands. Desperation gnawed at him still—he jerked, twitched, screamed into the musty air. Somber faces watched. Death lurked over his shoulder, and not one thanked for. One of exploitation. One of despair.

They gagged him so his horrifying cries that cracked her chest were silenced. Tears streamed down his face, eyes wild as he looked to his fellow Southers, for help, for prayers…for what?

What could she give him? How could she save him? Maybe if he was labeled a rapist it would make her feel better, but even if it were Jack Marin being hauled away, ready to disappear from this life, this death would not be deserved.

Was it up to her to judge that, though?

Rio trembled across from her, eyes on the ceiling of the barn. The other candidates looked away from the scene. Only she watched—partially because she was frozen in place, haunted by Gwen and the fact that she had watched her brethren be taken away for decades.

Even her children.

The hunters dragged him out while he continued to thrash with adrenaline and animalistic self-preservation. Desperation cloyed the air, and she was breathing it. They all were. The whole Farm was.

And the fact the Inaj in the morning factory lines were rendered to broken bodies and hollow faces made it all the worse.

Kowai gracefully stepped to the side to let the hunters pass. Immune to the guttural cries of the candidate, he motioned to something beyond her sight.

Four more hunters walked in. When their gazes landed on her cage, she nearly soiled herself.

They opened it up. A frenzy rose within her. Her hands flinched forward to defend, but Kowai's velvet voice carried through.

"It is not your time, so you can relax."

Her eyes nearly bugged at the word. *Relax*. Was that something he thought was possible in a place like this?

"You're invited to dinner," he clarified.

Rio swallowed his gasp. The hunters filed in, two crossbows on her neck, while another stepped forward with chains.

Adrenaline coursed, but at the same time, it froze her. There was no fight like the other candidate, but merely ice. Cold, cold ice as if she had been dumped into a pool of it. Her breath drowned in her throat, and her knees nearly gave out until the hunter righted her, turned her around and chained her hands behind her back.

"Take her to the bathing house and instruct the servants to change her into new clothes."

She looked down to her Souther clothes, the tight pants, the tank top, her boots, and the sweater atop it all. The capsule in her wrist pulsed.

"It'll be okay, Vi," whispered Rio. "Head low. It will be okay."

All her words lodged in her throat, but as she was calmly taken out of the barn, her ears picked up the soft murmur of another candidate.

"May they rise to the skies and the heavens beyond."

29

DINNER

THE BATHING HOUSE WAS FOR the Inaj servants, held within a sector of the royal estate. They stripped Violet and tossed her clothes to the side.

"Can you keep those?" she muttered to the woman scrubbing dirt off her legs.

The servant looked at her with confusion. Violet realized how futile that request was. Her death was tomorrow—the clothes did not matter.

Another servant gathered them up and took them out of the room. Her material hold on Calesal was gone.

They scrubbed her down and sprayed her with lavender scent. Her hair was washed twice just to get the dirt out, and Gwen's blood, still dried underneath her fingernails, was picked out.

A tear slipped down her cheek as the Inaj worked in silence. The door opened and Navee stepped through, pale green face revealing no emotion.

"They do this every year," she said. "They select a guest to join them for dinner. You are the woman candidate, and we don't get many of those."

Another servant brushed her cheek. Violet jerked away.

"Don't cry," the Inaj said. "They will drink your tears. You must be brave."

Her bravery resided in the clearing where Gwen's body decayed.

All of what she felt now was fear.

She was dressed in simple servant clothing, her hair braided down her back. It took everything within Violet not to flinch at each brush of fingertips at the nape of her neck. Because the last time she'd let someone touch her hair....

The night Gwen told her she was loved.

Navee stood patiently by the door until Violet finished. Two hunters waited for her. Violet's hands shook as they chained her.

When her gaze flicked up to their faces, it took every ounce of control not to balk at one of them.

Because behind that dark cloth covering the bottom half of his face, the tribal Inaj blinked at her. Those dark eyes—she would know them anywhere, because she had screamed at them after Gwen had died.

Navee sauntered forward and met the gaze of each hunter. Violet realized the other was Inaj too—younger, paler, but with that white powder to blend in. A powder one would only notice if they took long moments to spot it. If they would know to look for it at all.

A curtain lifted her observation because everywhere she looked, half-covered faces blinked at her, and she realized most of them were undercover Inaj.

Disbelief ate at her insides when she was led into the house. She passed so many servants, and the glances weighed with something unsaid. A plan? A coup? This was no coincidence. Something broiled underneath the gluttonous noses of the Crale, and Violet was surrounded by it.

As if they had studied a map. As if they had discovered *exactly* how to infiltrate it from a person who knew the Farm like the back of her hand.

It was Gwen's voice she heard in the back of her head amidst the heady silence.

Win, agia.

For the Inaj persevered, and the sole escapee of the Farm had lit that hope.

They turned down a stone hallway, the walls dancing with flame from the sconces. Fumes melted into the air, mixed with the haughty floras from the gardens. Hunters lined the walls—noticeably Crale. Deeper into the estate, the infiltration halted, and that worried her. How close were they to breaking the family apart? Even more so, the blindness she had to their plans drew her nerves back in. The tribal Inaj offered some comfort, but they were not here for her. She was the means to the end.

She didn't blame them. This was not her world. She was the traveler, the passerby, and she was not the priority.

The priorities were the lives shivering in the nearing winter outside.

Another stone room. Another turn. Soon enough, like the map depicted, two ornate wooden doors stood in front of them. Navee inhaled sharply at her back, pushed her finger into Violet's spine, and prodded her forward.

Was Navee's touch a comfort? Or a reminder that as she entered the room, part of their plan depended on Violet?

Or was it to shut up and let them do all the work?

Probably the latter. Violet's mouth never got her to great places.

Servants opened the doors and a warm dining room greeted them. A table decorated with winter flowers and vines stretched before her. Empty, high-backed chairs lined the sides, along with the one that dominated the head. Dining ware glimmered underneath the writhing flames atop the chandelier, and on the wallpapered walls, art of Gluttony's landscape hung.

At the far wall were two chains of iron, lazily hanging from the ceiling. There was no seat at that end of the table.

A guest is what they said. And she was the rare woman candidate.

Skies, if they made her eat any of the food, she was tapping that damned capsule and giving them the finger until her death.

The Inaj hunters drew her to the chains and locked her in, arms extended above her head. The tribal male shared a sharp look as if to say: *remember why she died.*

I will never forget, she returned the hard look.

As soon as the hunters took their place at the wall among the others, and Navee shuffled through another door, entering again with a herd of servants and goblets of water, the main doors burst open, and the Stradinth family strolled through. The servants and the hunters—Inaj included—bowed deeply.

"Ah, our esteemed guest," Stradinth said, frown lines deepening in his smile. "Thank you for joining us."

She said nothing.

Other Crale men filed in followed by a few women—their wives, she supposed—and then Kowai with the most gloriously bored look on his face. When his cold eyes met hers, his lips twitched.

Her scowl was surely going to be permanent for the rest of the night, but they were unbothered by it.

They took their seats, Stradinth at the head. Before she could question the two empty places, the doors opened again, and the servants bowed as Kiane sauntered in, frilly golden dress doing her non-existent curves a major disservice. Half of her hair was pulled back, and when she turned, Violet glimpsed the silver thing clipping it together.

She wasn't surprised to see Jack at her hip, dressed in an elegant black tunic and pants, knee-high boots as shiny as his green stare.

"Daddy." Kiane dropped and placed a kiss on Stradinth's cheek.

"Master Stradinth," Jack said politely.

Stradinth beamed at him, shaking his hand firmly. "It is an honor to have you join our family for our first Hospurin Eve."

"The honor is mine. I have been waiting for this day for a very, *very* long time." Jack smiled so *sweet.* So genuine.

She wanted to punch it off his pretty face.

The contrast of his warm brown skin and his dark curls with the appearance of the Crale was a bit of a shock. But the way heads turned his way, and the wives' gazes dripped down his body as he walked around to his seat, said enough. Kiane's look was sharp on the others, while Jack appeared oblivious of them.

"Bring the food!" Stradinth commanded.

"It really is just the best on Hospurin," said Kiane to Jack. She nodded to the Inaj servants and the hunters at the wall. "You can eat as much as you want, if you'd like." Her gaze flicked to Violet. "Even her."

Jack lifted his head. "I'm sure she would be delicious."

Violet gagged.

It went ignored.

"We are saving her for tomorrow—Hospurin is the celebration of our conquering of the lands. Of the day we declared our might over both the greedy and the gluttonous and took it for ourselves." Stradinth raised his goblet filled with blood-red liquid. "To our power. We thank the gods for blessing us with it."

"And we thank them for better meat than the stupid beasts that roam the mountains," said Kiane, raising her glass.

"We thank the sin, for giving us such pleasure in our food," said Kowai.

"For the food."

"For family."

"For the lands."

"For the—" one paused. Looked to Violet.

But she was ignoring them. Instead, she swung side to side in her chains, squeaking it enough so every head picked up.

Kiane sneered. "Did you have something to be thankful for?"

Violet lazily turned to look at her. She let her gaze roam Kiane's body. "I'm thankful you chose that dress. It's hideous enough to distract me from all the nonsense coming out of your mouths."

Kowai—to Violet's surprise—snorted into his drink.

"You look lovely, darling," said one of the wives, leaning over Jack rather closely. "That candidate looks sickly. She even has a blemish on her forehead."

Jack politely took the wife's hand off his lap and placed it on the table.

Violet gaped. Narrowed her eyes. "If straw and cat shit were blended together, you would be the final form."

The wife turned to her, red rising to her cheeks.

"Shut your mouth," snapped Kiane.

"Then gag me, you skiv."

"I want to kill it." Kiane stood abruptly. She stalked over to Violet, a dinner knife in hand. "I want to tear its throat out."

"Come on, Kiane," Violet said. "I know you can do better than that. Is the meat muddling your mind?"

Kiane screeched and slashed the knife. Violet flinched back, but it cut across her cheek. A hot sting. Kiane gripped her throat, dropping her voice. "Stop stealing the attention."

Violet pouted. "Is someone insecure?"

Kiane choked her hard. "I am going to kill you tomorrow." She lifted the knife where drops of Violet's blood slipped down. She licked it. "And I'm going to enjoy eating your heart. Just like I did to your Inaj woman's children."

Violet spat, "Don't you say a fucking word about her—"

"Shut *up*," she snarled. "I think I'm going to skip the poison on you. I want you to feel everything while I butcher you and watch you die." Kiane smiled and slid the knife across her lips. "And you know what, I think I'm going to make Jack watch."

Violet choked on her words. Kiane's hand clenched her throat harder. She grew dizzy, vision blacking in and out. A figure appeared—Kowai. He drew Kiane away.

"The food is coming, sister."

In reprieve, the servants' door opened and the tension fizzled out as trays were carried in. Charred corn, mixed greens, mashed potatoes, and spices that reluctantly made her mouth water. Bowls and bowls of it were scattered around the table, and everyone's eyes widened with hunger.

Gluttony.

Kiane scowled as she retook her seat. Kowai slid into his.

Jack removed the wife's hand off his lap again.

Heads leaned forward, and sniffs sounded in the air. Even Violet groaned and pulled as near as the chains would allow her, wanting to be closer…closer…wanting a bite—

The door opened again, and two servants hauled a giant gilded platter stacked with sliced meat.

Her blood iced. Hands grew clammy. The room swayed and she took a step back, then another as the servants placed it at the center of the table.

"A candidate," said Kowai. His gaze flicked to Jack. "Picked especially for you on this fine celebration."

"That is very kind of you, Kowai," said Jack.

Violet pressed herself against the wall in horror, mind reeling at just an *hour* ago when that candidate had been struggling for his life. The room seemed to close in on her, and her breaths grew heavy. That—that was what he was reduced to. She involuntarily gagged as bile rose to her throat.

"This is why I don't like inviting others to dinner." Kiane jutted her chin to Violet as she piled food onto her plate. "They always react, as if they aren't appreciative that we get to enjoy it."

"Relax, sister, you can take out your insecurities on the girl tomorrow," said Kowai.

Kiane glowered. "Why would you say such a thing?"

"You are going to ruin this dinner if you keep looking at her," he clarified. "We have more to be thankful for, such as the fact the wild Inaj never showed to get their trade—not that we were going to give them younglings anyway. Somewhere, in that little brain of theirs, they might have realized that it *indeed* would have been a trap to gather more of their kind."

Out of all the Inaj still in the room, no one bristled. They held their composure.

"We get the girl candidate, and they can have their slice of land." Kowai waved his hand. "It'll be ours within the month, anyway. My recon informed me of their current boundaries and their village location."

Servants filled the goblets. Navee was among them, and Violet noticed how she passed over Jack's.

She also noticed how Jack fingered the stem of his glass but never raised it. His plate was filled, and sometimes he would push the food around with a fork but never bring it to his mouth.

"I'm curious." Jack leaned back against his seat. "How do you plan on executing that? I'm sure I can give a few pointers."

"I have always enjoyed your input," said Kowai.

The passive-aggressiveness in the room nearly suffocated Violet.

Kowai started, "If we release some Inaj that we have now, the wild ones eventually will take them in. Patience is the key in weeding them out, and then perhaps we can expand to build a new farm. Coplan city nearby has an astounding population, and we must think about the Crale we need to feed there. It's worth it."

"And if they retaliate?" asked Jack.

Kowai blinked. "Why would they do that?"

"Never underestimate your enemy," said Jack. "It might be what brings you to your knees."

"Are you going to eat?" Kiane asked, voice softening as she looked at Jack. She shoveled a small bite of the meat into her mouth. "It's delicious."

Violet could feel Gluttony in the air. The Crale moaned as they ate, shoveling more into their mouths, or leaning closer to their plates as if it might sate the gnawing hunger.

Jack picked up his fork, twirled it in his hand. "I—"

One of the wives jerked forward, foam coming from her lips. Her husband next to her collapsed into his plate. Another head slammed down with a thump, then another, then another, until food covered their hair and they twitched in their seats.

"Oh, gods!" Kiane cried, jumping out of her seat. "What is happening?"

Stradinth realized. "Do not touch the food! It has been poisoned. Go—go to the kitchens!"

Some of the hunters at the wall rushed through the servants' door. Others stepped forward, hands on their longswords.

"Secure the estate!" Kiane commanded.

More rushed out. The tribal Inaj and his brethren lingered at the door, their movements defensive. As if they were guarding—

With the chaos at the table, no one, except Violet, noticed how they shut the door.

And locked it.

Seven out of the fourteen guests had collapsed on their plates. Every other one looked around or stood up abruptly, gasping in horror.

It was only Jack who leaned back, face bored. "Good guess, but it is actually the drink."

Confirming it, another member spat his drink out, black liquid staining the table. But it was too late.

His ears dripped blood, blackish foam coming out of his mouth. His eyes darted around and his arms twitched forward to catch himself, but the nerves of his body derailed from his mind, and he collapsed off the chair.

Kiane dropped her neighbor's head back on their plate and turned to Jack. "*What?*"

"Seize him!" Stradinth ordered.

The only guards left were the undercover Inaj. They did not move.

Everything about Jack Marin unraveled. The charming man gave way to the trained Commander. He gripped the fork and jammed it straight into the throat of his neighbor.

Black blood spurted out in four directions. Before the man keeled over, Jack gracefully whipped another dinner knife into the throat of the wife across. Her head thumped down. Her husband followed, blade jutting from his eye.

Jack was out of his seat, serrated meat knife in his hand, and pointed at Stradinth.

Stradinth gaped at his family. Too stunned, too shocked at the bloodbath to do anything but tremble.

"Ah, Master, you are always making it easy for me," Jack whispered in Stradinth's ear.

"My family…"

"Don't worry. You're going to the same hell as them. I'll see you there, eventually."

Jack drew the Crale's head back, his pale neck a moon

underneath the candlelight. He slashed Stradinth's throat ear to ear.

Kiane released a blood-curdling screech.

"Skies, can you shut up?" Jack let her father's body drop to his seat. He turned to her. "I've ripped out tongues before—do you know how hard it was not to remove yours with every word you spoke?"

He stalked around the table toward her. She was shocked as she raised the knife, hands trembling. He grabbed an empty tray and slammed it against her head. She dropped to the ground.

"I'll admit this was the most interesting holiday I've ever witnessed."

Violet's head whirled to find Kowai near her. She flinched against the wall. In her peripheral vision, one of the Inaj was advancing, a dagger in hand.

But Kowai only held up the keys to her chains and unlocked them for her.

Jack dropped the tray with an annoyed look as he took care of the last Crale and stalked over. "There's your place as Master," he said to Kowai.

"You weren't wrong about taking over a city," said Kowai. His gaze swept over his family, unbothered. "I'm thankful you distracted my sister so well."

"And that comes with the terms of leaving the rest of the Inaj land alone." Jack picked up a napkin and wiped the Crale blood off his face. He tossed it atop a head.

"Fine," said Kowai, turning around. "Take your half of the Inaj and get off my property. Along with the girl."

"I thought you wanted to hold on to her?" said Jack.

"She's nothing interesting to look at." Kowai sneered at Violet.

"That's too bad."

The wretched meat knife flung out and slammed into Kowai's throat. Black blood misted Violet.

"Sorry, slipped." Jack flexed his hand.

Violet gaped, looked down at herself and the Crale blood

covering her.

Jack nodded toward Kowai's crumpled body. "He wanted a deal with me to get his sister out of the picture, and his father dead, basically everyone dead, in exchange for no more candidates, or whatever the fuck his terms were. I didn't care. I was going to kill him anyway. I *especially* wanted to kill him because of his comments about you." Jack smirked at her. "You are interesting to look at, if you needed the boost."

She continued to gape.

"And then through their little Inaj message system—and your words about the map—these guys managed to contact her." He nodded to Navee, who leaned against the wall. "Who realized that you had wanted *me* to do something…and, well, it all came together."

He smiled brightly, as if he hadn't just murdered fourteen people in the last five minutes.

She was sure her heart was going to pound out of her chest.

"Now let's go, little Vi—sorry—*Violet*. We have some fences to knock down."

30

The Factory

For the most part, Violet held herself together, even though her clothes stuck to her with blood. Per usual.

Jack swaggered through the house, knife in one hand, fist clenched in the other. The Inaj had moved to the fight outside of the estate. People ran everywhere, and when a Crale advanced on them, Jack slashed them down without a second glance.

"I hate all of these people," he said.

They moved through the front doors. Navee brushed past her, her blade held aloft, as she led the kitchen Inaj through the garden with a roar of revenge.

Eventually, Jack slowed. Sighed. "You need to get it together," he told her. "I can't keep saving your life."

"I'm not asking you to," she snapped and moved past him.

He grabbed her arm. "What is your issue?"

She yanked it out. "Nothing."

"Violet—"

And when she opened her mouth to yell, her words were swallowed by the knife that flew into his shoulder.

Jack keeled over, falling to his knees with a grunt. His hand reached back to the knife, and with a hiss, he yanked it out. Blood poured, staining his tunic.

Violet whirled, but a fist knocked into her face. Pain flared at her cheekbone. Her vision blackened. She sagged forward, but before she could hit the ground, her hair was grabbed and she was dragged across the yard.

A scream tore through her throat.

Jack's eyes found hers, panic churning in them. He tried to stand but fell to the ground again, and Violet saw the second knife burrowed into his hip.

"I knew I should have killed you long ago." Kiane's rage-filled voice was as sharp as the burning on Violet's scalp. "Right next to your scum Inaj. It would have been a fitting death, and then my family wouldn't have been *murdered* by *him*."

Violet cried out, reaching to her head, but Kiane's grip was iron on her hair, and she dragged her past the open gates of the estate, to the right. To Violet's horror, the metal of the factory glimmered overhead.

"Kiane!" Jack's roar sounded.

"I'll be back for him," she seethed.

Violet was unable to get a footing the whole way there, ashes and mud slipping and sliding over her soles. She cried, but there was so much noise, so much chaos, that it was sucked away. Useless.

Another flash of light. *Gwen's dagger.* The turquoise blade beautiful amidst all the destruction, at the hip of Kiane.

Something within her snapped, and the heaviness to her chest reared back like a terrified animal finally realizing its cage had been opened.

"Do not let them see your fear," said Gwen. "No matter what you feel, you fight. You fight standing. You fight with your heart, your body, because this life is what you are dealt with, and to give it away would be a waste."

Violet patted the superficial gash on her head. Gwen had knocked her hard—harder than she was used to. But no remorse lay in the Inaj's eyes. She wanted Violet to know pain, and to know how to fight through it. Especially to fight when that carelessness seeped in and made her want to give up, to let it all go.

Just let it go, her mind said. Give up. The darkness is so sweet. You can start over. You can let go.

The threshold of the factory passed above her. The doors slammed shut.

"You do not stop fighting." Gwen lifted her chin, plated arms gleaming in the sunlight as she held her spear. *"Death will look you in the eyes, and you know what you do when it does that?"*

Violet wiped her sweaty forehead. "What?"

"You punch it in the damn face."

With a roaring cry, Violet twisted her body. Her scalp lit on fire, but it was enough movement for Kiane to lose her grip. Violet rolled free.

She burst up to her hands and knees. A hard kick landed in her stomach and her breath escaped her. She doubled over. Kiane's hand wrapped her hair again.

"Ever since you stepped in here, I knew you would be trouble," Kiane seethed, then laughed. Crazed. She dragged Violet, her boots squeaking on the clean floor. "But I didn't know you would ruin everything. My family, my home, Jack. I'm going to slaughter you. Just. Like. *Them.*"

The whole factory was metal—rigged belts crisscrossed throughout the massive space. Bleak lights shined down, blinding Violet. It was cold—abnormally cold. A refrigerator. And the smell—oh skies, the metallic, petrol stench reeked throughout, no matter the glistening machinery or polished hooks. Her grunts bounced off the plated walls as Kiane pulled her down the main aisle. To her right lined towers of shelves, packed full of bagged items and things she couldn't make out.

To her left, pristine conveyor belts. Giant axes hung above to slice. The line of belts continued until her vision watered from tears, the pain in her scalp overwhelming her senses.

Violet looked up and she wished she hadn't. Bodies—torsos, arms, butchered legs, all hung from rafters up above.

Horror cascaded through her. She shut her eyes.

"No matter what you feel, you fight."

Kiane shrieked and dropped her hair, only to grab her jaw. "No! Look at them. I want you to see what you will become! Your life means *nothing*, little candidate. Not to anyone in this world, except maybe that Inaj woman you grew close to. Boy, she might have been tasty, had she not been rotting old and wrinkly."

Violet screamed in anger. She swung her body and then her leg at Kiane's ankles. The Crale dropped and Violet lunged for her, pinning her down. "Do *not* ever speak of her in this vile place. You foul *conjua*." She slashed her nails across Kiane's face. "You fucking bitch."

Kiane clawed back. "But her children, *oh* her children."

"Arghhh!" Violet snapped and saw red. She breathed through it, controlled it, and channeled it at the female. She wrapped her hands around Kiane's neck, but the Crale twisted her wrist so hard that she let go. Kiane sent a punch straight into Violet's cheekbone.

Gwen might have taught her to fight against a worthy opponent, but the savageness in Kiane's movements was something different. Dirty. Exhausting. She was fighting Kiane's rage with her own, and no amount of training prepared her for that.

Kiane clawed at her. Violet recoiled. She elbowed the Crale in the face. A crack sounded and blood gushed from Kiane's nose. The Crale screamed in fury.

Violet scrambled off and ran to the rows of towers. The lights dimmed underneath twenty high shelves. When she managed to wipe the blood from her eyes, barely registering the sting at her forehead, she hurried away.

The Crale laughed—manic now. "You think you can escape me? Oh, now this will be fun!" Her voice bounced off the walls.

Violet's heart squeezed in her chest. She needed the upper hand. She needed a *weapon*. There would be endless scrapes and bruises using just their hands, and Violet was worried exhaustion would kill her before Kiane's demise because the stupid Crale didn't seem fazed by any punch.

Violet panicked, running the shelving units like she did alleys and blocks. *Just don't look up. Whatever you do, don't look up.*

But the butchered bodies took up her mind, the pallid green on them so evident. She had seen one of these Inaj in the line, and now...*now*...they were drying strips of meat.

She fought down the bile.

"Let's have some fun!" Kiane called. Metal banged. "Maybe some girl time? We can talk about Jack!"

Violet ducked into another aisle, barely catching the sight of pale hair. She looked around desperately. On one shelf, iron pokers hung, polished and clean. Like branding weapons.

She grabbed one and ran, footsteps light. A gasp told her Kiane heard and the Crale's speed picked up.

Violet turned down another row and ducked. Between the shelves, she glanced the ripped gold dress and the turquoise dagger wrapped by pale fingers.

"Come out, little candidate...come out, come out, wherever you are."

Violet drew in a ragged inhale. Her nostrils flared. She reached within her, for whatever bravery might still exist.

As Kiane padded, looked down another aisle, sighed loudly, and continued on to the next, Violet followed her movements. When Kiane turned, Violet was already pressed against the end of a unit and holding her breath. When Kiane's feet stomped, Violet moved, too, eventually backtracking in the direction of the exit.

"Okay, now I'm *bored!*" Metal hitting metal rang through the air. "You can't leave. The doors lock from the outside, unless you have a special key."

Violet blinked as she caught the motion of Kiane's body. The Crale stepped onto one of the conveyor belts, then waved Gwen's dagger.

And that silver thing binding her hair caught in the sharp spotlights.

"*Skiv,*" Violet whispered. Her hand tightened on the poker.

"After you, I'm going to take my sweet time with Jack." Kiane's voice wavered with heartbreak. She was blindsided by his actions. Tears slipped down her cheeks and she wiped them away furiously. "My whole family—*gone*. He's going to pay for this. They are *all* going to pay for this!"

Kiane stomped on the belt with her muddy flats. Violet edged along the aisle, closer to the belts. She reined in her trembling hands, steadying her breath. Focus, control.

The bottles on the shelf next to her caught her attention. She squinted. The writing was a scrawl of the Crale language, but within the glass, a translucent liquid swirled.

With each stomp, each bang of metal, Violet covered the noise of her screwing the cap off a bottle. She poured the thick substance into her hand and rubbed it along her arms. She hoped there wasn't a timer on ingesting it.

"Fight me!" Kiane said. "Come out of there, you dirty whore. Come face me like I know you want to! I'm going to kill you, and when I kill everyone else, I'll fry you up and hang you from the rafters like the rest of the scum!" Kiane twisted, eyes roaming everywhere. "You can die next to your little candidate friends, like that skinny one. I'll find a way to taste him. I'll make him *suffer*. Perhaps you can watch like you did your Inaj."

"Perhaps with all the threats you make to our lives, you are just afraid you'll die like the rest of them." Violet edged out of the aisle. Kiane whirled on her. "Like you meant nothing, like you did nothing, and with no one to remember you."

Kiane laughed. She pointed Gwen's dagger. "Is that what you think? Your whole city watches you blink on some screen. Do you think they care what happens to you? Do you think anyone cares about you? This is *my* world. I rule it. Your world tossed you right out, and I'll be happy to take you off their hands."

Violet stepped up to the belt adjacent to Kiane's. "Then what are you waiting for?" Her eyes narrowed. "Come do it."

Kiane's nostrils flared. With a screech, she lunged across to Violet's belt and raised the dagger. Violet parried it back with the poker. Twisted. Aimed for Kiane's head but the dagger met it with a clang, and Kiane pushed it away. Violet backed up. The giant factory axes shined above her head. The bodies beyond it.

Kiane jabbed again with a guttural cry. Her hair was a mess, eyes bloodshot, lips pulled back on her snarl. Violet ducked from the dagger, like all the times Gwen fought her with it, and came up on the other side of Kiane's arm. She grabbed it, nails digging into the Crale's skin, and drew her arm back. A painful cry flew from her lips, but Kiane dropped the dagger and twisted, catching it with her other hand. Violet jerked back. The blade slashed across Violet's stomach.

She bit her cry and jammed her foot into Kiane's middle. The Crale flew back and landed against a giant processing box. A beep echoed. The belt began to move.

Violet dropped to her stomach. The nearest ax arced over where her body had been. Ice slithered over her skin as the belt moved, and another ax slashed. Where her foot had been.

"Those are for cutting the head off," Kiane sneered.

Violet scrambled up after the ax line and lunged for the bitch. She feigned the poker. Instead jammed it against the back of her knee. Kiane crumpled to the belt.

"I'm fucking *tired* of you," Violet snarled. Kiane slit at her calf, but Violet kicked her face, sending her back. "You've ruined so many lives in this place, and you deserve to know how to die like them."

"I'll take a bite out of you first."

"I dare you."

With a roar, Kiane threw the dagger at Violet's head. Violet swiped it out of the way with the poker and advanced. Fury marked her face; revenge marked her movements.

Violet sliced the poker. The gold dress tore open at Kiane's stomach, black blood welling. She slashed again. A cut at her arm. Again. Again. Again.

Like the Crale had done to Gwen without remorse. For her being a nuisance.

Violet raised the poker again—

Kiane grabbed her ankles and pulled. Violet sprawled in surprise. She landed hard, her head hitting the rubber belt, vision dotting black. Kiane scrambled up to straddle her, using one hand to hold her wrists down, while the other grabbed the poker and pressed the long end to Violet's neck.

Violet choked.

The girl smiled—evil and hungry.

Violet got one arm free and pushed Kiane's baring teeth away.

"*Skiv,*" Violet growled.

Teeth snapped at her face. "Fucking—die already!" Kiane screeched.

Violet built enough distance to bring her knee up to the she-devil's chest, then her boot, and pushed the Crale away. She had the poker back and aimed a stab in the chest, but Kiane swung a leg and knocked it away. The iron skidded off.

Kiane tackled Violet off the belt and to the ground, pinning her again and spreading her arms. Violet screamed in frustration.

"I might just decide to have a taste now." She smiled, flashing her white teeth. Her lips brushed the skin on Violet's left arm. She glimpsed the oozing wound at Violet's wrist. "Oh look, there's already an opening for me."

"I *dare* you," Violet spat. "Bite me, bitch, and I will end you."

Kiane leveled her head with Violet's wrist, then licked up her arm. "You taste—"

Horror graced Kiane's features. The Crale quickly spat. "*Ada.*"

"Too late." Violet smiled.

Kiane's movements jerked, but she yanked Violet, and her left wrist, straight into her mouth.

Violet wasn't prepared for the fiery pain of teeth biting into skin. A scream tore from her throat. The room blurred, her only focus the pain. Fire. Agony. Inferno. She was burning. So hot. A hand wrapped her throat and she choked on air.

The poison finally took full effect.

Kiane went rigid. Her eyes widened and she recoiled, coughing into her hand.

Horror washed over the Crale's face. Black blood poured from her ears, staining her pale hair, soaking Violet's pants. Violet grabbed her shoulders and twisted so she straddled the Crale.

Violet gripped Kiane's jaw and kept it shut. "I'm not letting you spit it out."

With wide, terrified eyes, the Crale knew exactly what was happening to her. Soon enough, her arms lost movement and flopped numbly to the side. Blood leaked out of the corners of her mouth. Violet kept it firmly shut. She could feel the Crale's teeth stop, halted by something, and Violet smiled knowingly.

"Your vocal cords should be grating right now," she said. "The poison works in ten seconds. Ten measly seconds before the uneatable organs begin to shred themselves. You know…the stomach, the intestines. Well, yes, you know." Kiane's eyes flashed. Violet's grin deepened. "Then it renders the limbs unmovable, so the victim cannot fight. Very smart on your part. Not only do you finally shut the fuck up, but you also can't move while I finish you."

Panic flared in Kiane's gaze.

"Do you feel that?" Violet looked toward the Crale's stomach. "Like jelly, right? Probably hurts. Too bad you can't scream. But don't worry, the poison doesn't kill," Violet said. "That's what the belts are for. The hooks hanging above. No—no—you're going to look." She drew Kiane's eyelids back, forcing her to stare above. "Look at what you have done to all those people. You will die looking at them, knowing that you perished just as they did."

Kiane's eyes grew wild. She gurgled on the blood pooling within her mouth.

Violet cocked her head, puckering her lip out. "Oh, you want me to end it for you? Does it hurt, Kiane? Does it hurt to have your family murdered before you? Watch Jack end them?" She dropped her voice. "Knowing that he used you all along?"

Their gazes met.

"And the last gift I have for you is my little capsule of death.

I was prepared to take it out, but I thought it might be useful for you to have it. You just made it easier for me." Violet poked Kiane's lips. "That thing between your teeth? That is something special from my city, given to me when *I* decided I wanted to give up." She drew back. "I have no need of it anymore."

She jammed the Crale's jaw up. A crack of glass.

A deep green liquid dribbled out of the corner of her mouth.

Horror graced Kiane's pretty features until, slowly, her eyes glazed over, her face slackened, and the life left her.

"Sweet dreams, *conjua*," said Violet.

※※※

The pain in Violet's wrist didn't bother her as she stood. She wrenched the key to the doors out of Kiane's hair, grabbed Gwen's dagger, and walked away without a glance back.

When the factory doors slammed shut, her steps slowed, until she fully halted.

Everything within her stilled. Built and then stilled. Adrenaline slowed. Her limbs grew heavy. Her mouth opened as she gasped in air, and then it all washed away, leaving her to embrace her grief, everything that just happened…

She collapsed to her knees, lifted her head, and screamed to the twinkling stars above.

In that scream, she released. All of the hate, the anger, the numbness, the misery, the anguish, and the towering mountain built with her messy emotions. It poured out through her throat. Into Gluttony's sky. She screamed and screamed until she was sure the world heard. Her heart heard. Her soul stitched together from the fracture it had been for so long.

Tears poured. She opened her arms to the skies, Gwen's dagger warm in her hand. There was so much blood. All over her skin. A crescendo built, panic rising. She wanted it off—off—*off*—

She was sobbing now. Pain, there was so much pain. She wanted the blood off her. She wanted *her* hands off of her. She wanted everyone to leave her alone and cry and cry, and she wanted Gwen—

She gazed to the stars. Gwen. Her wrinkles. Her metal plates. Her cunning smile. Her knowing eyes. Her warmth. Her fingers through Violet's hair. Her affection. Her acceptance of the broken, exhausted Souther girl who never knew what motherly love was.

All the nights spent with her flashed, and the memories flooded as her tears did. But slowly, after she released her scream of pain that had been building ever since her mother turned away from her, ever since Reed was sentenced, ever since she shoved the dagger into Gwen's heart, she managed to smile. It was not happy, but it was in remembrance, because just then the wind blew her blood-matted hair, and she knew the Inaj was there with her.

Agia.

"Mia, mia," Violet whispered. *Mother. Mother.* "Stay with me."

Always.

Silence passed. She let her emotions roil. All of them. For her. She sobbed as she felt the years of pain and people who had died here. She felt the distance between her and Calesal and her old life that had died. The pot grew too full and spilled over. She opened an embrace to it. Sober. Ready. Willing.

Her breaths grew even. The world returned to her consciousness. There was a stillness to it.

Agia.

"Free," she said. "Free. Let them be free."

And after all that time, they were.

31

Burnt Food

THE ESTATE WAS EMPTY, THE barn was empty, and the cages were empty, so Violet took the road back to the gates.

All around her, the Crale lay dead.

Beyond that, she could spot the backs of a dark crowd moving down the road before her.

The Inaj.

Her lids drooped. Her knees sank. She caught herself as exhaustion hit her like a punch to the face.

"*Violet.*"

Rio appeared down the road and then rushed forward, catching her as she doubled over again.

"Where have you been? We've been looking for you...."

She noticed Jack's figure behind him, shirt gone to reveal his body beneath. Bandages wrapped his shoulder and stomach.

He gawked at her. Mouth open. *Surprised.*

Rio pulled back from their embrace. "What happened?"

"I killed her," she mumbled. "She dragged me to the factory, and I killed her."

"Violet—"

But something riled when Jack said her name. She nudged away from Rio and stalked up to Jack. Picked up her pace, and with a last burst of energy, tackled him to the ground.

Cold mud sprayed. Rio shrieked her name. Jack blew out a breath.

Violet reared her fist back, the other hand holding Gwen's dagger to his neck.

"I should kill you," she seethed. "For playing their game, and *now* you decided to do something about it?"

Jack snapped his mouth shut.

Tears streamed down her face. Violet choked on a sob. "Tell me you never ate them."

"I never, not once, had any of it. I wasn't allowed. Hospurin was to be my...initiation. I was not looking forward to it," he said quickly, grunting under her. She didn't give a shit that his fresh wounds must ache. "I didn't truly gain their trust until you were dragged in by stupid plans I suggested. Like I told you—I didn't think they would actually *work*." He wrinkled his nose, voice softening. "They were so blinded by their power that they didn't think failure could ever touch them."

His words echoed around. She sucked in a frustrated breath, willing him to see the way she *wanted* to hate him, but failed at convincing herself.

His gaze was too piercing, too knowing, for her false revulsion to be believable.

She placed the bricks high on the wall of her emotions, but it knocked down at the frown on his face. Metal went up, plastered together with steel nails, but it melted with the sadness in his eyes. Concrete poured, slicked over, and dried, but it crumbled when his throat bobbed at her dagger.

When he didn't fight her.

Let her take it all out on him.

A steadiness settled over her. Her mixed emotions about Jack, the teeming river she could never sail, eased its waves and she understood. Understood that part of him. The one that didn't regret but learned and accepted his defeat.

She had no right to hate him for the city. She had every right to hate him for Reed. For dragging Reed into his business and, in turn, taking him away from her.

But the word *hate* passed through her mind like a cloud, and it brought no emotions along with it. Eventually, as time worked its magic, the hate fizzled out. Perhaps that was her lesson in Wrath. All that energy went into lashing out with unrestrained fury, and in the end, it wasn't even worth it. It didn't solve anything.

So she had no reason to hold on to it.

When she looked at him again—at the Crale blood from his massacre splattered across his face—their messy history blurred.

"I want to punch you so bad," she breathed, fist still clenched.

"Do it," he mumbled.

She gritted her teeth and yelled, throwing her fist down into the mud beside his face.

He didn't flinch, didn't even blink. Ready for whatever she wanted to do to him. His eyes watered as he stared at her, and in it, she saw the pain he'd been through too. He let her into the thick walls of his mind, if only for a moment, to glimpse the realness. That he felt, too, that he suffered, and that while he masked it with annoyed or bored expressions, the pain still clawed at him, at his heart, the same way it did hers.

Violet's lip trembled.

They stared at each other, unspoken words of misery within their gazes. Surrounded by the terrors of sin, she could imagine the strings knotted prettily around each bone of her spine, her shoulders, her arms, and they extended to the hands of a puppeteer.

The Worldbreaker.

Little puppets in a massive, violent, and deadly play.

She couldn't envision him, but she imagined him looking down at a board of seven worlds and flicking pieces off, scorching land when it was ruined, and laughing when candidates thought it would be easy. That they could win.

"I don't want to be a game," she breathed. A tear slipped down her cheek and onto his face.

"I know," Jack mumbled.

"I don't want *them* to be a game either."

"I know."

"But it won't stop," she whispered.

"No, it won't."

A sob broke through her. She clutched the mud at the side of his head, reveling in the pain of the cold—something tangible that she could understand.

Jack's hand wrapped her elbow, tugging with a nod, and Violet willingly collapsed into his chest.

"Why," she sobbed. "Why-why-why-why...."

His hands hesitantly came around her back and clutched her tightly. "There will never be an answer for why. That is the reason it hurts so much."

None of their suffering was linear, but they suffered all the same.

"Time is not a friend," said Jack. "I didn't have it on my side. I am sorry."

Rio coughed, "It's not your fault. We wouldn't be here without you."

Jack's voice wavered, but he patted Violet's back. "We have to go."

Rio's hands wrapped her shoulders and helped haul her up. Amity poured between as they glanced around, eyes watery, at the abandoned Farm. Violet stepped away, wiping her face.

"The Inaj tribe used your friend's map to plan something. And I also have to finish my work." Jack looked to the ground where a long rope stretched to the estate, then the factory, and then to the front gates.

So they walked. They followed the Inaj as they passed through the Farm entrance gates and were soon on the dirt road leading to the nearest Crale town.

The Inaj tribe was much bigger than she thought—that, or they rounded up nearby tribes too. The latter was probably likely. They rode on the backs of dorelk, herding the town Crale away, while others gave blankets to the newly freed. Some Crale had brought their trucks and piled the pregnant Inaj and children into the back.

"There are Crale who wanted to see the Farm burn," explained Jack. "Destroyed. They never ate the meat, or anything like that. There just weren't enough of them to ever do something. And turning against the Farm meant death. An army was always needed to bring it down."

The herded Crale were clearly not sympathizers. They sat on the curbs guarded by tribe Inaj.

"This town will hold the freed Inaj for the time being until resettlement procedures can be paved out. Although, they've had plans for how they would adapt the victims back into the real world. It will be a difficult process, but the leader of one of the tribes—Nahele—is smart. Dedicated. He was one of the guards infiltrating."

A blanket was passed to Violet. Rio helped wrap it around her. All the cuts, the bruises that would arise tomorrow, felt minor compared to the crowd of confusion and anguish. The trauma would take decades, if not centuries, to recover from. Her cuts would take only days.

No matter how much she wanted to blame the Farm on Stradinth, his family, or all of the Crale for perpetrating this horror, in the grand scheme they only participated in it. But they did not create it. They—the candidates—did not create this horror, either. The Worldbreaker did. Whoever he was.

Nahele—the tribal leader who had turned her over—found his moment. Bloodied, yet walking proud, he clasped forearms with Jack. They spoke in hushed tones and by the end, Jack had a small smile on his face. "May you find peace, Nahele."

A backpack was handed to Nahele by another Inaj—not just *any* backpack, but Violet's. "This must be yours. We retrieved it from her home." Nahele turned to Violet. She took a small step back, but he held his hands out. "I am deeply sorry for the loss of Gwen."

Tribal Inaj turned and watched her cautiously. Jack, however, calmly took the pack for her and shifted to the side.

She lifted her chin. "I want you to honor her, the way you do your lands. I want you to never forget her, because if it weren't for her, you wouldn't have had me as leverage, and then you wouldn't be here. If it weren't for *her*, then the Crale would be celebrating Hospurin without a care in the world. So all of you—" Violet turned to them. "Don't you dare forget Gwen of Follin Peak. Remember her, honor her, for you would not be here without her."

Nahele nodded. "Her resting spot has been marked and a shrine will honor her for the many years to come."

"Good," said Violet. "Great." She held up the dagger. "I don't care if this is some special Inaj weapon—I am keeping it."

"It has already been yours, *agia*."

Violet stiffened but only said, "Take back your land." She reached up to her ear and touched the silver coil. "And heal."

He looked at her, with all seriousness. "Do not forget who the bigger enemy is."

"Now." Jack pulled a box of matches from his pocket and turned to where the rope ended. He lit the match and handed it to Nahele. "If you want—"

Navee stomped through the crowd, snatched the match, and threw it at the rope. She hissed a string of curses in Inaji as the rope burned. The fire stretched. Curved through cages, and soon the candidate's barn burned.

Then, with a rocking boom, the royal estate exploded.

"Might have doused that one a little extra," muttered Jack.

The factory, and all surrounding buildings, smoldered until the Farm scorched the night and its reign ended.

Jack stepped up next to her, hands in his pocket.

"Is that burnt enough for you?" he asked.

She turned to him, and he to her.

"Could have been better," she shrugged. "You could have—"

A thunderous reverberation shook the ground beneath them. Pockets of detonations ricocheted off of Srax Mountain in the distance, and boulders rolled below, slamming into cages, into the Farm, obliterating it.

"That wasn't me," Jack said sheepishly. "The tribe dug out mines and planted them on the mountain."

Rio whistled. "That's smart."

"Thank you," said Nahele. "Come, Navee, there is work to be done."

Navee first gathered Rio in a large hug and kissed his cheek. "Good luck on your adventures."

Rio blushed deeply. "Thanks."

"May the next world be better to you and those who live there." Nahele beckoned Navee and they disappeared into the crowd of Inaj.

"Bro." Rio scrubbed at his face. "She's, like, fourteen."

"Just a friend, then," Jack said.

"That didn't seem very friendly," Violet said.

"Did she have a crush on me this whole time?" Rio blinked. "Oh—oh skies, she did all those things…"

"You can stay, Rio," said Jack with a teasing smile. "Violet and I can move on tomorrow."

"I'm good. I'm okay. That is not necessary."

"How are we moving on? None of us have the…" Violet trailed off as Jack drew an Iris from his pack. "How?"

"The first time I was with her, she sort of slapped the gluttony out of me. It felt as if…if I didn't keep eating or consuming, it would be painful or glorious. There was a bittersweet feeling to it—like I would reach a high if I kept going, no matter how uncomfortable I grew."

He sighed. "I don't think she realized what she was doing, stopping me, because I felt that click in the world. So when the family would have dinners and I wasn't allowed to eat with them, I would have different servants bring me plates of food and I would force myself to go back into the sin—but with a locked door and all that. The servants knew what I was doing. The second time, I took one step out of the room, ready to ravage whatever was in the kitchen, and a big, burly servant pinned me down until I managed

to fight it. The third time was just as hard, but they were there…
helping me.

"You know, that's how it started—a dinner between the Inaj
and the Crale. The Sin was so new that it was seen as a disease. A
crazed disease. When the Crale consumed all the food, without the
respect like the Inaj have for eating only what was necessary and
not wasting anything, the Crale turned on the Inaj at the table and
tossed them in the hearth. Then ate them." He swallowed. "That
was how it all began."

Rio frowned. "The Stradinths were committing the sin all
along, with waste and such, not just the crazed overeating part."

"Yes," Jack said softly.

"You weren't actually sick when Stradinth had gone for his ride,
were you?" Violet muttered.

"No." He gripped the Iris—hard. "I went once and…it
reminded me of too much."

There was pain in his voice; Violet could see how it hurt for
him to talk about it. Maybe when he was ready, he would tell her
why. His lip even trembled for a second and she watched him take
a deep breath, chest rising and falling before his finger reached up
to graze his inner arm. Her brows puckered, but she said nothing.

Rio clapped his shoulder. "I think we all need a long bath."

"We have a place to stay. A room. For the night, before we
continue on tomorrow."

"Then let's go," said Violet.

32

SMOKES AND SHIVA

IT WAS A QUAINT, SMALL bedroom with an adjacent bathroom in an inn. Three cots were set up for them with fresh sheets.

"What happened with the other candidates?" asked Violet.

Rio dropped his pack to the floor with a thump. The Inaj servants had apparently kept, and washed, all of their original clothes and packed them for Jack to take when he left.

"When the uprising started and the Inaj burst through the door, everyone scattered." He shrugged. "They were told to go to the town, so they might be here. I'm guessing they went to search for the confiscated Irises."

"There were a couple of candidates in that crowd, Irises in their hands—so they made it out," clarified Jack.

Violet nodded.

"Are you hurt?" Jack turned to her. "May I?"

His eyes were on her head. The gash there.

Consent. Permission.

And to her surprise, she nodded.

"I'll get the dressings," said Rio, glancing to Violet's wrist. It oozed blood, but Kiane's bite never made it deep enough once she hit the capsule.

Together they all piled in the bathroom. Violet stripped her clothes off until she was only in a bra and underwear, and the men didn't let their gazes linger.

"You're going to want this." Jack handed her a small bottle.

"Thanks." She swigged it back, and—

"Shiva?" Her eyes widened. The glorious burning elated her. "How do you have—?"

"Perks of being an ex-City Commander."

She tilted the bottle back. Jack snorted.

They carefully cleaned her wounds—Rio stitching her wrist, Jack dabbing her forehead and then stomach. She winced, but for the most part powered through it. When she was done, they moved on to re-bandaging Jack and his shallow knife wounds.

When they were all bathed and dressed in simple sleeping clothes the Crale owners had left them, they barricaded the door and clambered into their cots. Rio passed out instantly, the bottle of shiva tucked into his arm. She plucked it out and took another swig.

Jack handed her a smoke before placing his own in his mouth. He lit a match, Violet leaning over so he could get hers.

When she inhaled, relaxation eased her back against her pillow. An indulgence.

Tense silence filled the room. In the distance, the Inaj chattered, weeping cries drifted through, mixing with Rio's soft snores.

"Your brother saved the city, you know."

Violet blanched. "What?"

Jack studied her, face unreadable.

"Because you deserve to know I was stupid," he said. "For lying to you, for—I don't know—never helping you. I abused my power and let it get out of control. The night before he was sentenced, I made a dire mistake. Reed stopped the damage before it became too bad, while Arvalo held precious contracts over my head and bombs planted at those locations. It was just like the Crale—I became blind with power and did not notice the one person under my nose who was delivering my downfall to my enemy. Reed willingly walked into a trap. He stopped the gardia wars. He saved the city."

"What?" she whispered. "He did it on purpose?"

"He *is* a good man. And believe it or not, I agree with you. He should never have been a part of my game. You aren't alone in your regret."

"The whole South hates you because of…what Arvalo did?"

"So let them hate me," he said. "My actions were blind. I had too much power, and I was young still, but I had glorious ambition. But I caused a war that went wrong. So they are right to hate me. I never deserved their respect."

Violet let his words play through her head. It was a sudden admission, yes, but he was stepping into the giant gray area that existed in their relationship. And he was holding his hand out for her to join him.

Jack watched her for a moment, eyes following her skin—her scars, her cuts, her bandages. They dipped to the bullet scar on her shoulder.

"I remember that night," Jack muttered.

"I remember getting shot as well, funny thing," Violet snipped.

"You weren't supposed to; if anything, your brother had reported you being extra difficult."

"And the others they shot?" A brow raised. "Were they being difficult?"

He said nothing.

"Why did you do…what you did?"

A loaded question. She saw the weight of it sit on his shoulders. He stared at his smoke, at the burning end of it, before he took it to his lips and inhaled.

"My brother, Lucien, and I lived a difficult life before it all, and the gardia was an easy way to make quick money. If you were loyal enough, and proved it, you could rise up quickly. I studied it all. I watched people, followed them, learned how the business worked, both the bad and good, and then I joined.

"It became easy to rise. I was always very good with people, so I charmed my way through the ranks and proved I was an intelligent asset and that I could do the dirty jobs. My hands are not clean."

"We know that."

"Calesal is a city built on blood, Violet." His eyes narrowed. "You know the harshness of it. But outside of the walls, it is worse." He swallowed some words and said others, "I commanded trade and commerce, so I knew what existed beyond."

"What was that?"

"Slavery," he whispered. "All of the people outside of the walls, but within our country's borders, are indentured to the city. Their pay is keeping their life. They work the fields, mine plasma, fish at sea…." His voice wavered. "It's all for the city, and no one but the government has any idea about it. And who would believe me if I said something? No one leaves the wall. For all they know, nothing else could exist.

"So I wanted to do something about it, but I got too wrapped up in the illegal business and the politics, and I thought starting a war would get me where I needed to be and begin the changes we needed to make. By the time your brother joined, I was making awful decisions and fighting against Arvalo all of the time. Instead of seeing the better, the power of what I had blinded me." He sighed. "I know how people talk about me—but what am I supposed to say? That I'm actually good? I don't even believe that about myself. The gossip morphed throughout the city, and the South suffers the most when things go to shit in the North or the Mid. So naturally, the South hates me, but like I said, I'd rather they hate me as the bad person that I am than love me for the person I am not."

"You're talking about Arvalo," she breathed.

"All that he shows the city is so *curated*. Perfect. They all think he is going to improve everything, when in reality, he just wants the throne." He took another drag. "I was the only person he feared. I tried to challenge him so many times because he took the wars and exploited them for all the violence it gave, and then threw a lot of the blame on me. Those bodies hanging on the bridge? Those were *my* men, sacked by Arvalo one night. Anything with initials? I never did that, but I'm not going to waste my time convincing people that that makes me a good person all of a sudden. I did *othe*r bad things. And the initial shit was stupid." He pinned her a knowing look. "I'm egotistical, god-like, even, but I don't need to sign my name for people to know my handiwork."

"Yeah, very valiant of you to say." She swigged the shiva. "Jack Marin, a man of many faces…." She frowned. "Are you okay, after…her?"

He blinked. "Why?"

"We all have our traumas…" she muttered. "Just because they're different doesn't mean one is worse than the other."

"Do you care about my traumas?" he smirked.

"No—well, yes. I care that you take care of them and not load it on Rio or me," she said defensively.

"Mhmmmm."

"I'm serious."

"Sure."

"Jack." She rolled her eyes.

"I'm okay," he said. "With her. I think. I certainly hated her and wanted nothing to do with her, but sacrifices come with survival, and in that moment, that was the decision I had to make. It will take time to get over it, but all in all, she was in love with me, I think, skies know why." He rubbed a hand over his face. "Everyone listened or was wary of her, so I wasn't harmed or touched, other than when I didn't give information about you."

She nodded. "I get it."

They paused to pass the drink, Jack bringing it to his lips and sighing deeply. A sigh that came from something that was still broken, but healing.

Just like her.

"You're not weak."

She glanced at him. "What?"

He was looking up at the ceiling. He took another drag of his smoke. "You're not weak," he said matter-of-factly.

"Why are you bringing that up?"

"Because you suffer through what you are dealt with in life, but the fact you are here, fighting, rather reluctantly at times, tells me you are not weak." He settled his other hand across his bare stomach. Violet caught the flash of a tattoo on his arm. "For some people, just staying alive is hard enough. Wanting to *be* alive is hard enough. None of that makes you weak. It makes you human. And an incredibly strong one at that."

Violet looked down, fingered the bandages on her wrist.

Jack was looking at it when she glanced back at him. "What was in there?"

"Nothing."

"She bit it out." His jaw hardened. "You *let* her bite it out."

"I didn't want it anymore."

"What was it?"

Her eyes burned. "Death. The Sins doctor gave it to me."

"So you made your decision?"

"For what?"

"To stay," he breathed.

"But what if I change my mind?"

His green eyes flashed. "Then I rip apart whatever damn hell you go to and drag you right back here."

She glowered.

"Don't you see what you've done? How far you've come? I know pain, believe me, I've been there before, where all you want is for it to be gone and you will do *anything* to have that happen, but it doesn't solve anything. Is your problem your pain? Your answer is to deal with it. To learn. To grow. Death is a fool's choice. It is a temporary fix, but you know what won't be temporary? When Reed learns you came after him, but you gave up on yourself and left him. Hm? When Jelan watches your tracker blink out, and she sees you didn't make it—is that who you want to be?"

The fact he mentioned Jelan had her stunned.

"He's right, Vi," mumbled Rio.

They both looked over to him to see his face buried in his pillow, one eye on them.

The tears were hot as they flowed down her cheeks. "I gave it to her because I wanted to live. So—so badly, because all she wanted was me dead, and I kept thinking no—*no*, I don't want that."

She sobbed. Jack stabbed out his smoke and took hers.

"May I?" he breathed, reaching for her.

Through the tears, she nodded, and his warm arms gathered her up, shifting so she curled on his lap, head against his chest.

She broke. And while her scream had released frustration and anger, her tears freed her heartache. For losing herself and then the painful path it took to find her way again.

"It's okay," he said, softly. "Let it out. I've got you."

And she did. She sobbed, tears falling down his chest. He was so warm, and it was beyond her that Jack Marin could be comforting, but skies, did she feel comforted. And safe. Very, very safe.

A huff sounded.

"Come on, Rio," Jack said.

The bed dipped, and another set of arms wrapped around her. Rio leaned into their sides, smelling of wood and linens. Both boys held her tight, Jack's head atop hers, Rio's head in her shoulder. Wetness stained her shirt, and she realized Rio was crying, and that made her cry more, so they cried together, wrapped in each other's arms, letting go of the horrors that had befallen them. Three lost souls, bruised but not broken.

"Tell me about her," Jack said. "This Gwen."

As Rio nuzzled her shoulder, Violet met Jack's gaze, that green blazing just a bit brighter than she'd seen it before, and she let herself fall into the warm comfort of it and her memories.

And so she did.

❃❃❃

"Well, that is quite a sight."

Violet scrunched her face. Blinked her eyes open. The morning sun slithered through the small windows. The sheets were a tangle around her—

Her cheeks heated as she'd realized Jack's arm was slung around her waist, gripping her stomach gently, soft breath on the nape of her neck.

Rio lounged back on his forearm, hair wet from another bath as he regarded them with amusement. He lifted his brows while popping the rest of his bread into his mouth.

She bolted up and scurried out of bed.

Jack's hand reached, as if protesting her pulling away, but then he opened his eyes and took one look at her, then Rio, who dramatically sipped his water, and a sheepish smile graced Jack's face. With a husky morning voice, he stretched his arms and said, "Good morning, everyone. How did we sleep?"

"Dandy," Rio returned, waving his hand to his lone bed. "All of the woodland creatures outside saw me shivering, lonely as I was, and then joined me for a cuddle session as you two were busy with—*that*."

Jack grinned.

Violet's brows lowered. "I must have fallen asleep."

"Drooling on my arm." Jack tousled his hair. "It was kind of cute."

She rubbed at her face, avoiding his gaze, but realizing how *rested* she finally felt. She had not woken once and had slept dreamlessly.

"You're always invited, Rio," Jack mused. "You can be the little spoon."

"The *littlest* spoon. As great as my ass is, I know how it is for men in the morning...and I am good on that, thank you very much."

A blush crept to Violet's cheeks. Both Jack and Rio noticed, and they exchanged grins.

"Whatever." She threw her hands up and stood. "I slept *great*. Finally. If you boys care. And I was warm thanks to the furnace that is Jack's body."

"Well, get ready," said Rio. "I want out of this world. I want to *eat* properly."

They slipped out of the inn with mumbled goodbyes to the kind Crale couple, and then took back pathways to avoid most of the Inaj. They had all agreed that a quiet exit would be best.

The trek was only a mile or so into the forest away from both the destroyed Srax Mountain and the resolute Follin.

"There," Jack said, pointing between the trees.

The plinth gleamed underneath the watery sunlight. They hurried to it, Jack pulling the Iris from his back pocket.

"When I came from Wrath, it was just me," Rio said, glancing between the Iris and the notch. "I'm not sure...."

Violet exchanged a sheepish look with Jack, who said, "Well, Violet kicked me away at the last second in Wrath, so I wouldn't have any idea."

Rio snorted, and turned to her, wide-eyed. "Really?"

"His Wrath-self was on a rampage; I had no choice."

Jack pulled up his sweater to reveal his burnt forearm. "Hm." He pushed it back down. "No damage done."

"Don't get on Vi's bad side."

"Rule number one." Jack smirked.

"Well, let's hope this works. All hands on the Iris," said Violet.

Rio nodded, breath fogging. "I'm so done with this skivvin' world. I'm ready when you are."

Jack hovered it over the podium. "The third adventure awaits us."

Both boys looked to Violet, who hesitated. She knew why she did. She glanced down to the turquoise dagger at her belt.

Win, agia.

Yes, mia, she thought back.

Violet stepped up to the podium, grabbed the Iris below Rio's hand, and nodded.

"Here we go," Rio muttered. "Let's find each other, please. I don't want to be alone."

"I've grown rather fond of you, Rio," drawled Jack.

"Can't say the same...yet," said Rio. "But I slightly trust you with my life."

"I can step back if you two want to make out," snapped Violet.

Jack's eyes lightened. "Sure, go ahead, give us some space."

"Later, Jackie," smiled Rio.

One by one, they each put their hand on the smooth metal.

The world slowed to the beat of her heart.

Jack plummeted the Iris down into its awaiting notch. A bright light blasted, followed by an alien warmth, and the world of Gluttony faded away. She felt that foreign tug on her navel, and clutched the Iris for dear life. Soon the light fell into darkness, and Violet fell with it.

33

Hira

JELAN

As Jelan was busy fussing around with one of the neutralizing components in a plasmic container, the detailed instruction book in one hand, a sharp bang within the penthouse jolted her.

"Finally!"

She recognized Lucien's voice and set the book down, marking her page before she rushed toward the noise.

Nearly nine weeks had passed since she moved in, and she had to admit her decision was one of the best. She was left to her lonesome most days, which she preferred, and the penthouse remained empty save for some unfamiliar voices Jelan didn't want to meet. Tivra had made an appearance every now and then, glowing and rubbing her belly. Just last week Lucien had gone to her baby shower and arrived home with bits of confetti in his hair.

He had respected her work and her space. All of the components within her lab required reading manual after manual, and she was now just wrapping up the last of it. Her experiments were sketched out and plastered to the walls, the details on notes posted at different machines, and a ridiculous amount of coffee mugs piled onto a small end table.

No one bothered her.

It truly was the perfect life.

But now, she was restless. She searched through the halls, high and low, wondering what she was even being nosy about.

A ruffling paper. A crunch of another. She dragged closer to the ajar door that was a couple of turns away from the lab—*her* lab.

"*I'm going to kill him when he gets back,*" Lucien grunted, followed by another thud. "I *knew* he was waiting for that girl—"

"It seems they have another friend, too," remarked an unfamiliar voice. A woman. Jelan paused, eyes widening, hoping she wasn't interrupting something…

But *that girl* caught her curiosity. Her gut told her it was Violet. It was normally Violet with that kind of tone.

Apparently, Jack too.

She glimpsed into the room. A wide office, towering shelves of papers and books, a conference table, and a giant wooden desk that Lucien sat behind. He took off his reading glasses to rub at his eyes in both relief and frustration.

Before one of the desks sat an older woman, legs crossed in dark pants and a long-sleeved black leather shirt. Interesting choice for an Elite. Her gray-white hair was buzzed at the base, while the top half was a tad longer. Ears pierced with silver, skin a lighter shade than Jelan's, and an aura that held both power and…death.

Jelan swallowed.

The woman whirled in her chair, observed nearly everything about Jelan by the dart of her brown eyes, and scoffed, "It's not good to sneak up on a commander and an assassin."

Jelan's eyes bugged. "I'm—I'm sorry—"

Lucien's frustration ebbed into a smile. He held a hand up. "No apologies are necessary. Lyla, this is Jelan, our Plastech engineer. Jelan, this is Lyla. Assassin, spy, general—all that."

"Nothing important." Lyla beckoned Jelan in. "Well, don't lurk. I'm sure you heard Lucien's tantrum."

Jelan entered and closed her mouth, choosing not to say anything.

Lucien narrowed his eyes at Lyla, then shifted back to Jelan. "We have news. From the Sins Screen." He motioned to a plascreen planted at the end of the conference table. The names listed in each of the seven columns had been amended to show only certain ones.

"Jack, Violet, and one other fellow named—" Lucien put on his glasses to look at a paper. "Rio Gaverra. They all transferred at the same time to the third world."

Jelan looked toward the screen and squinted.

Violet Sutton.

Jack Marin.

Rio Gaverra.

A smile twitched at her lips. "Finally."

"Jack and Sutton had been in there for over two months. And within the last twenty-four hours, their trackers, including Rio's, had been blinking red. I'm not sure what shit they got into but—"

Lyla gestured to the window.

Beyond it, cries arose. Shouted from the North's balconies, the Mid sector.

Celebratory cries.

"Gardia god," mumbled Jelan, trying not to think about the fact she stood in Jack Marin's office.

Lyla heard her. "Gardia god? Oh skies, Jack will eat that right up if he hears it."

Lucien snorted. "Don't feed his ego with that phrase."

"I always forget how popular he is here," said Jelan as the cries seemed to grow louder.

"You are from the South," Lyla said.

Not a question. Jelan turned to the assassin-spy-general. "Yes."

"I am, too," Lyla continued. "The South doesn't need a god. It's why there are none for them. Only the skies."

"Why do you say that?"

"Here, the Elites celebrate each other because of the riches they bring. Jack brought that, as well as established his name long before he was ever commander. He sat in on business meetings to broker deals, bought up land and developed on it. Proved his worth, more or less."

"All these cries are for his past," clarified Lucien. "Because he benefited the North and the Mid, and when that happens, the South suffers. No Commander has ever looked out for the South."

Jelan could wholeheartedly agree with that. If water poured into the North and the Mid, the South received the ending trickle to disperse within sprawling land taking up more than a quarter of the citadel.

"What's wrong with the South is that it is regarded as detached from the city. Another city in itself. It runs differently, burns fast, holds stubborn people—"

Jelan held up her hand. "I don't need you to convince me that you actually care."

Lyla smiled at that. "I felt the same way you did."

"How did you get out?"

"That's the thing, Jelan," said Lyla. "People think it is about 'getting out', when in reality, it is our home. Our place. Regardless of the poverty or not. This city is built to favor the rich, and the South suffers, so they hate. But they also crave more because they are neglected. So 'getting out' is an achievement in your eyes. You managed it, but not everyone will. So how do we fix that? How do we make it so no one actually wants to leave? How do we make it enough?"

"By getting rid of the Elites."

"But see, that's where the money is. We can't get rid of the money. We have to sort it. But no one wants an equal society with equal pay and equal this and equal that. It's boring, and eventually it fails. Eventually people get tired of it, and then the cycle begins all over again." Lyla fixed her with a knowing glare. "You know the answer. So here's the question again: How do we make it enough?"

Jelan blinked at her, uncomfortable at the thought she was even included in such a discussion. How would she know? She kept her head down, went about her day, enjoyed playing with plasma and then slept within the city, caged by the—

"Wall," she muttered. "You take down the wall."

Lucien smiled.

Lyla leaned back. "The very wall that constricted us in the first place. Forced us to believe that what was within was all that existed. So the opportunities became limited. The money poorly distributed. Certain classes benefitted; others did not. And now, some odd centuries since it has been built, we are here. Separated. Staring at each end of the city with hate. The Elites look past the wall, and the Southers do too. They all want more, but were not given it. And then here's the other question; what would happen if the wall came down and the country was open for us to roam free?"

Free was not a word Jelan heard often. The idea of it drove Violet insane. It did many people. Because freedom *was* associated with tearing down the wall. No one wanted to live in a cage.

"Um…" started Jelan. "Well, more jobs."

"Correct."

"New cities."

"Also correct."

"We'd probably have relations with other countries."

"True," said Lucien.

"And… and…I don't know. I'm sure a lot of people would feel better."

Lyla turned to Lucien. "I *told* you it had to do with morale as well."

"But you also think of the wall as a cage, Lyla, and not as a potential form of protection." Lucien leaned on the desk.

"Protection?" asked Jelan.

"It's more of a cage than anything," said Lucien. "But I have always wondered if it was built to protect us. Not cage us."

"From what? There are people outside the wall. The farmers, the mines, the fish, the—"

Lyla coughed, pausing Jelan.

Lucien's jaw ticked, but he said nothing. Jelan tucked that information away. *Something* outside the wall triggered him. Best not to do that in his home.

"Tearing down the wall is a goal that is very, very far in the future," said Lyla. "For now, we have to focus on the threats within it, at least."

"Arvalo," said Lucien, looking down at his papers, still agitated by something. He scribbled on a note.

Jelan's cheeks heated, hating how she made him feel that way. She didn't know she would say the wrong thing...whatever that was. Farmers? Mines? Fish? What in the world would promote a reaction like that?

"We need to get to him. My last spy—nearly four months ago—wound up dead. I don't know what he is planning, but the locks are tight within his own gardia," Lyla huffed.

It was then that Jelan noticed the slight dark circles under Lucien's eyes as he looked down to the papers. He shuffled through them, releasing a heavy sigh. And his support, the one he had built it all with, was gone, in those worlds and frolicking with Violet.

Lyla frowned, noticing it too. "I can call the council...."

"Yes, for Thursday," sighed Lucien. "I need this plan to work. I need my men to stop finding the bodies of Plastechs."

"And how are you going to get to Arvalo?" Jelan asked. "I'm sure he doesn't want to have a casual lunch with you."

Lyla snorted.

Lucien folded his hands. "Well, Jelan, we are going to a party. One he is hosting."

We. She didn't miss that.

"How will you get him to talk?"

A smile. He slid a ripped piece of paper across the desk. "We will need someone with more...expertise. Pay her a visit."

Jelan blinked at the note. "For what?"

"It's written there along with the address."

She grabbed the paper and her eyes scanned across the neat scrawl. "The one to take—?"

"Go," was all Lucien said as he nodded to the door.

"Goodbye, Jelan!" called Lyla.

Jelan shut her mouth at the dismissal. With narrowed eyes, she turned out of the office, pressed the elevator button for the ground floor, and stepped in.

There was no car waiting for her at the bottom. In fact, the driver was lounging at a café across the street with a newspaper splayed out in one hand and a cup of coffee in the other.

Her fingers rubbed on a harder paper, and she flipped the note. A very large bill was taped to the back, along with another scrawl.

No rides this time. Stay humble. And inconspicuous.

Wrinkling her nose, Jelan shoved the note in her pocket.

Her eyes stayed on the sidewalk until she reached the nearest Glide stop and used the last of the money loaded on her ticket to the lower Mid. The place he was sending her to was an unusual neighborhood—one she wasn't too familiar with—but one populated with a *lot* of gardens, greenhouses, smoke shops, and strange collections of medicines not filtered through pharmacies.

Jelan ignored the lingering gazes as the train pulled up and she took her seat. This train was one of the cleanest she'd ever seen, *sparkling* even, and she hated the feeling that her Southern roots dirtied it, even though her clothes were spotless, and she'd showered. But the stares were there, and she felt them like burns along her skin. She shoved her hands between her thighs and pointedly looked out the window.

Medicine was one of the top industries in the city next to Plastech. The Commander of Health, Alexia Javez, normally had her face smacked on the news for pioneering a new cure like the reverse of Corusgates, or working with labs to develop some new preventative for a disease. Beyond that, skin could be grafted and new faces could be created. People could become taller, hair could grow different colors, even bones could be re-shaped by some invasive surgery that might allow for wider hips, stronger legs, or broader shoulders.

That was mostly available in the North. Why such surgeries or changes were used was beyond Jelan, although she sometimes wondered if her burn scars could be faded. Then maybe it wouldn't be the first thing people noticed about her.

She was sure if she worked for Lucien for a while, she might be able to ask him about grafting new, smooth hands…

Her stomach sank and she looked down.

She let the thought taper at the back of her mind, and then pass. It was only a dream. But was it a dream for pretty hands? Or a dream to forget what had caused the scars?

It was two more train switches and a thirty-minute walk before Jelan was assaulted by the mixed smell of sweet florals and musky tobacco. A haze fell, fumed from steady smokestacks about the townhomes and small window shops. The sidewalk was riddled with moss between the cracks, and there was a constant stream of water along the curb, muddied with cars or plasbikes.

There were few people on the street, and they looked no different from any other Souther. She wondered how many drugs were funneling through the place. She also wondered if any of Jack's underground gardia was involved. Was that how Lucien knew where to go? Was Jelan supposed to pick up an order that might trash half the party and get Arvalo to spill his darkest secrets?

Doubt filled her, and her heart thumped with anxiety.

Unknown territory, unknown people, unknown medicine, unknown world.

She stopped in front of a shop with a sign that hung two loops' difference between one side and the other.

Indira Apothecary.

A bell chimed when she stepped into the cedar and sandalwood smelling shop. Jelan's head buzzed with memories—her mother praying before a eucalyptus candle, harvesting herbs from the neighbor's box garden, the smell of chives and eggs in the morning. In the rare moments where Jelan had *these* kind of remembrances of her mother, she tucked those memories away and reminded herself to write about it later.

"Are you fucking serious?" a deep, feminine voice snapped. "We're about to skivvin' close!"

Jelan's eyes widened. Not the *hello* she was expecting.

Thuds and bumps sounded from the back. Jelan turned toward the door, ready to slip out, when a deep-brown-skinned, plump woman about the same age as her, jammed through the towering shelves packed with labeled glasses and sidled to the front counter.

"Can I help you?" the woman asked, raising a bushy dark brow. Her black hair fell to her waist in a braid, while small bangs wrapped her ears along with a scarf atop her head.

Jelan blinked, opened her mouth, then pulled out the note from her pocket.

"I need *the one to take a man's pants and ego off.*" Her cheeks burned. *Skies*, she knew what it said, but it sounded *worse* aloud.

The woman straightened, balked at her, and Jelan had one hand on the doorknob when she said, "As I live and breathe, I thought I would be done with that stupid, *stupid* man after he went into the game." She pushed back her frazzled bangs. "Guess I'm destined to be plagued by him."

"I'm just supposed to pick something up," mumbled Jelan.

"Lock the door," the woman snapped. "And flip the sign. I'm fucking closed."

Jelan opened the door—

"No, you're *staying* if the god-commander bids it. Just lock the door from any other skivs."

She let the door shut again, and with a pounding heart, flipped the lock and then the sign.

The woman ducked underneath the counter, her supple, large figure maneuvering through the tables and stocks like water. While Jelan was very aware of her bodily space to avoid knocking any of the jars over, she'd place a large bet that this woman could navigate the shop with her eyes closed and wasted off shiva without grazing glass.

The woman shooed Jelan aside and yanked on a cord. A curtain shot down from the top of the door.

"You are?" She turned.

"Jelan."

"Hira."

Jelan shuffled awkwardly.

Hira looked her up and down. "Who sent you?"

"The brother."

"Skivvin' Lucien," she sighed and moved back to the counter, lifting the board atop it. She gestured Jelan through. "Let's get this over with."

"What is *this*?"

Hira's dark brows drew together. "You don't know what you're here for?"

"I was only given the assignment to come here." She held up the note. "And say this stupid thing. Is this what a poison is called?"

"Poison?" Hira blinked, her lips twitching. "Skies, you are new. What do you do for the commander?"

"I—I—Well, to be honest, I don't really know. I like Plastech engineering." Jelan shrugged. "They gave me a whole lab to work in."

Jelan didn't know why she was explaining more than she usually would—talking *more* than her one-word and reserved responses. Those were clipped, they told people to back off on information on her, but with Hira, her general energy felt not comforting but endearing. And not in the I-want-you-to-like-me way.

It reminded her a bit of Violet. The very *skiv-off* attitude that Jelan was drawn toward.

Hira scoffed, "You're very much Lucien's type."

"Excuse me?"

"Listen, I've been dealing with those two brothers, and all the other shitheads who work for them, for five years now. I know when they have an eye on someone." She rubbed at her lip. "That *poison's* name—which is a sedative drug—were Jack's words when he witnessed it for the first time. It worked so well that the people he was interrogating stripped their clothes and quite literally laid everything bare to him." She walked through the counter and motioned for Jelan to follow. "Now, let's go. It won't take long.

I have dinner with the chiseled man across the street and I *will* poison you if I miss it."

A small smile stretched across Jelan's lips, and Hira seemed to relax her shoulders. The woman probably expected Jelan to run the other way.

Jelan followed Hira through the labyrinth of shelves as high as the ceiling. There was a total lack of organization, save for the herbs, powders, spices and other things alphabetized. Beyond that, things were strewn everywhere, powders leaked from bottles, herbs hung dry from lines and shed to the wooden floor.

Hira bustled through a back door, revealing a quaint workspace. A desk was lined against dusty windows that overlooked a small garden and a glass greenhouse the size of the shop, if not more, all in the backyard. Two armchairs were squashed next to each other, one piled high with journals and books. Papers scattered about. Candles burned.

Jelan's hands tingled. This entire place was one damned fire hazard.

Hira moved to a row of cabinets on the far wall while untangling a key from her belt.

"You're letting me watch where you keep them?"

"Lucien's way of letting me know to trust you was that little sentence." She undid four locks, all with different keys, and the cabinet creaked open. Her hand reached within. "You can sit. Move the books if you want."

Jelan did just that before sitting at the edge, back straight. "So, who is Indira?"

"My cunt of a grandmother."

"Oh," said Jelan, coughing. "Do you work this place by yourself?"

"My mother is around, sometimes, but she usually has her skirts up with physicians in the North. It's how the Marin brothers learned of this place."

"You seem fond of your family."

Hira pulled out her ingredients and nudged the cabinet with her hip. "Hate them. Hate everyone, really."

Jelan didn't blame her.

They sat in silence. The only sounds were the clinking of glasses, Hira muttering under her breath as she measured gray-ash powders, and then the steady bubble of a beaker over a burner.

"So did they hire you, or were you forced to work?" Hira glanced over her shoulder. "Or give you a shitload of money?"

"All of them?" answered Jelan.

"I'm bored with my own thoughts most of the day. Care to explain?"

"Not particularly."

"Did you do something illegal?"

"No, but I guess I am now. Smuggling drugs and whatnot."

"So you *know* someone who did something illegal, and that put you under the gardia watch?"

Jelan bristled slightly at the open mention of gardia. Open for a conversation with a stranger, that was.

"My friend submitted herself to the Sins. She had some... entanglements with Jack through her brother. That stemmed to me eventually."

Hira stiffened, then shook it off. Jelan tabbed that movement to ponder over later.

"Who *doesn't* have entanglements with Jack Marin," huffed Hira. She poured a cerulean liquid into a gaseous container.

"He isn't even in this world anymore, yet he has his impact."

"It will be there for years, maybe even decades."

"You talk like you tolerate him."

Hira carefully rolled out a small sheet of paper, a dried-up, scab-looking thing within. She cut it in half and dropped it into the bottle. It immediately turned green. Then purple. Then finally a deep, dark magenta.

She stoppered it, lit a flame to the edges, and sealed it up with hot wax.

"I have to tolerate him," she said. "Not because I work for him. Sort of. But…" She hesitated. Sighed. "Well, we—my mom and I—were indentured to a couple of higher-up gardia people within Arvalo's command. It was like having a noose around our necks, day and night, only existing to work for them. Five years ago, Jack made a deal with one of the bosses underneath Arvalo and bought us out, then paid for the property and everything so it was in his name. We keep our practice, our land, as long as we are quiet about him and what he did. It took a while to grow used to him, actually, because he had such a reputation." She shrugged. "He then bought out the properties of this whole street, so no one has to move or worry about holding on to their lands."

"You don't think all of it was manipulation to keep you for himself?"

Hira smiled slightly. "Well, my mom was all about it, but of course, I was skeptical. A handsome man like him, with a killing past, suddenly wanting to buy us out? I acted like I was under manipulation because of it, but he just left us alone. For months, if not even a year, we didn't hear anything from him, but every time a bill came, one of his people would ride up, like clockwork, stamp a check on it, and then leave us with a gift basket of meats or rare plants signed by Jack." Hira met Jelan's gaze. "He's honestly one of the strangest people I've ever met. If not loyal. Very loyal. But I live in peace now because of him, so I tolerate them all."

"He has a whole city to get forgiveness from, though," observed Jelan.

"He doesn't care about forgiveness. He only cares that he rights his wrongs. Or at least, that is what he said in his letter before he went in." Another shrug. "I don't fucking know. He laughs at my jokes, so that counts."

Hira handed Jelan the bottle, small enough for her to shove into her satchel.

"Lucien knows what to do with it." Hira turned back toward the door. "It was nice to meet you, Jelan. The only feminine presence I have is my mother, and I'm close to giving her a muting potion. So…thanks. For the conversation."

Jelan nodded with a smile. "You, too, Hira."

"Now, I've got some things to shave." Hira unfastened the back of her apron. "I'll see you around."

When Jelan exited the shop, she was aware of a bounce in her step, a comfort on her shoulders.

For the first time in her life, she finally felt like some of her scattered pieces…

Had slipped into place.

34

THE THIRD SIN

VIOLET SLAMMED STRAIGHT INTO MUD.

The sticky, wet substance assaulted her, filling her nostrils, the lines of her small mouth, and even the ridges of her ears.

Her senses warped just like the last two times. Zapped out, blasted through, and then born anew. She gulped an inhale and nearly gagged at the thick, humid air, but also partially at the mud in her teeth. Violet struggled to her hands and knees, spitting it out and hating the earthy taste that reminded her of mud parties in her childhood yard with a trickling hose and annoying Reed.

The air wasn't hot, but it wasn't cold either. This world felt like walking through a giant water droplet. Sweat immediately glistened on her brows and upper lip.

Alas, the show, the game, continued on.

Through squinted eyes, she drew a semi-clean part of her shirt and wiped her face.

The dull ringing faded in her ears and sounds of the third Sin invaded. Caws of birds, a steady trickle of water, the brush of heady wind through creaking branches, and the occasional slither and slap of something…

Her eyes blasted open.

Gigantic, towering trees flush with green-blue vegetation reached so high the tops blurred above her. Vines as thick as her arms and legs, leaves and branches as thick as tree trunks in Gluttony. Another inhale and she gagged again.

Underneath the earthy nature, a rancid smell loomed like something had been left to rot for an absurdly long time. She tasted it on her tongue, a burning, and when she sniffed the mud, bile rose to her throat. She lifted a hand and watched the green-brown stuff slop off her skin and slap the ground again.

"Skies," she muttered with a prayer.

Not shit. Not shit. Not shit. Please, not shit.

Where was the calm, peaceful world that would grant her a *damn* break? The jungle surrounding her with mangled roots and rolling hills and massive flora did not bring any semblance of relaxation.

She lumbered to her feet and her boots immediately sank into the mud like it had the sand in Wrath. A groan spilled out of her.

The jungle floor was tangled with fauna. It was chaotic, looked annoying to sift through, and Violet wanted to whine at how little she could see.

Because it was all hazed by mist.

The mist itself seemed to move; curling around every living thing in the vicinity. It was so thick she couldn't see more than twenty feet in front of her. She took one step, a shiver running down her spine. How was she supposed to find Rio and Jack in this?

She trudged forward. One boot got stuck, then another, and she growled in frustration.

Skies, she had hoped for something better. Like Sloth. Maybe everything would have been easier in Sloth. It was laziness, right? Yes, that would be nice. The candidates in Sloth must be having a great time—for some reason that thought struck a nerve and a sharp, ice-like feeling pinched the center of her chest. Why was she stuck here when she could have that?

She breathed deeply—there wasn't anything she could do about it, and thinking it over wouldn't help her situation. Violet took one more step, boot squelching—

A low moan sounded behind her, followed by a croaking voice. "Pretty hair." A soft footstep. "I like pretty hair."

Her hands trembled. Heart raced. She turned, stumbling in the mud. A figure—a person—a—she narrowed her eyes. Something.

It stepped out of the gloom, bare feet slapping on a giant tree root. Its scaly arms hung as it lumbered forward, black eyes blinking furiously at her. A person, then…but they didn't look *alive*.

"Pretty hair," the female repeated. "I like pretty hair."

Her stare was so pointed that Violet took a step back. The female's hair was matted into thick locks, unwashed and greasy by years, if not decades, of neglect. As she drew closer, a smell enveloped her, and Violet covered her mouth as bile crawled up her throat. *Skies*, she smelled—

Dead.

The female drew closer, and Violet held up her blade. "Stop."

"Pretty hair. I like pretty hair."

"I'm telling you to stop." Violet's boot sucked into the mud, and she pulled to get it out. "Don't come closer, or I will hurt you."

The female was unfazed. "Pretty hair—"

Violet struggled faster, but her boot was swarmed. She grabbed her calf and yanked as hard as she could, but it wasn't coming out. The female's blackened teeth smiled, and her dirty, chipped fingernails reached toward her—

Violet slashed out her dagger to push her back. The weapon sliced off the female's finger with ease, and black blood sprayed onto the floor. The female paused, looking at Violet and then her finger, and then her head. "I like pretty hair."

"Get back!" Violet slashed again, missing.

Suddenly, the female's face twisted, lines of gritting anger baring her teeth, narrowing her eyes. With speed, she lunged.

The impact unhinged Violet's boot. They flew back. The thing clawed at Violet—no, her hair. She yanked on it, and Violet cried out in pain, her scalp still raw and healing from Kiane's damage. She shoved her hand into the female's throat to push her away.

"Pretty hair," the woman choked. "I want it! Give it to me!"

"Get—" Violet cried again as the the thing pulled. She swung the blade, almost hugging the damned gross body, and jammed the dagger into the spine. "Off!"

The female spasmed on top of her. Violet drew the blade out, the turquoise covered in thick, black blood, and shoved it off her. It coughed, more blood coming up out of her mouth, and Violet could only step back and watch. The damage was done. It was a fatal stab. But the thing did not still and die. No, it spewed out so much blood that it began to ooze out of the ears, nose, and even bulging at its thin, scaly skin until what was once a woman was all but a sunken sack of flesh and bones.

Violet backed up to one of the trees, breathing hard. She gingerly touched her scalp and winced. Her hand came away with blood. She would have to get that disinfected. She took another long, bewildered look at what was once a dead female walking, then took off running.

She ran. Or simply stumbled. Longer than an hour, probably. Moans, like that of the dead zombie thing, followed her. But the mist was too thick to see anything. She kept quiet, dagger out, ignoring the stabbing on her scalp.

She stopped for a moment, skin prickling as the shrieks continued to echo. Vile creatures, and the idea of their hands touching her skin, sent a deep, cold shiver running along her spine, into a roiling ball in her stomach.

And out it came. The feeling she had been trying not to bear. She heaved whatever contents were still in her stomach. Drips of sweat fell off her nose, down to mix with the horrid liquid, and she breathed heavily, hands on her knees.

This was running against the force of nature. So unlike the concrete and brick her palms were molded to, or the large expanse of desert in Wrath, or even the stacked branches and smushed boulders of Gluttony.

This—*this* was hard.

Violet wiped her mouth, noting the exhaustion pressing into her bones. The sheer terror racing through her after the mud-people encounter had her hands shaking, doubting the protection Gwen's blade could give her. It was also the restart of it all. Alone. Zero understanding of her surroundings. She would have to adapt *again*. And then four more times after this.

If she didn't die.

Hand on her blade, Violet squinted into the jungle. Bugs flickered on and off with lights, some the size of her fist, while a wet, scaly animal slithered nearby and under a bed of thick leaves. Violet spotted three tails with red lines flowing down the back and heaved once more.

When she was finally ready to come up, wiping her mouth, she leaned into the ridged, musk-smelling bark of the huge tree trunk and breathed. In and out. The dizziness slowly left her, and the stress of the situation clammed into her shaking hands.

Where was Jack in this world? Rio? She couldn't remember the last time she had been this unsure, this chaotic in her mind—her thoughts running races in her head. What was she supposed to do in a world like this? The sin could only be Greed. Or was it—

A snap of a branch. Violet whipped her head in the direction of the sound.

A figure stood, half-hidden behind a twisting set of vines. Silhouetted by the shadows of the swamp, she couldn't make out the features, but something seemed familiar. A deep *knowing* twisted in her gut.

The figure stared at her, eyes glistening. A blink and a shift in the growing pockets of light through the jungle canopy.

The breath whooshed out of her, until only a word—a name— echoed in the thick air.

"*Reed.*"

His smattering of freckles across his pointy nose greeted her. He stared for a moment as if registering her realness, then a cheeky smile twitched at his lips.

"Little booger," he said.

Hope flung her arms out. An anguished sound left her throat. "Reed. Reed. It's you—" Her smile faltered. "What are you doing here?"

She noticed his clothes—not a speck of mud on them. Her relief faded. Those blue eyes lacked their familiar spark.

He was wearing the exact clothes as he had to the Bloodswearing Ceremony. Dark jeans, plain shirt, and his old leather boots. No backpack—and he was clean?

"Miss me?" His voice had the same lilt; tentative, challenging, and light.

"You're supposed to be in the sixth world," she said, uncertainty pooling in her gut. "What—what are you doing here?"

"I came to find you." He cocked his head. "I missed my little sister. We were inseparable for so long."

Violet gaped. "That's it? That's all you have to say to me?"

Something slithered in her mind, like the three-tailed lizard. Unnatural, dark, deep. It entered into the crevices of her thoughts. And then it slipped underneath a rock.

She trekked forward. Even his shoes were clean of mud, but she stood in it. Covered in it.

He is fine. Why is he fine? Healthy. Happy. Unbothered. Why you—you're struggling.

"I watched you—I screamed your name and you looked at me with *blood* all over your hand—" She hyperventilated. Heat rose in her body. She wanted to hug him, to punch him, to yell at him, to stab him…

Ice pricked her chest. She clenched the dagger.

That slithering gripped her. Lurched her forward.

He is fine. You are not.

"Vi." He smiled.

He is fine.

You are not.

"You don't look well."

"Of *course*, I don't look well." She motioned to herself. "Why would I look well after I came all this way to find you?"

Carefree. He is carefree, while you shoulder all the cares in the world. It tricks you, makes you jealous, enrages you.

"How could you?" she asked, without even knowing her question.

His smile darkened.

Hurt him.

Her breath locked in her throat as she struggled against an intruder in her body. Her mind. The voice was foreign. Dark. But it seeped into her own thoughts.

The sin. The sin. The sin, the sane part of her yelled.

But it was strong and it swarmed her. A delicious cold gripped her chest—an ugly yet satisfying feeling that made her heart race. Even though part of her registered the sin, she craved more of the sensation, wanting to demand justice, wanting what *he* had.

He is standing there. Go get him. He is your brother. He hurt you.

"*No,*" she said to the coiling darkness.

You want it.

It was like two walls colliding in her mind, then seeping into one thought, one process. She couldn't decipher what was right and what was wrong.

A thread of a thousand emotions she didn't have names for pulled taut.

And then snapped.

Anger burst into her veins like red heat, and at the same time, a shadow appeared over her vision. She fought it—skies, she fought it.

It was the sin, but this sin ruptured through her jealousies and laid them bare before her. Her sanity bent toward it.

He left you. You had to watch your last family member fall apart and forget you. He even forgot you. He left you to look happy like that. He has been happy. His whole life has been easier than yours. Mama loved him, Meema loved him, and what did that leave you with? Dirt. Take it. Take it for yourself.

"You left me," Violet snapped. "How could you leave me? And now you're here? Living your best life without a care in the world. Is that what you want to throw in my face?"

"Maybe," he grinned sheepishly. "Are you jealous, little booger? That I was able to escape and you had to live in all that pain?"

"*Skiv.*" She twirled her blade.

"Give in to the feelings, Violet," Reed chuckled and twisted around toward a mishmash of vines. "It feels better when you give in!" He ran into the jungle, in the same way she had chased him for years of her life. With a playful grace, light feet, carefree.

She snarled and chased after him.

How could he say such things—

It's *not* him.

But *she* was the one who was left with nothing. She was the one who stared at the broken pieces of their family after he'd left. She suffered, and he looked happy.

And she just wanted to be happy.

For his whole life, Reed slid past pain while it knocked her down again and again. Why did she have to suffer while he basked in the freedom she had always wanted?

Take it. Take it for yourself. You want it. Take it.

Darkness clouded her vision, but her body knew where to go. She found better footing in the mud, gaining on her brother.

And you will do anything to have it.

And she would do anything to have it.

She grabbed a falling branch small enough for her free fist and flung it at Reed. "Face me! *Fight me!*"

The branch flew past him.

Reed stopped abruptly and turned around.

Before she lunged, another figure danced through the trees. She stilled, her entire chest a block of pure ice.

Reed turned toward their mother, warmth, adoration, *love* on his face.

Olive skin shined clean in the jungle. She stood on top of the mud, rather than in it—or swimming in it like Violet seemed to be doing. Their mother stared at her with bright blue eyes, dark hair piled at the back of her neck in a loose bun as it normally was. Had been.

"This isn't real," Violet breathed, shaking her head.

Mariana turned toward her daughter.

Violet's hands trembled.

"Violet," her mother breathed, that soft, lulling voice that had haunted her childhood.

Mistake. Mistake. Mistake.

She was a mistake.

"You have fought so hard, love—"

"No," Violet interrupted. "You do not deserve to call me that."

"Violet," her mother chided.

"Listen to her, Vi. You've done so well," said Reed.

"I don't want your pity," seethed Violet.

"Sweetheart—"

"No," Violet's voice was barely above a broken whisper. Her mother's hand reached, so close to cradling her face, to holding her, to taking away the pain aching all over her body in this wretched world. Violet shied away from it. "You barely touched me for all my life. You came home and went to bed saying *nothing*. You— you hurt me. Over and over. When you failed to show me *any* bit of love. I—" Violet finally looked up into the same eyes as hers. "You were hardly a mother, if not just another mouth to feed."

Her mother sighed. Her hand wrapped Reed's. She turned to him, gazing up at him with love. "You were always my favorite."

A helpless cry spilled past Violet's lips. Her legs weakened as she watched Reed smile. "You raised me well. You loved me."

The intruder jerked Violet's body forward, but it didn't have to. Violet was already reaching like a child who'd scraped their knee and wanted a mother's love.

"Mama," she whispered.

"I am so proud of you," Mariana said to Reed. "I have always been so proud of how strong you are, how brilliant you are. Look at you, all handsome and kind. I'm so, so proud of you, my loving boy."

Ice-cold jealousy spiraled in Violet.

Tell her how much it hurt to be unloved by her. Tell her how much you wanted her touch, her hugs when you cried yourself to sleep at night as a child. She gave it to Reed. To everyone but you. It made you so jealous. It made you hurt.

"*Mama,*" muttered Violet again. Still reaching. "Tell me—*tell me.*"

"I'm so proud of you," their mother said again.

To Reed.

He gets all the love, and you get nothing.

How does that make you feel?

Fury and frost snapped her into motion. Resentment built.

"Give it to me!" she cried and lunged.

The dagger was out. Her mother and Reed were two specks in Violet's blackened vision. She was falling, trapped, the intruder grasping the strings of her sanity and laughing as she became a frenzy in this jungle, hating how their mother looked at him, *wishing* it could have been her.

A hateful scream ripped from her throat.

The Sin. The Sin. The Sin.

Show them how jealous you are. Show them how much it hurt you.

"Shut up, shut up, shut up!"

Her hands were on her ears. Tears burned her cheeks.

You want revenge. That is what you want. To anyone who used you. Who left you. Who hurt you. Let it build, and show them what you want. Revenge. Show them.

A growl ripped from her throat. The darkness caved, and Violet clutched the knife, striking upward—

A point of a glimmering, night-sky sword was at her throat.

Pain hit her neck, expelling the darkness from her mind. Her vision cleared. She stared at the sharp, shiny edge of a sword, and then into the eyes of a small girl.

Violet's bloodsworn mark seared.

"Shut up?" the girl rasped. "You were the one screaming. 'Bout to drag every Endo from all over Iveyrez."

Violet's eyes bugged. She gulped down air hungrily. The girl's sword raised, up and down, with Violet's collarbone.

"Drop the dagger," the girl commanded. She was a hand shorter than Violet and her cropped black hair swished as she nodded toward Violet's weapon. Her delicate round face harbored dark eyes, slanted and single-lidded, black and serpent-like. She glared at Violet with unrefined loathing.

Human…ish. A drastic difference from the swamp-like people Violet had escaped.

Violet looked behind the girl's shoulder. There was no sign in the mud that Reed or her mother had ever been there.

Light broke through the canopy and caught the girl's light brown skin. Scales shimmered. Azure rivets followed her arms and stopped at her wrists, wrapping and flowing like a gentle stream along her skin. A bow stuck out on her back, followed by a pack of arrows.

The sword prodded Violet's skin again. "I said, *drop the dagger.*"

"Are you not a candidate?"

The girl wavered, brows furrowing.

Violet ducked to the side and swung out her blade.

The girl parried it quickly, not anticipating the attack. Violet danced with her dagger, ducking low when the sword swung over her head, twisting to reach vulnerable spots at the girl's side. They fought. Blades clashed.

"Go *away*," said Violet.

"I'm real!" the girl cried, swiping her sword to meet the dagger again. A snarl ripped through her. "The sin is gone. Stop—stop it!"

Violet grappled for the handle of the sword, twisting the girl's wrist back and letting it release into her open hand. With another shove, the girl splatted into the ground, mud flying onto Violet's clothes. Her eyes widened in shock.

"Woah," she gasped.

And then a wide, crooked-tooth smile stretched across her face.

Violet's chest heaved as she held the sword—damn heavy, too—toward the girl's face.

Violet scrunched her brows. "Who are you? I—you are real?"

A scowl. It seemed like the girl's permanent expression. "Of course I'm real, but the sin makes you see things. Bad things. Like those who have wronged you."

"Which sin is it?"

The girl lifted herself up and wiped at her pants. A dark shirt hung from her small frame, while a small pack wrapped her waist.

The girl held out her hand. "Sword first."

Violet looked at the glimmering black blade. "What is this stuff?"

"Nostor. A metal. Found only in Iveyrez." She waved her fingers and when Violet didn't relent, she sighed. "It is indestructible. You can light it on fire and it will burn through anything."

Violet nodded, flipped the sword so the hilt was facing the girl. She took it. Sheathed it.

"And the sin?"

"Envy."

"And your name?"

A hard look. But she gave in.

"Anaya."

35

ANAYA

ENVY.

The land of jealousy and fatality because of it. That cold, miserable sensation along Violet's skin was curious, and the dark shadow lingered on her shoulder the whole trek toward somewhere. Anaya hadn't given any indication of *where* they were going, and Violet figured out pretty quickly that there wasn't a single destination. Or any destination. This world was as desolate as it was murky. Once she found better footing on the writhing roots and patches of grass, Violet looked up and studied her surroundings. It was the same every step, every breath, and she grew consistently more annoyed at the never-ending stench.

After Violet had sneezed for the thousandth time, Anaya finally whirled to her. "If you are going to follow me, at least stay quiet."

"It's not my fault your world reeks."

Anaya fixed her with an icy look. "It's not my fault the Sin kills the host from inside out either."

"Funny." Violet slopped mud off her arm. "Was it better before the Sin happened?"

"Ah, let me look back on my five-hundred-year-old memory." Anaya leaned on her sword, feigning thought. "Yes, better."

"You're rather smart for being what, twelve?"

Anaya laughed darkly. "Twenty years, asshole. And I had an engineer for a papa. Hm, what do you have?"

"Issues," Violet said.

"Well, you don't need to tell me the obvious. *You left me! You left me!*" Anaya mocked and pointed the sword. "Everyone leaves you here in Iveyrez."

"Aw, does Anaya have abandonment issues as well?" Violet pouted. "Does she want a hug?"

She growled, "My papa was one of you. A candidate. And then the Sin finally got to him six months ago—among other things. My mother died because some Endo was jealous of her baby—me. My papa raised me in a village far from here, where most sane Endoliers still are."

Violet was incredulous. Her gaze flicked around them. "People live here?"

"Are you not going to say sorry to me for my horrible childhood?"

Both girls narrowed their eyes at each other. Challenging. Anaya's gaze dragged over Violet's muddy body again, a spark in them, and Violet drew her guard up.

"So you're half-human and half-Endo—"

"*Endolier,*" Anaya corrected. "The Endos are the ones who are gone to the sin. Can be candidates too. They roam this world, their mind a jumble of jealousies. They don't know how to care for themselves or bring themselves back to life because they are sick with envy."

"Okay," said Violet. "So you're an Endolier. Envy is the sin, and Endos are anyone taken by the sin. How...what determines that? How do you go and never turn back?"

Anaya gave a hard look. "When the voice in your head takes over."

Violet balked. "You can hear it?"

"Yes, and it will tell you to take and kill for a petty thing."

"My envy surge didn't seem very petty."

"Then you must be amazing."

Violet glowered. "Do you know the Worldbreaker?"

Anaya scoffed. "People are afraid of the man. He's all pale and scarred. But he controls the Sins and the worlds and goes between them as he wants. Like magic."

"He doesn't need a portal? Or an Iris?"

"No, only his glowing hands."

Great, she groaned.

An animalistic moan sounded, and Violet's head whipped to a lone Endo a distance away. Through the jungle fog, it bumped into a tree and a string of words fell out of its mouth. Anaya glanced at it like it might have been a fly, then went back to picking at her nails.

"How are you not like—" Violet waved her hand to the Endo. "That?"

Anaya lifted her chin to the hazy jungle around them. The tall, semi-glowing trees, the blue-green vines, and the limitless end of it.

"What's there to envy here?" Her dark eyes flicked back to Violet. "It started off with simple things. Clothes, food. But now the sin makes you hallucinate your deepest envies, and if you aren't quick enough to get rid of it, you turn into that." Anaya frowned. "And there's no coming back from that, no matter what you do. They're as good as dead. The voice took over. Whatever person was there is gone."

A pang jolted Violet, and she quickly searched around them, fearful that those blue eyes belonging to her brother and mother were going to appear.

"They will show up for you again," said Anaya. She walked up to one of the giant tree trunks and placed her hand on it. "All the ones you wished had loved you."

As if the tree sensed Anaya's touch, a flare of blue-green sparked beneath the thick bark like veins of blood, as it traveled from the roots and disappeared into the canopy.

Violet gasped.

"Put your hand on it," said Anaya.

Violet wavered but took a step. Her palm met the rough, slick wood and it warmed beneath her fingertips. Another flash of color burst from the base and shot up like a firecracker.

As if the tree were saying hello.

"They are alive." Anaya's lips twitched and she removed her hand.

"No shit," replied Violet.

Anaya grinned fully, her smile reaching the sides of her face. Her front teeth bulged out, bigger than the others. "No, really. Everything here is woven into each other. It is different from what I hear. I have met humans before, and your plants just… grow—blah—boring." She placed her hand back on the trunk and shut her eyes. "Here, they are much more than that. The Abos trees are the roots of this place and *very* old. These guys…" She gently patted the tree, opening one eye to Violet, "…have been here for hundreds of thousands of years."

Another flash of color. A low hum vibrated underneath Violet's palm and she recoiled, but Anaya smacked Violet's hand back on the tree. "It is talking to you."

Violet gaped. "And saying what?"

"That you're a little bitch."

Violet stepped away with a glower. "You think you're funny."

"I *am* funny." Anaya grinned. "And I think you're easy to make fun of, which I like to do."

Violet's glower deepened. "What are you doing out here?"

"Wandering, wishing, hoping."

"Optimistic."

A cunning smile.

"Do you have a place to stay?" asked Violet.

"Are you trying to get in my bed, human woman?" A teasing gaze.

Violet's brows lifted. "Do you want me there, half-Endolier?"

Anaya made a show of looking Violet up and down and wrinkled her nose. "After a bath, I might think about it."

"Skiv," snorted Violet.

A smile rose to the Endolier's face—

A clash of metal and a scream tore through the air.

Their heads snapped toward battle sounds. With only a glance, they both bounded off into the jungle.

The mist hovered around them, but Violet followed Anaya's light steps—she knew this world, she knew its dangers and seemingly the workings of the sin better than anyone did. She also knew, somehow, how to skirt around one of the massive trees without splatting into one.

Violet unsheathed her blade, ready for whatever Endo might surprise them. But the scream was human and familiar.

"Shouldn't they know not to scream?" Anaya snarled.

"They probably do now." Her heart hammered. "I think I—yes, I definitely know them."

Between the curve of a tree branch and a massive trunk, cowered Rio, kicking out his feet at the pack of Endos clawing up at him. Some were as scaly and morbid as the one Violet had run into, but others had more color—more life to them, except the blackness of their eyes. A sign of them too far gone. They all whispered different wants, moaning like a choir.

Jack was at the base of the tree, fluidly slicing his shortsword through Endo after Endo. He was covered in their blood. His face tight, if not annoyed at Rio's uselessness.

"Well, the two lovebirds found each other," murmured Violet.

An Endo barreled toward Jack's back, long, sharp fingernails ready to dig into his skin. Violet ran forward and threw the dagger. It whistled over Jack's shoulder, embedding into the Endo right between its decaying eyes.

Jack looked up. "Oh, nice of you to finally join us." He glanced at the Endos hounding Rio—maybe five or six. "Do you mind—oh, you made a friend." He winked at Anaya as he grabbed one of the Endos and jammed the sword between its shoulder blades. "Look at you, little Vi, being all social."

Violet shoved an Endo at him.

Jack, a teasing grin on his face, volleyed the thing's head off and turned to her. "You look awful."

She couldn't say the same about him, so she simply scowled. He laughed.

Anaya gave him an incredulous look and whirled, a blur, whipping her body like a snake, and slammed her sword into the skulls of two Endos back-to-back.

Violet retrieved her dagger. "Always the damsel now, are we, Jack?"

Jack shoved her out of the way and drove his sword into one behind her. His dark shirt hugged his body from sweat. "This is just the warm-up."

"Then why did Rio scream?" asked Violet.

Anaya took down the last two. Rio, pale and trembling, hugged the tree branch and shook his head when Anaya nodded for him to get down.

"One of the things took his dagger soon after we landed. He was screaming then, too, so it wasn't difficult to find him."

"Take me back, take me back, take me back," Rio pleaded.

Anaya gave Violet a look. "This—is a candidate?"

"You warm up to him," said Violet. "Rio, meet Anaya. She's a…local."

Rio took a deep breath and shimmied down the tree. Jack reached out to hold a hand, and Rio grabbed it, steadying himself. "Always the gentleman."

Violet snorted.

"Anything for you." Jack gave Violet a dirty smile. She sneered playfully right back.

Anaya's dark brows drew together. "Are you…?"

"In love?" Rio smiled at Jack. "Absolutely."

"You get used to it," said Violet, kicking the ashen corpse of an Endo.

Rio stretched his arms above his head. "Something about venturing through deadly sin worlds makes you grow closer to one another. They were spooning this morning and left me *out* of it. The skivs."

A blush rose to Violet's cheeks as Jack's gaze turned to her. She dropped her head and pretended to clean her dagger.

"Is that normal?" asked Anaya.

"To what?"

"Tumble with each other?"

"I mean, I wouldn't say that we wrestle much…."

"She doesn't mean that." Jack clapped Rio on that back. "It's the wrestling but without clothes."

"And things going in places," clarified Violet.

Rio's face reddened. "Oh—with each other?"

Violet turned to Anaya. "The answer is no."

"What are you?" Jack asked Anaya.

"*Jack,*" whispered Rio. "You don't just *ask* that."

"Well, I want to know. Her scales are cool."

"Endolier," she said. "Half-human too. My papa was a candidate."

"Bummer," said Jack with a frown.

By Anaya's strange look, Violet stepped in. "You can ignore him. He thinks everyone ends up liking him."

"And he also has a habit of picking lint off his clothes to make himself look cool," said Rio.

Jack only grinned.

At that, Anaya cackled a high laugh and Rio's brows flew up. She had a loud laugh, but a funny one, and soon enough, they were all chuckling.

"So what's this sin?" Rio asked.

"Envy," said Jack and Anaya at the same time. Their eyes narrowed at each other.

Anaya looked up. "The sky is getting dark. We need to get to a village."

Rio muttered something about it already being dark.

"There are villages?" asked Jack.

"Empty ones." Anaya's eyes roamed the brush. "I stay there, but we will need one of the bigger huts now that there's more of us."

Jack stepped forward. "How can we trust you not to eat us?"

"Jack," Rio moaned. "Huts. *Huts.* Maybe we die by this little creature's hand, but at least there will be a roof."

"I think she is fine," shrugged Violet. "If she wanted to kill me, she would have done it a while ago."

"*Jaju*," Anaya smirked. She turned to them. "I will help you, candidates, as long as you take me with you to the next world."

"Deal," Rio stroked the branch. "Anything. Deal. But there must be food."

"Is that even possible?" Violet asked. She had never thought about it before. If she had, maybe she could have moved on with…. She shook her head, looking away from Jack's knowing gaze.

"If it is possible to get me out of this world, then do so." Anaya's eyes were on the jungle brush again, narrowing.

"I don't see why not." Rio cringed away from stepping on another Endo corpse. "If I can have a night where people don't want to eat me, then I'll call it a great night."

"A *fantastic* night," clarified Violet.

"Better than sex—"

"Mmmm, don't go too far there," said Jack.

"Well, Jackie, with a body like that, I'd imagine—"

A whoosh filled the air, and instantly weapons were drawn.

Anaya lowered her bow. She walked over to some brush a distance away and yanked up what looked like a pig by its hind leg. An arrow stuck out of its eye.

"Dinner," she smirked.

❀❀❀

It was a long trek, and by the time they reached a clearing of swamp and giant trees, Anaya claimed this village was a good choice. The candidates took one look at the Endolier and then the hut-lacking area, before Rio muttered, "Great, Vi, you picked up a crazy."

Anaya's sword found Rio's throat and lifted his chin so he looked up. "Call me crazy again and I'll cut your balls off."

Rio blinked above them. "Oh—well, I take it back then."

Jack and Violet followed his gaze and above them…*was* a village. The small treehouse town existed seventy or eighty feet high, built around the giant trees with bridges connecting them.

Anaya showed them the rappelling vines that worked with pulleys to get up and down from the jungle floor when needed. There were many predators in Envy to be aware of—and not just the Endos. By her judgment, the village was free of any other stragglers, and any home was up for the take.

After stepping into the loops and pulling herself up, Violet edged onto the sidewalk platforms, the only barrier between her and the drop being some wooden posts. Heights were never an issue for her with the towering buildings of Calesal—or the fights she had on top of some of them. It was a bit of a relief to be away from the ground. Occasional shrieks echoed, followed by moans or laughs. Jack arrived last, towing the pig on his shoulders, and together they ventured across the bridges to a two-story home hugging a tree.

The giant, faintly blue-black trees were the heart of the land and the energy of the jungle, calling to its inhabitants and fueling them with life. As babies, children were left for a night within the tree, watched and celebrated by the adults, Anaya had explained.

Anaya jammed her dagger into the door and unlocked it. She let the it creak open and they all peered in.

"Looks fine," said Rio, raising his foot to step through—

Jack hauled him back and nodded to Anaya. "Shit like that is how you end up in trouble, little damsel."

"Weapons out. We need to scope it. Crawlers can be hiding out here."

"Crawlers?"

"People on the verge of becoming Endos," Anaya explained. "They are no fun, and desperate. A lot of them smoke *fonteyn* to ease the transition. It is a sedative."

"Druggies on the brink of no return," said Rio. He waved his arm to Anaya. "After you, then."

Jack shoved him forward. "Come on, Rio, use your manners— the ladies have done most of the killing so far."

Rio hesitated, and Violet nudged past him, stomping in. "Stop being fussy."

She walked the wooden floors, careful of the ones that might creak.

They each took a room to check. Violet drifted into the kitchen—a brighter space compared to the rest of the house. It was strange to see how modern and similar it was to Calesal. Cabinets hung ajar, dishes lay in a curved, clay sink with a spout, while pipes pumped from the water reserves in the tree. A dusty, woven rug lay under a table for four, and chairs were pulled out, as if someone had gotten up and never pushed them back in. Violet tugged a cabinet open, cringing at the squeak, and took a whiff. She shut it quickly, gagging.

There was a hearth embedded into one wall laid with mortar and stone. It hadn't been swept since the last occupants had lived here. Darkened char and ash spilled onto the wooden floor. A large pot hung between two metal poles.

She thought she should feel pity for being in the eerily empty home. It had not been evacuated on purpose. It seemed that lives were created here and then torn again. She guessed this house was abandoned more than ten years ago by the thick layer of dust and cobwebs on everything.

A creak of a floorboard and Violet whirled to the entrance, holding out her dagger. Anaya's dark eyes narrowed at her. "You think you would succeed with that?"

Violet sheathed it. "The fight between us said differently."

"That is what you think." She smirked. "The house is secured. We have to blind the windows with sheets if we want any light, skiv."

"Skiv?" Violet smiled. "That is very demanding of you."

Anaya studied her, eyes roaming. "I can be demanding in other ways."

Violet gave her a pointed look and brushed past her. "Not my type. Too short."

Anaya cackled.

After they stripped the beds of their linens and nailed them against the windows, Rio lit a fire in the hearths, one in the kitchen and one in a sitting room. On the upper level, there was a round basin big enough for one body. After finding the waterline, Anaya rappelled down the tree and kicked it open, quick and silent in the night.

They decided who was the smelliest and then sent them to the bath first. Anaya smiled smugly when Rio leaned in, sniffed her, and gagged. She climbed up the ladder and took a very long time bathing herself.

Violet had found extra clothing in one of the two bedrooms, enough for everyone. She washed the simple shirts and pants in the kitchen sink with soap from Gluttony, and then hung it from various places in the house. The water upstairs finally drained, and Anaya shouted for Jack next.

Outside on the balcony covered by tree foliage, Rio skinned the boar—she learned the actual name—and sliced it thick.

Violet was washing the plates and utensils when Rio ducked under one of the drying shirts in the doorway. "I think we have enough to last us a year."

They stuck the meat into the cleaned pot, inhaling as it sizzled.

"Damn, does that smell good," Violet said. But still, she grew nauseous as she looked.

He threw a comforting look. "It was an ugly beast anyway. Anaya says they're vicious and highly annoying."

"Sounds familiar," she muttered.

Once Jack was done, he sang Violet's name from above. She scowled to Rio's giggles while grabbing dry clothes. She climbed the ladder.

"Does that face mean you smell the reek on yourself?" Jack drawled as he left the bathroom with only a linen wrapped around his waist.

She halted at the sight of him. He lifted a hand to push back the wet curls from his forehead and a sharp jaw revealed on his newly shaven face. Water droplets shimmered along his body, lingering muscles lost from the commander days, but still lean and taut. Down and down along his abdomen, to the V beneath his navel that was a giant arrow pointing—

She blinked, asked quickly, "Where are the towels?"

"Under the sink." He stopped before her. "Are you...ogling me?"

That snapped her out of her daze. "Oh, get over yourself."

"Don't stare at me like that, or else I might start thinking Reed's little sister *is* all grown up."

A pang bruised her chest at that. *Did he only view her as that? As a perpetual child who needed looking out for?*

She lifted her chin. "Nothing I haven't seen before."

"Did those other times make you all red in the face like now?" he teased.

Her blush deepened.

Violet kept eye contact with him as she grabbed the hem of her shirt and lifted it over her head. Jack stilled, mouth open. She unbuttoned her pants next and pushed them down her legs, mindful of how her back curved. In only her underwear, she shook her hair out from its braid, stepped out of her pile of clothes, and sauntered to the bathroom.

Before she entered, she pulled her black, stretchy bra off and tossed it behind her head. She aimed to shut the door but looked back as Jack took his gaze from her, to the bra before his feet, and then back. His hand grasped the towel tightly.

"Looks like my clothes slipped first." She puckered her lip out.

"Is that an invitation?" he asked.

"In your wildest dreams, Jack Marin."

She shut the door.

"You have grown," he said through the wood. "You *wicked* little thing."

❀❀❀

Violet was glad the water was cold.

After scrubbing the blood of Endos off her skin and out of her hair, Violet let the bath drain and then rinsed herself off again for good measure. The soap laid out smelled sweet and she lathered it in every crevice.

The clothes, provided by whoever had lived here, were on the looser side, but they were clean, dry and comfortable.

She went down the ladder, calling for Rio. He was quick leaving the kitchen, his eyes meeting hers with an amused look. He leaned to her ear, whispering, "Whatever you did to him, that was fucking hilarious. Broke one of the dishes. Let me repeat, *hilarious.*"

Suddenly nervous, she strolled into the kitchen where Jack lounged on one of the chairs at the small dinner table and Anaya stoked the beast at the hearth. She had gathered more food worth eating because rice boiled atop the burner, followed by a pan of green vegetables sizzling.

The clothes Anaya was wearing swallowed her whole, while Jack's—

Violet laughed, her eyes crunching. "What is *that?*"

His clothes looked like they were four times too small for his body, pressed tight into his skin. The pants revealed his ankles and the bottom half of his calves, while the shirt stressed against his arms.

"The tiny devil took the bigger clothes." Jack met her stare with loathing.

"When I don't have to wear tight breeches, I take the opportunity," Anaya snipped from the hearth. She pointed the spoon at him. "I think they fit you fine."

The look Jack gave her would have made Violet rappel straight down to the Endos, but Anaya returned it with a smile. Tiny devil and lethal commander. A dangerous game.

Violet took the seat across from him at the dinner table— already laid out with plates and utensils. She caught a glimmer, and she picked up a piece of broken glass, raising a brow at Jack.

Anaya huffed. "Little Jackie had a tantrum."

"She's already picking up the nicknames, I see." Violet twirled the bit of glass.

"My grip is strong." He flexed his fingers slowly and directly in Violet's vision. Long, strong…she bit her cheek. She was also playing a dangerous game.

She put the glass back on the table and stood to stir the veggies, then turning off the burner. They arranged the pots underneath towels and placed them at the center of the table.

Just as Anaya forked the strips of boar onto a plate, Rio strolled into the room, toweling his hair and grinned. "Dinner time?"

"It almost feels normal," said Violet. "Almost."

"Bring it here!" Rio slid into the seat. Anaya plopped the boar on the table and the boys wasted no time putting it on their plates. "Gotta love me some meat. Right, Jack?"

Violet scooped food on her plate. "Is it big enough for you, Rio?"

"I personally prefer the juicy, wet, and fatty pieces," Jack said.

"Wow." Anaya sat at her seat. "We do have something in common."

"Yes. I do love my girth." Rio smiled as he shoveled some in his mouth. "I also love taking bites so big they make me choke."

They all snickered. The ambiance in the room relaxed, and Violet was able to sit back, take her time, and enjoy the company.

Once they began eating, there was silence. Anaya was quite the cook. The spices were different, musky compared to the savory ones in Calesal or the earthy ones of Gwen's cooking in Gluttony. She hesitated on the meat, having only put a small, thin slice on her plate. Underneath the table, a barefoot caught hers and tapped.

She looked up, meeting Jack's knowing gaze.

The foot rubbed. A comfort. He knew. He struggled too. But he was there, and he understood.

36

GREEN

STEEL PLATES COVERED HER ARMS. *White hands gripped them, polished nails digging into Violet's skin. Underneath the plates. They ripped it off.*

Violet screamed, but a hand slapped over her mouth.

"Don't cry, little candidate." Kiane breathed over her. She held up the bloodied plate. "I'm fixing you."

Another tug at a different slab. Kiane ripped it off, tossed it, and the metal clinked on the floor.

Violet cried, shaking her head.

"I need to make sure your wounds are okay." Kiane dragged her finger along the next plate. "It would be so terrible if they festered."

A rip. Violet shrieked.

A slap on her cheek.

"You must stay quiet, or else the monsters will come for you in the night."

But Violet blinked at the monster. The pale-haired, white-skinned horror pinning her down, ripping plate after plate after plate—

"You're not leaving," Kiane said as Violet's vision blackened. But she opened her mouth, and a deep, familiar voice sounded, "Come back to me."

Violet lurched.

"Bucket," said the voice.

A pail skidded across the hardwood and thrust into her chin. A hand gripped her hair and turned her face. She vomited into it.

"It's okay." A hand soothed her back. "I've got you. Come back to me."

Tears splashed into her bile. Tremors shook her body. Violet recoiled from the bucket, and the hand, tugging her hair away.

The hands immediately retreated.

When her vision cleared, Jack was frowning at the bucket. Anaya knelt by Rio, whose face glistened with sweat. His hands shook as he ran them through his hair.

The only source of light was the crackling fire in the hearth of the living room. It hadn't taken long for them to clean up dinner and make four beds of blankets and pillows on the floor. The quiet night of Envy—Iveyrez—chirped with crickets.

Long silence passed. Violet breathed heavily, rubbing at her eyes. She gasped, looked at her arms—

No plates. No wounds. No blood.

"I—" Rio swallowed. "I thought I could forget, now that we are in a new world. But they kept making me eat and I couldn't…." He touched his lips. "And then they took my hand."

Violet stared at her bare feet.

"You can't scream like that," Anaya said softly, looking at the both of them. "Not at night. There are terrible monsters that hunt at night."

"They can't control their screams," defended Jack.

"Then we must gag them."

"You're really a bundle of joy, aren't you?"

"Lower your voice, commander," she hissed. "I already told you."

Rio glanced at Jack, and Jack only frowned. "I couldn't sleep."

Rio grimaced.

"So he told me bits about your little city and your backgrounds," Anaya said. "But during the night, we must be quiet. There have been…villages torn apart by terrible animals that are not from this world."

"Not from…?" Rio paled and buried his head into his knees.

Violet's gaze had moved from her feet back to her arms.

No plates. No blood.

No pain.

"I think we all need something to drink." Jack reached over to his bag and pulled out a large bottle. Not the shiva they shared, but something…

"Gluttony liquor." He unscrewed the cap. "Nasty stuff. The Crale would drink loads of it and pass out all around the estate. On the stairs, in the shrubs, on the toilet." He shook his head. "But it will help."

"Drink enough of it and you might not dream," murmured Violet.

Rio snorted and reached his hand out. "Good."

Jack passed him the bottle and Rio downed a gulp.

"Does it burn?" Violet asked.

"Oh—skies," Rio groaned, his eyes watering. "Like…fuel. Or—gah—my mother's cooking."

"Gimme some of that." Anaya scooted up as Jack poured a glass. She sniffed it, nose wrinkling, but shot it back in one… two…three long gulps. The others looked at her incredulously. She smacked her lips and smiled. "Yummy."

Rio side-eyed her, scooting away.

Anaya crawled to hand it to Violet.

Violet plugged her nose before taking a long sip. With all the shiva she had consumed, the burn was minimal, but it had a fuel-like taste to it. She coughed into her shirt. "Skies, that is strong."

"Well, since we are all up and need happier spirits, we should play a game." Rio smiled. "To get to know each other."

Anaya tip-toed out of the room and came back in a minute later with four glasses. "I like games."

Violet scowled. "We are already in one."

Jack snorted.

Anaya gave her a sour look, but poured the liquor into each glass and once it was distributed, Rio said, "If one of us says something, and you've done it, you drink."

"You do realize I'm not from your world," Anaya said.

"Drink if you've been a skiv about a game," Jack said.

Anaya daggered him with her eyes and took a drink.

"Drink if you've never been to another world," Violet said.

Anaya slid her narrowed gaze to her and drank. "Fine then, drink if you have slept with someone in this room."

Rio wiggled his eyebrows and clinked his glass against Jack's. "Knew it would come out soon, buddy."

"I thought we were keeping it on the down-low." Jack sipped his, smiling.

"Really?" Anaya's eyes bugged, and she looked to Violet.

Violet merely shrugged. "Drink if you have woken up in a place you very much wish you hadn't."

Rio, Jack, Anaya, and Violet all raised their glasses and sipped.

"Drink if you have ever been victimized by *the* Jack Marin," Violet continued.

Rio all but tipped the glass upside down into his mouth. Violet took a long drink, enjoying the burn. Anaya, confused, looked at Jack. "What are you?"

Jack lazily leaned back on his elbow, smiling, unoffended. "Not the most-liked person in our world."

"Guess he didn't tell you everything, especially the fact people hated him. He ran part of our city," Violet snipped. "And a gardia."

Anaya's confusion remained.

"Gardia—gang," Rio corrected. "Lots of bad people. Pew— pew. Lots of plasguns."

"Plash-guns?"

"*Plas*guns. Plasma guns. They shoot little bolts of plasma… colorful, glowy power. All that."

"Hurt like a bitch, too," Jack said.

Violet nodded. "There's also plaswhips, plastasers, and our lights."

"Ah." Anaya nodded. "Like the Lord of Envy."

The three candidates blanched at her.

"The what?" Jack asked.

"He has those. His group does too. The glowing weapons. He uses it to kill Endos and others to control them. His underlings hunt people—candidates who need rounding up, Endos, mainly. Like game. It is where the night monsters come from."

"There's a Lord of Envy?" Violet gaped. "And he has plasguns?"

"All kinds of stuff. Long vines that can cut off your fingers, big tubes that shoot fires—or plashama—"

"Plasma."

"Phlasama. It is all in his village. They have the power there. They took it all for…something. I never figured out what."

"So he hunts people, kills the Endos, and rules over this world?" Jack surmised. "Is he like you?"

"No," Anaya said. "Human. Like you three."

"Where is his village?"

"Ten iluns from here." Anaya pointed toward the kitchen. "Your table is there."

"The what?"

"The portal," Violet breathed. "She is talking about the portal. You're saying you know where it is, even though we haven't got the Iris?"

"The round thing." Anaya held her hand up and did an obscene motion.

Rio choked on his drink.

"The Iris, yes."

Jack asked, "How do you know all of this?"

"Like I said, I didn't used to live in this area of Iveyrez, but where there are more lagoons than trees. My mother had been on a hunting mission and they caught my papa, and then they fell in love." Anaya rolled her eyes, but tilted her head with a smile. "And had the wonderful me. I ended up in this area because the night monsters started to find our villages—big beasts that blended into the dark. Normally we set traps for big predators and then sedate them for release farther away, but these ones are smart, and so my village was set to move to another one, but that was when my papa disappeared. A night monster took him."

Rio's eyes widened. "How?"

"The monsters don't massacre. They kill every now and then, but they take Endos and candidates. So one night, I woke to glowing eyes staring at me, but they took my papa and vanished. I decided not to join my village and go after my papa. He was already having trouble with the sin, but when you are in a village, there are ways to help. Envy can hardly be fought alone. There was already word of the Lord of Envy and his compound filled with non-Endoliers and candidates of the Sins, so I came here to find my papa, but I haven't seen him. What I *have* seen are your people, with their glowy weapons in the village. I think they have to serve in the compound first before they can get your round thingy."

"And the village is surrounded by thousands of Endos," Rio said, face paling. "I think I saw it when I landed here. I was a distance away, but I climbed a tree to get my bearings and there were all these people wandering, growling at each other, and in the middle of the horde was a fortress with a giant tree that a villa wrapped around. It looked as big as the factory grounds at the Farm."

Anaya followed up, "I have been watching it for a while now. There are always more people than homes, which is strange. I think there is something underground where mud tunnels roam. But the ones I looked for have all been blocked off."

"What do candidates serve as? Guards?" asked Violet.

Anaya nodded.

"Well, that explains why a handful of candidates go to the fourth world every couple of months." Jack rubbed at his jaw. "But I'm more curious as to why they need guards in the first place. Why they care or need exiles to serve time before they go. Seems like the Lord of Envy hijacked the process."

"There is an operation there. I think they create the night monsters. Some higher-ups—humans like you, candidates probably, dressed in all black who patrol there. They work for the Worldbreaker." Anaya swallowed. "I don't know what they are building there, but this land isn't what it used to be. Less game. Less animals, in general."

"This ain't a game no more." Rio heavily chugged his liquor.

"They take Endos, too." said Anaya. "A group of them now and then. I've watched them corral those around the walls of the compound. My village used to say that the Lord of Envy had a cure to give Endos their souls—their lives—back, but they never believed it. So many villages lost to the Sin, and then they would go to the compound and beg for a cure. They never came back."

"What if we catch an Endo?" asked Violet. "Douse ourselves in its blood and sneak in that way?"

Anaya shrugged. "They don't just let Endos in all the time unless they are ready for another round of the cure."

"And how often is that?"

"Once a *hunu*."

After watching Anaya count her fingers, Rio sighed, "A week. Once a week."

"And when is the next round?"

Another shrug. Count of fingers.

"Seven days," interpreted Rio.

"*Hunu* is the crest of our moon, Fovana, and the time it takes—so you said a week? Yes. The call of the moon is powerful to Endoliers, and it adjusts with the color of our scales." She rubbed her arms, that shimmering cerulean a beauty in the firelight. "So on the full moon, they are more blue and more resistant to water. We can also swim in the lagoons for longer periods of time without breath."

"How long?" asked Rio.

Anaya twisted her hand back and forth. "A *kolava*? An hour? You learn at a very young age, tossed straight into the nearest lagoon and the village watches you bob and then sink."

"I'm sorry, what?" Violet's eyes widened, meeting Rio's paling face.

"The babes can swim. It is in our blood. Along with *shunu*."

"*Shunu*?" asked Jack. "What is that? Does your human side affect it?"

A shrug. "I don't think it's as powerful as a true Endolier...."

Anaya held up her arms over the brown blanket on her lap. The blue scales shimmered again, and with a long breath, her gaze hardened. The scales morphed, changing, like ripples of color one by one, into the coffee color of the material. Even where the scales weren't visible—smaller—the color changed, and her normally light brown skin darkened to blend with the blanket, until only the pale outlines of her fingernails were visible if one knew to look for them.

Rio gasped. Jack's brows raised, thoroughly impressed, which was not a look often seen on him. Violet's mouth parted, and she leaned over to Anaya where her arms should be. Every now and then, she caught the outline of her limbs, but the scales continued to adjust within the flickering firelight until Violet squinted but could see them no more.

"That's camouflage," said Jack.

"Stupid fucking cool," mumbled Rio. "*Stupid* cool. I can only twist my tongue one way or another, and that hasn't got me anywhere."

Anaya grinned. "I can see in the dark, too. My papa called it night vision."

Rio's expression brightened.

"So we have seven days before they corral Endos to bring into the compound. If we can infiltrate them through that, hopefully getting the Iris beforehand, then we can break for the portal and get to the next world," said Jack.

"And catching the Endo?" asked Violet.

"There are empty bedrooms upstairs. We can hold it there," said Anaya.

"Are you okay with using your people? Killing them like you did?" asked Rio softly.

Anaya knocked back the rest of her drink in heavy gulps. She swallowed it like water. "They are long gone. No matter what *cure* the other surviving Endoliers have whispered about, I doubt it makes one normal again. That part of being alive—"

"Conscious," muttered Violet.

Anaya nodded. "Is gone once they look sickly like that. Or when their eyes turn fully black."

Jack huffed a breath and glanced between Violet and Rio. "We only need one Iris."

Rio groaned. "Not me."

"Me either," said Violet quickly. "I don't want to go through that again."

"So you have already dealt with it?" Jack turned to her. "Because I haven't."

"Nor have I." Rio chugged back another sip, his cheeks red. "I was too busy frolicking with your dead-walking cousins."

He nudged Anaya and she pushed him right back.

"We will bring you back." Jack smiled at Violet. "Promise."

The alcohol was working, because Violet's lips twitched at his charming expression. She found herself nodding. "If it brings us closer to the next world."

Jack cocked his head. "What do you envy?"

"Well, she suffers from lack of love." Anaya grinned.

"Typical," teased Rio. "Don't you have something more exciting to be envious about?"

"*Typical?*" Violet whirled to him. "At least you have a mother."

"Talk about your mother, Rio," tested Jack.

"What?" Violet set her drink down. "No—"

"Well..." Rio leaned back on his elbows. "She loves to squeeze my cheeks. On my face now, mind you, but when I was a babe, I'm sure it was my booty too. She also makes us hot chocolate when we were upset. She has the best voice for lullabies—I mean, she used to sing all of us to sleep every night while my father read the paper with his shiva. It was so loving, comforting..." Rio's smile grew tight, and his ears reddened. "I was truly so loved and cherished... well, except for when I went through my uncontrollable diarrhea phase, but that wasn't my fault, but my allergies to cheese—"

Violet chucked a pillow at Rio, which smacked him in the face. "I'm not envious of your bowel issues, Rio."

Anaya cackled.

"Reed said you liked to collect things that were..." Violet whipped toward Jack. He slid her a smile. "...green. Do you like green, Violet?"

Her heartbeat stilled. Cold tingles lashed down her spine.

"Why do you like green, little Vi?"

Her gaze snagged with his. The green in them blazed. Called her in. Tugged at her heart.

Freedom. Isn't that what you want more than to be loved? Is that what green meant to you? Isn't that what Gwen meant to you?

His eyes dragged her into that darkness. So like the foliage, the jungle—the expanse of it. There was liberty there. Unrelenting freedom. No chains, no walls, no anything.

It lured her in so much she leaned forward, drawn, until something in her pushed and pushed until she was crawling to Jack.

Freedom. Freedom. Freedom. Why does he have it? Why not you?

"I like your eyes," Violet purred.

"Thank you," he said, but his voice sounded muffled, like a thick pane of glass existed between his mouth and her ear.

Her vision clouded. This was a familiar feeling. She should fight it, but something in her pressed her forward. Freedom. She wanted it. Her heart thrummed with cold desire.

Green like the forests over the wall. Green that called to her, begged her. Freedom. Green. Freedom. Green. Until the words morphed together and all she could feel was that ice-pick sensation in her chest.

Take them. They are beautiful, aren't they? Take them. You want them. Why does he get to have that freedom and you don't?

Pain drew at her heart. She struggled to breathe.

Get it. They will make you feel better. Go—

Something grabbed her arms and slammed her down. A hand slapped across her face.

"*Anaya,*" growled a voice. "That wasn't necessary."

The pain ricocheted all over her body, and Violet gasped as the darkness swarmed in a frenzy and then winked out of existence. Her vision cleared. Her hearing returned. She could taste the musty air and feel the burning on her cheek.

Her bloodsworn mark flared.

"Pain brings them back," came Anaya's voice.

Violet blinked and found herself on the floor. All three heads stared down at her.

"Did you get it?" Rio asked hopefully.

Violet flexed her scarred palm and nodded, still disoriented.

A hand hauled her up and Jack smiled, dimple and all.

"Good girl."

37

Southers

VIOLET LINGERED IN BETWEEN A large branch and the massive, slippery trunk of an Abos tree. She had her Droanian leathers wrapped around her hands, covering her scars, and providing exquisite grip as she sat in the gloomy foliage of the jungle.

It was early morning. The sun poked through the upper canopy in bright, soft rays, waking up the dark floor.

She watched the ground a distance below. Yawned hard enough it cracked her jaw.

Endos blankly milled about, walking here and there, bumping into another, and then shrieking into the air at the audacity of it. Their greasy swamp hair matted to peeling gray scalps, and even the scales on their arms muted in color, so unlike the blue-green vibrancy of Anaya's.

Beyond the horde, just as Rio had said, a fortress sat surrounded by a thick stone wall. It must have been a quarter of the height of the tree she perched on, which was an impressive size in itself. Vines snuck down from the surrounding Abos trees. They crawled over the wall, through cracks in the stone, and then scaled the numerous buildings inside, until they reached the epicenter—a home made of stone and wood, built into an Abos tree at its center.

A gate stood at the western side, guarded by men in silver and black plates with shining plasguns resting in their gloved hands. The minute she saw them, she thought they were Redders.

The guards higher in command had curving swords strapped along their backs, white-plated like a plasgun, but ringed with dim, translucent gray. A training circle was set, and guards were getting ready for combat. One stepped in and drew the blade from his back. The moment it was in front of him, it *ignited*.

She nearly lurched out of her recon position. An orange hue wrapped around the white metal like that of plasmic signs in Calesal. When the guard twisted and turned, the plasma sizzled the air.

Another guard stepped forward and drew his own blade. It ringed blue when he triggered it.

And then they fought.

The clash crackled through the jungle. Her heart thundered as the hot plasma collide, but she imagined one sword would slice through the other, it merely met in a peak of bright light, before the swords were drawn away and they continued fighting.

She was surprised to see no rain of molten energy. The blade molded, curved to the sleekness of the internal metal, and she was certain that if one did meet an arm, that limb would be long gone.

She remembered Jelan's drawings. Countless prototypes and ideas that went over Violet's head. Jelan hadn't fashioned a *plasblade* like that, but her ideas were structured around such a thing.

The guards continued to fight, and the more Violet watched, restless in her perch, the fouler her mood became. Her head ached, she was exhausted, and she didn't eat much once the sun rose and they agreed to short naps so dreams wouldn't happen.

Above all, she loathed the commander.

She was distracted by him, how she wanted to gouge his eyes out during the envy surge, but also how his body had looked so lean when he'd stepped out of the bath, his lips when they smiled at her and those damn dimples—

Good girl.

Her scowl deepened.

What she wanted, what she was *envious* of—she looked pointedly to the world and threw her hands up—was to forget all of that. To pretend he was nothing, and that she wouldn't notice those little details, like how his eyes had a ring of dark green around the outside—

Violet huffed and leaned back in the crook. The Endos milled about a distance away. She pouted in her position and kept her eyes on the fortress, but eventually they drifted out of focus, and in her thoughts, Jack spun in a new light.

❄❄❄

When a calm bird noise jarred her, Violet shimmied down the tree and landed quietly on a gnarl of roots. She was far from the horde of Endos, but some still meandered, and she drew out her dagger in case one found her to be appealing. Her scalp tingled as she ducked under a vine.

After all the times her neck had been grabbed and her hair yanked, the sharp pain of it dulled. Anaya had been quick to ask at breakfast why Violet had a yellowish bruised ring along her neck, and Violet merely mumbled about a crazy skiv, an iron pole, and the number of times death had spat in her face that night.

Even now, when Anaya padded up to Violet's position and lifted a brow, those dark eyes fell to that bruise, her scowl deepening.

A warmth swelled within Violet. She'd hardly even known Anaya for a day, but there was a ferocity in her gaze when they recounted Gluttony to her. A vengeful camaraderie.

Violet wondered what the Farm would look like if Anaya had been set loose on the Crale.

"Anything?" she mumbled.

Violet shrugged. "I didn't know they had plasblades. I'd never seen such a thing in our city."

"I'm talking about movements."

"Four guards at the gates. They change every two hours. No sign of the Lord. Twenty-seven guards around the wall, some stiff-backed, some bored-looking. But the wall is too slick to attempt to climb." Violet frowned. "They train and then have a break for lunch."

"Then after mealtime," confirmed Anaya.

"We won't go in at night?"

She nodded her head toward…some direction. Violet's internal compass was nonexistent in this place. "Endos are like bugs compared to what lurks at night."

"Goody," deadpanned Violet.

They met up with Jack and Rio beneath the pulley for the village. Rio's eyes did not stop moving from the foggy tree line, while Jack lounged against the mossy bark of an Abos tree. His gaze flicked to them, lingered on Violet, and then he went back to watching Rio.

"Anything from your recons?" asked Anaya.

Jack rolled his healing shoulder. "The south side is a dead zone. Plenty of vines if we want to give climbing a try, but there are archers in the trees with plasarrows. They were shooting at the Endos on my side for fun. I also think they were drunk. I was surprised to see little commandment because that kind of behavior is what allows people like us to slip through the cracks." He huffed a laugh. "There is a very heavily manned door that slants underground. Do you know what that is?"

"Probably why the tunnels are caved in," said Violet.

Rio mumbled something, eyes darting to another part of the tree line.

"What's wrong with him?" Anaya wrinkled her nose.

"He's been like this since I retrieved him." Jack shoved off the tree. "I think something spooked him."

"Envy?"

"That or bugs. He is not very fond of the spiders here."

Violet gave him an incredulous look. "And why are you just standing there?"

Jack didn't look at her, but instead rubbed at his tired face. "I am watching—"

She interrupted him by stomping over to where Rio had drifted. His boots were sunken into mud enough that it caked the cloth of his pants beneath his knees. As she drew closer, she noticed the sweat glistening his skin, the tremble in his hands. And he wasn't just mumbling nonsense.

"*Maria*," he whispered. "No, wait—Maria, come back. Come here. Don't say that to me."

His knees sagged as he stared at a thin tree and pleaded with it.

"Rio," Violet said softly. "Look at me. What is going on?"

Her words didn't reach him. He trudged another step toward the tree. "Maria, no—I tried. No, I want to be there, but I can't because I'm—no, I'm—I *know* Mama doted on you, but I tried, I *tried*...."

"Rio," Violet called again. She reached for him, fingertips brushing the side of his arm. Her other hand was at the hilt of her dagger—

He turned abruptly at her touch. When those wide, terrified eyes met hers, they were wholly black.

"The sin!" she called, removing her dagger.

"Maria," he mumbled incoherent nonsense. "No, I don't want to do that to her! No—stop! I won't hurt her!" Tears streamed down his cheeks, and before Violet could tackle him, he darted off into the forest. "Come back! No, come back!"

"*Shit*," snarled Violet. She rushed after him.

He turned to the right. Paused. "Estelle—no. I know I wasn't the best, but I was the oldest! I had to take care of you. Of everyone!" A sob choked out of him. "Please don't turn your back on me, *please*."

Violet lunged to grasp him, but his sweaty arm slid out of her grip. He jerked away, horrified by her presence, paling by the second. "Maria, Adriana—I *tried*, mama! I did what I had to do—why do they get your love? Why do they not have to sacrifice it—no, please *mama*!"

Heartache tore through her chest as she chased him again, but Rio ended up stopping himself by running straight into a tree. He clawed at it, punched it until his knuckles split open. "I tried! I tried! I tried!"

"Rio!" called Violet.

She wrapped her arms around his waist and tugged, grinding

her teeth against the force of him. "Stop—they aren't real! I'm real. Listen to me. Hear my voice. You tried and you did your best. Your mama loves you. *Listen to me!*"

He paused, fingernails chipped and bloodied. "Violet?"

"It's me," she cried into his back, pulling him away from the tree. "It's me, Ri. You're alright."

Rio immediately stopped fighting, but the lack of resistance flew them back. The breath knocked out of her. He twisted. She heaved for air, and when she gulped it, she crawled over to his trembling body, straddled him, and grasped his face between her hands.

"Stop it—Rio—no—" She jerked away from his flailing palm. "I swear to the skies I will hurt you—"

A rush of footsteps told her Jack and Anaya had caught up. But Violet ignored them, pressing her knees into Rio's chest, her feet onto his thighs to steady them.

"Maria—don't do that. Don't tell me that. It was for you—it was all for you and you want to reap the glory? I am here because I fought for you and our family!"

"You are here, Rio—"

"You need pain," called Anaya.

"I don't want to hurt him," snapped Violet. "I know—I know, Rio. You can cry. You can be mad at them. You can let it all out."

His lovely brown eyes peeked behind the dilation. She breathed a heavy sigh of relief.

"Fight it," she said. "You overcame it. You tried for them. You did it. Now we are here, and you are loved." A sob racked her chest as she remembered Gwen telling her that when she needed it. When she was broken, unbelieving that she deserved such a thing because her own mother didn't give it to her.

Rio had fought for his family, and suffered in the Sins for it. It didn't take much for Violet to realize what he was fighting—the envy of seeing his family fine without him. It would send her into a panic too.

And that kind of thing was not something she could slap out of him.

So Violet leaned down and hugged him. Buried her face in his shoulder and gave him the tightest hug of her life. The last time she'd hugged someone like this…it wasn't even Jelan. Not even her brother. This kind of touch was foreign to her, but she did it. Did it because she loved Rio and knew the plagues of the South.

Slowly, he settled. A ragged breath met her chest.

"Steady," she said in his ear. "I know. I understand."

Another inhale. A deep sigh of an exhale. A sob racked through him. His arms slowly wrapped around her and squeezed.

"Violet," he croaked. "*Violet.*"

"It's okay."

"They hated me." Wetness met her cheek. "Skies, they didn't need me. After all I'd done for them. They said they were better off without me and I—I snapped—and felt so cold. So, so cold…."

"I know."

Footsteps walked up and Violet lifted her head.

Anaya held a flower in her hand. Jack behind her, lips thinned, eyes blazing. Not sad, not ashamed for letting Rio get so far, but icy. Feral.

"If you sniff it, it lessens pain," said Anaya softly.

Violet clambered off Rio and helped him up.

He still trembled. "I hate this sin. Skies, my head is pounding."

The white, long-petal flower beckoned, and Rio nodded thanks to Anaya. He bent toward it and sniffed. Hard.

Anaya's lip twitched.

Rio's eyes rolled back into his head, body collapsing. Strange attitude forgotten, Jack lunged before Rio's head smacked a gnarl of roots.

"What—" Jack started. Rio's head lolled and drool slurped onto Jack's arm.

"Is he okay?" Violet asked. "What—is he dead?"

"Rio, come on! Rio—hey, Ri Ri, wake up!" Jack gently laid him on the ground. Violet crawled to Jack's other side

"Skiv," Anaya snorted. "He's alive. The meeter flower knocks out the smeller."

"I thought it was for pain?" asked Violet as Jack checked Rio's neck for a pulse.

"Pain relief by putting them to sleep." Anaya's wicked smile grew. "He will wake up by nightfall feeling better. But he did sniff a lot."

Jack's scoff was between impressed and annoyed. Annoyed because he was the one who had to carry Rio back to the house. Impressed because Anaya knocked Rio out while he was still vulnerable to the sin attacking again.

"Skiv," said Violet, lips twitching.

38

PLASBLADE

JELAN

"I DON'T THINK THIS WORKS...."

"You look great."

"Yeah, but the holster for a plasgun? There?"

"We can exchange it for a dagger."

Jelan frowned at Lyla. She kicked at the flared midnight-blue pants that shimmered like stars. She definitely liked that Henry, Jack's interior designer and clothing aficionado, had given her a dress with pants to begin with. Yet the minute Lyla had strolled through the door with two plasguns and four daggers, all with pretty holsters, Jelan knew the clothing was not *just* for her comfort.

Lyla scoffed as Jelan fussed with the holster. "It goes the other way."

"Thanks for the help," grumbled Jelan as she flipped the straps until it properly clipped her calf. She glanced at the weapons laid out on the bed before her. "I've never used, or even held, a plasgun before."

"Not even to study it?" Lyla leaned back against the window. "You've spent nearly all your time in the lab managing the plashield. Don't be nervous now."

I'm always nervous, Jelan wanted to say, but she picked up a dagger and said, "There isn't an abundance of plasguns in the South for me to experiment with, sorry."

Regardless, the workings of the plashield were different from the firing sort of the plasgun. The shield was meant to stay put and block the heated bullet of the gun. It needed to stay controlled, whereas the gun's barrel encapsulated the plasma and shot out so fast it maintained its small form, but once released and slowed within its target, there was no control. The plaslights spoke for that too. All of that was in a controlled environment. Jelan had nearly burned half her face while fighting with the scalding substance in its neutralizing environment. Trying to *control* the damned energy and still have it maintain a shield form felt nearly impossible.

The elation had slowly leaked away after all these weeks spent in the lab. The top engineers in the city—as far as she knew—had managed what she was trying to do. But the grit in proving herself, in proving that those sketches weren't just dreams, pushed her along.

But the idea that her work might possibly influence the fate of the city was not something she could comprehend. It was not factual.

Lucien withheld information, but the money already flooding her usually embarrassing bank account was enough for her to keep the questions off her tongue. Also, now that Jack, Violet, and this Rio Gaverra were in the third world, still so far away from coming back, Lucien was normally locked up in his office with Lyla, or one of the other generals, floating in and out.

Jelan had wandered into the spacious kitchen more than a few times during the night for a snack or drink and watched Lucien sip a dark liquor from one of his crystal glasses, the weight of the city on his shoulders.

He would never show it to the others—then again, he didn't need to. With Jack gone, their gardia was fractured. A gaping hole in its heart. The system poured on without an important valve, and soon it was bound to leak. Clog.

Explode.

But he didn't rush her. He checked in every now and then to make sure she was comfortable and also reminded her about her breathing appointments which have helped tremendously, but otherwise, he firmly remained out of her lab, his breath down the necks of nearly everyone else.

Lyla had let Jelan drift into her thoughts while she padded over to a portable plascreen and scribbled notes with a unique pen. Jelan's hands itched to explore the handheld screen—something she'd never seen before moving in here. Something that existed only in the North, apparently.

"Is he ready?" asked Jelan.

The door opened, and in stepped Lucien. Dressed in a fitted tux, hair slicked back and freshly shaved, Jelan thought the man had just walked out of a photoshoot. His gaze landed on Jelan and he paused on the threshold. He cleared his throat, a smile on his lips. "Are you ready? We need to go over the plan."

Jelan nodded, a shiver running down her spine as his gaze passed over her again.

"This is recon, more or less. We need names. I'm sending four groups to infiltrate the party and gather as much information as we can. This party is for the release of a new weapon—nothing like the rumored one. All of the City Commanders will be there."

Lyla grunted.

Jelan motioned to her dress. "I'm guessing this is too late to ask—" *Because I'm a damn pushover, that's why.* "—but why am I going?"

"Because you will know what to pick up on in the conversation, especially if someone talks about the real weapon."

"I still don't understand…."

"These parties are filled with ego; bragging about achievements, boasting about their awards and flaunting their pride. My other spies are my military Plastechs, still unknown to Arvalo, but it is better to have more than one as it is a large party, and they will be talking in different words that I wouldn't be able to pick up on. Words that could give an idea to what they might be building or point us in the direction we need to go." He smiled, a spark in his eye. He handed her a card. "Also, because they don't know you. Your name for tonight is Gena Levinson."

Fine. She would go and she would listen. As long as she could leave at a reasonable hour and revive her introverted energy in her lab.

Her lab.

Skies.

Lucien held out his arm. "I'm sure you won't have a hard time getting information."

"Why?" She furrowed her brows.

His breath brushed her ear. "Because I would spill all of my secrets to anyone who looks like that."

Jelan was sure her blush didn't cool until they were in the sleek car and zooming through the streets of the North.

❀❀❀

Lucien dropped her off with an entrance ticket, her fake identification, and two guards before the sprawling red carpet that he was destined to step out on. Large cameras flashed for the various city magazines and newspapers as notable names appeared in glimmering dresses and sleek tuxes.

Guided by her guards, Jelan climbed the large staircase. She presented her invitation and fake ID at the side door for non-notable persons, and with a gruff nod from the towering bouncers, she entered.

And her eyes burned with tears. Elated tears.

Because she stood in the giant atrium belonging to the towering skyrise of Plastech Industries.

With the glittering, expensive crowd around her, Jelan became very aware that she was the only person from the belly of the South. And yet she stood, invited by a commander himself, within the fortress of her dreams.

The atrium was an edifice of cream stone, sleek steel, and

thick columns like chess pieces ready to be played. Balconies hoisted above, filled with important-looking guests who chatted and laughed, bubbling glasses of krinder in their hands. Along the corners and walls, plasma displays in tubes whirled in whites, blues, and purples, giving the atmosphere a celebratory vibe.

A five-tiered fountain burst with clear water from the center. Chandeliers hung low and illuminated the blue banners of Plastech Industries' symbol; two hands cupping a writhing ball of plasma.

Jelan would have been the only one to notice how lined and clean the palms were, even though it was a simple drawing. Hers would never look like that. She ignored the crawl of ice down her spine as her guards beckoned, keeping close. The number of people in the room had her curving her shoulders, wanting to seek out a corner to hide in. Her heart picked up its beat as she tucked her hands within the starlight folds of her pants. The perfect Elites here would stare, ask questions, wonder why she had such awful hands and why she had never fixed them. And she'd be unable to answer.

"Look," one of the guards—Bronto, a giant, russet-skinned man with small streaks of gray along the sides of his head—said. "This part is always fun. Lucien hates it."

"Jack normally loves it," the other guard said. Ashan. White skin, a dark beard, and a crooked nose. "Lucien would rather sneak through the back than face the cameras."

"I don't blame him," said Jelan, turning.

The red carpet for the famous guests ascended the stairs and continued through the yawning doors. Velvet ropes fenced the carpet and newspersons pressed up against them, some yelled at by bouncers when they got too close.

"Alexia Javez, and her wife, Venara," said Ashan.

Alexia Javez, Commander of Health and Biology, was a sight to behold with milky skin contrasting her long, inky hair. A deep, wine-red dress held in her lithe figure. Her face was sharp, her aura similar to Lyla's, giving Jelan no reason to wonder how she held such a position within the city. She commanded respect, and she got it. Without a doubt.

Others filed in after, names shouted that Jelan didn't know, but they were easily identified as renowned Elites. They waved, smiled brightly, posed for the cameras and answered questions.

"Hunt Covokai," said Ashan.

The Commander of Public Works and Rescue. His sharp chin jutted out, gray beard neatly clipped along it. He looked as though he'd rather be anywhere else.

"Ellis Pofer and…" Ashan narrowed his eyes. "Oh, he has a new girlfriend."

"Maren Honsin," clarified Bronto. "They were seen getting drinks at the Blue Front last week."

Commander of Transportation and Recreation. A close-set, blue-eyed man with a tiny beard along his chin. His bronze skin gleamed with hints of sweat on his bald head. His girlfriend clung to him, breasts ready to jump out of her purple dress. Jelan thought they looked like someone had shoved two large pomegranates underneath her skin and called it a day in the operating room.

"Then the one and only…" smiled Ashan. "Lucien Marin."

"Skies, he wishes he could teleport right out of there," said Bronto.

Her lips twitched in a small smile as Lucien, now-Commander of Trade and Commerce, made his way up the steps, hands shoved casually into his pockets, brown eyes wary as he looked around. The newspersons screamed at him, asking numerous questions about Jack, then others about his romantic life and what he had been up to.

"His first public appearance since then." Ashan frowned. "Gah, he should have practiced."

"He never answers questions; that's for Jack."

Based on Lucien's stiff appearance and glances toward his left, she could sense that Lucien also felt something missing. Jack was supposed to be there, and while Lucien would never mention the weakness, to her it was obvious that they held a deep, brotherly bond severed by the Sins. Lucien's courage to move on without him, even stepping onto the carpet when he could choose to go through the back without any questions, told her that he was trying his best. Along with facing the consequences of his brother's—*their*—actions.

Actions she became more aware might be false and mere rumors within the South. The only taste of gardia Jelan ever got was with her brother joining Arvalo and through proxy by Violet. Violet hated Jack Marin, but according to their trackers, Jelan supposed that hate had dwindled.

Unlike most people who wanted to live and breathe the hatred of the Marin commandment, Jelan had never quite developed her own opinion. Buildings had exploded in the South during the penultimate night of the gardia wars before Reed was sentenced. Still, the main war was between the gangs, fighting for territory and control using drugs, shiva, power, and more between the Commanders. It had kept the streets in the South quiet in the late hours, gunshots ringing, alarms blaring, and the shattering of glass, but Jelan had learned to despise all of them for not figuring out their shit and using the city as its war ground.

Based on the Commanders' glances as they stepped near the end of the carpet, there was no friendship between them, only tolerance. If friendship had ever existed, it had been fractured by the wars.

"And him," said Ashan with a slight growl. "Juss Arvalo."

The Commander of Plastech and Media stepped up wearing a crisp suit on his lanky body. She judged he might be in his mid-to-late-fifties by the frown lines along his mouth. His white skin told her he didn't spend much time outside.

A smile stretched his lips and Jelan thought it looked practiced. But it reached his eyes as he waved to the cameras, posed, and beckoned behind him.

"Oh shit, he brought the kids," said Ashan. "He never does that."

Arvalo had five kids, apparently by five different women. But that was a rumor, and a squashed one at that after their apparent mother was found dead from an overdose of a drug called honeycrush. It was a yellow powder mixed with nearly ten different pharmaceuticals that could be pilled or snorted to alleviate pain ailments.

It had been a big story within the city because the youngest, Mai, had only been five years old at the time and was found covered in the drug next to her mother's body. Jelan remembered her own mother crying about it and then lighting a candle, repeating Mai's name over and over to help that little girl through such trauma.

Apparently, her prayers never worked.

The crowd loved it. Loved how Arvalo walked up to his adult children—four boys and one scowling Mai—and embraced them. The cameras flashed and one of Mai's brothers nudged her. She put on a smile that never reached her eyes.

Jelan hated that she felt bad for Mai. Because Arvalo's main focus was on the boys and Mai eventually stood to the side, silver dress hugging her thin frame, jaw sharp from the constant clench. She watched her father embrace her brothers and not spare her a glance.

"That daughter, if her gaze could incinerate the room," snorted Ashan. He turned to Jelan. "Didn't she date your friend? Reed's wild sister?"

"Something like that," said Jelan bitterly.

"Almost stabbed her at a party because she stole Jack's ring." Ashan chuckled.

Jelan flashed him a dubious look.

Why Mai had targeted Violet and continued on with their tangled history was beyond Jelan. But Violet had been in a very dark place, a place where Jelan could not reach her, and in the end, Mai snapped something.

Anger. Hate. Resentment. Violet stopped being the uncaring, depressed skiv Jelan had been used to, and instead carried bitterness like a backpack, as if it held her together.

And then Kole had brought the guilt.

Once Arvalo was done doting on his kids, the Commanders posed for a final picture before dispersing. As Lucien caught Jelan's gaze, before a crowd hounded him, Jelan spied Arvalo flash a scathing look at Lucien.

And *that* look was the gardia. While this room was posed and entrancing for the five City Commanders, the lurking animosity set them right back in their place. The gardia, their military, were still at war with each other despite their public appearance above ground.

Because everything about the gardia was Underground. Under the table. Illicit and mainly functioning within the South. There was always a balance. A dark side to the light. And since it was such a sprawling citadel, a gang just wasn't the proper term for it. It was more political, more prevalent, and their power of commandment enabled the illegal activities while the Empire turned its head and Redders focused on more conspicuous crimes.

Skies, if the tension in the room were shiva, she'd be drunk off her ass at this point.

Lucien eventually sidled out of the crowd and beckoned Jelan. Ashan and Bronto stayed near.

"What's being revealed?" Jelan asked as Lucien placed a glass of krinder in her hand.

His gaze snapped behind and she turned. Arvalo was shaking hands with a man—a familiar man at that—and whispering to him.

"That right there is Chun Akard, newly promoted Plastech Head Engineer after the last one…" Lucien gave her a look. "You know. The unveiling should be…ah, there it is."

Jelan narrowed her eyes at the name. Very familiar.

His head craned and Jelan followed, aware of how his arm brushed hers. High above, to the collective claps of the guests, a covered item descended from the ceiling of the atrium and stopped above the fountain.

Arvalo took up a microphone and smiled. "Now, my fellow guests and the Citadel of Calesal, I present to you a new, advanced weapon headed by Plastech Akard."

The sheet dropped and Jelan gasped with the crowd.

A sword. The cool steel rimmed with translucence. The hilt was a sleek white with insignias on the back and the front. The body stretched in a straight line until one side curved like a crescent moon and met the other at the sharp, gleaming tip.

"I present to you: the plasblade!"

It ignited a rich, royal blue.

"Damn," Ashan said behind her.

It began to morph through different colors of the spectrum, and Jelan could hear, if not feel, the delicious thrum of plasma and the heat that escaped it.

Another flash of light and heads turned as Arvalo pulled a plasblade from his side and it sparked a bright orange.

"Mr. Akard, the demonstration." Arvalo handed off the sword to the Plastech.

Akard took the weapon with grace and turned to a statue Jelan hadn't noticed. The stone and metal structure sat on a plinth before the fountain. With a hiss, Akard arced the sword. It sliced through the body of the statue like butter, the plasmic heat simmering at the edges of obtrusion.

When she turned to see Lucien's reaction, he was already watching her with a grim expression. "Nice, right?"

"Unnecessary," she said.

"Most weaponry is unnecessary, but people love to develop more to instill fear."

"Right," she breathed. The crowd bellowed, clapping a roar in her ears. Jelan noticed Alexia Javez huddled next to her wife, arms crossed with a look that could kill.

At least they weren't the only ones unhappy about it.

"Now, let the celebrations begin!"

39

Not Your Game

Violet lunged, spinning to Anaya's side. She switched the blade to her other hand, aiming it back until it met Anaya's throat.

Anaya roughly pushed her away. "Again."

Violet took up her position across the living room, sweat dripping down her face as she handled the blade in her non-dominant hand. Anaya nodded once and Violet lunged again.

There was frustration in her moves, but if Anaya noticed, she didn't say anything. It had been like this for two days—scouting in the trees outside of the fortress, hunting for food, felling the roaming Endos, and then training in the evening until Violet's legs almost collapsed from the strain. She hardly noticed her muscles protesting each movement because the pain fueled her purpose.

Metal met metal with a piercing clash. Violet growled as Anaya parried to her left, then met another of her stabs at her right. Violet had trained with Gwen, but Anaya had a ruthlessness about her that was addicting. Her combativeness had Violet throwing every ounce of energy into her thrusts, her swipes, and her defensive counters. The world around them drifted away until it was only blade versus blade. She reveled in it, to physically *feel* something and to be able to push herself to her limits.

The dagger was slick in her hand as Violet careened it toward Anaya's side. Anaya crouched below, letting the metal swipe above her head, before jumping to Violet's throat. Violet dodged—barely.

The blade nicked her, but she felt no pain. She wrapped her hand around Anaya's outstretched arm, twisting so she was forced to drop her blade and went in for the headlock—

An elbow slammed straight into her face. Violet stumbled back, vision blurring.

"Douche." Violet rubbed her nose. It wasn't hard enough to have broken anything, but blood seeped out and she let it fall into her cupped hand. "I want a rematch."

"Get rest, Vi," Anaya said, wiping her own sweat. She sported nicks and bruises along her arms and neck. "I'm exhausted."

Violet didn't notice, and more so, she didn't care. She sneered. "Giving up so easily? I never thought I'd see the day."

"This has been my life, human. I am more used to it than you. Don't tire yourself because you are angry about what happened."

"I'm not angry about anything except your reluctance to fight me." She found a spare towel and wiped the blood. "I can play dirty, too."

"I'm tired, Vi." Anaya brushed her off. "And smelly. I'm taking a bath."

Violet frowned and plopped down on the floor. Rio's hums filled the domestic noises of the house. Jack lounged out on the balcony, sipping his liquor. The bath faucet cranked on and water gushed out from above.

Rio had recovered from Envy well, thanks to the meeter flower. He had woken up high enough that he couldn't quite form his words at first, before he turned to Violet and thanked her for not beating the sin out of him.

When the Sin took over, Anaya had said it was superficial things. Hair, clothing, possessions, homes, resources but even that resulted in killing. Bloodbaths in every village because someone would take one look at the cloak on another's back, one they didn't have, and they would slit any throat for it. Soon it turned deeper, more dark and twisted, and the hallucinations had begun even when no one was around. Envy for family lost, love, freedom, admiration, recognition; and it taunted the victim until they were so consumed with their resentment that they lost themselves.

"No one has exited for a reason, Sutton," Dr. Evek had said. *"They are not supposed to."*

In the end, she still did not know the reason behind Dr. Evek's words. Was it because it was so easy to die here? Or fall victim to the Sin? In reality, candidates died yes, but more often they survived and slowly moved on until that fateful sixth world where Reed was. Was that the answer why no one came out—did it have something to do with the Worldbreaker?

Her gut told her yes. *They are not supposed to.* But how would Dr. Evek know that? The Empire slid the candidates straight to the entrance with a bleak and routine goodbye, but Violet attributed that to their general shittiness.

But there were plasguns, the new plasblades, things directly *from* her city. Perhaps it was never the sin keeping candidates trapped at all.

She sheathed the blade and rubbed at her temples

"You need sleep."

She picked her head up. Rio leaned against the doorframe to the living room, towel flung over his shoulder. A streak of char lined his forehead.

"I also need to face the Sin one more time." Ice bloomed in her chest as if Envy agreed.

"You should eat first." He stalked into the room and plopped down next to her. "Dinner will be ready in…I don't know, actually. Whenever it is ready."

Shoulder to shoulder, both Southers gazed at the fireplace. Long, yet comfortable, silence passed until Violet turned to him. "Do you feel better?"

Rio sighed. "Sort of. I keep replaying it in my head though, partially because I haven't seen my family in so long and they were just… *there.* Real. I didn't want to leave the hallucination, even though it would have consumed me if I had stayed. I could feel that voice taking over while I simply watched from afar." He nudged her shoulder. "I'm…happy you understood."

Violet leaned into him. "You have six sisters, right?"

"Unfortunately," said Rio. He chuckled. "I mean, I love my sisters, but I'm convinced they were born to drive me insane."

"They wouldn't be siblings if they didn't."

"But if one of them were in the Sins, I would go after them." Rio leaned his head on Violet's. "If only to make sure they didn't feel alone."

Her throat tightened. She quieted for long enough that Rio wrapped his arm around her and drew her closer. She let him, because with Rio it was only loyalty and comfort. With him, since the moment they met, she didn't have to be anything but her broken, tired self, and he would accept it all.

"The doctor who gave me my tracker said something to me," breathed Violet. "She said, *'No one has exited for a reason…they are not supposed to.'* What do you think that means?"

A pause. "Why haven't you mentioned this before?"

"Because she also told me to off myself early on to make an impact," she said. "So I thought she was only trying to pity me."

"Well, she can go skiv off for saying such a thing, that's for sure." Rio's hand tightened around her shoulder. "I'm happy you didn't though, because it was really nice watching the Farm barbecue next to you."

She snorted.

"But I think with the talk of the Worldbreaker, the game is probably just a benefit to them in one way or another. I think if it were truly for redemption and to break the curse, we wouldn't die so easily. This… guy, or whatever… wouldn't let the Sins manifest so much, right? He'd control the clan wars or stop the Farm so they could only focus on producing their oil.…"

"Ahnsa, right?"

"Yeah, the Crale used it for everything, and I remember hearing them talk about their shipments—*massive* quantities. I mean, by the way they talked about it, I would think that much oil could power four Calesals. If not more. And you saw their towns, right?

They were not using it themselves."

Silence fell over both of them. Minds running, Violet tucked under Rio's arm as they stared at the wall. She wanted to open her mouth to continue discussing it, but her growing fear of this Worldbreaker's power kept her mouth shut.

"Also—you said you loved me today."

Violet turned to look at him. "I did but as a—"

"Are you about to friend-zone me?"

She snorted. "Yes."

A teasing look. "So I guess I should return the ring, then."

"I'm sure Anaya will love it."

"I don't have a pair of tits. She won't marry me."

"If she does accept, can I officiate your wedding?"

"Only if you dress up like the noodle man on Eighth."

"His beard is so long."

"He's the only one I want," sighed Rio. "I love him. He would feed me all kinds of noodles. Maybe I should propose to him."

"I think that is a good idea," said Violet. "Then I will dress up as him at your wedding and, plot twist, you accidentally marry *me*."

Rio laughed. "Perfect plan."

Silence fell over them and the door to the balcony opened. Violet's heart picked up.

Rio dipped his head close to her ear. "You still on him, yeah?"

"What does that mean?" she scoffed.

"You know—since the eyes thing—"

"He lured me into it," she whispered. "How about you? Are you done crying about your mama?"

He narrowed his eyes, lips twitching. "Harsh. You aren't very good with parental figures, are you?"

"I prefer not to talk about it."

"You have some stick up your ass in this world, little Vi." He smirked. "Wanna talk about it?"

"I literally just said—"

"Jack?" Rio gulped.

Violet looked toward the door.

Jack stood rigidly, eyes blazed, heavily dilated. "What do you think you're doing?"

Violet pulled away from Rio and both scrambled to their feet.

"I don't know." Rio held up his hands. "I wasn't doing anything. Jack—"

Jack's hand was on his blade and Violet immediately stepped between the two. "Jack, stop."

"You don't get to touch her." His eyes blackened until there was hardly any green left. "I see you. I know what you're doing. Hah. I *know* that look."

"He's in it. *Vi*," Rio panicked, stepping backward.

The danger looming around Jack had her hesitating. One flick of his hand and the blade could be out and in Rio's neck.

She walked over to Jack and placed her trembling hands on his chest. "Jack, this isn't you. Come back."

He didn't seem to notice her. He took another step forward and she was no match for his strength.

"Rio, leave—"

"But, Vi."

"*Now.*"

"Do not talk to her," Jack growled, removing his dagger. "Do not look at her like that."

Rio scrambled out of the living room. Anaya's voice crawled from the hallway, "*What's going on?*"

Jack went to lunge for the doorway, but Violet threw her body in his way. He looked down at her and blinked—

She slapped him across the cheek. Hard.

He blinked again. Green returned, dilating in and out with the black. He looked at her again and she snarled in his face, "You better come back to me, Jack Marin, or so help me I will gut you if you hurt Rio!" She pushed at his chest. He backed off. "Put that damned blade down *now*."

"Is dinner—" Anaya poked her head in.

"Dinner will be late!" Violet shouted. "Go drink. I got this."

Anaya took one narrow-eyed look at Jack and then retreated. "*Skivvin' men. Always with this shit.*"

Violet grabbed Jack, who blinked blearily, and dragged him out onto the balcony. She slammed the door and whirled on him. "Are you good?"

He was blinking faster now, hands going to his head. He calmed himself with some breaths and then, as if remembering, turned to the liquor bottle and chugged some of it. "Yeah."

She snatched the bottle from his hand.

"You can ask," he said. "You know. Last time I checked you had a voice. Foul as it is."

She set the bottle down. "What was that about? You know— you about to absolutely obliterate Rio for talking to me? What? Is this some protective male shit you have going on?"

"You were…cuddling." He gripped the railing.

"Skies forbid I cuddle with another male. Obviously, it means I'm about to sign my heart over to them." She rolled her eyes. "You owe him an apology."

"Yes," he sighed.

"Tell me," she breathed, suddenly nervous. "Tell me what that was…"

Her words caught in her throat. His eyes trailed her over, wholly green now, as if he were seeing her for the first time. His mouth parted, then closed.

"I'm not going to dagger your eyes out," she spat.

"I know you aren't." He stood to his full height.

"Then why are you looking at me like that?" Her heart hammered in her chest. He took careful, prowling steps toward her. She barely had time to blink before his lips were inches from hers. His scent of fire and salt invigorated her so much she held her breath.

"The issue is—" His finger drifted along her jawline. "Have you thought about what *I* might envy?"

"My fabulous personality?" she breathed.

He leaned in, not amused, and her back met wood. His hands

dropped to either side of her and he pressed in, long fingers wrapping around the railing. It creaked at his grip.

Thoughts eddied in and out of her head, but no darkness was called forth as Jack surrounded her, his warmth seeping, his dark curls slipping onto his forehead. Her mouth parted as he studied her, like a predator with a very mysterious prey.

"Maybe I envy all those living in luxury back in the city, with ease and ignorance of this...pain. Maybe I envy those who are running my gardia." He inhaled sharply. "Maybe I envy that blue in your eyes that reminds me so much of my home. Maybe I envy those who have not stained their hands with blood like I have, and live in a world of innocence." He dipped, lips on her ear, and whispered, "Or maybe I envy Rio because he shamelessly flirts with you, touches you, and you him. Because I *want* that. Only me. And perhaps more."

"It's not like that..." she breathed. "With Rio. It's not."

Her saying that didn't make a difference to the darkness of the Sin and what occurred. The power, the need, roared from him and she could hardly breathe. He restrained himself, even as he dragged his fingers slowly along her skin, until goosebumps erupted and she shuddered against him.

"Then what's it like with me?" he breathed, emotion flashing over his face. There was a flutter in her chest at that—a foreign, uncomfortable feeling.

"With you," she swallowed. "It's different...and weird. Very weird. I don't know. You're some big, bad killer—"

"And?"

"You've done horrible things in your life for power..."

"Go on."

"You sleep with women for pleasure or gain, and you use people for your benefit. You used my brother. You used your men. You used me..." She tilted her chin as Jack cocked his head, his lips so, so close to hers. "You used me in Wrath to get you out. You've done all this—"

Jack whispered, "If I'm so bad and horrible, why are you still here?"

He meant physically here. Trapped by him against this railing as the night moaned and chirped with whatever prowled.

"If I'm so bad for you, then leave." He pressed even closer. How much was closer? They were basically molded into one...

She stayed put. Instead, she lifted her hands and let them drag up his chest. Jack's breath grew heavy. But why did this feel so daring? She trailed the collar of his shirt and then the mark on his neck—

He grabbed her hand and pinned it to her side. *Sensitive spot, then*. Thick lashes lowered. His other hand came up to her jaw and she melted into its warmth.

He breathed against her lips, "Are you going to leave?"

Slowly, she shook her head.

"Even with all that I am?"

She nodded.

"Then, what's your next move, darling?"

She threaded her other hand through his hair and yanked her lips to his ear, where she whispered, "I'm not a game, Jack Marin."

She dipped under his arm and headed toward the door.

"What? You think I'm playing a game with you?" he called.

"If you ever want more with me, you go apologize to Rio right now." She yanked the door open. "That's *your* next move, got it?"

A smile. Dimples and all. "Yes, ma'am."

40

CRIMINAL

JELAN

THE PARTY, TO JELAN'S DISMAY, continued on and there was no sign of her leaving, let alone any discussion of plasma.

Most guests were more interested in gossip between their counterparts than the glittering, deadly sword that hung above their heads. There was a sister to the development too; a plasdagger. Both the blade and the dagger could retract into their hilt and provide for a stealthy carry.

Jelan was buzzing with the ambitiousness of it. Why hadn't she thought of plasma wrapping a blade? Her sketches were more... practical. Less advanced, save for the plashield that still lay unbuilt back in the lab. If these people celebrated such accomplishments, what would they say if she achieved her own product?

If. Jelan groaned. She couldn't say if. She needed to say *when.* The anticipation of finishing it, holding it within her scarred hands like the Plastech Industries insignia, thrilled her.

She leaned against a column, watching Chun Akard and another Elite play a chess game. The board lit within the lines at certain moves; gold for important pieces taken, red for each pawn removed, and so on.

She frowned at one move. The Elite man sighed in frustration while Akard leaned back in his seat, smug. His eyes flicked to her, dragged along her dress.

"Do you like plasma?" He smiled at her.

The Elite man ran a hand through his hair as he studied the board.

Jelan ignored the dance of her heart at the energy. She twirled a hand in a braid. "It…lights things up. I like that."

He snorted. She was thankful she could keep her expressions to a minimum because within, she was scowling.

She quickly grabbed another drink, filling both her hands, as he said, "Chun Akard," and extended his palm.

"Gena Levinson." Jelan motioned to her glasses. "I have to keep up with the rest of you."

He gave her an odd look but only smiled and clinked his glass on hers. "This new development deserves a celebration. I like that. Were you watching the chess game?"

"I think it is interesting."

"It takes a lot of skill to beat these men. They have been playing since they could talk, and every day, around lunch, there's usually a chess game going on to keep our minds active." Akard dragged his eyes over her. "It is what leads to magnificent developments."

She reined in her shiver because if she wanted any information to hand over to Lucien, the Head Plastech would probably be a great start. "It truly is a magnificent development. What do you plan on doing with it?"

Akard opened his mouth, but the Elite man moved his piece and sighed, "Your move, Chun."

But Akard's eyes remained on hers.

"Go ahead, sweetie," Akard said. "Play a move."

She bristled as eyes wove over to her, not expecting the attention beyond their simple conversation. She swallowed, shot back her entire glass and regretted it. Because these men sipped their drinks, not downed them like Southers.

She smiled sheepishly and stepped forward.

Her eyes swept over the board and a small smile curved at her lips. Ignoring the gazes on her mangled hands and the clench of her stomach that always came along with it, she grabbed the rook and moved it to a square.

The Elite smiled like a fool as he snatched her queen. "Your loss, Chun." He placed it with the rest of his conquered pieces. Plasma gilded the board at his capture. "Sorry, sweetheart, this game takes practice—"

Jelan moved her rook once more.

The men around her quieted, the Elite gaping at the board as it flashed a victory blue.

"Checkmate," said Jelan.

"What—" the man lunged forward, glaring down at the board and searching for a lie. With each passing moment, his face fell, and the cool shock of humiliation brought a smile to her lips. "I can't believe it."

"Lucky move, I guess." She flicked a braid behind her back. The beads clinked. She turned to Akard. "Thanks for the win."

A burning at her back had her turning. Up above, alongside the other Commanders, Lucien stared at her with pride bursting on his handsome face. He raised his glass, lips moving, "*Good job.*"

Jelan shrugged and fetched herself another drink. The men around still stared at the board and then back at her as she weaved away.

"Wait!"

Akard sidled up next to her. His eyes drifted over her body again. "Have you ever seen the inside of a plaslab?" Honeyed desperation laced his voice and Jelan tried not to gag. He was what, forty? Fifty?

And her height at that.

But she didn't want to disappoint Lucien, and she especially didn't want Arvalo to have the upper hand at the expense of her nerves.

A movement caught her eyes.

She nearly dropped her glass.

In the far distance of the party, Ahmad Gregory, her estranged brother, leaned into Arvalo and whispered in his ear while pointing into the milling crowd. Her heart rolled into her stomach, a cold sweat crawling at the back of her neck.

Gardia members were not supposed to be here. Her brother was *not* supposed to be here, at the hip of Arvalo.

Akard's hand brushed her arm and snapped her out. She hurriedly blurted, "I'd love to see it."

She took Akard's arm, giving a hesitant look back at Ahmad, who still hadn't noticed her. Her gaze involuntarily flicked to one of the balconies, where Lucien leaned on the stone, watching her with cool eyes.

Not her. Akard.

She nodded. *Trust me.*

He narrowed his eyes, then reluctantly nodded back.

"Your guards don't need to come," said Akard. "I'll take care of you."

Jelan looked to Ashan and Bronto, and to her dismay, she waved them off. "I'll be right back!"

They balked at her, moved to follow again, but she hurriedly shook her head and let Akard lead her to the elevators. He flashed his ID and drew her in. The doors shut on Ashan and Bronto's concerned faces.

Skies, she was in deep shit. Was this how Violet felt when she got into trouble? No, Violet would have lounged against the wall and been unfazed by the power in the room. Jelan tried to calm her racing heart. Lucien said they needed information, and she was going straight to the heart of it.

"You're a silent one," said Akard.

She leaned into the comfort of the dagger strapped to her leg.

"I like to observe," she mumbled, forcing a smile on her face. "And plasma. I think it's great."

She sounded like a damn robotic record player.

The doors opened. Fourth floor. She was sure Ashan and Bronto had watched which floor they'd stopped on.

Before her sprawled a space that laughed at her own. The entire floor was a working plaslab, save for a few office rooms, one labeled 'Chun Akard'. Taking in the spotless floors, the glass walls, and the giant plasmic neutralizer at the center, Jelan had stopped breathing in awe.

"Great, right?"

Fabulous. Exquisite. Amazing.

She had half a mind to never leave. Skies, the things she could do here, the potential of her work and all those sketches. Her hands tingled in anticipation.

Akard led her forward and proceeded to give a tour, simplifying his vocabulary so *Gena* could understand. Jelan already knew what every piece of equipment did, but her fascination was not fake.

He finished the tour outside the door to his office. She dreaded this part, because it meant—

A beep sounded at his hip. Akard looked down at the pager. "Oh, I have to answer a few questions to reporters. We should go back."

"Oh, okay," she said sadly.

He led her back to the elevator. They descended. She leaned on him, fingers reaching into his pocket—

When the elevator opened, there was an onslaught of reporters and Akard zoomed out. "I will find you later!"

Once he was gone, no crowd stood there. No one saw her. She was a wraith in the shadows, invisible to the power in the room. Ashan and Bronto were looking away…

So Jelan stayed within the elevator and let the doors shut again. She pressed level four and went back to the lab, Akard's key card in her hand.

She hurried over to his office and swiped the ID against the scanner. It blinked green. The door clicked open. She stepped into the dark, wide space with its huge desk covered in papers, lounge chairs, a giant plascreen, and shelves of books.

Time ticked in her head. She didn't ask him a damn thing, but being in his office? Even better. Right? She didn't even know where her daring came from. Spontaneity and thievery was not her thing, but here she was, breaking and entering. One look at her hands told her she *couldn't* get caught. At least not with fingerprints. And Akard would never mention to Gena that there couldn't be security cameras near plasma labs because unspun energy disrupted it.

But Jelan Gregory already knew that.

She gave herself five minutes to look around. Nothing weird in the bookshelf, nothing on the coffee table other than simple notes.

She saved the most time for the desk. The papers included congratulatory letters, scribbles of degrees and money for parts, notes with quick thoughts and—

Her foot stepped underneath, where space should have been for a chair. Instead, she kicked a hollow wooden obstacle.

She dropped down to her knees, finding the compartment and swiping the key against it. No scanner here. Only a large padlock that was keeping many secrets.

She sighed. She never thought she'd have to use the technique that Violet had taught her.

She pulled the dagger from its sheath and whittled with the lock, sweat beading at her brows as she earnestly pressed, willing it to click open.

And like a soft heartbeat, it did.

She put the dagger back and opened the long compartment. Out came extensive rolls of blueprints. She unfurled them on the desk and bit her horrified gasp.

The lock at the door buzzed. Opened.

Kole *Akard* stepped through.

He blinked. She gaped back.

"Did you find it?" Chun Akard called from the elevator. "Son, hurry, I need them for the reporters."

Kole swallowed. Stepped into the room and grabbed the pair of glasses near Jelan's elbow.

"Yes, I did!" he called to his father.

"Bring them here, boy. Now!"

"Coming, Father!"

Kole's eyes drifted to the blueprints in her hands.

"Now!"

Kole flinched at the anger in his father's voice.

"Best you leave a minute after me. There's a staircase to your left. Go down five floors. Take a right. You will find the servants' entrance." He nodded to a map case. "I'd take one of those, too."

"Kole…" Jelan started.

"I still expect drinks," Kole said without a smile as he backed out of the room. "And now an explanation. Wait for one minute once I shut this door."

She nodded.

The door shut.

Jelan's heart thundered in her chest as she counted the agonizing sixty seconds. Once she reached the end, her scarred hand met the cold of the doorknob. Soundlessly, she opened it, checked that the hallway was empty, slipped out, and darted toward the staircase. Down five flights, out the door, then to the right, she met the bustling kitchen filled with people. They hardly spared her a glance as she shimmied to the doorway and then out into the back alley behind the Industry's skyrise.

Disorientation hit her, but Jelan was used to crawling amidst the shadows and hiding. She just didn't know where she was going.

It took nearly an hour to find her way back to Lucien's building.

When the elevators to the penthouse doors opened, guards were there, plasguns at ready.

Jelan held her hands up. "It's me. Just me."

"Jelan?" called a voice. Lucien. The guards lowered their weapons and let them pass. "Where in the skies have you been? I was looking all over for you at the party, and then you weren't there...." He ran a hand through his hair. His eyes flicked to the map case behind her back. "Oh, did you get a souvenir?"

"I stole it from the guy's office. He showed me. Then I went back in...." Her heart still raced. She hadn't thought. Just did. Because seeing her brother around the arm of Arvalo, needing to prove herself, the elation after the chess win...

Lucien looked as if he was about to hug her, so Jelan stepped out of the elevator quickly and strutted into the living room. The lights flashed on, sensing her enter.

She took the case off her back, popped the top, and lay the blueprints on the coffee table. Her mind was a dull roar, adrenaline pumping from her daring act.

Before glancing at the map, Lucien brushed her arm, letting her know he was there. Wondering if she was okay.

When she looked at her hands, trembling, a haughty laugh escaped her.

His brows drew together.

But Jelan only giggled, "I just stole—" She looked up at him. "From the fucking head engineer at Plastech Industries."

He smiled. "That you did."

Her grin bit into her cheeks, scrunching her eyes. She laughed again, coming off the high that had started when those elevator doors had shut and Kole had—

"Shit," she said. "Someone saw me."

Lucien's face dropped. "Name?"

Jelan's gaze flicked to the map. Now in proper light, and with time, she could fully take it in. It was clearly a map of Calesal, but with certain points marked in bright red ink. Notes littered it.

"Name?" said Lucien quickly. "We need to get to him—"

"What is this?" She pointed to one of the red marks and the note written next to it. "The plasmic degree of this...is like a bomb."

"Jelan, *name*."

"He doesn't know anything about this." She met his gaze. "He—he let me go. Saw me in the office and told me how to escape and to bring the map case with me. He isn't a danger."

"I'm not going to ask again," snapped Lucien. "If even one person knows that you had your hands on this—that your face could be sketched and then led back to the Marin Empire, that we even knew to look for something like this, it could cause another war. The city is worth protecting for maintaining this secrecy. I need his name, Jelan."

Her mouth opened and closed. But she remembered the way Mr. Akard had yelled at Kole, how Kole had flinched. "You can't kill him. Please. Please don't kill him. He's innocent."

Lucien blinked with confusion. "Kill? I'm not going to kill him."

"Then what are you going to do?"

"I'll make that decision when I know who this person is."

Jelan swallowed. "No torture, no killing. Not with him. Give him a new identity and a comfortable life. I—however you gardia people work this sort of thing. But no *killing*."

Bronto shifted at the door, Ashan purposely looking away from the interaction.

Tone it down.

But Jelan ignored her mother's voice. She held her shoulders back despite how much she wanted to disappear as Lucien's hard gaze bore her down. A Commander. A gardia Commander.

"No killing," Jelan mumbled again.

Lucien held out his hand. "No killing."

So Jelan sucked up her fear, her insecurity, and clasped her scarred hand with his calloused one. She bit a yelp as Lucien jerked her forward, her shoulder meeting his arm. He bent toward her ear, warm breath on her skin. "Tell me the name."

"Kole Akard."

He squeezed her hand. Let it go. Turned to Bronto and Ashan. "Kole Akard. Find him, blindfold him, bring him to me."

"Here?"

Lucien thought for a moment, then looked back to Jelan's pleading face. "To the Mid-sector location. Take Hira's serum. I want to vet him before I do anything else."

"Yes, boss," they said and turned out of the door. The elevator dinged.

"You're going to use truth serum on him?" asked Jelan softly.

"He could be as innocent as you say, but I have to make sure. There is no room for mistakes. You have to understand the consequences of what you just did."

A shiver descended down her spine. "Are they—will they be after me?"

"Most likely, but it is best if we squash every single thing that could lead back to you and us. I'll send one of Lyla's spies to drug Chun Akard so he doesn't remember much about the night before, attributing it to too much drink."

Jelan shoved her hands under her armpits. She couldn't control her shaking. She was wanted now.

"I think I need a drink." Jelan dropped onto the couch. "A strong one. Perhaps just the bottle."

"I will get that for you, but..." He sighed and then knelt down before her. "There are no morals in this world. You have to understand that. This city was built on blood, walls erected to cage or protect. What good is that plasblade going to do except destroy more and threaten more?"

Jelan blinked back the burning in her eyes.

"You did good, Jelan. There's no right and wrong here, but you did good. Splendid, actually. I cannot risk another weapon being used against this city. All of the Commanders are at odds, and no one even knows the sides in this damned thing. It is a mess, but this is a start. Stopping Arvalo is right."

"I know."

His hand brushed her dress. "I will get the drink, and then we will study the map, since neither of us are good at sleeping."

She merely nodded as he stood and stalked over to a bartending tray. He poured the deep brown liquor she'd watch him sit out on the balcony and drink. When he handed her the glass, she took a long sip.

"It is a map of Calesal?" He sat on the couch across from her.

"With high-degree plasmic points," she muttered again, looking at the map. "There are also two points at the exact location of the Sky Arches."

"What is..." Lucien turned the map. "Aether?"

Jelan shrugged. "Never heard of it. Maybe it's a type of metal? The special metal to construct the arches?"

"That's a good guess," said Lucien. "I've never heard the word. Perhaps Hira would know...."

Jelan perked up at that. "Is she allowed—could we invite her here?"

Lucien gave her a long look as he swirled his glass. "I will need to vet her, too."

"She'll flay you."

"I know."

"So you'll invite her?"

"Yes," huffed Lucien. "In three days. Jenkins, too. We are going to have a busy penthouse very soon."

"Oh, why?"

"Meema's lease at her elderly home is up. Now that she has been recovering and on medication...." Lucien smiled into his drink. "She is very, *very* fun."

Jelan knew that. Knew that well.

Silence passed and she studied Lucien, that slight agony on his face she was used to recognizing. It existed on hers too; when the loved one was gone and one found themselves reminiscing about them. The pain ignited all over again at the gaping hole Violet had left in her life, but instead she turned to Lucien, a smile on her face.

Wanting to give him hope. Wanting to *believe* in this hope.

She cleared her throat. "When all this is over and Jack is back, what do you think will happen?"

"When my brother is back..." Lucien swirled his glass with a twitch of his lips. "Arvalo's head will depart from his body."

41

MASOCHIST

"**STOP MOVING.**"

"You're yanking too much."

"I haven't done this in a while—"

"Then why did you volunteer?"

"Because I *can* do it. Do you want it loose or tight?"

"Tight," said Violet, lifting her head again.

Jack tugged on her hair and finished weaving the braid at her scalp, now brushing the nape of her neck. She ignored the shiver that ran down her spine.

"How *do* you know how to braid hair?" she asked.

"Kids like me." A shrug. "I get along with them."

She scoffed, "Big, bad Jack Marin playing with kids?"

"I may be able to kill a man very quickly, Violet, but that's not my only personality trait."

She bit down on her flinch as his breath brushed her ear. Tingles erupted within her. Another shiver.

Jack's nimble fingers reached over her shoulder. "Hair tie."

She handed it to him. He wrapped the bottom of her braid, placed it gently on her back, and sighed, "Good enough."

When she reached back to feel the braid, her brows lifted in surprise. "You weren't kidding."

"I used to babysit."

She turned her head and met his playful eyes. "Really?"

"When there were assassins out for my head and I had nothing else to do," he deadpanned.

"Lovely."

She stood from her cross-legged position, Jack following her.

Her eyes met his curly locks. "I could braid yours."

"I like the sexy, tousled look." He ran a hand through his hair. "Maybe later."

When a single curl fell and kissed his brow, she swallowed hard and turned abruptly back toward the kitchen, exiting the living room.

Jack's low laugh followed her.

Anaya squatted by the hearth, roasted venison smoking the room and making Violet's mouth water. They'd managed to find some eggs from tiny colorful birds. Like she had done in Gluttony, Violet had left a stash of berries in the nest. Anaya had given her shit for it on their way back to the treehouse, but Violet merely shoved her into a mud pile and hurried away, fighting a smile.

Now clean and in a better mood, Anaya flipped the meat so it charred on the other side and then sat on the floor. "Do you see that little thing on the window there?"

Violet's head snapped to the sill nearest her, where a colorful lizard of orange, green, and blue sat with an arched head and a curled tail.

"What is that?"

"A nomulasa," said Anaya. "A chameleon, my papa called it. Go near it and it will change colors."

"I'm not falling for that like the meeter flower."

Anaya cackled. "It's not deadly. It's like an Endolier. Changing skins and whatnot."

Violet's brows flew up. "Really?"

"Try to touch it and it will show you. They are everywhere in Iveyrez."

Violet thought of a million other things she'd rather do than touch the chameleon, but she continued. She neared the thing, as long as the tip of her middle finger to the start of her wrist. Its big, scaly eyes blinked at her, but it did not move.

"Don't be a skiv," said Anaya.

"I'm not being a skiv, you twat," snapped Violet.

"Twat?"

"Add it to your vocabulary." Violet waved her hand, and at the movement, the lizard's tail shimmered black.

Black.

It seemed unnatural on the thing, and it reminded Violet of the nostor sword Anaya kept near her at all times. Its eye blinked and Violet could have sworn a whirring sounded.

"What a strange creature," murmured Violet.

She reached a finger out to touch it. Poke it. Lose a digit. She didn't know—

A long, pink tongue flashed out and caught her finger. Violet shrieked in surprise, vaulting back as a sticky substance met her skin. The chameleon flicked its tongue again and slithered out of the window, back into the jungle expanse.

Anaya laughed loudly, clutching her belly. "It is harmless."

"It's strange to me." Violet wiped her hand on her pants. "But it is cute. I have to admit."

Anaya pointed the spatula at her. "You need to get the Iris."

"I'm aware."

"What are you jealous of? Me? My stunning beauty?"

"I'm certainly not jealous of your small height."

"Skiv," scoffed Anaya and Violet lifted a brow. Anaya continued, "Rio taught me...."

The front door slammed open. "Speaking of the man."

Rio hurried in. Blood marked his cheek and a leaf stuck out of his hair. He looked around, frazzled, and blurted, "There's a hunting party out for candidates. They know we are here. And..." Rio swallowed, paling. "He's coming. The Worldbreaker is coming in two days, they said."

Jack entered the kitchen, toweling his wet hair. "Two days?"

"A hunting party?" Violet asked.

Anaya slammed her spatula on the table, groaning in frustration.

"Is that bad?" asked Rio. "That must be bad. All of these things must be bad."

"The hunting party is the first thing to deal with," said Anaya. "We've managed to stay quiet with the night monsters, but the party is looking for fresh candidates to take back to the compound."

"We don't have the Iris yet."

All gazes turned to Violet, and she winced.

"Did they see you, Rio?" asked Jack.

"I don't think so. I was up in the tree when I heard their conversation. There were at least fourteen in the party, all candidates themselves, and one of them mentioned that you, Jack, were in the third world."

Jack exhaled. Rubbed at his face.

"I know," Rio said. "But word traveled from Gluttony, I'm guessing."

A knowing look passed between the three candidates.

"So what?" Violet tugged at her braid. "He blew up the Farm. I'm sure it ruined their oil production, but in the end, this Worldbreaker leaves the candidates to these elements and sins like…what else are we going to do if we fight to stay alive? This whole thing is bullshit."

Rio rubbed at his face. "I just want some skivvin' sleep."

"Everything is more connected than it seems and the hierarchy is beyond me. From what I understand, the Worldbreaker stays in the main world—given that two worlds on that screen are the most populated, it is either the fourth or sixth," said Jack. "But he can freely travel between all the worlds and has some control over them. So he's connected to all of it. Like a…walking portal, so to speak."

"Have you ever seen someone *appear* at the portal in the compound?" Violet asked Anaya.

Anaya shrugged. "If they do, they do it at night. Or when I'm not looking."

"We can't remove our trackers, can we?"

"There's no way to take the tracker out. It is in the neck, and there are too many arteries or ways to kill yourself before you get to it," said Rio.

Jack turned to Rio. "You said this hunting party is looking for candidates, right?"

"I think they are a couple of miles out. I managed to go around them and run straight here because they were stopped by a horde of Endos. They are headed this way, though, and should be here by nightfall."

"That gives us three hours," said Jack. "We need to eat, turn off all the lights, get the Iris, and make this place look unlivable." Jack took Violet by the jaw and stared into her eyes. "Is this triggering you?"

"It is annoying me." She removed his hands from her face. "I don't know anything else...."

"My scales are cool." Anaya lifted her arms to flash them in the light. "Don't you want something like that?"

"Not really."

"Well..." Anaya clapped her hands together and glanced at Jack, then nodded to Violet. "I guess since this shit is so perfect and she doesn't envy anything else, we should eat."

Violet sagged with relief. "I'm starving—"

Arms wrapped her body, covered her mouth. Jack whispered in her ear. "Not you, darling."

"Get the rope, Rio," instructed Anaya.

Rope? Violet said into Jack's hand.

Rio disappeared while Jack sat Violet in one of the dining chairs, pinning her down. She flailed and he shushed her.

Rio returned with shredded shirts tied into a long rope. Violet gasped into Jack's hand as Rio began to wrap it around her, securing her body to the chair. Her arms were restrained to her side, her thighs pressed tightly to the wood.

"Now the gag." Anaya grinned.

Jack's hand moved and Violet opened her mouth to let out a string of curses, but Anaya was quick, shoving a wad of cloth into her mouth and wrapping another around it.

"Skies, you can make it so easy, Vi." Rio patted her shoulder. "Now, time to eat."

"Here, let me help you." Jack pushed her chair up to the table while Anaya plopped three food-filled plates down. Jack brushed Violet's hair back. "I want to make sure you're comfortable. You can see, right?"

Violet grumbled into the gag.

The three sat in their seats. Rio tucked his napkin into the collar of his shirt, Anaya licked her lips, and Jack clapped his hands, a smile on his face.

"This looks delicious, Anaya. You really do know how to cook," said Rio.

"Thank you so much." Anaya shoved her fork into a hunk of meat. "I have been hungry all day. I couldn't wait to dig into this."

Jack moaned dramatically. "Holy shit."

Rio dropped a strip into his mouth, then slammed his hand on the table. "Amazing! Take my money!"

"I wanted something juicy, something mouth-watering," explained Anaya as she took a bite. "And—I did just that. *Yum.*"

Violet scowled, purposely looking away from their plates. Her stomach rumbled loudly and Jack cocked his head. "Someone's hungry."

"Look at it, Vi." Rio dangled a piece in front of her face. Juices dripped onto the table. "Just look at it. Doesn't it look delicious?"

She averted her gaze to the ceiling.

A thump hit the table and Anaya was leaning over it. On it. She grabbed Violet's jaw and forced her to look at the meat. "I'm offended. I worked so hard to make this food the most delicious thing you could possibly imagine…."

Rio slapped the strip of meat against Violet's cheek.

"There, yes, feel the texture, wouldn't that be so nice to chew?" Anaya petted Violet's hair with her other hand.

"Skies," snorted Jack.

Violet's stomach rumbled again.

Anaya now had her knees on the table. "Do you want a bite?"

Yes. Yes, we do.

Violet nodded her head.

Rio dragged the strip under Violet's nose. "Big, deep breath in."

Ice pricked at her chest. Violet jerked toward the food, moaning. Rio pulled the meat away and plopped it into his mouth.

Violet snarled and her vision blackened.

Take it. You want it. Kill them and take all of it. You are so hungry. Why do they get to eat and you don't?

Violet jerked forward again, her fists clenching. *I want it, I want it.*

"Her eyes are pretty black. I think she's good," Jack's voice crawled through the darkness. "Go gentle—"

A hard slap met Violet's cheek. Her head whipped to the side, and Envy slithered away. Violet's hand burned.

She blinked back the blurriness in her vision.

"I said go gentle." Jack scowled.

"Sorry." Anaya smiled.

A clink hit the table. The silver of the Iris glimmered. It rolled, and before it could fall off, Jack caught it and stood it up as a centerpiece.

"Well done, Vi." Rio pointed his fork. "You know, the Iris would make a nice candle if you think about it."

Jack stood up, came around the table, and began to untie her. His knuckle brushed her temple. "You did well."

Anaya placed a filled plate in front of her. "Eat up."

Jack removed her gag, and Violet, mouth dry, grasped a piece of meat.

"Fuck *all* of you."

❄❄❄

When Violet was freshly bathed and in a better mood, she dropped downstairs. Tension lingered throughout the house as night descended on the jungle. The fires had been put out; the house was dark. Rio was packing their stuff in case they needed a quick getaway, and Anaya was camouflaging herself on the rooftop as their lookout for the hunters.

In the darkness, she found Jack in his usual spot, lounging on the floor of the balcony, back against the house. Violet spotted through the window that his shoulders were tight, jaw hard as he thought, long and hard, while looking into the firefly-filled jungle expanse of Iveyrez.

When she opened the door, his head snapped to her. And then he relaxed.

"Smoke?" he offered.

She shook her head, surprising both him and herself.

"How are you?" she asked.

"Fine. Why?"

"Aren't you tired of being hunted?" She leaned her back against the railing. "I sure am. It's getting a bit old at this point."

"It boosts my god complex," he said. "Everyone wanting me, that kind of thing."

Violet glanced at him, half-surprised to find those eyes already on her, studying her, unsaid words within them.

His soft expression tightened and Violet scoffed, "Do you ever drop the act?"

"What act?"

"Oh, the one about being both the worst and the smartest in the room."

"Well, I *am* those things." A slight smile. "But if you're asking if I ever relax, the answer is no. Not really."

She blinked at that. "Not even back in Calesal?"

"I was responsible for a city, Violet, and even if I had a million drinks of krinder, I still had my head down in some papers, trying to solve some issue." He leaned his head against the wall. "It's been a long time since I felt peace."

"Are you finally going to tell me your tragic backstory?" she teased.

"No," he said, and the way his voice wavered had her playful demeanor slithering away. "I'm not ready for that, yet. At least, I don't think I am."

"Oh." She picked at the scabs on her hand. "Yeah, it's okay. You don't have to."

"So what do you do to relax?"

She plopped down next to him. "Drugs," she deadpanned.

He snorted.

She continued, "Sex, too, but even that can be too much work with the wrong partner."

"A very true statement," he sighed, then whipped his head to her, eyes flashing jokingly. "I can do all the work, if you want to give it a go."

Heat rushed to her cheeks. "'Give it a go?' Is that really how you're going to ask me to sleep with you?"

"I promise you will be very relaxed at the end."

"I'd literally rather volley myself off this balcony," she said, tasting the lie.

"Well, I can wiggle some fingers, or a tongue, to make you feel better after you break all your bones."

"It's about the pacing of it." She wrinkled her nose. "You can't just go poking your fingers into places and think it's going to send them into the next dimension. You gotta—" She rotated her fingers, curled them. "And find that little, but *amazing*, spot."

"*Then* they start getting all whiny and frisky. So you have to pin their hips down and find the nub to end all nubs." He licked his lips. "Fuck me, I miss that."

Violet was very aware of how the heat cascaded down to her core, also very aware of how Jack's long fingers curved and arched while he was trying to show her. He was still talking, actually, but her heart was in her ears at the influx of pleasure drawing her into a place she'd never imagined with…

"Violet?" he whispered, and then his voice deepened, "do you want me to show you?"

"I know you said those words the other day…." She swallowed. "You don't actually see me like that, do you?"

A long silence passed while he looked at her. His gaze flicked to every bit of her exposed skin, to the way her nails dug into the wood of the floor, to the incessant flush of her cheeks, and then to her lips.

He was leaning closer, and Violet didn't wait for an answer before she said, "My brother will kill you."

His hand reached to cradle her jaw. He grabbed her hip, and she bit her surprise as he pulled her onto his lap, those bedroom eyes boring into hers. She could feel, if not hear, the rapid beating of his heart, matching her rhythm.

"I kind of want to let him," he breathed upon her lips.

He looked at her, between her eyes, then back down to her lips. "May I?"

She nearly scoffed, but the way his hands gripped her, his breath mixed with hers, and the yearning curiosity in his face all had her heart pounding out of her ears, heat pooling low, low, low…

He waited for her yes.

So she lifted her dagger to his neck and said, "Go ahead, kiss me."

Amusement shined along with the challenge. "*Violet.*"

His throat bobbed against blade. He angled his head, fingers squeezing her hips hard enough that warmth flooded through her. Demanding, craving. His heart pounded underneath her hand while the other held the blade steady.

"What?" she asked innocently.

"This might be turning me on," he said.

"Masochist."

"Something along those lines."

She lifted the dagger so it was underneath his jaw, meeting that blazing freedom within his gaze.

"I said kiss me, Jack Marin."

A pause. A breath.

He leaned in without a care in the world. Like nothing could separate this moment or keep him from what he wanted.

Their lips brushed gently, two souls whose slates were wiped clean and they were fresh, innocent for the first time, exploring the idea of bodies and feelings like kids with sugar. Tentative, nervous, filled with uncertainty, but fueled by curiosity.

When she pulled back, astonished, and lifted her gaze to meet his, their walls crumbled down.

A Souther, a Commander. A wild woman destined for nothing, and an ambitious man who had lost everything.

And yet, within it all, something changed.

Snapped.

And unraveled.

Jack pushed her hand and the dagger aside. He reached for her face and collided his lips with hers.

The dagger slid from her grip. Her hands wrapped the back of his neck as passion overrode her. It was a dance, a drug, a frenzy of tasting the sweetest fruit and wanting more and more and more…

Kissing him was euphoric. And yet she hadn't expected it to *be* this way. He kissed her like she was chocolate. Touched her like she might turn into a ghost. A tiny whisper in her head told her Jack Marin was not supposed to be gentle, yet every touch was made with a semblance of care, his lips and tongue expertly molding into her own with patience that suggested maybe, just there, kissing each other, Jack would be satisfied.

His need grew, as did hers. Their teeth crashed before he gripped her jaw and held her mouth against his. She parted her lips willingly. His tongue dove in to meet hers and she nearly scoffed into his mouth.

Dominance was her thing. She was used to the control.

So she took it.

She grasped the soft curls at the back of his head and pulled, hard enough that his lips left hers and his sharp jaw tilted upward. She rose on her knees.

"Damn," he breathed heavily. "You kiss like you hate me."

"I do hate you," she muttered against his lips. "I hate everything about you."

"Then hate me some more."

Her mouth twitched. Before she could kiss him again, before she could even process a thought, Jack changed his mind.

He flipped them so she lay on her back, pressed into the worn wood.

Her hands shot out to take control, grasp his shirt, pull him closer, but Jack chuckled and found her wrists, slamming them above her head.

"I think I've met my match," he murmured.

And when he kissed her again, she melted into those lips, into the warmth of him as he hovered over her. Her thoughts muddled—she didn't know where this was going, but skies, she would risk it all to feel this way with a man. With anyone.

He groaned into her mouth at the way she bit his lip and tugged on it, and she gasped when he ground into her, his hardness—

An inhuman scream ripped through the air, and they flew off each other like a bomb had exploded between them. Just as the scream had started, it stopped, and a sickening squelch followed, coming from the upper level of the home.

They spared a look at each other. Her lips swollen and her shirt rumpled. His hair disheveled. They breathed, gaped, and Violet knew that whatever had just happened between them, reality had separated it with that scream.

She scrambled up. Her heart pounded in her chest, cheeks reddening. Regret? Did she regret it?

His mouth parted.

She twisted away, rushed through the door, and ran upstairs before she could give it a second thought.

42

Bots

"**You skiv. You damn skiv!**" Anaya's voice called.

"I didn't know—"

Violet burst through the door, Jack right behind her.

"—that he would bite me! It hurt!" Rio held up his bloody finger and paled. "I think the tip is gone."

Violet whipped to the windowsill where that nomulasa, the chameleon, was back again. And whirring. Loudly.

"Is that normal for a lizard?" Rio asked as the tail shimmered black like it had before.

"I've never seen." Anaya squinted her eyes, and a moment later they widened. "*Nostor*. Get back!"

The tail glistened black again. Those ringed nostor eyes blinked. And then it transformed.

The tiny chameleon stretched and morphed. Within its joints, glimmers of nostor twinkled, reconstructed, until over and over the metal plates slapped one after the other, lengthening the legs, its neck, the head.

The side of the house ruptured in cracks of wood, splitting the window and destroying half the room. Rio and Anaya dove for the opposite side, where Violet shielded her head, all the while her heart pounded in fierce realization.

No wonder nostor was familiar.

Because it was covering the gigantic machines that had attacked in Wrath.

"Run!" called Anaya.

The metal added more and more to its limbs and head. Within moments, an enormous scaly lizard blended with the wood. It whipped its head, the size of half Violet's body.

And it roared.

Jack pulled Violet to the door, Rio after him, while Anaya grabbed her sword and hissed right back.

"Now is not the time for that!" called Rio.

The giant robot lizard whipped its taloned tail through the wall to the bathroom. Wood snapped, cleaving into hundreds of pieces.

They raced for the ladder, Jack shoving Violet and Rio down while Anaya smiled at the lizard. "Come and get me, you twat."

Jack grabbed her arm. "Later, evil one."

They ran down through the house, gathering their already-packed bags.

Wood rained. Violet looked up in horror to see the scaly foot of the lizard peering through the ceiling. It removed its foot, shoved its head through, and that tongue darted out.

Anaya ducked and slashed her sword above her head. It cut through the pink and black tongue, watery blood slopping down onto her. The lizard screeched in anger—not pain, *anger*—and it reared on its legs. Pounded back into the ceiling. A gaping hole shattered, and they all managed to dive out of the way, back into the kitchen.

To Violet's horror, as the beast fell through the ceiling, its massive body blocked the front door. Jack seemed to realize it, too.

He bristled. "I don't have a plan for this."

"Well, you better think of one!" Rio grabbed a pan from the clean dish rack.

"Did you not think to mention these?" Violet was on her feet, ripping her dagger from her belt.

"I don't know what it—" Anaya started. "The night monsters don't transform like that!"

A thunderous crack shook the house again. The balcony door

shattered as a giant cat, striped with white and deep green, barged through.

The cat flicked its large yellow eyes over them. It was not natural—but the way it looked at them, how it growled at Anaya's sword, matched Jack's icy gaze—it acted villainous. Human, even. Behind those eyes, gears whirred. It thought, calculated, determined, and then attacked.

Jack prepared for it. He notched a wooden arrow. Fired. It struck the cat between the eyes.

The arrow…dissolved.

Rio gasped in fright. Anaya groaned.

The cat growled as the lizard lumbered into the kitchen from the hallway. The four pressed against each other as those eyes— those conscious, knowing eyes—studied them. Understood them. Watched as the breath convulsed in Violet's throat and sweat beaded on her brow.

Violet, heart thumping so loud she could barely hear another feral growl, flinched as Jack's hand brushed her arm. She looked. Looked into those eyes wondering if it would be the last time she'd ever see that marvelous, enviable shade of green.

A sharp prick met her neck. She reached up and yanked out a dart. The obsidian metal shimmered and a soft blue light blinked on the end of it.

When she glanced up to her friends, similar darts stuck out of their necks. Rio slopped to the ground, eyes wide. Jack's knees sagged. Anaya halfheartedly thrust her sword as the cat advanced, another beast appearing on the balcony behind it.

Violet slowed, her limbs becoming heavy and sluggish. Her legs jellied beneath her and she collapsed to the ground. Hot air surrounded, and the sharp edges of teeth met her skin. No groans from her friends—even her breath hardly made a sound. Her awareness never slipped, and a fearful jolt run through her.

Ada.

But there was no shredding of her insides, or blood, or the general carnage the poison showed.

One of the cats—the white-and-green-striped one—picked her up with its mouth and then, with a satisfied huff, it bounded out the destroyed balcony door and leaped off the ledge.

Violet couldn't react to the drop, but the cat-beast landed softly on the ground. Fireflies blinked around; the rest of the jungle undisturbed by what just happened.

"Perfect," said an unfamiliar voice. She barely registered the dark figures cloaked by the night. "Take them back to the compound. The Lord will see to them."

Violet dipped, and it took her a moment to realize the cat was *nodding* to the masked hunter.

She was awake, conscious, the whole time the beast carried her in its maw. It continued overland until Endos scattered the area, their dark silhouettes growing thicker by the second. Her body hung like a wet towel, while the cat's giant teeth wrapped around but did not puncture her. Whatever she had been darted with rendered her consciousness to some small, observable witness.

The cat began to slow down until gates groaned open. The beast lumbered past towering walls laden with blue moss and thick, twisting vines. The compound.

She glimpsed three other beasts in her peripheral vision—the lizard, a deep brown creature, and a beige cat sauntered in behind with each of her friends limp in their mouths.

Her beast wandered in. Burly soldiers milled about in the dark foggy night until they noticed the cat and paused, gazing on with plated helmets and stone faces. She noted their plasweapons, those sleek plasblades up close.

The gates shut behind them. The Endos' moans became distant. Her gut leadened and Dr. Evek's words whispered in her mind.

"No one has exited the Sins for a reason, Sutton...they are not supposed to."

Oh gods, she wanted to cry. Or vomit. Or scream. She didn't want to keep losing, she didn't want to fail, again and again, to this stupid game.

The beast carried her on, until, surrounded by the ominous stone buildings and the towering Abos tree at the center, they reached a courtyard of thorny trees and brown flowers. Then it dropped her straight into the mud.

Paralyzed, she could only stare into the canopy above. Boots sloshed around her until a particular set of steps drew closer and a face peered down. A man—an Elite, judging by his trimmed brows and abnormally bright eyes. His graying hair was cropped short, slicked back behind his ears. The piercing of a bone threaded one of them.

He smiled at her, his front two teeth gapped. "Did you have fun braiding each other's hair and getting your precious Iris?" He glanced behind her, where the thump of bodies told her Jack, Anaya, and Rio had been dumped as well.

Spied on. The chameleon must have been spying on them.

He snapped his fingers and a guard lifted her with ease. Her head lolled. She caught a flash of black. Each one of those beasts had turned back into small, unassuming forms.

One stone building loomed above, two gaping metal doors yawning open. The bleak plaslights of the courtyard disappeared, and sconces of twisting white plasma lined the long hallway.

The guard carried her in. Up close, the building held an unusual aura. While built around the tree and within a jungle, the interior looked nothing like what she might have pictured. The floors sparkled, made of a shining red-brown wood. The walls were painted a dark green and lined with bars of that obsidian metal. A protection? A decoration? The nostor was everywhere, making this fortress nearly indestructible.

The guard turned three times, backtracked down one hall, passed eight identical doorways—meeting rooms, or cells, she didn't know—and turned into one. He dropped her on a cold table, never once making eye contact with her. Speckles of scales crawled at his neck beneath his collared uniform. He cuffed her to the table at all limbs and retreated to the doorway. Three other doors slammed near her.

That Elite man swooped in.

"*You*," he started, flamboyant in his gestures. He wrinkled his nose at her muddy, beast-blood appearance. "Why they gave me the order to track you down, I'll never know. You don't look very—ah, how should I say it? Capable of burning down an entire factory and slaughtering the Stradinths? Hm, yes, that about sums it up. I'm very aware that Commander Marin had an involvement, but you were a frustration for a long while." His lip curved. "The girl who sacrificed herself to the Sins...for *love*."

He took a step and then recoiled from the gunk along her skin. "The effects of the tranquilizer should wear off within the hour. You might thank the tigerbot for not impaling you with those teeth. They are still in production, you see. Nasty things." He sighed. "Now, I have some questions for you—or well, Lord Honter does. He's the overseer of Gluttony and you, my dear, put a drastic dent in his ahnsa production."

She wished she could claw at his face. Disgust and boredom leaked in from his expression.

He must see her struggling. Her eyes watered with the lack of blinks. She could begin to feel her fingers, and her ears twitched at the sounds of metal crashing and groaning around her. A factory, a facility. Building, forging—whatever this place was.

"You must have questions, though—many. In due time, they will be answered. Or not. Lord Honter might decide you are... disposable after what you did." He leaned forward. "I haven't seen a woman candidate in a very, very long time. Sometimes it is a surprise to see the...lesser sex succeed. But alas, I have been Lord for an abundant time in this wretched world. When you—" He waved his hand. "Get your speech back, you may call me Lord Arok. Or my Lordship. See? I'm gracious. Not as gracious as Lord Honter will be, though."

The Lord of Envy. It hadn't taken much to figure it out, but by the way he handled himself, he seemed to not take pride in ruling a world. He was pure Elite, and to have left the lavishness of the skyrises in Calesal for this decrepit place boggled her.

Envy exuded from him. Whenever he mentioned the other Lord, he scoffed lightly with distaste. Jealous. Resentful.

Was it power that Arok wanted? Or something that could have never been offered in the citadel? Something that could have only been offered by the hand of someone who ruled the Sins—the Worldbreaker. So there were Lords for each Sin, infiltrations of her city's plasweapons, and now—by the look of Arok—there was a way into the Sins without bloodswearing oneself. She could never imagine this man going through the rage of Wrath or the horrors of Gluttony.

A tight smile. "Your mind is churning with all the details. It is such a delight to show the candidates that the Sins aren't really what they seem. I hope some time we can enjoy a dinner—"

The soft clacking of boots flowed down the hallway.

"Ah, Lord Honter has arrived." Arok straightened and walked out of the door, his brows lifting in surprise at the arrival. His face paled two shades, and he bowed deeply to the floor. "My liege, I was awaiting Lord Honter. You and the rest of the Fringe weren't expected for inspection for two days...."

All Violet could do was glare at the doorway while her heart hammered.

The mysterious figure stopped before the frame and cleared his throat. "Lord Honter has been disposed of by the Master."

Everything in her body turned to ice. That voice—*that voice.* Not the Lord, not the Worldbreaker.

No.

It was Reed.

43

REVELATIONS

WITHIN HER BODY, SHE SCREAMED. She cried out, but the only sound that left her was a harsh breath. Her fingers scraped the metal table. She tried, over and over again, to scream his name, but her mouth could barely open.

"Disposed?" Arok said, a shake to his voice.

"He let the candidates ruin the Master's ahnsa production. He is not pleased at all." There was the same light flair to Reed's voice, but within it, darkness swirled.

Her lips began to move, but she could only whisper, "Reed. Reed."

"This all has nothing to do with me. I caught them as you requested." Arok scoffed. "Don't you see what I'm dealing with here, training his abominations? Just last week a robot malfunctioned and destroyed nearly all of my recovered Endos—who, mind you, were ready to be sworn into the commandment."

"I can pass it along to the Master that you have an issue with his decisions."

Ah, there was the lighthearted threatening she was used to.

"You can keep that to yourself, young liege," Arok snarled. "You might have risen through the ranks quickly, but remember who was here before you."

There was silence before a hand wrapped around Arok's throat and squeezed. Arok's eyes bulged. Reed laughed darkly. "I always loved playing with you, Arok. No wonder the Master gave you this lost cause of a world to rule."

"He…respects…me…."

"It seems that respect is dwindling." Reed let Arok go, who fell to his knees. "Remember your place—"

"I have the girl." Arok drew a harsh inhale, hand at his throat. "The one who destroyed the Farm. She's here, right in that room. Do with her as you wish."

All her brother had to do was take a step and turn. He was so close, and her lips were moving faster, feeling returning to her fingers. Her body trembled as she mouthed his name, but still no sound came out.

The one thing in this entire universe that she was here for was outside the door, a breath away, but she could not fight the paralysis.

"I have no time for petty candidates." Her heart sank. *No! No!* "You may dispose of her if you wish, or let her go. The Master will judge your actions regardless of how you handle a candidate that has gotten out of line."

Arok managed to get to his feet, his eyes flicking to her as she struggled on the table. He watched her coldly. "As you wish, Captain Sutton."

Captain? *Captain?*

You and the rest of the Fringe.

Could Reed move in between worlds like the Worldbreaker does? How was he…how was he even here?

"I'd suggest to *dispose*," Reed said. "The more you try to tame something wild, the more it thinks about biting you."

Words Meema always used to describe Violet. She was sweating from exertion, but Reed's footsteps were already retreating.

"No," she croaked. "No. *Reed.*"

The steps paused. Squeaked as they turned. Her heart picked up. *Come*, come. Look in the room. See her. See your sister.

But Reed only said, "You have the other candidate, though, don't you?"

"Which one? I have four in total."

"The commander from Calesal. Your new recruits mentioned him ruling the Farm at the side of that bitch."

There was a surprise in Arok's voice. "Jack Marin?"

"*Commander* Marin," corrected Reed, to Violet's bewilderment. "Bring him to the interrogation room. I want two sets of plascuffs on him and six guards at all times. And clean him up; I don't want him smelling like shit."

"I can talk to him now—"

"*I* want to speak with him," insisted Reed. "We have history."

"Yes, my liege," Arok bowed.

"Sunrise," was all Reed said before those boots padded down the halls again, the gait of his walk so desperately familiar.

Arok straightened his robes and stuck his head in her room. "Lock her in here. I will be back soon after I deal with Marin."

The guard nodded and shut the door without sparing a look. Darkness consumed.

And to that darkness, she breathed, tears spilling down her temples,

"Come back. Come back."

She drifted off to unwanted sleep as the tranquilizer settled her bones, but was brought back awake by the rising sensations in her body. She could fully move her mouth, her limbs—as much as the restraints allowed her—and then her head. Her jaw cracked as she stretched it. Her tears had long since dried, the pain replaced by the severe ache in her body from being in one position for too long. She jostled and twisted, but the manacles held her. If only she—

She angled her head down. Her dagger. Gwen's dagger. She had never been more thankful to sheath it. She nudged her hip on her wrist. With each rub, it slowly slipped until it clattered to the table, and she hissed at the loud sound. Holding her breath, she waited; ready to throw her body on top of the weapon when a guard burst through, but no one came. Still, she calmed her racing heart and listened.

No footsteps, no door slams, no coughs or murmuring voices. No yawns at the early hour. Anaya, Jack, and Rio would be in this same hall, strapped to a table. However, Reed—*Reed*, she still couldn't believe it—would be questioning Jack. In the same room as the man whose blind ambition resulted in so many losses, and her brother, if Jack's admission was true, deliberately handed himself over to save the city.

There was no right or wrong. They were only humans who failed, now facing severe consequences. Underneath the Worldbreaker, though, all of their actions felt minuscule. Like flies clambering for a spot on a split, ripe pomegranate. The worlds. Power. They were all pawns in his game.

What game was Reed playing? *Captain?* The authority in his voice? Calling the ruler of the Sins *Master* instead of Worldbreaker?

Reed was on the *other* side of a line so blurry that Violet didn't know what it even stood for. The sickening realization hit her. She needed the truth, needed to talk to her brother, needed to believe that Reed was not actively working for the Worldbreaker because he decided to, but because he was thwarted and threatened into it.

He'd used Meema's quote and Violet clung to that. He wasn't gone. Just lost. Just severely, hopelessly, undeniably lost. He'd see her and remember that he had family waiting for him—family fighting to reunite with him. In the end, that was all that mattered.

She needed to move. And fast.

As quietly as she could, she used her hip to nudge the dagger toward her. With each scrape, she paused to listen. No one barreled in. She twisted her fingers awkwardly to reach it, barely grasping the handle—

A door banged down the hall. The dagger slipped out of her fingers and clattered to the floor as footsteps echoed—slow at first, a pause, then growing faster. She took a giant inhale, scooted her body to the opposite side of the table, as far as she could go, and then on her exhale she jolted herself toward the other side. The table careened and fell, smashing onto the brace of the chains with a crack. Her right arm and leg yanked free, shackles dangling, and she grabbed the dagger and worked as the footsteps grew louder.

The door opened to reveal a guard with tired eyes that widened at the sight of her—"Hey!"

She unlocked the last restraint and lunged for the guard. Dragged him in and threw him at the table, where the corner met his head. He slumped unconscious to the ground.

"Hi." She smiled.

A plasblade gleamed at his hip and she took it with hungry eyes. The weapon shimmered in the hallway light. The gleam of the white handle molded to her hand and immediately warmed in her grip. It lightened at the touch, matching her strength. When she thumbed the small insignia of a diamond, it blazed to life, the rim around the iridescent steel humming a steady orange.

She ran the edge into the metal of the chains. Sparks burst from the impact, but with a little force, it sliced through, leaving her with bracelets of metal around her ankles and wrists. She had never seen a plasweapon this effective. With another swipe over the insignia, the light retracted into the blade. Another symbol marked the back, and with a touch, the entire metal retracted into the handle within a blink. Left with just the hilt, she shoved it in her belt, blew a kiss to the guard, and quietly shut the door.

Back in Calesal, she had marched onto the stage with every intention of submitting herself to the Sins to find her brother. She still held that desire, but now, that ache of being so close to him warped into fury. She would throttle him for calling her disposable, whether he knew it was her or not.

And then she would hug him, and then throttle him again.

She paused in the hall. There were twenty-four doors in total. Based on the sound of them slamming last night, she landed on one across and four down from hers. She drew Gwen's dagger, messed with the lock, but it didn't budge.

She grabbed the hilt of the plasblade, ready to slice through the handle, when the door swung open.

"Hey," said Anaya.

"Hey," said Violet. She spotted the two unconscious guards

behind the Endolier. "Did you sleep well?"

Anaya shrugged. "Could have been better. I had a dream about riding one of those cats." She nodded back to the guards. "They interrupted it."

"That's rather rude."

"That's what I said." Anaya stepped out and shut the door. "You have one of those phlashblades? I only got this." She held up two plasguns and a taser.

"Maybe they thought I was more lethal. They clearly misjudged."

"They always misjudge the tiny ones."

Violet smirked. "It's their death, then."

"Rio isn't here. They took him away shortly after we were chained up and that stupid Lord came in to grumble about his poor job. Also something about the Fringe group being here." Anaya sheathed her weapons. "The guards taking Rio mentioned something about a testing room. We need to get to him now."

Violet nodded but looked away. "My brother is here. He's a captain. Whatever that means."

Anaya paused. Looked at her, face softening. "Really?"

"He's one of the Fringe—the higher-ups of these Sins…I don't…" Violet looked down at her dirty self. Anaya looked even worse after being drenched in lizard-bot blood. "He is going to interrogate Jack since they have history."

"They tumbled with each other?"

"I'm sure they wrestled, but sexually? No. At least, I don't think so." She groaned. She hoped Jack wouldn't have made out with her if he had already tapped her brother. That would be…

Oh, skiv, she was going to throttle the gardia Commander, too.

"Go." Anaya nudged her. "Find your brother. It's why you are here."

When Violet looked back to the Endolier, she felt the untruth of those words. Yes, she wanted to find her brother, but instead she had found something else.

"Partially," said Violet with a slight, warming smile. "But I found you, too. Or, well, you found me."

Anaya wrinkled her nose, but her dark eyes flashed in understanding. "You look like shit."

"I like you, too," muttered Violet. "Meet at the entrance when…?"

"When this stupid place runs red." Anaya smiled.

They moved down the hallway. The scales of Anaya's body were shifting to match the stone walls. Violet drew the plasblade hilt, thumb near the insignia. When they reached a fork, they nodded to each other, each taking a different route.

Her mix of emotions settled into a lethal calm as she walked the empty halls, prepared to strike. She hoped the foul sight of her would make any run-in pause long enough for her to silently take them down, like she had with Gwen a world ago. Renewed hope pressed her forward.

Labyrinths of tunnels twisted and turned, some sloping down beneath the earth. She tracked her path back to the wide main entrance. It was before dawn—or the grayish light that was dawn in Envy. Four guards stood at the entrance, faced outward. She pressed her back into the wall and took a steady breath.

That small, tiny, innocent-looking tigerbot roiled something inside her. Is that what she looked like? Ignorant and submissive? What if she, inside, decided to transform into a foul, vicious beast?

She knew Gwen would smirk at her and say *unleash it all, agia.*

In these tunnels, Arok slept somewhere. Soundly. With the knowledge that she was strapped to a table ready to be dealt with in the morning.

She slipped past the main entrance, following the hallways that sloped into the ground. No interrogation room would be near the entrance, nor near the cells either if they wanted to muddle a hostage's mind enough. Especially with how well Reed knew Jack.

She paused before one spectacularly decorated hallway. Arok was an Elite, and judging by the massive, obsidian-gold-embroidered door, this area was home to his living spaces. Two guards stood at the post, relaxed and tired. She paused around the corner, leaning just enough to glance at their plasguns, hilted plasblades, and shining armor.

Radios echoed in their ears. The guards listened, mumbled back and stepped aside as the door opened. Arok swept outside, robes gliding along the linoleum, and a nasty scratch along his face. Red, yet healing, he must have sustained it after Reed accosted him. Unless...

No. While Reed might have sounded evil, he wasn't violent. He'd rather use his words to hurt than his fists, and that scratch didn't seem human by the length of it.

"Find me the medic and have them meet me in Interrogation Four. Afterward, I want to make sure Subject 421 has settled after its outburst." Arok began walking the other way. "Set the girl candidate up in a chair. Bring a vial of itoh. That will loosen her lips."

The guards nodded and stalked down a different hallway. Left alone, Arok walked, his back to her as she crept out and followed him at a distance. He turned, ambling on until seven hallways and a long peruse later, he reached a door. One in particular that had six guards, like Reed commanded.

Violet's heart thundered. Partially because Reed was so near, but also because those guards were dressed like war machines, plasweapons strapped to all sides of them. No matter her cool weapon, she was no match—

"You know, escaping might have been a better option than following me." Arok glanced over his head. He tapped his ear. "They already told me what you did to one of my guards. Why didn't you leave?"

His eyes found hers as she looked around the corner. The guards bristled, straightening. Arok swiped his wrist at an adjacent door, and it clicked open.

Violet brushed the insignia.

Arok scoffed. "You're curious, aren't you?"

She stepped out of her alcove.

"Well, come on then. You're already this far along, and well..."

Clicks of weapons. A line of guards stood behind her, helmets and visors covering their faces. "You don't have a choice of leaving now."

She didn't say a word as she walked forward. Arok held his arm up. "Ladies first."

"You aren't going to take my weapons?" she asked quietly.

"Killing me wouldn't get you anywhere, would it? Except for more blood on your hands, girl who burned the Farm."

When she walked into the room, she noticed the chairs, all facing a window. And through that window...

Jack relaxed back against his chair, smugly smiling at Reed, who leaned against the far wall, an unreadable emotion behind those eyes.

44

JACK AND REED

HER KNEES SAGGED.

Arok pushed her to one of the chairs. "They just started. They won't be able to see or hear you. If you so much as mutter a word, a bullet is going into the back of your head."

She slumped into a seat, reining in her screams for Reed. Emotions hounded her. Tears pricked her eyes. Right there. He was right there. She couldn't take her eyes off him as he and Jack were enveloped in their tension-filled silence.

Reed's hair had grown longer, the dark brown curling at his shoulders, held back by a twisting nostor headband around his forehead. That smattering of freckles looked washed out on his light brown skin—like he hadn't seen a ray of sun in a long while. His nose sported the childhood nick from when he had careened into a pole. Body tall, with muscles underneath his tight leatherwear and flowing black cape. Hands gloved. Boots neatly laced and shined.

Those eyes, the same as hers, stared at Jack. Jack met that gaze, but there was a stiffening to his shoulders, a guard that flashed up. Not a friend, not a gardia member, not even an enemy.

"Did you drag me here to gawk at my beauty?" drawled Jack.

Reed said nothing.

Violet lurched slightly, but settled back quickly and covered it with a cough. Arok's gaze burned the side of her face, looking for leverage like any power-hungry and envious person would.

"Can you at least offer me a drink?" Jack sighed. "You saw many interrogations with me; you know it is the procedure."

"I don't follow you anymore."

Reed's voice was sharp, no charming, carefree lilt to it.

Jack smiled. "Well, I know that. You made it clear when you took the hand of a Redder instead of mine."

"You think I wanted to do that?" said Reed. He pushed away from the wall, cape billowing behind him. "Did you think that was how I was to end my job with you? By leaving the city, my life, indefinitely?"

"In those last few weeks I did not know what was going on inside your head," said Jack. "You betrayed me."

"I saved you."

"I did not deserve saving."

"How did you even get into the Sins?" Reed paced, glancing to the mirror.

Violet's heart lurched. A plasgun clicked behind her. She kept her rear in the chair.

"Let's recap the whole damn thing for the audience." Jack waved to the mirror. "Where shall I start?"

"You don't need to—"

"Hm, the night it all went to shit. It's always a fun story to tell. For weeks there was a plan to raid the bridge, get into the government sector, and therefore into the Empire's Circle where I could challenge the despicable Neuven for the throne. So we could finally destroy the walls, release all the indentured slaves outside of them, and actually function as a fucking country. *A bold dream* is what you said to me when I first laid it all out to you."

Reed's jaw clenched, but he said nothing.

"You supported me, even though you didn't like me at first. You couldn't look me in the eye when you first sneaked into my party four years ago begging for a chance to help your family and provide for them. For your *sister*, who had gone off the rails then, and you were so desperately worried for her—"

"Don't talk about her."

"I'm sure you have questions, don't you? About where she is? What she might be doing right now?"

Reed's steady blink was the only answer.

Violet's heart cracked.

No, ask about me. Tell Reed I'm right here. I'm right here!

"No? That's sad. She is alive, by the way, last time I saw her." A deep smile showed one of Jack's dimples. "Moving on. That particular night was when a spy for Arvalo within my gardia was revealed—someone you knew about."

"I only learned about Faroh hours before anything happened."

Jack stared at Reed, searching for the truth. Reed stared right back.

"Faroh had slipped my plans to Arvalo, and the ambush by Arvalo was set. And *you* didn't say anything to my men when you led the mission to take the bridge."

"I didn't say anything because so much would have been compromised if I did."

"How would saving the fifty men I sent to secure the bridge not have been worth it to you?" Jack sat up, icy anger roiling from him. "How did it not compute that ending the entire damn thing would have been better?"

"You say this now, Jack, but you were different then. You were so wrapped in your own head and your want—no, *need*—for power that if I came up to you and said it was all about to fail, you would have chained me back at the penthouse and continued on anyway."

"No, instead you did that to me."

The tension, the swirling anger within the room, was suffocating. Arok huffed a chuckle next to her and sat back. "The gardia—such petty things."

Jack continued, "You used one of Hira's potions to drug me, Lyla, Cairo, and the rest of the circle, and then chained my brother and me to the floor in the command room. My whole house was unconscious, and then you take the team for the bridge and still walk there, aware that Arvalo knew, that the Redders were hiding there, that fifty men were about to either die or be bait for the Sins. So you charged the bridge, took down a good number of

Redders, actually secured it, but Arvalo let you. He let you have it because—"

"Because he was going to use your gardia and the work to get himself into the Emperor's Circle and challenge Neuven. Instead of you." Reed's eyes flashed. "And then when the government alarms went off, Arvalo changed his plans."

"You had a chance to fight him off," said Jack. "You had fifty men."

"I could have had a hundred, two hundred, but it wouldn't have mattered."

Jack tapped the table. "Because…"

"Because Faroh had found your contracts. And those contracts meant that I had to show up to that bridge and speak with Arvalo."

Her eyes widened. Faroh? The annoying ex-friend of Reed's, Faroh? The one she lost her...

She scowled.

Jack filtered to only a primal, lethal calm. "And one of those contracts was…."

"My sister."

Violet's blood chilled.

Jack clenched his fist. "Arvalo had wanted to bomb the whole city."

"There was a plasbomb planted at each location of the contracts." Reed walked to the table, leaned on it. A heavy weight lay on his shoulders, his eyes filled with misery and confusion at the memory. As if he were reliving his work, his command, in the surrender of Jack's entire ambition. "He told me that if I didn't yield Jack Marin's gardia and entire command, every bomb would detonate. I refused, at first."

"Then the school in the South was the first to go down."

Violet wasn't breathing.

"I refused again," said Reed.

"The infirmary in the Mid."

"And then he looked me in the eye, and told me an exact location underneath my guardian's house that only Violet and I ever knew about because we'd crawled under there to catch a cat."

"*Violet*," whispered Arok. His head whipped to her. "Oh—*oh*."

But she couldn't care. Not as she slid out of her chair and fell to her knees, silent tears streaming down her face.

Your brother saved the city, you know.

"So I surrendered," sighed Reed heavily. "I won't apologize."

"I would never make you apologize."

Reed's gaze snapped up. Met his ex-commander's. "You had a vision, Jack. You did. But it is all over now."

"Because of the Master?" taunted Jack. "Tell me, Reed, does his power make you want to bend as you did for me?"

"Fuck you," Reed growled.

"While nothing ever happened between us, you sure are always desperate to get on your knees for power." Jack's lips twitched. "Did you succeed this time?"

In a flash, Reed's plasblade was at Jack's throat.

"No!" Violet lurched forward, palms sweaty as they collided with the glass. "Reed! Reed!"

Jack's gaze flicked to the window in the barest of movements.

Violet cried again when her body was slammed back into the chair, and the cool metal of a plasgun pressed to her temple.

Jack didn't flinch. He maintained eye contact with Reed.

"If you degrade the Master once more, I will kill you," growled Reed. "This is not a joke, Jack."

"I'm not laughing." Jack smiled as the plasma hummed a breadth from ending his life.

Arok cackled. "This is better than watching shirtless men battle each other."

Violet looked at Arok incredulously, her breathing labored and short. The room dizzied around her—

"Don't faint," the guard said behind her.

"So you decide to get on your knees for the Worldbreaker instead of crawling through the Sins back to your sister?" mused Jack. "The very person you were sentenced for in the first place."

"It's more complicated than that."

Jack looked lazily at the plasblade, then back to Reed. "I can't imagine it being any more complicated. You're dressed in his shit, you smell like crackling coals, you weave a sword better than the last time I saw you, and boss around everyone in this damned place like you're a Commander. You're a part of the Fringe, right? A captain?"

"A captain of the Master," said Reed roughly. "You of all people should know that there's always someone greater, bigger and we all just end up working for them. Dying for them and their cause."

Jack's jaw clenched.

Reed motioned to his uniform, the plasblade unwavering. "This is the reason why no one leaves the game, Jack. Because in the end, the Master rules all seven worlds and the candidates' lives. I had no choice in the beginning, but now...now I would die for his cause."

"No," Violet breathed. The thought of Garan, Gwen, Isolo, and even Anaya's papa passed through her head. Her heart cleaved in two, each of Reed's declarations a punch to her hope, her fuel, over and over.

A beat of silence passed. Reed retracted the plasblade, and a serious look came over Jack.

"Do you like knowing you abandoned your sister?" muttered Jack.

Violet trembled in her seat. Skies, it was so hard to breathe—so hard to breathe properly. Her lungs must not be working. They were closing—closing, closing, closing...

"How is she?" grumbled Reed while he sheathed the plasblade.

"Alive," said Jack. "And—"

In the Sins, here. Looking for you. Here, here, here.

"—not as depressed anymore. She was working for Arvalo and in the sheets with his daughter."

"Skies." Reed looked up to the ceiling. "And what was she doing when you left?"

"Probably being a nuisance."

Arok snorted.

"Well, Mai Arvalo didn't quite like her and wanted to get rid of her, so I set up to have Lucien rope all of her friends under his wing in case there was collateral damage. Her one friend...Jelan, is being overseen by Jenkins. They're safe. Your guardian, Coco Mathan, should have moved into my penthouse and is being cared for while also taking medication to reverse her Corusgates, thankfully, since you left her contract to me and—"

"Violet? What about Violet? You're talking around her."

"Little Violet..." Jack said slowly.

A tear slipped down her cheek. She didn't know... didn't know Jack had done all these things. Why didn't he tell her?

Because you hated him, the rational voice in her head said, *and you wouldn't have believed him, that's why. And clearly Reed believes him, and you believe Reed, so believe that Jack had cared for your problems.*

"Where is she?" Reed's face flashed with panic. He shook his head. "Tell me, Jack."

Jack only smiled. "When I left her, she was surrounded by friends, kissing a very attractive man, and with a heart on the mend." His gaze sharpened. "In Calesal."

Violet's heart sank. All true, except the obvious last bit. But why wouldn't he tell Reed she was in the Sins? Here? Traveling with Jack?

"You made out with *him*?" Arok blanched. "Skies, the things I would do for someone who looked like *that*."

"So she's fine," said Reed.

"Better than after you left her." Jack scowled.

"Hopefully Lucien tells her the truth about me, one day. When she's ready."

Jack frowned. "I'm sure he will."

"Thank you, for Meema."

"I didn't do it for you," said Jack as he fumbled with the handcuffs. "I did it because watching your sister lose herself and her only piece of family left was more traumatizing than my allergic reactions to lemons." Jack shrugged. "But it is over with. Since she is in Calesal, obviously."

Reed stood, nodded, straightened. "The Worldbreaker will want to meet you. You will be a great addition to his army."

Jack sat up and winced at the burn of the plascuffs. "What is this army?"

"An army of the Seven Worlds. Candidates are important because some have abilities—"

"Abilities?"

"—to portal. But they have to pass through the Sins first."

Jack leaned forward. "As a test? A game?"

"To weed out the weaker ones."

"You think a cannibalistic Farm is a way of *weeding out the weaker ones?*"

"You did well. Had that one girl wrapped around your finger, didn't you?"

"I did what I could to survive."

"The Master likes survivors," said Reed. "You would be a great asset. I've already discussed your work in Calesal with him. He is intrigued."

Reed went to the door. Opened it. Violet was up, out of the chair again, but a guard's hand wrapped her arm and lugged her back down.

"I'm not speaking with him. Nor am I joining him."

Reed flashed Jack a solemn look. "You don't have a choice."

"I'm afraid I'll have to prove you wrong on that," said Jack.

Reed pinned him with a long look, then turned to the guards. "Take him back to his cell."

"Can I stay here? It's a bit cozier," said Jack, looking at the bleak ceiling and barren walls. "Something about the art calls to me."

Reed rolled his eyes and said to the guard, "I want him in the courtyard to await the Master." He slammed the door behind him.

"Reed!" Violet called but a gloved hand slapped over her mouth.

"Violet."

She whipped her head to the mirror, where Jack stared at it. Searching, unable to see her, but knowing she was there.

"He's not gone," he said.

While hot tears rushed down her cheeks, and panic was barely kept at bay by those walls, something relaxed in her at those words. Words by Jack. Comforting her in the weird way he did, that somehow translated and soothed her subconscious.

Arok swiped his key and opened the door. "Take her to the stock room before the Master gets here." His cold gaze met hers. "I'm curious about something."

45

OPERATION

THE FARTHER AROK LED HER through the hallways, until the tunnels were earthen, carved mud, and drips of tree roots, the more the smell grew metallic—not the smell of blood, but of fresh machine, and the zap of hot plasma on metal. It was so strong it tingled her nostrils and lingered at the back of her throat as if she'd swallowed it. Arok gingerly touched his face the whole way there, muttering curses she'd never heard on the lips of an Elite.

At the end of a particular hallway, buried far beneath the muddied ground, a giant metal door mounted into the stony wall. With a swipe of his wrist, a light blinked and the door slid open.

Beyond the door, beyond the flap of plastic blocking the chilly air, lay a cavernous lair the size of the Aariva. Or the Farm. Or maybe even Tetro. Giant roots trailed down along the walls, cradling it, hugging it. Underneath the Abos tree, it held more than she ever expected to see, and…

Her words left her. Arok strode around and looked on at the massive operation with disdain. "The Master left me this to look over. After their little talk, it got me thinking…a man who would fight to keep you alive, and a brother who doesn't know you are here, can most definitely be used to my advantage."

She had to give the man credit, at least he realized that senselessly killing her wouldn't gain him any favors.

"I'm a glorified mother to all his little creatures," he scoffed and motioned to the cut on his face.

Creatures was a good word for it. The metallic smell came from the decayed bodies of beasts she'd never seen in her life—some like the tigerbot, others winged with the bodies of lizards, or horned, thick beasts twice the size of pakiks. More and more were sectioned off as the room led on, farther than she could see. Screeches littered the air, and she realized the door must have prevented the sounds too. Test subjects—like the supposed Subject 421 that scratched Arok's face. She wondered which beast managed to do it.

The area at the front was used for the molding of nostor to bodies of various beasts. The very thing that allowed them to transform from an inconspicuous spying chameleon into a war machine lizard. Both men and women engineers worked tirelessly welding the obsidian metal into joints, nerves, bones, and arteries. They were on an assembly line like that of the factory at the Farm, but there was no consuming Inaj here.

Arok let her walk, where more creatures lined up on assembly, and one worker jammed some socket to test them. The creatures on the table writhed and grunted, coming alive at the jolt of power. Nails and teeth lengthened, bodies morphed, and even fire erupted from some mouths. Darts—like the one she had been struck with—shot at targets large distances away.

"It's interesting, isn't it?" Arok said, flatly. "They gather these beasts from all these different worlds, stock them with that foul metal, and then power them up into these creations. And I'm meant to oversee it. No Farm, no Wrath, no mind games like Lord Lonu of Lust—he always gets the best, damn him. No, I was left with these festering beasts."

She tried to control her panic at the operation. It was bigger than the Farm, and the chaos…the destruction that existed in this very room would tear Calesal apart within hours. Her head craned to even glimpse the full mass of some of the creatures. Her breathing grew shaky as her attention was dragged down the center pathway, where workers hovered around a fence, looking down into a pit.

Arok noticed her attention. "Go on."

Her body screamed not to.

Cold pressed against her neck and a plasgun clicked.

"Move! Move!" Arok shooed some of the workers at the fence. The shrieks grew louder, echoing off nature's walls. "We have a visitor! Despanin?"

"Yes, sir?"

"Which one are you working on?" The engineer pointed. "Ah, good. Let us show our visitor a test run. Then I'd like you to bring out 421. I want it resolved for...this." He turned his face and the engineer nodded, his own dark skin riddled with more scars than she'd ever seen on someone.

A giant pit extended in front of her, big enough to swallow the width of a skyrise. Cages littered the walls where creatures—alive and aware—paced with impatience. Guards walked the metal platforms above, long plasrifles held at the ready. The static of plaswhips crackled. As she stepped up to the barrier, it was as if the eyes of the creatures followed her, marking her move.

"You are awfully quiet for having caused such a burden," Arok said. "Don't you have any questions for me?"

"Are they...do you control them?"

Arok nodded to the engineer—Despanin. He spared her a long look. "Their consciences are manipulated and engineered for what we want. It is not control, but commands. Their bio-mechanical minds understand our commands as a human would. They are aware, alert, but they are designed without basic animal necessities."

Weapons. They were weapons with human understanding.

"How many are there?" she asked thickly.

"Over four-hundred subjects and counting."

"And what are they used for?"

Despanin shared a look with Arok, who shrugged. Oh, he definitely had no plans for her leaving.

"There are many different uses, but the primary ones are war, sur-veillance, infiltration, and...." Despanin swallowed. "Annihilation."

"Lovely," she muttered. "Is this what you do to the Endos, then?" Their faces screamed yes. "You use the Endos for testing? So there's no changing them?"

"Well..." Despanin trailed, sharing another nervous look at Arok.

Arok leaned close. "If we can do this to these creatures, what makes you think we can't do it to you too? Build you for something better? Command you for our bidding? Wipe your consciences and fit you to be a walking weapon?"

"Did you change your mind now?" Violet snapped her gaze to his. "You going to turn me into one of these...things?"

"Why wouldn't I? You heard Captain Sutton; he said to dispose of you, but I won't risk an advantage when I hover his sister over him. Maybe the Master would like to see you through the trials too. Just like your skinny little friend."

She snarled at the mention of Rio. "Where is *he*?"

"Safe and sound, away from the rest of your little group." Arok smiled. "The Master will enjoy meeting you all."

"Wouldn't he want to see me first? To make sure I'm...worthy of being such a subject?"

"You burned down the Farm, girl. I can't say I'm not curious about what else you can do."

"Maybe Captain Sutton should see for himself." Her voice steadied. "Call him. Call my brother."

Arok thought for a long moment. During that time, Violet's heart hammered aggressively against her chest. The animals screeched and clawed at their cages. One, in particular—a large, black cat—eyed her with uninhibited awareness. That creature did not look commanded or controlled.

"Prove it," Arok said.

"What—?"

But she was cut off, lifted, and shoved into a caged elevator. The door slammed and she bounced up, grappling for the thick wire. "No—*No!*"

The lift began to descend. The creatures went wild. Arok folded his hands and shot her a sinister smile. "If you want an audience with Captain Sutton, your brother, for your precious little reunion before I tear you up and stuff you with nostor and reap the rewards when both Marin and Sutton bend their knees, then I must have a reason to call him. Face one of the creatures and kill it successfully, and I'm sure even the Master might greet you."

"But they can't be killed!" she cried, panicking within the lift as it lowered and lowered until it passed the top of the pit. "They're weapons!"

"Then you will need all the luck this world can give you." Arok cackled. "Release Subject 421. Let's see if the girl satisfies its rebellious nature."

The lift stopped and unlocked. Bile crawled up her throat. Fear—pure, unrelenting fear roiled through her. The plasblade at her hip meant nothing. Nor did Gwen's dagger. All around, sheets of steel shot down and hid the creatures that were not Subject 421. The cracks of metal hurt her ears, but were nothing like the sound of her heartbeat. Across the room, that sleek, black monster prowled in the darkness of its cage...

The bars groaned, then lifted. Slowly. A low growl released from its lips, its haunting amber eyes never moving from hers. It waited, watching, until the bars had disappeared into the wall.

And then it stepped out.

46

NAVO

IF SILENCE WERE A KILLER, she'd be nothing but ribbons by now.

That's how Subject 421 looked at her as it prowled out on giant, quiet paws. The sheen of its glossy fur repelled the light, meshing perfectly with nostor so that it didn't even *look* like a machine. Around its middle was not fur, but rippling scales of shimmering black. As large as the tigerbot, yet more lithe, it blended with the shadows along the wall, rendering itself almost invisible, save for the shining amber eyes. She drew a sharp inhale, and its tail flicked in response—it was embedded with sharp needles of silver the size of her forearm.

As it stepped out of the shadows, the color of its coat morphed to match the gray earth.

Despanin's voice echoed, "Panther mixed with the adaptable coats of a chameleon, and the stings of a venomous jelly originating from…." A rustling of paper. "Sloth, actually. It's one of our newest and most advanced species. Additional features include breathing and fluidity in water from the konav serpent here in Envy; the ability to see in the dark, natural for a panther; a keen sense of smell, and the ability to taste blood or matter and smell, track, and locate the recollection of said blood or matter within its bio-library for the rest of its life. Main category: infiltration, but the subject fits well into the other categories as well." He cleared his throat. "Status: Advanced. Aware. Difficulty obeying commands.

Rebellious. And with a kill count of…." A weighty pause. "Six-hundred-and-forty-two Endos. Along with four other beasts."

"Was that the final count when it escaped?" Arok asked.

"More or less," Despanin answered.

So she was fucked. Royally, truly, ridiculously fucked.

"I'd suggest leaving the lift!" Arok called. "I'd hate to have to fashion a new one."

The panther-serpent waited for her, as if it didn't want to bother with slicing its claws through the metal. It sat. *Sat* on its hind legs and flicked its tail.

Swallowing, Violet unsheathed her plasblade and let the metal shoot out. She pushed open the cage door, never taking her eyes off the cat's as she stepped out.

The cat stood. There was something beneath its gaze—wariness. Workers banged on the barricades above. Violet flinched. They *wanted* her to die. They wanted her to fail, and for these abominations to destroy everything in its wake.

Unleash.

Amber eyes. A twinkle behind them. A conscience that matched hers. The banging riled up the cat and it emitted a rumbling growl that stood the hairs on her arms. Its needle-tail flicked.

Violet thumbed the diamond on her plasblade. The orange plasma ringed the metal, humming and heating. The panther recoiled back and bared its teeth.

"Oh," she said. "You don't like that, do you?"

As if in response, the panther huffed a yes.

She had noticed the coiled plaswhips around the guards and workers, ready to strike out if a beast disobeyed. Morphed and molded to be brutal, yet by brutality itself.

"You can understand me," she muttered. She swiped her thumb over the diamond, and the plasma sputtered, retracting, leaving only the metal blade. "No plasma. I promise."

Behind its unnatural gaze was a comprehension like her own, something that had once breathed and lived as a predator, untamed and free. This beast knew that terrible mix of fury and fear when something wild was trapped. She had been there, walled by her city.

Within its mind, the command to kill pushed the cat forward, but it snarled and flared its nostrils, drawing back into the shadows. Plasma leered, metal tinging the air. The bangs grew louder. Although they had designed this creature, they did not account for the fact that once something had tasted freedom, it would never, ever forget that sweet flavor.

Reed had said it best—or Meema originally had.

The more you try to tame something wild, the more it thinks about biting you.

Violet sucked in a sharp breath. A blink of those eyes.

Unleash it all, agia.

Violet threw her weapon to the ground between them. Gray-camouflaged paws hastily stepped back. It sniffed the air and chuffed.

"Kill her!" Arok cried above. "Why is it not doing anything?"

Even Arok's voice provoked a reaction from the cat.

"They suck, right?" Violet smiled and dropped to her knees. "All they want is for you to kill. But you know more than that. You know they are using you, and so you act out." She breathed deeply, and the cat prowled forward.

But for some reason, the fear ebbed away. It drew closer, curious yet wary of her. She held her hands out in peace. It sniffed the air again but did not growl. It gave a wide berth to the plasblade on the ground, and as it drew closer, its fur rippled back to black.

"That's it," she said softly. "Show yourself. Do not hide."

"Command it!" Arok cried.

"I—I can't!" Despanin stuttered. "It blocked itself from our system. It—how did it override it?"

The cat bent its head before Violet, nostrils at her ear, and sniffed. Its fur rippled again in response. She could hear the whirl of unnatural bolts and nostor as it blinked. But it blinked in some absurd truce—a trust between two caged creatures yearning for freedom.

"Subject 421! Exterminate it!"

"I don't think I like that name for you," she muttered, the voices of everyone so far away. "How about Navo? It means 'nomad.' One who never settles and always continues on, to the next adventure. It used to be a popular name in my city, long ago, before the walls went up. Yeah?" A nudge and a...*purr*? "Do you like that, Navo?"

Navo chuffed a response.

Beyond their peaceful interaction, alarms began to shriek, echoing around the cavern. Arok was snarling profanities and ordering the workers. Doors slammed shut. Despanin cried out in frustration, banging his finger on his tablet to command the cat.

But Navo was no longer his to command.

Violet unsheathed Gwen's dagger and sliced her palm. "I will bond you to me, and I to you, so that you never operate under their clutches again. Do you accept?"

Navo grunted and bent down to the dribbling blood from her palm. Its sharp tongue hurt, but with widening eyes, she watched as the wound instantly bound back together and closed up. "Oh skies, you can heal."

Static tinged the air, lifting the hair on Navo's body. He roared and stepped around Violet, shielding her as workers evacuated and guards loaded their plasguns. Navo gave her a look, and then glanced to his back.

Violet balked. "You want me to...?"

Plasguns fired.

Navo lunged in front of them, wisps of shadow and smoke regenerating its body. Violet dove for the plasblade and, without hesitation, climbed onto Navo's back. He barely let her settle before she clutched around his neck and he leaped at the wall. He scaled the pit with ease, vaulting over the lip and scattering a group of guards. His tail whipped and lashed. The needles embedded into bodies. Their skin crawled with purple, until they choked and foamed at the mouth, collapsing. Dead.

"Violet!" a familiar voice called. One of the guards removed their helmet and Rio—wide-eyed—revealed himself. "You got yourself a pet!"

"Rio!" she shouted. "How are you—?"

"Bad directions." Rio gave her a sheepish smile. "Can I hop on?"

"Navo, grab him. He's with me."

Rio clambered on, wrapping his arms tightly around Violet.

Navo roared and they buried their heads down as the plasguns rang again, but Navo took most of the hits with ripples of nostor. He destroyed machines with his tail as he bounded away from the pit, his hell, and toward the steel door. Arok was slamming his hand into the reader in desperation.

The door slid open and Arok stepped through, shutting it with a terrified look.

Navo slid before he careened into the door. Violet hurriedly looked around—

"Give me your plasgun," she said to Rio.

Rio didn't hesitate, handing her the sleek thing.

She pointed to an overturned fuel bank and fired. It burst into flames that rocketed to the ceiling.

"Okay, arsonist, what now?" Rio clutched her firmly.

She stared at the curved claws of the panther-beast, glimmering nostor glaring back at her. Anaya's words popped into her head.

You can light it on fire and it can burn through anything.

"Trust me," she whispered to the cat.

Flame beckoned. Violet nudged Navo toward it.

Navo stepped his paw within, then the other, and with a steady voice, Violet commanded, "Break the door."

With bright, flaming paws, Navo reared back and slammed them into the metal. It shredded with ease. The panther did it again and again until the door was just a singed circle.

"Where are the others?" Violet asked as Navo leaped through the door and patted out the fire. She spied Arok running up ahead.

"Anaya went to find you since you would have been with Jack. I was supposed to hide, then found some uniforms and ended up getting called to that factory," said Rio.

"Okay—wait, grab him, Navo."

Navo scooped up Arok with ease, the Elite bellowing a high-pitched scream of terror.

"Main entrance, Navo." She turned her head to Rio. "We need to get out of this world, now. The Worldbreaker is coming."

"What about your brother?"

Violet's heart clenched. "He's gone."

Rio didn't need a further explanation. Instead of a response, he brushed her arm, she nodded in permission, and he hugged her from behind. She sighed deeply.

Navo whirled through the hallways, sending guards and servants to the walls like he knew the place inside out. They steadily rose and Violet felt like she could breathe properly as the murky smell of the jungle reached them.

They dropped past the cell rooms to grab their bags, along with the Iris inside Violet's. Rio breathed a sigh of relief and they clambered back on the panther.

When Navo bounded away, Violet squinted ahead.

A shimmer of something. Violet yanked on Navo. "Stop!"

Within the center of the hallway, a form shifted with its background until Anaya loosed her camouflage. "Were you about to run me over? Wait, you have a pet?" Her brows furrowed, looking to Navo's mouth. "Is that…?"

"The Lord of Envy," said Rio.

He bellowed and Anaya drew close. "May I?"

"I just need his wrist to unlock the main door." Violet patted Navo's fur. "Hop on."

With the help of Rio, Anaya lumbered on the back of Navo and gasped. "This is skivvin' cool."

Navo grunted in response.

Violet nudged her heel. "Jack's at the courtyard—hurry!"

"Let me go! Let me go!"

"Can I kill him?" asked Anaya.

"He's all yours."

"Skies, I hate this job! Let me go! Fucking—"

Navo reached the main doors and with one billowing growl, the guards scattered, the pants of one wetting. When one lifted his weapon, Navo twisted and flicked his tail, splattering blood and guts onto the wall.

Rio hissed.

"Wave your stupid wrist," Violet snapped to Arok.

"No!"

"I'll help—" Anaya dropped down. She held her hand out for Violet's plasblade. Violet lit the blade up and Anaya sauntered around to Navo's mouth. "You can drop him, you lovely beast. Yes—yes, you are so lovely."

Navo purred in response and Arok fell to the ground with a thunk. A flash of orange plasma later, a shrieking cry from Arok, and Anaya swaggered to the door with—

"Holy fucking skies," said Rio.

Violet gaped.

And Anaya waved the severed hand of Arok at the lock. The door hissed open, revealing the gloomy jungle outside.

"Here, you can have this back." Anaya tossed Arok's hand at him.

Arok screeched in pain as blood oozed from the stump on his arm. Anaya only smiled at him and clambered onto Navo's back again.

"Hurry, Navo," said Violet.

They raced through the muddy walkways until they reached the supposed courtyard. Jack kneeled there shirtless before the plaswhips of multiple guards, fresh gashes along his back.

The portal for the Iris stood a breath behind him.

At the sight of Navo, the group of guards stared wide-eyed, backing up. Navo needed no command from Violet because the beast knew—knew by the whips in their hands and the men victim to them—that they were the enemies.

Violet gasped and slid off of Navo. She rushed over to Jack, falling to her knees before his bowed head. His hair was matted with dirt, dripping with humidity and sweat. She carefully lifted her hands and brushed his curtained face.

"Jack," she whispered.

"All right, which of you twats did this?" Anaya cried, plasblade humming in her hand. "I'll rip you apart for hurting him! Which one of you was it? You know what—actually—I'll enjoy murdering all of you."

Navo roared in response, tail swinging. The guards shook, looked at each other, and then ran.

Violet grasped Jack's face. Lifted it.

Her heart broke as he trembled beneath, that cunning commander gone to a terrified man, shaking with fear.

"Violet?" he breathed.

"I'm here. I'm here—Rio, can you do anything?"

"He'll be okay, but we have to go," he said, looking around the compound. "I can't tend to it right now. Every guard in here will be rushing to—"

Jack doubled over into Violet's arms. He burrowed his head into her shoulder, clung to her, and she let the mass of him brace against her. This powerful man, reduced to this.

Cold fury spiked through her.

Anaya roared again at the group of guards, echoed by Navo. The men dispersed in fear, dropping their weapons, and Navo pounced after them, Anaya on his tail.

"Get the Iris," Violet said to Rio. He rummaged through her pack, pulled it out, the silver glimmering, beautiful within this destructive environment. Violet attempted to stand, Rio at Jack's back to steady him.

"I'm here, I'm here, I'm here," she reassured him, and he tightened his hold in response. "Anaya! We have to go!"

"But I'm not finished!" The sickening squelch and hiss of plasma. "They hurt Jack. They hurt him—and I will kill them all!"

Navo roared again.

"Anaya! Now!" commanded Violet.

The Endolier huffed and slashed once more at a guard, cutting into his leg. She pointed at the guard. "I'm coming back for you."

The guard soiled himself.

Anaya strolled over, Navo at her back. "What about your pet?"

"Navo is a free animal. He can do what he wants," said Violet as she managed Jack's tall body.

Navo huffed a response. He looked at Violet with those bright, knowing, intelligent amber eyes, then out toward the jungle.

"Be free, Navo." Her blood warmed, remembering their bond. "I will see you again."

The panther looked again to the wall, then back at her. Violet pleaded with her eyes because where she was going, there was no freedom. There would be more pain—four more worlds of it.

"Go," she urged. "We will meet again."

Navo blinked. *Thank you. We will meet again.*

Violet blinked back.

The panther turned, howled into the expanse of the jungle and the towering Abos tree above, then bounded to the compound wall. Within three leaps, Navo breached the lip of the stone and disappeared over it.

He would run. He would live. He would be free within this world. He'd destroyed their compound, and there would be no more cages for him.

"Jack, I need you to hold the Iris." Violet pushed at him, but his large hand just pulled her closer to his chest. "No—*please*, grab the Iris so we can fix you up in the next world. We need to go—"

"Violet," he whispered into her neck.

"I'm right here—"

"Violet?"

Ice dumped through her veins.

Violet turned her head, meeting the gaze of her brother, who paled four shades as he gawked right back. Those blue eyes, that smattering of freckles, the nicked nose.

Memories flashed in her head. Reed pulling her close under the bed sheets as a child, covering her ears to the late-night screams and gunshots. Reed bringing her peppermint tea with honey. Wrestling matches in the backyard. Toys broken and noses smashed. Hands held as they ran from Meema. Doors slammed when their mother only congratulated Reed on passing his test, while Violet had scored high on her diorama.

Smashed hand-made figurines. Cardboard soaked with tears. Her brother's dirty fingernails scraping her skin, rubbing her waterworks away.

Tears slipped down her face. He took a step forward, hands reaching as if to wipe them again—

Violet snarled and lunged.

She tackled her brother to the ground. Mud splattered his pristine uniform.

"How dare you!" she screamed. Clawed at his leathers. She shook him, drew him up to glare into his eyes. "I thought you were hurting. I thought you were going to die when I saw half the screen turn red that night. I came here for *you*, and you're working for him!"

"Violet," he breathed again. "I thought—" His gaze flicked to Jack.

Jack spit up blood and quirked a lip. "Might have lied."

"Lied?" Reed's face flashed with confusion. "Kissing a...." Fury blazed and he snarled at Jack. "My sister? *My fucking sister?*"

Reed reared up, pushing Violet off of him.

Violet's fist reared back and slammed into Reed's cheek. His head whipped to the side. Spit flew out of his mouth. He fell to his knees before her.

"Why didn't you fight?" Violet cried, shoving him. "Why... why...why didn't you come back?"

"There *is* no coming back." Reed wiped at his face. "My question is why are you in the skivvin' Sins?"

"Because I needed you!" A sob broke through her. "You said '*if you ever end up in those worlds, I'll tear apart each one of them and bring you home*' and I would do the same for you—I should have done the same for you, so you weren't going to go off and work for the Worldbreaker. For the person who ruined every world he took over!"

Reed grabbed her face. "You absolute idiot."

"I'm not an idiot!"

"You were bloodsworn into the Sins!"

"She did it herself, actually," muttered Rio.

Reed looked at Rio incredulously and then turned back to Violet. "You chose this?"

Violet wept. "I chose you. I chose my family. But…you never came back."

"I'm not your life, Vi." Reed wiped her tears. "You should have lived. I would have wanted you to live."

"Without you?" she blubbered as she punched him in the chest. "How could you say such a thing?"

"Because you would have been safe from all of this, from all those candidates *he* killed that day. The trackers you saw go out."

"He killed…" Her eyes studied Reed, and up close she spotted the scar along his neck, as if a dagger had slashed it, but never followed through. "Oh skies."

"You stupid, stupid idiot," said Reed as his face scrunched and his eyes watered. He tugged her into his arms. "I hate you. I hate you so much for being here. You fucking idiot. You could have lived."

Guards poured out of the hangar.

"We have to go!" Rio called.

Within Reed's hug, her brother's whisper came, "We cannot be siblings in these worlds. Not in front of him. Do you trust me?"

Violet pulled back. "What?"

The world shifted. A powerful wind swept through the trees, and the atmosphere darkened. Plasguns lifted, blades swung out and ignited. Reed grabbed her face, kissed her on the forehead, and pushed her away. "He's coming! Go!"

"No!" cried Violet, but arms wrapped around her, yanking her away from her brother. She reached, clawed at those arms, at the blue-green scales covering them. A screech tore through her, but Anaya held tight, dragging her through the mud and back to the portal.

All around, the world of Envy gushed with heavy wind. A flash of lightning streaked the sky. So like the Bloodswearing Ceremony.

Reed stood and rubbed at his cheek where she punched him. He watched as she screamed and reached for him.

"Hold on to Jack, Anaya! I'll pull all of you through!" Rio cried.

A whirl of luminescence swirled next to Reed. A man stepped out between light folds, arms glowing with twisting lines of filigree. Stark-white hair to match his pale skin. Gray eyes landed on Violet's.

A mouth that fell open.

With a smile.

Rio slammed the Iris into its notch, and the world bled into darkness.

PART III
THE FATE

47

THE FOURTH SIN

ALL FOUR BODIES CRASHED INTO warm stone. Violet's elbow hit hard enough that she wailed and clutched it, face scrunched in pain.

Her ears screeched with a high-pitched sound. A moan passed through. She blinked through the blazing rays—not daylight, but bright bulbs of all kinds of colors, dulled through shifting chiffon. Still clutching her elbow, she shuffled to her feet, only to have Anaya in front of her, shaking her.

Anaya yelled something, but Violet's hearing had not returned. Anaya pointed to the ground, and Violet's head swiveled.

Jack lay unconscious on the floor, blood leaking from his back. Rio was just coming to, clearly disoriented, before he rolled into Jack and scrambled up.

Anaya yelled something again.

Violet inhaled, her smell arriving. She doubled over immediately, astounded. A drug swirled in her body and everything heightened. Sensations intensified, and her heart throbbed in her chest. Like it wanted to get out—to release.

The fourth Sin.

Another breath and a smile curved along her lips. Worries eddied from her head. Feelings, so euphoric and tantalizing, sang within her. She tilted her head back, eyes heavy-lidded as she greedily sucked in the sweet, honeyed air; warm to the touch, threaded with fine silk. It invigorated her, enveloped her being, and tugged at her core.

She dropped her injured arm and turned to Anaya, giggling, "I can't believe I saw Reed. He looked so terrible."

She giggled again.

Anaya laughed back. A cry ripped through their haze, and Violet's smile dropped. She caught Jack again—the blood, his parted lips, his slow-moving chest—

Let go. You have suffered pain for too long.

She hardly noticed the dried tears cracking the skin on her cheeks.

I can take your pain away.

Violet stuttered—sound skidded back.

"We have to find a doctor—I can't do this on my own!"

Panic flooded her. Violet dropped to her knees beside Jack and said quickly, "What do you need me to do?"

"Help me flip him—oh skies, he shouldn't have landed on his back, but I didn't even know if we would all make it, so I didn't think..." Rio brushed his hair back. He carefully pushed on Jack's arm while Violet eased the commander over his side and onto his stomach. "We need to stop the bleeding. Anything can help."

Violet dropped her backpack and tore her shirt off, flipping it inside out so mud wouldn't cake Jack's wounds. She lay it over half his back. "Anaya, we need your shirt—"

"I can't *feel* anything—oh—oh wait—oh twat." Anaya was on her belly, sliding her hands over the floor, farther and farther, until she sprawled out and embraced it like a lost lover. "I feel... *Violet.*"

"I know," she said.

Rio swallowed heavily, sweat licking his skin. "This Sin is hard to work in."

"What Sin is it?" Anaya giggled. "I love it."

"It is Lust," breathed Violet.

Even with the grit of Envy, familiar warmth pooled in her core. It burned—*hard.* Heat rushed to her cheeks and she fumbled with packing Jack's wound.

"We just need to stop the blood." Rio coughed and squeezed his eyes shut. He shuddered. "The lashes aren't deep—more superficial, but he can't lose too much blood because it won't help the healing. And I don't know if there is supply, let alone human blood supply..."

A crash swept through the mishmash of feelings. Anaya jolted from her rendezvous with the floor and whipped out one of the five plasblades at her belt. The blade ignited a bright red.

"You do not step near the commander," she growled.

Violet was too disoriented to even realize they were on a grand, open-air veranda that led straight into an exquisite, sprawled sitting room and kitchen. A figure stood near the huge island laden with eight stools. A shiny silver platter lay at their feet.

The apartment was shadowed, little light appearing save for whatever city bled at their backs. There was whirring and rumbling, like the roar of motorbikes or wind passing between towers.

"*Alexander!*" the figure cried. "*You received your wish!*"

Anaya stepped up, waving the plasblade. "Try one thing and I'm lobbing your head straight off."

The figure gasped and stepped forward, hands raised. "Please, I mean no harm." It spoke with a honeyed accent—smooth, buttery with a high lilt. "You may put your weapon away. No one here will harm you."

"I don't believe a damn word you say," snarled Anaya.

"My wish?" called a voice. Another figure glided out of a hallway, wrapping a robe around their waist. "Did you get my favorite candies, or were they sold out again?"

The figure stopped.

"Lights on."

A warm white light—cozy, enticing—ignited the large apartment.

The two figures gaped at the scene. Violet gaped right back. Even Anaya's plasblade wavered and her jaw dropped.

Black-and-silver-dusted skin gleamed underneath the pleasant light on the two males. Carved jaws, curved bodies, and painted nails. The one who dropped the platter had cropped hair to his ear; thick locs painted silver at the ends. His chest was adorned with jewels of all sizes, arms laden with even more. Tiny brows, full lips, a ring through one nostril, he rested a hand on the counter and sighed, "Alez, you should have been more specific about your wish."

The other—Alez—was mesmerizing to look at. Both of them were, but Alez had a shining, silver aura about him. His locs drifted past his shoulders and were dipped with bright blue at the ends. Giant hoop earrings graced his ears—ears that were butterflied. Both the tip and the lope pointed, like wings about to take off.

And atop it all, tiny horns the size of pinkies jutted from their heads.

Alez raised his voice to no one in particular, "Call the medic!"

❀❀❀

The other male's name was Nadar. Both Alez and Nadar were Auriens—one of the four main species in Carcadia.

The City of Clouds.

The City of Lust.

After Alez quickly introduced this and begged Anaya to put her weapon away, the medics arrived. A stretcher rolled in, followed by at least four nurses and two doctors. Violet grabbed Jack's hand, still shocked as the mix of species walked in—pure moonlight skin with glittering wings, light-blue toned with scales like a snake, and olive-hued with long, flicking tails sticking out the back.

Some were a mix of different ones.

"Please step away from the patient—"

"No," blurted Violet. Her hand wrapped Jack's wrist. "He can't go to a hospital. We are..." she exchanged a look with Rio. "Jack's terrified of them. Hates it. If he wakes up in a hospital, he will—"

"Shit himself," interrupted Rio.

Violet stared at him. "That or *freak out.*"

Rio grimaced.

"No hospitals. We do things privately here in my home." Alez waved to the medics. "Take him to the nearest guest bedroom. He will be comfortable there. I have met many candidates before and know how overwhelming it all can be, and you four look like you have seen the bowels of...." Alez wrinkled his nose. "Something horrifying."

Nadar shuddered.

"Let them take him and I will answer any questions you have. We have extremely high-tech medical advances. His wounds will be closed within the next fourteen hours, but he might need more time to rest and finish his healing..." Alez held out his hands.

"We aren't leaving him," said Anaya.

Alez blinked at Anaya as if seeing her for the first time. His eyes dipped to her scales. "You are certainly a rare creature."

Anaya camouflaged her arm with the plasblade. "If you do anything to him, I'll enjoy killing you."

Alez smiled at that. "You're a fun one too." His gaze moved to Violet. "I see you're more human. I don't see women candidates much."

"We won't hesitate to hurt you if you try anything," seethed Violet.

He lifted his hands. "We will see your comrade fully healed."

The medics moved to brush Violet and Rio aside. She wavered, but with one look to Rio, and then Anaya, she allowed them the space.

The minute Jack was on the stretcher and rolled down the hallway, Anaya following right behind, Rio stood. Walked around Jack's blood puddle and heaved Violet to her feet. He wrapped her in a tight hug, cheek pressed to the top of her head, uncaring that her hands remained at her side, or that her eyes stayed on Jack's stretcher until he disappeared.

A laugh bubbled out of Violet. Rio stilled, pulled away to look down at her.

Her lips split into a giant smile and another laugh escaped. Irrational. Wild. She didn't have the tears to cry or the mental ability to process any of the shit that had happened, so she laughed. Opened her mouth, flashed her teeth, and cackled.

Rio blinked down at her, but amidst the bot blood and mud and the fact he was still in guards clothes, he cracked a grin and snorted.

"Alez—"

"Now, now, Nadar, my love. Let them feel it. This is the world of sensation, isn't it?" Alez cleared his throat. When they turned, he was beaming, hand raised to the billowing chiffon. "Go out onto the balcony, darlings, and behold the Sin of Lust."

Rio walked toward the curtains. Violet followed.

Her jaw dropped.

This *world*. It was as if Calesal took a thousand drugs, the motorbikes lifted to race through the sky, and plasma shined five times brighter. The city boasted twisting skyscrapers of marble brushing through the clouds. A citadel. Alive. With a heartbeat and euphoria and verandas where diverse creatures danced to thumping music and lights—the lights full of color she'd swear she had never seen before.

Violet grinned.

"*Lust.*"

Everything was sensuous. From the verandas with flickering lights, bridged like lovers holding hands in smooth, cream stone, to the bodies in skins of blue, green, black, and pure white, to the waterfalls—Violet gasped—*waterfalls* drifting out of pockets in the buildings like glitter. Vines and flora meshed with the technology of bright lights, metal columns, and plascreens. Or screens. She didn't know.

She honestly didn't care.

She was just in love with it all.

Between those interlocking bridges, hovercars danced and defied gravity. It was the whirring sound—the sound of engines that didn't honk or emit grueling noises. No, they purred. A car, the top half gone, whipped past. Voices shouted, dark-skinned and lithe bodies danced, and one even pointed to her, waving.

She raised a hand back. They zoomed on.

She turned to Rio.

Tears streamed down his cheeks. "Is this when we finally get a break?"

She thought of her brother, of the last things said between them, and then of the man who stepped out of those magic light folds and smiled.

Even if it was for a day, even if it meant they could sleep and feel safe, Violet knew she would fight for her friends to have that. They deserved it.

So she opened her mouth—

"You are safe here." Alez strolled out with an unopened bottle and glasses. "I promise you that. There are only a select few spots candidates drop in Lust, partially because of the actual drop if one happened to appear in mid-air. That was hundreds of years ago, where a candidate would…." He pointed his thumb down. "Splat. But now, we generally have a timeframe to expect candidates, however, I never thought I would get *four*. Let alone a little rare one and a young female."

Rio lingered close to Violet.

"Those who receive candidates take oaths to care for them. It is a duty of Lust—to make one feel sensationally at ease."

"It is just…hard to believe anyone will be nice to us after the other worlds," said Violet.

"You are *very* welcome here." Alez's eyes were too…homed in on her. He clapped his hands and smiled. "Let's celebrate!"

48

Tone it down

JELAN

"**This place?** *This place! Oh my fucking skies!*"

Jelan nearly soiled herself at the outburst, gloved hand adjusting one of the neutralizing tabs on the circular metal plasma bay, while the other poked the writhing substance hoisted within. It shifted from blue to green, the color only settling when confined unless otherwise manipulated.

Jelan blew out a steady breath and leaned back from the substance, pressing a couple of buttons so a thick glass tube erupted around the plasbay, securing it.

The sound of Hira's shrieking voice spread throughout the penthouse, rousing servants as Jelan took off her gloves and left the lab. She wandered the few turns of the hallways until she reached the foyer, fixing her gaze upon Hira as the woman gaped at the magnificent chandelier above.

"It's a lot," said Jelan with a smile.

Hira's gaze flicked to her, taking in her singed overalls and the brush of ash over her skin. "You don't look ready for dinner."

"It's only the afternoon."

Hira shrugged, gazing down to her long, billowing dress of quilted fabrics and brushing back her waist-length black hair, held back by a headband. "Close enough. I deserve to raid their expensive alcohols after Lucien made me take the truth serum and relay my deep, dark secrets." She rolled her eyes. "How are you, skiv?"

"I'm fine." Jelan smiled, in higher spirits now that Hira was here—she'd been anticipating her visit for a long while since her heist a couple of days ago, leaving her alone most of the time in the penthouse.

Hira's energy took up most of the room, boastful and bright, and Jelan reveled in it.

"Well." Hira motioned her hands. "Show me what you've been doing. What's this secret project all about?"

"Actually, I was just finishing up—"

Hira frowned. "Nonsense. You look like you haven't had a proper night's sleep in forever, and with Lucien probably having a big project breathing down your neck I'm sure you don't take breaks." Hira held her arm out. "Now show me what you're doing. I'm sure it's a lot more interesting than the penis enlargement potions I've been making for my neighbor."

Jelan gawped at her. "Is that a thing?"

"No." Hira smiled.

Jelan giggled as they walked down the hallways back to the lab. When she opened the door, Hira gasped at the plasbay that took up the center of the spacious room. The plasma writhed like a blob, balanced by its container.

"What are you—" Hira shook her head, unable to shape her words. "What are…what are you doing?"

"I'm building a plashield."

"A what?"

"Plashield. Like a shield, but with…" Jelan rubbed her hands together. "Plasma."

Hira snorted. "I figured that much. So, like…how?"

"Well, I have to manipulate the plasma enough so it stays in a consistent shape and more or less listens to me, and then I have to connect it to a small neutralizer so I can retract and ignite it at will, all the while telling it to maintain its shape…" At Hira's dazed look, Jelan shifted uncomfortably. "I—well...I sketched it out with the degrees of heat so I know how thin it needs to be at the sides so it's more easily manipulated and you have no idea what I'm saying."

Hira whirled on her, bright, big smile blossoming on her face, crinkling the lines at the sides of her eyes and scrunching her bushy brows. "I have no idea what you're saying, but it's cool. So damn cool. No wonder Lucien has a hard-on for you."

"What?"

Hira's eyes widened, sheepish. "Never mind. So can I get the first prototype and plashield my mother from going through my room?"

"I was thinking more about helping the city, but I don't see why not," said Jelan.

"I'd love to help."

"You know about plasma?"

"Not a clue."

"Oh," said Jelan. "So how do you—"

"Moral support," said Hira. "I'm fucking good at that. When I want to be. Well, when I actually like people. Which isn't often."

Jelan looked at her, lips twitching. "I don't see why you can't keep me company, but there are dangers to this—"

"Honey, this is nothing. What actually scares me is how fast my neighbor shoots back the penis enlargement potion and walks around like it suddenly burst from his pants."

"Men," said Jelan. "How dare they."

"*Exactly,*" Hira beamed. "How dare they. Speaking of annoying men, where the hell is that brooding brother?"

Jelan hadn't seen Lucien in a day or so. Not because she'd been cooped up in her lab, but because he'd gone out to vet Kole and had not come back. Jelan had spent the time diving into her work and hoping Lucien stuck to his word.

"Well, he said he would be here for dinner—"

"*Skivvin' shit! What is this place? Where in the skies—what—this ain't the South. Stupid skiv! Where am I?*"

The hoarse voice shrilled more than Hira, and Jelan was thankful she wasn't playing with plasma at that time, because she could have sworn the glass rattled.

Hira whirled on her. "Who is that?"

"The one and only," sighed Jelan.

Meema lumbered through the foyer when they got there, sneering at the paintings on the wall, and then at the peaceful trickle of the fountain. "Skivvin' Elite shit."

"Ma'am, your room is this way—"

"Now what in skies' name is that?" snapped Meema, her wrinkled, sun-spotted brown face gazing up at the naked bust of a statue that led into a small art gallery. "Who carved my tits from my younger days? Hm?" She whirled on the servant next to her, and his face blushed as red as his hair.

"Wasn't me," he squeaked.

"Who the skiv are you?"

"I—my name is Fin. I brought you here, ma'am. Did you need a refreshment?"

"What? A drink? Who the—" Her pale gray eyes landed on Jelan. "*You.*"

Jelan had been both looking forward to and dreading seeing Meema again. When Jelan had first stepped through the door of the Suttons' cramped home in the South three years ago, she'd made enough of an impression with how many times Meema pointed out how quiet she was and how much she and Violet needed a bath. Soon enough, the old woman had warmed up to her and stopped questioning when Jelan would quietly appear. But Jelan and Violet had come home drunk numerous times, raided the fridge, and woke the woman up enough that Jelan had earned a love-hate card.

Loved because Violet suddenly settled down and stopped trailing her brother so much. Hated because Violet had a friend and they got into a good amount of trouble during that time.

When Meema's memory had started going downhill, Violet had stopped inviting Jelan over. She gave excuse after excuse to meet elsewhere, citing that Meema wasn't allowing others over. That had been that—and Jelan had spent those years believing Meema hated her and not that her memory was out of order.

"I remember you," said Meema, fixing her plain, long-sleeve shirt. "You used to eat my food."

"You used to feed me," said Jelan quickly. At that point in life, her father was out of the picture and Ahmad was slowly growing distant. Jelan hardly knew how to fry an egg.

Meema was the one who taught her.

"You had a knack for baking. And a tooth for oranges. You loved my orange brownies."

"I loved everything you made for me," mumbled Jelan.

Meema huffed. "I don't remember much right now, but at least I'm here in the present. And those…" A pained look crossed the old woman's face, tugging at Jelan's heart. "Those two kids. My two kids are in the damned game. Skies, I need a drink."

"Water?" chirped Fin.

"Who—what? Who are you?"

Fin looked like he wanted to drop into a puddle at his feet. "I'm Fin, ma'am."

"I think she means the alcohol, Fin." Hira shuffled. "Short-term memory doesn't seem to be there for this one."

Meema's gaze snagged on Hira. "Who the skiv are you?"

"I'm skivvin' Hira."

Meema studied Hira with a long, judging look, and Hira did not back down under that gaze. Meema only huffed and then shuffled to the living room, followed by two more servants and a knee-wobbling Fin. The guards carried four bags of Meema's belongings down another hall where a row of bedrooms lay.

"Coco Mathan, or Meema, Violet's guardian," clarified Jelan. "Violet Sutton. Reed Sutton. All of that shit."

Hira's gaze widened. "Oh—oh."

Jelan merely waved her hand. "I'll catch you up on everything later."

"Sleepover?"

A pain tugged at Jelan's heart as she was reminded of how often Violet used to say the same thing. She rubbed at her chest, and then smiled. "Only if you don't hog the bed."

"Deal."

Jelan followed as Hira bounced on her feet, eyes eagerly watching Meema as the older woman sat on one of the couches and awaited her drink from Fin, prompting Hira to roll her eyes and take over for the lanky boy.

"If she's anything like my grandmother, she'll want a lot more of the good stuff than that." Hira snatched the glass and poured generously from a crystal bottle of liquor. "Her memory might be whack, but her tongue is not."

"Thank you," whispered Fin, and he disappeared out of the room, mumbling something about getting Coco's pillows re-organized.

Hira held out the glass to Meema, who again flashed the herbal woman a judging look, which Hira returned gladly, and sipped.

"Are you sure that doesn't interact with any medications?" asked Jelan.

Both Meema and Hira turned to her.

Meema spoke first, "If I'm to know that my butt-nugget, turd-brain kids are in the game, then I will have as many drinks as I want."

Hira nodded in agreement.

Jelan refrained from rolling her eyes. "Thought I'd ask."

"You always kept her in line," said Meema. "The weed flower."

Jelan snorted at Violet's nickname. "Apparently not enough."

"Now she's in the game with *him*."

Hira flashed her a look and Jelan mouthed, *Jack. She hates him. As most do,* Hira mouthed back.

Meema rubbed at her head. "This damn medication is making things fuzzy. Memories come back, and then I lose them."

"I can make you a remedy for the aches," offered Hira.

"Perhaps it's the alcohol," reminded Jelan.

Meema scowled, and then looked to Hira. "I need the strong stuff, not some Elitist shit—"

The elevator dinged, saving Jelan from more of Meema's whines. She whirled, leaving the two in the sitting room as she walked into the foyer.

Lucien stepped out, finding Jelan instantly, his rugged, tired face brightening. She smiled back, unsure of what to do with her hands, so she shoved them in her pockets.

A part of her had wanted to hug him after going so long without seeing him. And that was weird. Very weird. She became aware of the warmth along her shoulders, the blush that crept to her cheeks, and how dirty she was from being in the lab. Skies, she wished she had showered, scrubbed herself clean, made herself look presentable.

Lucien noticed. "Hard at work?"

"I'm getting there...." Jelan trailed, eyes finding the figure that exited the elevator next.

Kole beamed at the sight of her, even though they hardly knew each other. He glanced warily at Lucien, then back to her. "Jelan, you look—"

"Messy?"

"Happy," said Kole. "Well, much happier than when you were caught stealing from my father's office."

She cringed. "Yeah, about that...."

Kole held his hands up and the translucent bandages for plasburns wrapped his wrists.

She snapped her head to Lucien. "I said—"

"It was necessary," said Kole as Lucien remained stoic. "I, well, I wouldn't calm down because I had no idea what was going on, but I'd take this over being with my father any day. Arvalo's gardia was at my house all the time, and my mother would...." Kole rubbed his face. "Both of my parents bent to his will the minute my father accepted the Head Plastech job. I hated being there, hated watching them talk about the most awful things. I've told most to Lucien as he vetted me—"

A mutual understanding settled between the two men. Lucien nodded for Kole to continue.

"—so he knows everything I learned there. It's why I came to you in the South that day. I was desperate to get out of that damned house. Every week I'd be stopped by one of Arvalo's guards because there was so much risk in what my father was working on. I had no freedom, no anything. And of course, I missed her too. So I thought befriending you might help, and they'd allow me to hang out with you since my other *friends* were too far up the gardia's ass." Kole smiled sheepishly. "I was so damn confused when I saw you holding those blueprints in my father's office."

"Believe me, I was too," said Jelan.

"But I'm happy I did, because I hate what my father is doing for Arvalo. He's always been a workaholic, but now it's like he lives and breathes Arvalo's farts. I'm not kidding—" Kole snorted. "So I knew letting you go would have someone after me who wasn't Arvalo. But I was desperate for anything."

"He's cleared and provided me with a good amount of information about the structure of Plastech with Arvalo." Lucien's face paled. "And also about the disappearances."

"And?" asked Jelan.

"I thought the bodies were enough to point to Arvalo and whatever he was up to," said Lucien. "But it's worse. A lot worse."

Jelan's heart thundered in her chest. "What?"

Kole cleared his throat. "I was always so confused when they talked about thousands and millions for the plasblades because what? Are they planning on giving them out to citizens here like sweets? No, they're being shipped off to the government sector."

"Along with plasma technicians, biologists, others I didn't even realize had been going missing," said Lucien.

"The bodies are from the river." Kole rubbed at his face. "They are also people who threw themselves off of the bridge before they could be trafficked to the government sector."

"And where do all these people and plasblades go?"

Lucien looked to Kole, whose hands trembled.

"They'd only said this once, and the person who muttered it...well, they were carried out of my house in a body bag." Kole rubbed at his eyes, sucking in a deep breath. "They said Greed."

❀❀❀

There were a lot of questions looming around in Jelan's head, but as she sat down for dinner, the biggest one was how in the skies did this gaggle of people end up at the same table.

"How's the plashield coming, Jelan?" Jenkins stuffed his fork into the chicken, smirking at her from across the table.

"I'm getting there," said Jelan.

"What does that mean?"

"It means don't ask her about it," snapped Meema.

Kole coughed. Hira smirked in her drink.

Lucien sighed, "She's allowed breaks. She spends nearly all of her time in the lab."

Jelan blushed, unease whipping through her at the fact she wasn't working on her prototype. She had managed enough in a short amount of time, but taming the plasma was the hardest part, because it morphed and did what it wanted, and when it was out in shield form, released like that...

She put down her fork, suddenly losing her appetite. She hated how her shoulders curved and she wanted to shrink away. Perhaps they were judging her for not doing more. Perhaps Lucien was regretting his decision to hire her. Perhaps she dreamed too much like her mother warned her about, and those sketches were to remain in the imagination.

Tone it down.

Her mother prayed to the skies, lit candles, turned to some outward thing in order to tame the fire within Jelan. When Jelan cried, her mother would turn toward her little altar and ask for guidance, and then when she received it, she would hug her daughter and give her comfort. Telling her the skies would guide and answer any of her prayers.

Jelan hadn't prayed to lose her family, she'd only prayed for them to let her free.

"—Arvalo is getting stronger. My spies have told me that he is gathering his circle closer to him, leaving little room for eavesdropping or finding out his plans." Jenkins swirled his drink. "And then Ms. Scarred Hands over here became a thief."

Jelan clenched her jaw.

"I was thinking of making a potion that could help with your mind. Herbal supplements for clarity, processing, all that stuff—" Hira turned to Meema excitedly.

Meema huffed. "Fine."

Underneath the table, Hira nudged Jelan's foot with a roll of her eyes—

Knuckles dragged on her thigh. Warm heat splashed against her cheeks as she subtly flicked her gaze to Lucien's hand and then to his ever-stoic face.

But those knuckles rubbed. Hesitated. Waited for her to push him away.

She held her breath.

And then he continued.

Jelan could barely focus on the conversation, which really consisted of Meema grumbling about the Elitish food and Hira chuckling at everything she said. Kole mainly stayed quiet, clearly uncomfortable and still processing the last few days, but there was an ease to his eyes and…and…

Lucien's knuckle trailed high on her pants, brushing the pocket before he pulled away.

Jelan released her breath.

"—and then there was some cream that could totally burn away my hair. See?" Hira pushed her hair behind her ear, showing off the reddish bald spot on her scalp. "But imagine if I drop that over my neighbor—oh, imagine if I actually gave it to my neighbor with his penile enlargement serum—"

Kole choked on his bite. Jenkins got up, slapped him on the back, and the bit of chicken splattered on the plate. Kole's face turned a brilliant shade of red as he mumbled thanks.

"I can hook you up with a dosage," Hira said, turning to wink at Jelan.

Jelan dropped her head, letting her braids fall around her face as she hid her smile.

"I'm good, thanks," said Kole.

"You could make some real money selling that," Jenkins said. "Even if it isn't real."

"Could have given it to my four ex-husbands," said Meema.

"Four?" Lucien's brows raised. "And all of them—?"

"It's why they're exes, boy." Meema waved a servant away.

"So what's the plan?" said Jenkins. "With Arvalo. I mean—we are all stuck with trying to take him down. This ragtag group, except you, Ms. Mathan." Jenkins pushed his glasses up. "Where do we begin? How do we stop him? He is trying to step over all of the commanders' roles. Alexia Javez has been complaining about him, going on about how he won't leave her alone, or how he wants her to strike up deals with efficient Plastech instruments for her hospitals."

"Arvalo is trying to tone it down—" began Lucien.

Tone it down.

Jelan dropped her fork to her plate with a loud clatter. She stood out of her seat, chair scraping the wood.

"Jelan?" Kole perked.

"I know how to do it." Her gaze met Lucien's. "I know how to make a plashield."

Jelan turned, abandoning her dinner and exiting the room. Hira mumbled *thanks* for the food before saying, "Wait! I'm coming with you!"

Jenkins's voice followed her through the halls. "You got to push them, the young ones."

※ ※ ※

Jelan furrowed her eyebrows at the energy. Looked from one mediating tab to the other.

The energy morphed like a blob, taunting her, asking her if she dared try to tame it.

Tone it down.

"Do you know—" Hira started, then shut up at Jelan's focused face.

Her experience with the energy, and herself, was confined to spaces. Fit in the box that people make for you. Don't step outside, don't make a scene, don't blast through the barriers, and dream.

But she didn't need to tame it. It was a molten ball of colorful energy, twisting and turning within a mediator table. It shouldn't have been that hard.

So instead of taming it, she merely...

Stretched it. Gave it an endpoint where it could mold the shield form, whereas on the journey there, the plasma could do whatever it desired. A sort of freedom that existed within a walled city. A sort of freedom Jelan never thought possible.

Her scarred hands found the knobs, and Jelan let the plasma suck into the bracelet prototype for holding the shield. The metal container warmed at her touch.

"Back up," Jelan instructed to Hira.

Hira did so wisely.

She took one of her prodding tools, messed with the plated switch on the side of the bracelet, and then with a gloved hand, she flicked the sensors that would normally scorch the skin. The tendons on the hand would trigger the shield and awaken it.

The plasma, encapsulated in a tiny silver container that justified its field shape, shot out.

It met the block barrier from the knobs on the neutralizing table.

Within, the plasma morphed, did what it wanted, stretched enough like a thin film of colored veins and iridescent haze.

Hira gaped, then burst from the chair. "*Jelan.*"

Mouth parted, Jelan took a step back from the writhing blue plasma.

That ended.

"You did it," breathed Hira. "You fucking did it."

The heat from the plasma warmed her cheeks. "Throw something at it."

"What?"

"Not anything made of plasma, though, because that would be absorbed by the shield."

Hira lowered the lamp.

Jelan turned to the room, eyes roving for an object. Elation was nearly bursting from her chest and drew a smile to her lips. She grabbed a paperweight atop a bed of scribbled notes and turned.

"You might want to step back."

Hira shuffled away, a giggle escaping her.

Jelan nearly giggled. But first...

She tossed the paperweight at the shield.

A resounding boom shook the room as it met the shield. Smoke stung her eyes and charred part of the curtains from the flash of plasmic heat.

And then the paperweight rebounded off it at a blurred speed.

Hira yelped as she ducked. Jelan barely hit the floor before the flying projectile burst into the linoleum walls of the lab. A roaring crack shook her bones, and when she looked up, fissures extended from the impact spot. Debris drifted through the air, particles clambering to the ground and painting nearly everything in the room with bits of stone and dust.

If Hira hadn't moved, the projectile would have pounded through her.

But the woman merely looked at the crater in the wall with wide, brown eyes, and then she laughed. Cackled. Rolled onto her back and clutched her stomach.

A laugh burst through Jelan as she rose to her hands and knees. The lab was a mess, the shield zapped out after the impact, and the blue plasma was now swirling within its small container again.

They shared one look, tears in Hira's eyes, and then they erupted into fits of laughter.

The door flung open and Lucien's concerned face appeared, body already in a stance to fight off an intruder. His guard was behind him—plasguns out, eyes darting from every crevice to look for a sign of danger.

Lucien's gaze fell to the two laughing girls, bewildered. "Are either of you hurt?"

"No," giggled Hira. "Not at all. Well, almost. Jelan nearly blew a hole through my body."

Jelan wiped her eyes where tears of laughter had shed. "I did it."

"Did what?"

"She made a *shield*. A plashield." Hira lumbered up to a sitting position, in awe at the amount of dust on her.

"You did?" Lucien's eyes widened, turning to her.

"It needs a lot of work." Jelan struggled to her feet, blushing. "I probably shouldn't have started with a paperweight."

"More like a raisin next time."

"Oh," said Jelan, glancing at the bowl of nuts she'd procured from the kitchen for lunch. "That would have been better."

She and Hira shared another look, and Jelan clutched her stomach through another fit of laughter.

"So neither of you are hurt?" Lucien motioned his hands, and the guards exchanged places with servants. They already held mops and other cleaning supplies.

Hira and Jelan ignored him.

Hira beamed at her, stepping forward. "You did it, baby."

And Jelan, pride ricocheting through every fiber of her being, glanced around the destroyed room, cheeks hurting from her widening smile.

Because here, now, she knew exactly what it was like to stand within a dream.

"I fucking did it."

49

LOCKED

AS THE DAYS IN LUST passed, Violet, Anaya, and Rio constantly hovered, rarely leaving the bedroom Jack recovered in: a sprawling, yet cozy white and gray space with a gigantic, plush bed and floor-to-ceiling windows that could tint completely with privacy. A blue fire roared in a towering hearth. There was an accessible balcony, along with the most enormous bathroom Violet had ever seen. The shower alone could have been a whole bedroom in itself.

At first, they stayed with Jack because of concern. Anaya paced the room, sometimes peeking out the window to gasp at the new world, then shaking her head and carrying out guard dog duties as medics came and went. Rio would hover over the drip line connected to Jack's forearm, typically checking his pulse or questioning the medic about their aqua-hued bandages that quickened the healing.

Each inquiry was met with patience. Each glance at their blades or the way Violet's hand went to it every time there was a knock on the door, was met with revered understanding. One medic—the moonlight skin Jonxai, who had slots on the back of her uniform for her glistening wings—asked to examine one of Anaya's collected plasblades out of curiosity. Anaya then decided, after her eyes roamed the Jonxai, that she would give an up-close demonstration.

Violet placed her plate in the strange, robotic dishwasher and turned, reaching for her glass—

It was gone. She frowned, looked around the kitchen and then to the sitting room where Anaya and Rio had passed out while watching a Carcadian film. Alez now flipped through the channels and gave Violet a wave.

She ignored him and padded back to Jack's room.

Then Violet sat and watched. Watched as Jack's chest lazily rose and fell, watched the hands that touched him and fixed his bandages, watched as the hover cars zoomed around the hundreds of beaming skyrises when night descended over Carcadia. She stared at her hands, at the grit stuffed under her fingernails despite the numerous harsh settings she put the shower on. How they had clutched Navo's fur. How they had gripped her brother's leathers. How her knuckles ached from punching his cheek.

How he had whispered to her, like it was to be only their little secret…

We cannot be siblings in these worlds. Not in front of him.

Do you trust me?

Violet brushed her wet hair behind her ear and curled up onto the couch next to the bed. Night descended again, Lust a honeyed haze that only arrived during the dark hours. It tickled the back of her throat, hugged her heart. The room dimmed in Carcadia's nightfall, other than the soft lighting from the bathroom Rio insisted they leave on.

Jack tended to move or flex in his sleep. The medic kept him unconscious to help with the healing, but Violet could tell that as the days went on, Jack's subconscious grew more restless.

"He's a strong one, that is for sure," said one medic as they rolled him over and peeked under his bandages. Their headlamps shined on his injuries. "He is healing incredibly fast. Faster than I've ever seen."

Violet glimpsed the faint red marks that had once been lashes. Relief flooded through her.

The other nurse dropped their voice and replied, "I've never seen such a mesmerizing human before." A giggle, her olive-toned skin glimmered. She reached to adjust the sheet, and a mole the size of a quarter mark, poked from her wrist. "I wonder if he'll be at any parties. I'm absolutely going. He would just be delicious. Perhaps after my other shift later tonight."

Violet glared. The one turned her head, and Violet quickly closed her eyes, pretending to be asleep.

"Well, I'm about to reverse the sleep tonic. Maybe you can ask him in a little bit." The first medic pushed a liquid into the tube connected to the bag. "But I think he's taken."

The nurse shrugged. "Is anyone really taken in Carcadia?"

"She hasn't left his side."

"She can join, too, then."

Violet steadied her breathing as a rush of desire swirled through her. Perhaps that was what she needed to stop feeling so stiff all of the time. She'd let her hands drift between her thighs countless times in the shower, eddied on by the sin, but even as she breathed heavily, forehead pressed into the tile while she bit down a moan, it still didn't feel like enough. Lust begged for more.

They giggled softly. He shifted again, sighing deeply. The medics packed up their stuff, turned off their headlamps, and shut the door quietly when they left. It locked automatically—an install from Alez. Only the bracelets on Violet, Anaya, and Rio's wrists can unlock it.

Violet opened her eyes. Let them adjust to the room before they landed on Jack. His hand clenched the sheet at his waist, chest bare, lips parted. His facial hair had grown scruff, but Violet didn't mind it. It made him look rugged, more senseless, and it enticed her.

She tossed the blanket off of her and padded to the bed. She clambered on to the middle, inches from Jack's sleeping form, and when she felt she could be close enough to feel his body heat, but not touch, she sighed her head into the pillow.

Perhaps it was incredibly creepy that she watched him as he slept. Perhaps it was also because she didn't think she could get away with staring without him being medicinally knocked out. His nose was straight, but the slightest bump emitted from the center. Three tufts of brow hairs lingered closer to his eyelid than the rest. There was a mole in the crevice of his right ear. A small bald patch of his beard made up the size of a fingerprint at his left jawline. A scar lined his temple. His eyelashes curled into his cheeks like they hugged the entire time he slept.

The first night she had felt so lonely on the couch, so when she knew Rio and Anaya had been fast asleep, she crawled up into the bed and lay like this. She had done it every night since then.

Gazing at him didn't make her think about her brother. Watching him breathe tugged her hopelessness away. She couldn't explain it, wondering if Lust was the reason she felt at peace when Jack was near. Things suddenly... didn't matter anymore. Her thoughts slowed, as did her heartbeat, and she would always fall asleep eventually.

She'd realized the previous night that it was safety. Jack made her feel safe. It boggled her to even think back on Wrath and how much she wanted to claw his teasing smile off. She still did, sure, but it was different, because this time she felt the tug of her lips, wanting to smile back.

She curled closer, still not touching. Her eyes fluttered shut and her breath evened. Warmth spread from her brows to her toes, a peaceful bubble that allowed her to rest finally. She looked forward to this harmony every night.

"Vi."

Her eyes flew open.

Jack stared at her. That blazing green the missing piece. He looked well-rested, slightly drowsy but alert. "Are you okay?"

She scrunched her brows. "I'm not the one who was whipped."

"And I'm thankful for that," he breathed, voice a rasp. A shudder ran down him.

She lurched up and grabbed the glass of water that was left on the table.

She helped Jack sit up and tilted the glass for him. Drops dripped onto his chest, but the rim met his lips and he drank deeply. The entire thing.

He sighed, "My throat feels like I swallowed Wrath's desert. Thank you."

"You've been asleep for five days."

His eyes widened. "Really?"

She nodded. "Do you want more water?"

"I'm okay."

"Okay."

She fumbled with the empty glass before placing it on the other side of the bed. "How do you feel—?"

Jack tugged her arm. She careened into his chest, slapping her hand to catch herself. His grip was tight.

"It's Lust," he breathed.

She nodded.

"Are we safe?"

"For now."

"Anaya and Rio?"

"Healthy. Fine. Out with our host, who is a kind man, so far."

"And you're okay?"

She nodded again.

"Promise?"

"I'm okay. Even after my brother. I'm… I'm okay."

Jack searched her eyes, looking for a lie, but she did not back down. He continued, "The Worldbreaker?"

"Saw us when we left Envy. Smiled at me. No sign of him. But we haven't left the apartment, or room, really."

"Your brother?"

"Said we couldn't be siblings in these games," she blurted. "Also, to trust him."

"Trust him when he says something like that," said Jack. "Nothing else. Not at the moment."

She nodded.

"Where are we?"

"A rich person's apartment. His name is Alez. Has a partner named Nadar. Lust is called the City of Carcadia."

"Anything interesting?" He glanced to the door and with ease, ripped the IV out of his arm and removed the pulse monitor off his finger.

"Cars fly. There are too many skyscrapers to count."

"The sin?"

"Only comes out at night."

"Problems?"

"Not yet."

"You've eaten?"

"Yes, and it's pretty good food."

"Anyone got the Iris?"

"No."

"The door?"

"Locked," she breathed.

"Good."

He leaned up and crashed his lips to hers.

Violet reached for him, fingers curling around the back of his neck and into his hair. She pulled him closer, and Jack groaned into her mouth. He was needy, as breathless as she was. His hands roamed her sides, settling on her hips, and yanked her atop of him. He pressed her down, and when she ground into him, he broke the kiss and moaned, "Skies, Vi."

She captured his lips and he eagerly followed. Their tongues danced. Her hips rocked again, feeling the generous hardness there. His hand skimmed underneath her sleeping shirt, up her back, and he paused when he realized she wasn't wearing a bra.

"Have you left the room?" he asked between kisses.

"I couldn't leave you," she answered truthfully.

"You're an idiot."

"So I'm told."

Jack pulled her tighter and flipped them without breaking the kiss. His warm, skillful lips molded to hers like honey and butter. He nudged her legs apart and settled between them, the only pieces of clothing separating their regions being her skin-tight shorts and his briefs. She gasped as his hardness rubbed at her. He groaned right back.

Lust was a frenzy within her. The minute her core burned, she was filled with sweet need. His hands lit firecrackers on her skin, his kisses like lightning that shocked her, over and over, dragging her into their fervent little storm. The cloying haze of the sin had her hands roaming over his chest. He wrapped his arm underneath her back, bringing her closer to the firm ridges of his body. His scruff scraped her jaw and with each deep kiss, she lifted her hips up. Wanting to be closer, wanting more than what she'd done to herself in the shower while thinking of him…

Jack broke the kiss. He reared up, fingers under her waistband—

"Your back," she said through her daze. "Don't hurt—"

"I really don't care right now," he growled.

He yanked her shorts down and tossed them away. His eyes met her center and his expression darkened. Hungered. Starved. She crumbled underneath it. She'd never felt so lost, so sensationalized within her body beneath a vulnerable stare. Jack was going to ruin her.

He ran his finger up her slit and she whined.

"Good girl." He sucked in a breath. "You're so wet for me."

She melted to that finger as it teased her, circled her bundle of nerves and her entrance. Jack caught her gaze, his lips quirking. He pressed on that nub, and she grasped his other arm, digging her nails in.

Lust was a drug and it danced within her.

Let go. Let go. Let go.

Her other hand dipped beneath Jack's briefs and wrapped around his hardness. A choked gasp escaped his lips as she pumped him. The trickles of his arousal met her fingers and that urged her on further. Jack ground into her hand.

Their needs erupted in the room. Months of pain without pleasure. Jack seemed to completely forget his injuries, or the fact he'd slept for so long, powered by a longing in his gaze as he bent and kissed up her neck, thrusting into her hand.

Two fingers entered her, and Violet crumbled underneath his power. His palm wrapped her neck, fingers squeezing the sides, breath at her ear. "Like that, baby?"

"Yes," she answered.

He curled them and she arched, a desperate moan leaving her.

"Fucking skies," he muttered against her skin. "You feel amazing."

Her hand wrapped his wrist, pushing his fingers in as far as they would go. "Don't stop."

"I wouldn't dream of it."

He pumped those fingers, in and out; building a crescendo in her that Lust pranced with. Euphoria flooded, shortening her breath.

Take him. Take all of him. Let him bring you to your peak and further.

Her body tightened and grew heavier. Jack's face buried into her neck, as he found that glorious spot and urged her on.

"Come for me, baby," he exhaled.

"Jack," she whined.

"Yes, come on, you can do it."

Her vision dotted. She clenched her eyes shut, toes curling as every nerve in her body intensified. Her skin crackled with heat.

A loud moan escaped her, but Jack quickly shut it with a deep kiss. His hand wrapped the back of her neck and pulled her closer, bruising, both groaning as they rode through their highs. They chased the feeling of the sin, of ecstasy, into a catalyst of rich need. Desperation flooded their kiss.

She clutched his arm tightly, stopping his thrusts, and ground onto his fingers, letting her body reach the peak of her orgasm. Her world spilled over and breath left her. Stars twinkled behind her eyelids. Jack shuddered above.

There you go, the sin whispered. *Bow to me.*

Violet peeled her eyes open to find him heavy-lidded, staring at her mouth.

Stickiness covered her hand inside his briefs, and Jack hurriedly reached for the box of tissues at the nightstand. He pulled her hand out, wiping everything, and tossed the bundle onto the floor.

"Skies," he muttered. "I don't usually come that fast."

"It's okay."

"I just—when you…" He shook his head. "Just *you*."

"Me?"

He searched her eyes, studied the way he kneeled over her, the bare skin of her stomach where her shirt had ridden up, to between her legs, and then back to her face. His hand brushed her hair back from her forehead as his eyes went from dark to that bright green. Un-dilating.

"It was the sin," she said. She could feel it slithering away, partially satisfied, but ready to awake at the next sensuous touch.

"The sin." He nodded. Swallowed.

She glanced away.

Silence passed between them, and Violet didn't know how to interpret it. One moment he was unraveling before her—every thought, every feeling available just for her to see. And now his wall was back up. He must have hated being vulnerable. Both to her and the sin.

"Can you pass me my shorts?"

Jack snatched them, ignored her outstretched hands, and slid them gingerly up her legs. He fixed them around her hips. Took a breath. Double-checked that they looked right. The brush of his fingertips at her low abdomen had Lust curling within her.

Violet clambered up, unsure of how to respond to him…re-dressing her. It was minuscule, something he didn't even think twice about, but her mind reeled and his gentle touches burned her thighs.

"Welcome to Lust," she said with a small smile as she hurried off of the bed.

She was halfway to the bedroom door when Jack said, "Vi… thank you for staying by my side."

She didn't turn her head. His gaze scorched her. "You're welcome, Jack."

She fixed herself, ignored the rustling of sheets, and cracked the door open to scoot out.

Alez was there. Two bubbling drinks in his hand.

"You look rested," he beamed.

Heat rushed to her cheeks. He snorted.

"Ah! The last of the four is awake." Alez shoved his face in and grinned at Jack who looked bewildered, now wearing pants.

"This is Alez," said Violet. "This is Jack."

"And these are your drinks. The medics gave you the go-ahead to move around. Explore Carcadia! Don't worry, I've made reservations for dinner and did some shopping for you two while you... caught up." Alez plopped the tray into Violet's hands and then headed back into the hallway. "We leave in two hours!"

Violet placed the tray on the floor, took one of the drinks, and chugged the whole thing. There was a sweet, pleasant burn, and definitely something alcoholic in it. Warmth filled and her lips quirked.

"That's comforting," Jack teased, swooping by her to grab the other.

She scowled and paraded to the bathroom, slamming in behind her.

The showerhead drowned out Jack's laugh.

50

RICH

"AURIENS BITE."

Alez leaned over the lavish dinner table to flash his sharp canines. "Not for sustenance or anything of the sort, but for the *truth*. We can bite, and whatever lies you've been told will unravel before your eyes. Whether it was years ago or just yesterday. In turn, we find out the truth about you as well; your words, your person, and any illusions. We taste and feed off emotions—so if I were to bite a suspect being interrogated, I would taste any lies through not only the toxicity in their blood but also his emotion. Our venom can…enhance the emotion too, if we want."

They all sat cozily at a dinner table within a giant, three-story restaurant foyer. The place was packed with elegantly dressed guests; Jonxai with their white skin and wings, Auriens with their long locs, afros, or braids, the olive-toned skin of a Quinam, tuft tails flicking underneath their seats, and then the mesmerizing blue of the single-lid Lovuphal with ridged dark strips like the tigerbot.

By the time Violet had exited the bathroom, she was ushered to another guest room and greeted with shopping bags piled on the plush bed.

Her hair was curled and sprinkled with glitter, her makeup done in lengthy flicks of eyeliner and dark lipstick. Her dress was shimmering silver with a deep V-neck that showed the stickers of crystals adorning the valley of her breasts. She crossed her leg, adjusting the long dress, thankful the heels were not that high.

To get to the restaurant, they had to ride in one of the floating cars. A giant one. Rio had death-gripped the door handle the entire time, while Alez repeatedly told Anaya to stop leaning half her body out of the window. Eventually, he gave up when Jack wrapped his hand around Anaya's belt for safety so the Endolier could enjoy her awe. They floated between the buildings of the city, and Violet dipped her head out of the window, gaping, nearly the whole time. The car followed the air traffic and ascended high into the sky, where shifting clouds hazed with colorful spotlights. Music thumped. People danced on verandas. Ships and cars of all sizes honked. The buildings were wet with glitter, the sin cloyed through the air, and for the first time, Violet was excited.

As the others continued to talk, Anaya nudged her from the left, her legs widely spread so that Violet was crushed between her and Jack. Violet turned to the Endolier, who, for the fourth time, gestured to her outfit.

"It looks great," muttered Violet.

Anaya had chosen the most dramatic, brightly colored, feathered top Violet had ever seen. Even Alez's brows lifted when she exited her bedroom. Rio had spat out his drink. Jack had whistled.

Anaya loved color, and that was understandable since her world had been bleak. She'd even transitioned her scales to match the feathers, but it could not compare to the top.

"Why thank you." Anaya grinned. "I picked it out myself."

"I can tell," deadpanned Violet.

"What's your favorite emotion to taste?" Jack asked Alez as he swirled the blue wine in his glass.

"Lust is the most common, it tastes like berries. Happiness tastes like sweet syrup. Anger tastes like the hottest peppers— not a fan of that one, but some are. And fear tastes like the most deliciously spiced chocolate. Decadent. Raw. Rich. Pure." Alez smiled softly. "But Auriens don't go around biting without consent unless one is under criminal investigation."

"But you have tasted fear…" trailed Violet.

"Some have a flash of fear when they are about to experience something new," smiled Alez. "It's normal. And delightful."

"In that case, as long as the environment is safe, the Aurien may push forth other emotions to help said bit*ee* calm down or find pleasure, but it is usually very pleasurable and doesn't hurt," said Nadar.

Alez continued, "Before we adapted to Lust, Auriens were heads of species relations and promoted peace as well as enforcement. We still do, but our city transformed under Lust's effects, and Carcadia found itself with nearly thirty-million additional citizens within the first one-hundred years. So while we are still peaceful, in the end, Lust is too…involved with itself to focus on such things. The foundation of harmony still exists, but horrors arrived such as trafficking, non-consensual acts, drugging, and more."

Rio frowned into his drink.

"This world has its up and downs. As natives, we know what it was like before—there was a high intensity of pleasure and lust—but now it is the basis of every business within the city due to the Sin. Otherwise, the parties here are exquisite and most people are very, very kind. Although, yes, Auriens can bite for the truth, and Quinam can sense emotions with their tails more intricately than an Aurien, Lovuphals have incredible telepathic abilities if you hold eye contact with them long enough. Still, all these things are not something we flaunt."

"And Jonxai?"

"Have wings." Alez winked.

"My question is if everyone is having sex every night, how are there not like… a billion babies?" Rio asked.

"Birth control. It is a requirement until one might intentionally find a partner and agree to have a child together. Both males and females take it, doubling up the protection," said Alez. "With sexual diseases, however, those do transmit, but there are free clinics to have testing done, and most do once a week—you are all clean, by the way."

Violet sat up. "*Excuse me?*"

Rio paled. "Did you—"

"While I was unconscious?" Jack glared. "What the—"

Alez held his hands up. "It is only spit! We only need spit, and we want to make sure our city is safe from other world's issues."

"You could have asked," mumbled Violet.

"Well, a glass that you drank from does the trick," winked Alez. Violet exchanged a glance with Rio, who frowned.

"I don't know what any of that means." Anaya waved her hand, changing the conversation, "So you are not...unhappy?"

"I wish the Sin weren't the case, because there is the trouble of over-indulging to the point others don't want to participate. We try to maintain some order among the Qors, the twenty-four territorial rulers of Carcadia—me being one of them—but it slips because it is a world of feeling. Rape, pressure, torture, the Ungona, elisian-advanced drugs, trafficking rings—they exist. Some are corrupt, though. Lust isn't very pure, so to speak." Alez huffed a laugh to himself. "Once the Sin takes over for the night, it is hard to maintain composure, as I'm sure you've felt. It also means messes and lack of cleanliness—picking up after wild nights, I should say. That is the downside of Lust, or any sin. There is no reprieve, so any semblance of an organized life is gone."

Anaya frowned. Violet knew the woman was relieved to be out of her world, but there was always confusion with the usual amazement—why did the next world get to live so lavishly, and she had to trudge through tragedy in Envy?

"So Lust's days are its nights?" asked Jack.

"You can't sleep through Lust; it is uncomfortable," said Nadar.

"But during the day, there is a break?"

"More like a recovery," laughed Alez. "You need time to recover before you indulge again."

"Don't I know it." Anaya sprawled in her chair. "So you...rule the city?"

"A Qor is not so much a ruler, rather than a position to help establish order. I am Qor Alezander Konta. My territory is quite big, but I do my best to keep the peace and prosecute when things get messy. There are other Qors who are…more lenient with things when there is money or other benefits involved. It is more of a volunteer position. We have other businesses that help keep the money and status flowing. Restaurants, clubs like the Un—" He shook his head. "Entertainment things. Especially revolving candidates. The city loves their candidates except when my people want a taste."

"And what about the Worldbreaker?" Violet asked.

The table stilled. Even Jack tensed next to her, while Alez paled. The restaurant ambience continued, unaware of the tension.

"I think it is time for elisian drinks," mumbled Nadar. He motioned to a waiter and ordered a round for the table. The other waiters came to clean up their empty plates.

"We do not talk about him here." Alez dropped his voice. "He has eyes. Everywhere. Anyone talking about him, badly, or really at all, is seen as a traitor. You are killed for it or taken to his world."

"Well, we've almost been killed in every damn world, so what's the difference?" Violet leaned over the table and kept her voice at a whisper. "Which one is his world? Does he visit here often? Do you know what he looks like?"

"*Girl.*" Alez's stare was haunting. A shiver ran down her back, but she ignored it. "Do you know what you are saying? I know things, but if I talk…it could drag him here."

"So he visits often."

"More often than I'd like."

"So we have to be careful."

"His captains visit more. The Fringe. His other commander groups. Lust is heavily regulated."

"For what?" pressed Violet.

"What do you mean?"

"Well, he seems to benefit from something in each world, so what is Lust's benefit?"

"Violet…" Jack warned. He squeezed her thigh under the table, but she ignored it.

"Doesn't it bother you to be reserved and happy in this world while the other Sins suffer?"

"Violet," gasped Rio. "Put that attitude away."

Alez's color returned. "She is fiery, Jack. You weren't kidding."

Jack flashed him a glare. Alez smiled sheepishly, cleared his throat, and leaned over to Violet.

"We do not talk about the Worldbreaker or his captains because Lust survived and, for the most part, thrived in the Sins. We are a diverse, peaceful people, with females, males, and those who like to switch between the two or identify as neither. I'm sorry to know you have had so much pain in the last worlds and lost those you cared about along the way. And I'm sorry your brother is under his command."

Violet's eyes flashed to Rio, and he guiltily looked away.

"I can tell you his world is the sixth. I do not know the sin, though. I can also tell you to be careful because he not only started your curse, but he controls the worlds and the candidates. You must understand that. If he is plotted against and if it is found to be my world, the whole city could suffer. I cannot allow that." Alez brushed her cheek, tilted her chin up. "I like the fire in you, but here, that fire must be contained. There are too many spies in this city, too many people who benefit and like what he did. They do not rebel like the other worlds. Remember that."

Before Violet could open her mouth, Jack squeezed her thigh again. "Enough," he commanded.

She bit her retort and leaned back. Extinguished the flame. Anaya nudged her again, but this time it was to give a slight nod.

I'm on your side.

"Have a fun night, young one. You have made it this far. You should reward yourself." Alez winked at her.

The waiter returned with the so-called elisian drinks—bubbling, purple liquid that smoked out of the glass.

"Elisian is derived from the native flowers that grow near the waterfalls. It is a drug, and if infused with alcohol, can be strong at first for candidates," said Alez.

Anaya picked up her glass and chugged a long sip. A moment later, her eyes bugged, and she groaned, "*Oh…that's good.*"

Violet drank hers quickly, wanting to rid the sour feeling in her mind. She had been excited to come into the city, her brother and everything about the Worldbreaker far away, but the more Alez had talked about the benefits of the sin, the more it made her think he was on the Worldbreaker's side.

Jack's hand rubbed her thigh. Up and down. Farther up, farther down. His fingers found the leg slit in her dress, and when the tips brushed her skin, she stiffened. Lust slithered in.

It is just the sin, she reminded herself. And if Jack wanted to participate in the sin with her, then it was okay. There could be worse things.

But the *sin* didn't make her yearn to be close to him, to see those eyes, bright and alive. The sin didn't make her angry when she glimpsed the healing red marks on his back. The sin didn't make her feel guilty when she caught him tracing the lashes in the bathroom mirror, a dreadful, haunted look on his face. She keenly remembered him flinching and shuddering at the whips in Wrath.

There was pain, a deep, unending wound within Jack, and Violet wanted to kill anything that dared to touch it.

His fingers danced on her inner thigh. She sucked in a gasp. Jack laughed at something Alez said, the tension forgotten. Nadar was nursing his fifth drink, Rio gazed at the piano player on a balcony above, and Anaya admired her feathers.

Jack's hand neared her core.

Oh, it feels so good, doesn't it? purred Lust.

Violet gripped the table as Jack brushed her wetness.

Good girl. You're so wet for me, Jack had said.

Her head dizzied. Lust reached out its hand, seducing her to take it.

The sin, it was just the sin.

No, a part of her said. *I don't want it to be just that.*

Violet stood abruptly from her seat. Her bloodsworn mark seared. A heady daze made her lose her balance and it took a moment to realize the elisian took effect. Her thoughts were further away, muddled.

"Violet?" Jack asked, hand gone, concern on his face.

"I need to pee," was all she said. "Come, Anaya."

"What?" The Endolier turned to her. "I don't have to go—"

"Yes, you do," urged Violet. She grabbed Anaya's arm and hauled her up. "I need help with my dress."

"Follow the toilet signs," said Nadar. He turned and whispered to Alez, who nodded and pulled out his small plascreen. "We are going to see where to go next."

She exchanged a look with Jack and flashed him a smile. He narrowed his eyes.

"I'll be back," she said.

The moment they entered the bathroom, Violet stalked to the sink. She leaned over it, squeezing her eyes shut.

"Vi—"

"I just need a second," she said.

"He wasn't shutting you down, it just wasn't the place." Anaya sidled up next to her. "I'm not happy with it either after everything that happened in Iveyrez. But for now, I'm safe. I'm not hungry, I'm not tired all the time...." A hand rested on Violet's shoulder. "As for your brother, he's fine—"

"It's not just that," muttered Violet. She opened her eyes and gazed at her reflection. She looked older, more put together. Her body had filled out the dress and curved in ways she didn't know it could. Even her breasts had grown, and it pained her to think how undernourished she'd been back in Calesal. She didn't look...the same. Not like Reed's little sister or the chaotic girl on the street who was usually drunk or depressed.

She looked more...her.

The door opened and two females, one Quinam and the other Aurien, walked in. Anaya flashed them a saccharine smile. They disappeared into different doors—the stalls.

"Then what is it?" asked Anaya.

"I feel guilty for feeling good," said Violet. She turned to her friend. "After all that I've seen, the guilt has been eating me alive. I'm dressed in these fine clothes and looking like an Elite, and I feel guilty for it. For the fact that I could possibly have a moment of happiness, especially with Jack—"

"What about Jack?"

"Well…we…"

"Tumbled?"

"Not entirely."

Anaya smirked. "Was it good?"

"Fantastic."

"Maybe this world is meant to teach us that feeling good is okay. In parts." Anaya shrugged. "It will take time, but maybe you just need some good di—"

"Ladies."

They turned to the voice. The Quinam entered the parlor from the stalls. A sweet smile split her face. "You're candidates."

Not a question. The Quinam's dark eyes flicked to their palms. Violet slid hers into the folds of her dress. The Aurien exited her stall and brushed up to the sink nearest Violet.

"No, just travelers," said Anaya.

The Quinam laughed. "You're funny."

Anaya and Violet exchanged a look. Violet turned back. "Do you need something?"

"I was wondering where you got your top." She nodded at Anaya. "It is eye-catching."

Anaya beamed. "Oh yes, it truly is."

"And your arms… you truly are a rare creature."

Violet saw the Aurien move too late. Teeth flashed out. Twin fires lit at her neck and Violet keeled over, caught by the Aurien's arms. A heady sensation flooded through her, one of calm and a smile passed over Violet's face.

Anaya slopped to the ground. A dart stuck out of her neck. The Quinam flicked her tail and hauled Anaya up with her hands. A great mole was plastered to her wrist, and Violet could only stare, unable to say anything. Her thoughts meshed together.

The medic.

"Definitely human." The Aurien's teeth were replaced with a pinch of a needle. A flood of sweet elisian overwhelmed Violet, sating her nerves and making her slump into the Aurien's embrace. "Message him that we are on our way. We are going to be *rich* after this catch."

51

THE UNGONA

THERE WERE HANDS. HANDS EVERYWHERE. Voices, loud and in her ears. The room was big, filled with hundreds of bodies, some pressed against her, slick with sweat. A blindfold was wrapped tight around her eyes. Light accents yelped, while some seemed to complain in another language. All around, male and female voices echoed. A crowd? A club?

"What the—" She struggled, sagged into her body as the sweet elisian rushing within slowed her movements. Her thoughts. Panic didn't rise—it couldn't. Her mind wasn't allowed to freak.

Arms held her upright. She lingered between sober and drugged.

Drugged.

Kidnapped.

Violet jerked away from one pair of hands, only to find another on the opposite side, grabbing at her. They kept going, the hands relentlessly tearing her dress off, cold fingers sending chills along her body. Fear began to rise. "Anaya? *Anaya!*"

A sharp voice snapped. "Give her more elisian. She needs to calm down before the bidding."

Liquid dripped into her open mouth. Violet tried to spit it out, but soft hands held her jaw. "That's it. Drink it. You will feel better."

The hands washed her naked skin with a cold rag, and the scent of raspberries drew her in. She couldn't struggle—the elisian didn't let her. It embraced her again, and all Violet could do while her mind screamed was let it happen. Her hair was brushed, her skin painted, and new clothes—thin fabrics on her legs up to the middle of her thighs, a silken one-piece on her upper body.

"Let go of me," she snapped. She managed to jerk her hand away from the cream being rubbed on it. She patted her hips. No plasblade, no things.

"Your items will go with you to your room once you have a bidder."

"What bidder? Where am I? *Please*," she begged, but could not cry. The elisian drugged her, making it hard to stand, let alone flex her fingers.

"Relax—"

"She needs to get to her room! A female candidate, gods, we will be rich because of her."

"Please…" Violet begged.

"Shhh, you will be okay."

"Get her in the room!"

She was hurried somewhere, and a door slammed shut behind her. The room muffled all the sounds beyond. Her steady breath filled up the space.

A hand removed the blindfold, and Violet blinked back, eyes wet as they searched the room.

Black curtains hung around, but otherwise, the room was bare. A soft purple light illuminated from the top, like bits of stars on the ceiling. Violet took a step forward, her hand going to wipe at her face—

Her arm was grabbed and turned. A Quinam with dark eyes. Not the same one that drugged Anaya. Blue hair. She regarded Violet.

Violet yanked her arm back. She was slow, her body protested. She stumbled and fell into the wall.

"You will fetch a high price, and we need it." She stroked Violet's cheek. "The bidders will love you. You will be okay."

"Okay? What do you mean, okay? Where am I?"

"The Ungona."

"What—" but Violet's tongue was heavy and numbed. She shook her head.

"The Ungona is only the best bidding show in Carcadia. You and your rare creature are the prizes."

Rare creature. Rare creature.

A long, shrill bell rang, sending a chill through Violet. The female looked her once over. "You are the show. It begins now. A high price will come from you."

The Quinam yanked a thick red cord that hung in the back corner of the small room. "Don't do anything bad." Then she vanished.

The world changed. Behind Violet, the curtain went up to reveal a translucent window, and through it...

Violet felt any remaining confidence leave her. People. Thousands. Staring at her in her display window atop the rows and rows of others. Like trinkets in the front window of a toyshop.

Levels of these windows spanned numerous floors. They were filled with scantily dressed people who turned and bent and danced for those in the seats. Violet pressed her hands against the glass, searching—

She spotted Anaya a couple of windows over. Oh skies—Anaya was fighting the drug, kicking out, punching the barrier that led to a substantial drop to a stage below. Four stories below.

"Anaya," she muttered. "Anaya." She couldn't scream. She needed to get out. The door behind her was locked, the space small. It closed around her, pressing in. It was going to trap her. She was already trapped.

Breathe. Breathe. Breathe.

Her mind was in chaos. The crowd roared, and a voice rang out, but it was not in her language. Across from her, the crowd sat in four galleries, one stacked atop the other, the first two with tables and servers and rich-looking Carcadians. The bottom two were for theatre seating. Some pointed…to her. Then to Anaya, but the show started at the windows on the bottom level, and it moved. Fast.

One by one a booth was lit up while the rest dimmed, giving the body within a display. The figure would dance, beckoning, performing, selling. Paddles raised as the crowd placed bids. Some, as the light illuminated their booth and they danced, enjoyed it.

She wasn't unused to the low news of trafficking sex workers back in her city. It was an underground business, but it was nothing filled with so much flair as this.

Horror ran through her mind, but still her body betrayed her. All she could do was press against the window, calling Anaya's name. The Endolier gave up on kicking at the glass, movements slowing. She looked around, caught Violet's gaze and said something. Mouthed. She pointed to the crowd and then mouthed something again. Violet's vision hazed. She stumbled. There was too much elisian in her system. It detached her conscience from her body.

Anaya mouthed again, screaming it. Violet's vision cleared for a moment.

It was a name.

She mouthed a name.

Jack.

Then she pointed.

"Jack?" Violet croaked, already sagging back against the glass. The elisian worked in waves, and during this wave Violet desperately searched the crowd, but there were too many people. Jack was here? Was Rio? Were they in the booths too? From what Violet could tell, only a couple of other male humans were scattered at the top level with Anaya and she—the prizes of the night. But none of them were the boys.

The elisian surged. Her ankles gave out. The lights flicked so fast, those auctioned off danced or slumped against the window, unconscious. Violet's legs wobbled and she collapsed to the ground, hands and knees.

The door to Violet's room opened and the Quinam woman stepped in with a vial of swirling blue liquid. "Smile big—you will get your reward after."

Violet wanted to protest. Another wave tilted the room around her. The Quinam gently held her jaw, opened her mouth, and dumped the vial in.

Violet had no choice but to swallow.

Everything sparkled. The sounds of the crowd and the announcer's booming voice intensified. The Quinam's coaxing voice, her beautiful eyes, the tufted tail tickling Violet's arm had her bursting with warmth.

"Good girl," the female said, caressed her cheek, and then exited.

Violet reached for the door, or the female, she didn't know. Her body was not her own, reacting to everything with sensual warmth and arousal.

Anaya's booth lit up and she growled beyond it. Feral. Still, hundreds of paddles lifted and people even stood, yelling at each other, waving their drinks in protest. Numbers and symbols rolled on a screen above them, reflecting against the glass. She watched as it rose, higher and higher, until finally it blinked and the crowd clapped.

The next candidate smiled through the window, eyes heavy-lidded from the drugs. He was auctioned away. The light flashed again. Her body finally listened and she backed away from the window.

She needed to hide. But they knew. She was last. The highest price. She would fetch them money.

Brilliant purple-white light lit up the small space, blinding her. She lifted a hand to cover her eyes, looked once out the window to watch as a frenzy started. So many paddles lifted. People roared, stared, gaped at her. Hands of all colors pointed.

On the third-tier gallery, a familiar figure waved frantically.

Violet crawled to the glass. "Rio. Rio. *Rio.*"

He watched her with his big doe eyes, panic running along his face. He turned—

She locked eyes with another.

Her number rose. The crowd's shouting deafened.

Jack looked ready to murder. He yelled and pointed to her, fear and fury flashing across that beautiful face. So beautiful, right? And the hands that had held her, been in her…the elisian warmed her blood and Violet flashed a bright smile, hoping to lure Jack in. She wanted him again. She felt safe with him.

He dipped his head to his neighbor—Alez. Again and again, Jack would lean in, whispering, and the paddle would lift. The number rose. Alez waved him off, waiting a few moments before raising his paddle to continue the bidding.

Jack was trying to get the Aurien to win, but a portly Quinam above beat the price each time, his tail wrapped around one of the two females beside him. He smirked at Violet, eyes haunting as he lifted his paddle, over and over, determined. Jack noticed. He muttered something to Alez, then to Rio. Alez frowned as the number rose until it lingered at a final one, and then flashed. When Jack turned away, a satisfied smile tugged at Alez's face.

The fat Quinam grinned in victory.

"No," she muttered. She threw herself against the glass in her last batch of energy.

Alez dropped his paddle to the ground. Rio had vanished. Jack angrily talked with the Aurien, looking up—

Violet's door opened and she was dragged back.

"A high price indeed." A Jonxai woman sneered at her, wings fluttering. "Get her ready for Qor Nockona. He doesn't like to wait."

She was changed and robed, then hurried within a lift, the city of Carcadia spread at her back. It rose and rose. They led her to a room with a wide-window overlook on the city and an even wider bed. She trembled.

The servants shoved her against the wall, cooing and coaxing as they lifted yet another vial to her mouth. Violet failed at batting them away. Her mind didn't want anymore, but her body ached for it. Needed it. Craved it.

"Shhh, open. This will help you forget."

Perhaps that was for the best. Violet willingly opened her mouth.

The sweet liquid filled. She swallowed. Another vial was out. Kisses peppered her skin, luring her. Violet didn't fight the next swallow of elisian.

The door shut. She was left alone.

Her vision blacked in and out. She collapsed to the ground. She tried to lift herself up, but she couldn't fathom how hands worked or how to get her fingers to move. The room danced, blood warmed and coursed—

A frustrated gurgle escaped her mouth. In an aim to lug herself to stand, she jolted too far and crashed into a wooden table, knocking over a cream vase. It shattered on the floor. She blinked through the next blackout of her vision.

She snatched a shard. Once a long piece lay in her palm and she focused hard on strengthening her grip around it. Blood welled, but she couldn't feel the pain.

Footsteps padded the hallway outside.

Kill. Kill. Kill.

Her heart thundered—she glanced at the bottles on a table, the round hooks nailed to the four bedposts...

A desperate sound left her. As the steps drew closer, Violet mustered for a semblance of control over her body.

The knob turned. A tall shadow stepped in and quickly shut the door.

She lunged, swinging the shard, but her energy lacked and she fell short. Still, she surprised him, and they collapsed to the floor.

The figure twisted them until her arms were pinned above her head, the shard having fallen out, and Jack looked at her with amusement from inches away.

"This was certainly a different kind of treatment than what I paid for." His voice was hoarse.

"J—Jack," Violet sobbed. "It's you."

He released her hands. "You think I'd let it be anyone else?" His gaze studied her, falling onto her neck. "An Aurien bit you?"

A relieved exhale left her.

He pulled her up and into his arms as her body finally gave out. Warm. A comfort. She buried her face into his neck, and he rubbed her back.

"When you didn't come back from the bathroom, we sent a female to check and they said no one was in there. Alez threw a fit, used his Qor status, and sent half the waiters out to look for you. One said they saw Anaya's hideous top and a Quinam carrying her. The snatcher said Anaya had too much elisian and was bringing her home. Alez checked his little portable plascreen and found the announcement of two females at the Ungona; rare creature and human candidate."

"Anaya…" breathed Violet.

"She's fine, although she didn't need much help. Her suitor was tied to the bed, naked, before Rio managed to find her. Anaya had been waiting for him longer than she would have liked." Jack kissed her neck. "I'm so sorry."

"Jack." Violet wrapped her arms around him. "Don't trust Alez."

He hugged her back tightly and buried his head within her neck. "I know."

Someone yelled outside—Alez's voice. *"I want this place shut down! Atrocious! How could you let something happen? Where are your credentials? No—go get me your superior. This will be evaluated by the Qors."*

The door opened and Alez stepped through. "My darling, I am deeply sorry. I shouldn't have…I should have been more careful. The Ungona is only operated because most prizes are consensual. However, I think Anaya's shirt caught some eyes in that restaurant, and an opportunity was presented."

Jack tightened his grip on her, sighing deeply.

"I had never seen a price so high for a candidate." Alez smiled sheepishly.

She hiccuped.

"Do you have something to cover her with?" asked Jack.

Alez searched the closet and pulled out a robe. They wrapped Violet up in the soft thing. With a lurch, Violet was up and cradled in Jack's arms. She clung to him desperately.

"Gods, they gave you too much." Alez frowned.

Alez escorted them out, swiped a badge against an adjoining door, and called out, "Mager, my sweet, you can have your fortunes, but I won't be needing you for the night."

"Really, Alez? You bought me out again for nothing?" A female Jonxai swaggered to the door, pale wings peeking over the tips of her shoulders. "Why do you always do this?"

"I'm offering you to leave the Ungona for a better life, but it seems you never want to listen to me."

She leaned against the door. "What else am I supposed to do within this Sin? Watch dakárt?"

"The sport is renowned."

"It's boring." Mager waved her hand. "Go enjoy your drinks." Her eyes locked on Jack. "*Oh*, unless he is my replacement? My, my, I've never seen a finer—oh. You're a candidate. And so is she. Are they both for me?"

Jack smiled. "Qor Nockona is open. And unconscious. Sadly, she is not available. Nor am I."

"That Qor! Hah!" She chuckled. "You really hate the man, Alez. Madam Drona won't be pleased to hear her biggest customer has been subdued. I'm guessing this pretty little human was meant for him? I heard she fetched a high price." Mager paused, white brows creasing. "Oh dear, she doesn't look good, though. How much elisian did they give her?"

"Too much." Alez frowned. "We must go, Mager. I will see you soon."

"*Fdon*, Alezander."

When the door shut, they all hurried to the elevator, Jack careful with Violet. Everything was hazing, morphing, twisting. She almost vomited with how fast the elevator dropped. Jack gripped her tightly, whispering little nothings to keep her awake. At some point, Anaya and Rio joined them. Then a cadre of tall Aurien guards. They paced through the packed hallways and giant foyer, Alez snapping at his phone the entire way until they reached the platform out front lined with hover cars.

A large, sleek-roofed vehicle slid up, and they piled in. Violet was barely hanging on to consciousness the whole ride, nestled into Jack's side with his arm protectively wrapped around her. Anaya passed out the minute the door shut, and Rio sighed as she drooled on him, but he said nothing. He removed her shoes and twisted the Endolier around so her head lay in his lap.

There was a threshold with this elisian, she heard Alez mutter. Something about it being sensitive to the candidates when they first arrived, but also when it was given in concentrated doses, it acted like a tranquilizer, drugging the victim so heavily it might cause permanent mental damage.

Jack's arm tightened at that. His face must have looked a certain way because Alez was suddenly coaxing him, calming him, explaining that what Violet and Anaya had been dealt was minimal compared to when that threshold of damage occurred.

Then someone mentioned something about a bucket. There was vomiting. Her vision blacked. She was lifted and on solid ground, wrapped in a warm chest. Sleep overtook her as lips brushed against her forehead.

52

DOWN

"THERE ARE NOT ENOUGH GUARDS."

"Do you want me to pull half the city, Jack Marin?"

"As much as it will take to protect them."

A scoff. "The Ungona is shut down for the time being. We had a quick vote last night to enact better regulations for those who want to auction off themselves and enact in prostitution—"

"I think you're lying."

"Excuse me?"

Violet rubbed her eyes and stepped out of Anaya's bedroom, leaving the door open. It took nearly two minutes to reach the sitting room where Alez sat on a couch, steaming drink in hand, and Jack paced back and forth before a giant plascreen. Calm music creeped out of the speakers.

Rio lounged on a chair, tapping his temple. He beamed when he saw her. "Oh, hi, Vi. I see you're trying out a new hairstyle."

She glowered.

Jack whirled, spotting Violet, and concern flooded him. "You're up. How are you feeling?"

"Like shit," she said.

"Well, you spent the better part of last night vomiting and then took up most of the bed...."

Violet's eyes widened. "You stayed...?"

"With you? Of course. Someone had to hold your hair back," he said.

Blush crept onto her cheeks, but she paraded toward the stack of hangover tonics on the kitchen island. She shot back two of them.

"They went to the *bathroom*, Alez." Jack went back to fuming. "They shouldn't be in danger there."

"I'm aware of that, Jack, but things do happen." Alez waved his mug. "Just two weeks ago I was groped at a party. Another month ago a candidate was caught in the bidding war of trafficking gangs. We managed to snatch him in time before we lost track of him at the bottom. A year ago there was an instance where one candidate popped into the world, took just a breath and was snatched on the spot." Alez rubbed at his temple. "We are in a city of tens of millions of people. I can't control it all."

Violet dropped her third shot of tonic. The glass shattered on the marble, and Alez popped up, surprise on his face.

"Oops," Violet said. "My motor skills must not be working, along with my memory." She took another tonic and threw it against the wall. "But things have been…coming back to me. Even though elisian is great at fogging the details. If *my* memory serves me right, your little medic with the mole was also the one who attacked us in the bathroom."

Alez paused. He blinked those big eyes and held a hand up. "Excuse me? My *medic*?"

"I had a hard time believing it, too, but after catching up with dear Anaya this morning and realizing that you were the only one to call her a rare creature, and the workers at the Ungona called her the same, things simply clicked."

"You are mistaken," Alez said.

Alez had wound closer to Violet, his fist shaking. He reached for his pocket.

Jack stormed across the sitting room. "I swear to the skies if you touch her—"

Anaya rippled into sight, her scales un-morphing from her surroundings. The Endolier held the end of a plasblade, flicked the sigils so the metal sprung out and burning plasma lined it, and swung.

The blade went clean through Alez's neck. His head thunked onto the floor amidst the tonic. Anaya nudged the blade into his body and it collapsed.

Violet wrinkled her nose.

"I hated his voice," Anaya said. "And his laugh. And his stupid face."

Jack gaped. Rio stuttered for a moment and then howled with laughter. "What the fuck?"

"*Alez?*" Nadar's voice came from the hallway. "My love? What was that noise?"

Anaya swung the sword. "I'll take care of him."

Nadar ran into the room. His eyes found the mess on the floor and Alez's decapitated body sprawled on it. A curdling scream erupted from his mouth. "Alez? *Alez?*"

Anaya cackled a laugh. "You're next."

"She's not socially trained. We are working on it," said Violet.

"*What have you done?*"

"You were selling us out," snarled Anaya. "It was your medic with the little mole on her arm who drugged us. It was your little boyfriend who called me a rare creature, as did the workers at your little Ungona. Which they let slip that *you* owned." Anaya lifted the humming plasblade. "Any last words?"

Nadar's face twisted in anger. "I hate you fucking candidates." He lunged for a button on the wall, his fingers barely missing it before Anaya lobbed another head off.

Anaya retracted the plasblade and shoved it in her belt. "Our bags are all packed."

"Damnit, I liked their shower." Rio pouted.

Jack huffed a laugh. "Where are we going to go now?"

"Down," was all Violet said.

❀❀❀

Violet had wiped the blood off Anaya's face by the time the hover taxi arrived at the apartment. Freshly changed, packed, and with food stuffed into their bags, the four of them piled in. Just like in Calesal, the taxis were marked with orange stripes and glowing with yellow lights. Up close, the driver was—robotic. A dark gray and glittering sort of machine, the oval head swirled and beeped out a mishmash of an alluring language.

"We want to go down. To the ground," said Violet.

It registered her voice, her language, and blinked gray plates over its glowing blue eyes. "To the bottom *za Carcadia*. Fourteen *havs*."

A button jutted from the car.

"Scan your identification," the driver beeped.

Jack flashed Alez's identification card to pay. It blinked blue, then green, and then the door opened to the taxi. A small bridge met the edge of the veranda. "Confirmed, Alezander Konta."

"Goodbye, Alez," deadpanned Jack as he tossed the identification out of the vehicle and into the open air.

Lust was bleak during the daytime. The city was a haze of gray buildings and clouds. There were fewer hover cars, less traffic, and most verandas or buildings were abandoned, the citizens tucked in for sleep after a night of Lust. Mist sprayed on their faces and Anaya reached her arms out, reveling in it.

"I love this city," she grinned.

Rio turned from the front seat with a bewildered expression. "Thankfully, we can get lost here after your murder."

"Exactly." She beamed.

The descent to the bottom was a long ride. Violet nursed her headache the entire way down and kept her eyes shut. The driver was…good for a robot and maneuvering a flying car, but as the buildings blurred around her and she felt the occasional drops, she spent the rest of the time making sure her stomach didn't flip again. At some point, Jack's hand rubbed at her back as she took long breaths.

By the time the car slowed, night had started to arrive. Colorful rays from buildings replaced natural light, doors were flung open, and the first of Lust's participants appeared. Music screeched on. Humidity permeated the air, and the smell of sweat and cooked meat reached her nose. She gagged slightly as the driver blared, "The bottom. Good day."

They stepped out onto the wet sidewalk amidst the thrash of other hover taxis and glanced up.

The bottom of Carcadia.

It was as if the city's heart beat beneath, then pumped and rose like blood up the skyrises around them. Walking bridges shifted over their heads, coated dark and silver with bursting lights. Restaurants, clubs, cafés, and stores lined the street that hundreds walked on. Bodies danced, talked, throbbed, shuddered. The light mist of rain from the plethora of waterfalls made the streets glitter.

The bottom was more battered than the extravagance of Alez's apartment or the restaurant they had been to. Here the emerging people were dressed more simply, yet flashy, and less confined to the long gowns or suits that most had worn yesterday. Along with their backpacks, Anaya had shoved quite a few bags of the clothes Alez had bought them.

"Let's find a bar," said Jack. "At least to lay low. I'm sure there are hotels here."

"We don't have any money," said Rio.

"We have someone who can camouflage well enough to steal some keys." Jack shouldered his pack.

They walked the streets, eyes wide at the chaos of it all. When night settled, everything began. Lust swirled again in Violet's core, but the emptiness of her belly kept her focus. She couldn't take her eyes off the rushing cityscape—from the multitude of flashing signs, to a pink glitter waterfall, to a giant hoverbus that flew through the tight traffic spaces along with fifty other hovercars. Within twenty minutes, more bodies piled onto the street and the four of them blended in.

"There?" Rio pointed to a lucrative bar with an unhinged metal and neon sign. A few Jonxai dressed casually entered, laughing. Plascreens flashed within and it reminded Violet about bars in the South where people went to watch the North's sports.

They headed that way and the door peeled open for them automatically. A flash of red light marked their entrance, but only a few heads turned their way within the packed bar.

A long bartop wove like a snake, drinks of all colors, smoking and bubbling, piled on top. The bartender—a portly female Quinam whose tail was dyed blue, cried to another bartender in a different language. The Aurien bartender yelled back, and the female cackled a high laugh.

Screens littered around the walls, some scrolling news with twists of a different alphabet, others a sport where players tackled each other, and many more. Booths and tables packed the place, nearly every one filled until Rio stood his full height and motioned to the back. They packed into the booth, exchanging glances.

Before Rio could open his mouth, a waiter flicked long, bright red hair behind his head and sidled up to their table. Human. Completely, utterly human.

A bright smile split on Jack's face. "Adrian, you skivvin' dog."

The waiter's eyes bugged. His narrow face, deep-set blue eyes, and an assortment of freckles beamed in bright, crooked-tooth surprise. "Jack fucking Marin?"

Jack stepped out of the booth and opened his arms for a hug. "Good to see you, man."

Adrian shook his head. "How did you get in the Sins? I—what are you doing here?"

"The short answer is that I lost the gardia wars," Jack said. "Long answer is…very long."

"And now you're in Lust…."

Jack studied his friend. "Do you work here?"

"Yes, I do because—"

"Why is this the most casual conversation for this situation?" mumbled Rio.

"Why does he have so many spots on his face?" Anaya said.

Adrian looked at the rest of them, eyes narrowing on Anaya. "They are freckles."

"Does your hair catch fire?"

"If you light it." Adrian cocked his head at her. "Do you turn into a snake, little Endolier?"

"If you piss me off." Anaya grinned.

"Who is this group, Jack?"

"My travel group," said Jack.

"You guys walked into the right place, because you can find any kind of help for candidates down here." Adrian shrugged. "I went into the Sins maybe five years ago? Right when this shit was getting all his fame and stealing the hearts of everyone." He nudged Jack. "I've been working here 'cause I like it. The owners are great people." He motioned to the Quinam woman behind the bar. "She offered me a job in exchange for a place to sleep and some food, and I just… never moved on."

"Why are you in the Sins?" asked Violet.

"Thought I'd take a little vacation," teased Adrian. "You're a pretty one. Why are you here?"

"Thought it would cure my shiva-addiction."

"Isn't that what we all say," laughed Adrian. "I'd love to catch up, but what can I get you guys?"

Before awkward silence could ensue, Jack drew Adrian in, lips on his ear. "You—what?"

"Oh, look!" Anaya clapped her hands and pointed to a screen. "My handiwork!"

Rio slapped his hand on Anaya's mouth and smiled. "We don't have any money because this one needs some self-control training."

Adrian gawked from the Endolier to the plascreen above the bar. The news played and the familiar hallway of Alez's apartment panned through, followed by shots of the spilled tonic and broken glass. Two bodies were covered in black fabric.

"She…did that?" said Adrian.

"He sold her and Violet to the Ungona," muttered Jack.

Pure shock passed over Adrian's face. "Really?"

They all stared at him, and he combed a hand through his hair. "Man, there's going to be some parties tonight."

Violet's brows scrunched. "Why?"

"Because we all fucking hate Alez Konta."

And as if to match Adrian's statement, nearly the entire bar pointed to the screen and erupted in cheers. Drinks slammed the tables, liquid splashed, people turned to their neighbors and hugged, and even the bar owner shouted, "Round of drinks on the house!"

"Let me see about some rooms for you." Adrian winked at Anaya. "We are celebrating tonight."

Beneath Rio's hand, Anaya beamed.

53

SPECTACULAR

ADRIAN RUSHED BEHIND THE BAR where he dipped his mouth to the Quinam female. Her eyes popped open and she turned to their booth with a gap-toothed smile. She ushered Adrian away. He flashed them a thumbs up.

Adrian guided them to the back of the bar and a tight hallway beyond. The crinkle of Anaya's shopping bags filled up the space as they turned another corner and entered a plush sitting room filled with couches, tables, a cooking area, and a handful of other candidates.

Adrian dramatically gestured to the four of them as they all filed into the room. Eyes lifted. Some halted on Jack, who stiffened, while some split bright smiles, oblivious of who stood there.

"Now, now, we all have had some dealings with this one right here." Adrian squeezed Jack's arm and left it there. Violet narrowed her eyes at the motion. "But if a candidate makes it to the fourth world, you know they've been through the skivvin' shits. So no fighting, bitching, or killing. You all know the rules. We play nice here because we all need a break and because we don't want nothing to do with the overruler of this game."

"You all know the Worldbreaker?" asked Violet.

For once, no one paled or looked at her with solemn eyes. There was no tension or uproar, just nods and eye-rolling. Adrian whirled on her. "Well, none of us know the guy, but seeing as we all served our little sentences in Envy, you know that everything is ruled and controlled by him."

"We also don't wanna go to the sixth world," chimed another candidate with glitter on his lids. "It is easier to lay low here and hide."

"I will have to go 'cause my sister needs the money, I'm sure of it." Another candidate slapped his thigh. "Soon though, soon. It is good here."

"Also!" Adrian snatched Anaya's arm and pulled her out. "We have a savior here! Alez Konta is dead 'cause of this one!"

Silence ensued before an eruption of cheers.

"I landed on that skiv's balcony and he was out giving me to some trafficking shit within the day," said Glitter-Eyes. "Fuck him. Good on you, little one."

Anaya had a permanent grin on her face. She bowed. "Thank you."

One candidate stood—long brown hair pulled back into a bun and intense gray eyes. He strutted up to Jack who pushed Violet back when she took a step to defend him.

The candidate held his hand out. "The name's Vince. Three years ago, my daughter was kidnapped by that big trafficking scheme in the Mid, and it was your boys who stopped it all. You might not have any idea about it given your power but—"

"I remember," muttered Jack. Agony passed over his face. He stared at the man's hand. "But I don't deserve that."

"She's alive because you stepped up all those years ago and challenged the heads of the city." Vince still held his hand out. "I always wished I could personally thank you. Just didn't think it would be in these circumstances."

Jack opened his mouth and then closed it. Violet was a bit surprised to see his reaction. There was no salty smirk or clipped words. No lifting of the chin to cling to whatever power lingered, or even the faintest cold glare. He looked like a vulnerable man standing among the shattered walls of himself that he erected throughout his years ruling Calesal. A true man, one whom he might not feel comfortable with, one who had grown and viewed whoever he was back in Calesal as some distant memory.

Clearly, his impact would remain. She wondered when those whips lashed, they had torn out his charade along with his skin.

Her hand found the belt loop of his pants and she wrapped a finger through it. He seemed to relax slightly and then clasp Vince's hand. "You'll have forty more men to thank for that. I was merely the overseer."

"The Sins strip our own sins, don't they? After each world. Like skin to be shed." Rio clapped Jack on the back. "Maybe there is redemption after all."

Jack scoffed and pulled his hand away. "It is still a mad, fucked-up game."

"Isn't that life?" muttered Violet.

Adrian smiled at her. "It truly is."

After the reconciliation, Adrian showed them to two rooms. "I'm sorry we don't have more. There are beds big enough for two in each—"

"Perfect." Jack grabbed Violet's hand and dragged her inside one. He slammed the door to Rio's cackle and Adrian's confused murmurs.

Jack let her go, and Violet stayed by the door, watching as he dropped his bag on the floor. He sat on the bed; elbows on his knees, hands covering his face.

It was a tiny room of four white walls, a single lamp, clean sheets on a double-person mattress, and two pillows. A shared bathroom down the hall. Violet sagged in relief. The ambience felt more comforting, more inviting and safe, than Alez's apartment ever did.

Her eyes turned to Jack. "What do you need me to do?"

That interaction had rocked him. His hands shook and he took a few deep breaths before saying, "Nothing. You being here is enough."

"I'm not the…hugging type," said Violet. "Rio was a one-time thing."

"I don't need a hug."

"Okay," she mumbled. She slid her back down the wall until she was cross-legged on the ground.

They sat in silence; Jack's head in his hands and Violet gazing at the bare ceiling. The thump of the bar vibrated the room. A great cheer. Eventually, Violet rummaged through her bag and pulled out a pair of clean leggings and a simple sweater she liked from Alez's shopping spree.

She stripped and slid on the new clothes, brushed out her hair with her fingers, patted her cheeks to bring out the color, and smoothed her brows out.

"You seem comfortable like this," said Jack.

"It is more familiar."

He didn't say anything back.

She braided the top half of her hair. "Are you done moping about the weight of your sins?"

He snorted. "You're the one to talk."

"You look rather unattractive when you are feeling sorry for yourself."

He stood. "Tell that to the snot I had to wipe from your nose in Gluttony and Envy while you slept."

She glowered. "Also a one-time thing."

"Doubtful." Jack studied her. "Have you recovered from last night?"

"I think most of my fear flew out of me when Alez's head left his body."

Jack smirked, dimple and all, and ran his hands through his hair. His shirt lifted, revealing the V of his lower abdomen, the line of hair trailing underneath his belly button into his tight-fitting pants.

Her heart picked up. Violet tied off the end of her braid and flicked it behind her shoulder. "Want to go celebrate Anaya's murder?"

He threw his head back and laughed.

Violet thought it was the most beautiful sound she had ever heard.

Let go. Let it all go. The worries, the pain. Let it drift into the wind and give in.

And she did.

The night consisted of partying, drinking, and more partying. At some point, Violet was straddling Anaya on the bar, and to the cheers of the crowd, she licked up the elisian in Anaya's navel, then the powdered sugar at her collarbone, and then the juicy fruit at her mouth. Their lips touched and Anaya grabbed the back of Violet's head, pulling her close in a sweet, sticky kiss. When Violet lifted her eyes, Rio was fanning himself and Jack was grinning.

Lust purred throughout the night. Jack danced on her, pressing her against the bar, kissing her neck. Rio tongue-wrestled a Jonxai, disappeared, then came back shaking his bloodsworn hand. Anaya went to start a fight with said Jonxai and then disappeared herself for a long while before coming back with lipstick on her neck. Adrian had made himself busy with another male candidate while Vince sat on the bar happily pouring drinks into patrons' mouths.

Beautiful bodies of all sizes ground into each other. Moans permeated the air, the honey taste of the sin laced with the happy celebration that extended throughout the streets of the Bottom.

Violet downed her elisian. Music swathed along her bones. The lights wrapped her in a euphoric trance. She opened her mouth, a smile tugging on her lips, as she allowed herself to feel.

To forget. To forgive.

To be free.

A hand slipped in hers and she turned. Anaya, sweaty and heavy-lidded, bounced to the music, dark hair moving like gallops of ink. Violet looked at their hands, awed at the friction between them. There was a heady jolt in her core. A haze along her vision. The lights sparkled like the stars, and the music thumped like a heartbeat.

Violet danced, pulled close by Anaya. Steps away, Rio had his eyes closed, head tilted back as he swayed.

It sang along their veins and for once, the four of them felt no pain, no heartache, no fear. Darkness would not touch them in this euphoria. The lights splashed along her vision. The city, the eclectic and welcoming Bottom of Carcadia, opened its warm arms and embraced the four lost souls in a mesmerizing heaven.

Anaya and Violet danced close, fingers sliding on each other's skin. Every touch was a soft firecracker. Every breath tasted of sweet mint and raspberries. The Auriens, Quinams, Jonxai, and Lovuphals around them swayed to the music. Violet spun in a circle, pulled close in safety by her friend.

And when the girls were close, Anaya's gaze drifted to Vi's lips and Violet connected them.

The kiss was sweet, smooth. Her mouth tasted of the elisian drinks—hints of citrus, a deep, iced pomegranate, and sweet berries. Violet brought her hands to Anaya's face as they kissed, living in their ecstasy.

After moments, they pulled back for breath, and the girls smiled wide, giggling. Violet ripped her sweater off, wanting more skin, more touch, anything that could add to the inferno within her.

Violet fell into the arms of a male Quinam, his tail wrapping her arm, and they danced. He spun her around and he leaned in, expertly roping her hair behind her ear before kissing her jaw. A female Jonxai glided over with wine-red hair. Those iridescent wings shimmered behind her back. She smiled, teeth gleaming like starlight. She gripped Violet at the waist, tilted her head, and kissed her.

Embrace it. Feel it. Let it consume you.

She burned like the brightest star in the sky, and Violet never wanted it to stop.

The Jonxai pressed against Violet's back as the male gently slid his lips along her neck. Her skin shuddered with each stroke, each caress.

The female pulled from the kiss, just as the male did. Empty. Cold. But their fingertips still slid along her skin as they danced together.

Jack stepped around, power, heat thrumming from him. The Quinam male leaned toward Jack, and Jack gripped him by the jaw and brought their lips together.

Violet's eyes widened in surprise. The female slid her hands along her body, over her curves, along her hips, breathing hot against her skin. But Violet was entranced by the two males kissing—Jack, as his jaw tightened and his strong hands moved.

Something ignited within her as she looked at how he claimed the Quinam's mouth. At how much Jack liked it.

Jack pulled away, as if sensing her eyes, and turned. Her knees weakened under his gaze, those green eyes swirling and bright in the shifting colors of the room. His beauty halted the breath in her throat. His dimple poked out and it slashed heat into her core. Hands slipped around her waist and pulled her toward him.

"Vi," he whispered.

Her heart throbbed against her chest, and his beat back. An answer to hers. *I am here. I am here. I am here.*

We are here.

"Jack," she breathed.

And they crashed their lips together.

In yearning, in haste, they tasted each other, devoured each other. A thought eddied into her head that this was the most euphoric thing of her life. He was Lust in a man, wrapped in an irrevocably beautiful body. He moaned against her, strong, calloused hands rising to cradle her face.

They fell into each other, finding a home. She pulled him closer, harder. Their kiss deepened. Tongues danced as their bodies did. He slipped his knee between her legs and she gasped, core igniting. She ground her body against his, closer, closer, closer, and she pulled away for a breath in this ecstasy. She let her hands roam down his chest, until she slipped them beneath his shirt while his nails scraped down her back. Jack brought one hand to her jaw, grinning against her lips, while the other found her ass, cupping, squeezing.

One moment they were dancing, devouring each other in an indescribable sensation, the next Violet threaded her hand with his and was dragging him down the hallway. The lights flashed with the beat. Jack pulled her roughly to him once they were alone in the back hallway, hurrying to their room. He stopped her, pressed her against the wall and she yanked on his neck, tugging him closer.

With ease, he moved her into the bedroom, locking the door. It was dark and she breathed once before his lips captured hers. Every feeling, every touch was heightened and electrified. He roamed his hands, dragging fingers across her nipple and squeezing. She gasped in his mouth and pushed him back.

He blinked. "Are you okay—?"

Her hands went to his shirt and she ripped it straight down. Jack's eyes flashed in approval.

"Never better," she purred, tugging his shirt off his back. Her eyes hungrily took him in—toned muscles from his training days as a commander, broad shoulders…she didn't really care, honestly. He was beautiful all the same.

Jack hoisted her up, hands on her rear, and pressed her into the door. His lips were bruising, full of chaos and electricity, and fire… such a warm, lovely fire that ignited from inside. The ache at the center of her thighs grew in earnest.

"Vi," he groaned. "If we keep going…I won't be able to stop."

"Don't stop. Fall with me." Her breath caressed his lips and she tugged on his curls. "Sin with me, Jack."

His hand wrapped her jaw. "That's a dangerous thing to say."

She smiled. "Ruin me, Jack Marin."

"Who knew you were so naughty." Those bedroom eyes locked onto her bra, and with a single movement, it was unclipped and on the floor.

He dipped her head to the side and kissed up her neck, her jaw, along her ear, and she gasped, a tiny sound escaping her. He chuckled. Trailed his tongue back down her skin until he reached one of her breasts and pulled it into his mouth. Teeth grazed her nipple, bit gently, and Violet shuddered underneath. He ground into her, holding her to the wall, his arousal evident.

She reached for his belt buckle, but he paused his meal and

carried her to the bed. "I want my time with you. A long, *long* time."

"I want to…." She kissed him again, ecstasy shocking her at the way his lips met hers, wrapping her in sweet, shameless desire. "You deserve pleasure, and I can give that to you."

His thumb drifted over her lips. "You want to feel me?"

"All of you."

"Spectacular things don't come all at once, darling." He drifted lower and lower, pulling her pants with her. "Well, except for you, after I'm done with you tonight."

He ripped her underwear off in one go, the lacy thing discarded across the room.

He kissed up her thighs, grip bruising. She was already a mess, hands clenched into the sheets, back arched to meet him. His warm breath met her core. Tongue flicked teasingly.

And then he yanked her into his mouth.

Moans bubbled out, and she arched her back. He ravaged her, sending her to some infinity where stars danced behind her lids and a fire roared within her. His fingers entered, curling and flexing, and she gasped on her breath.

He chuckled into her skin. "You like that?"

"Don't stop," she breathed. "Don't you dare stop."

"As you wish," he rumbled and moved his fingers faster while his tongue worked and licked, shattering her into an inescapable euphoria. Lust heightened every feeling, every motion, to a blaze in her core as the crescendo built, and Jack groaned along with her moans, urging her, teasing her skin and the most sensitive part of her body.

"Come on, sweetheart," he mumbled. "Come apart for me."

"*Jack*," she moaned. Her hands tangled in his hair.

"Baby," he growled. He pinned her hips down as she wriggled against the ecstasy, cries growing louder. She couldn't think. She couldn't breathe.

He brought her to the edge.

And again.

And three more times after that.

He found that spot within her, curling his fingers into it and begging her on. He explored her, journeyed through her passion and euphoria like it was the best adventure of his life.

She grasped his arms and tugged, yearning, needing him. He crawled up along her body, kissing her neck, then her jaw, before the corner of her lips. His fingers found her mouth and propped it open. "Suck."

A command. She willingly obeyed, eyes heavy-lidded.

"Good girl," he whispered.

She flicked her tongue, tasting herself on his fingers. His face grew dark as she drew her cheeks in to suck harder. Her hand slid over the bedsheets to his pants. Jack undid his belt buckle and let his slacks slide down. "You want this?"

"Yes," she said and drew him to her lips. "Please."

"You're protected?"

She nodded. "They gave me a shot back in Calesal."

"Good."

Whatever frenzy between them had dwindled into something more slow and passionate. A calloused palm trailed the skin on her thigh as he angled her, bending her knee in. Jack lowered himself between her legs. His tip nudged her entrance.

Their gazes locked. His striking face watched, studied, memorized her every detail. She did the same, from the ridge of his nose to the curve of his eyes to the scar at his neck. The puckered heart of his swollen lips that made her feel so many things. The gleam of those green eyes she always searched the room for.

She nodded. His hand pressed into the bed beside her ear as he leaned down and captured a kiss.

He slowly rocked his hips, sliding into her. Her lids fluttered. She moaned into his mouth. Gasped. Inch by inch, he glided in, and his eyes glazed over in pleasure. A sharp exhale breached his lips.

He grasped her jaw. "Look at me," he commanded.

She did.

"Are you okay?"

She nodded. She wrapped her legs around his hips and tugged him closer. He pulled out, thrust back. His lips parted with heavy pants, brows drawn together. Violet clawed at his arms and Jack grabbed them, pinning her wrists above her head as he buried his face within her neck and picked up the pace.

And together they joined. Their story passed before her eyes as he claimed her, made love to her, something so precious and passionate she didn't have words to describe it. Her moans filled the air as Jack grabbed her hip and drew her closer, angling himself deeper.

A circumstance, yet a truth of certainty. That they both wanted to be there, as they were, in each other's arms while their labored breaths grew heavier, and the pleasure built to its peak for both, but mainly for Violet. Jack urged her along every time, taking care with his hands, every touch of his something that might have rivaled the intensity of Lust. Like every sound she made was only a notion for him to keep going, with his lips, with his hands, with himself. Everything.

The sin bowed and sang, but more in harmony, a celebration. He released her hands and she pushed at his shoulder, flipping them. She straddled, rode him, bowed her head back. His eyes rolled as her hips did. Eventually, he rose and pulled her into his safe embrace, thrusting from beneath. She whined into the blissful air. He groaned against the skin at her neck.

"That's right. Press your thighs in. Embrace it. Feel it. Get on your knees," he said between desperate breaths. "Sin for me, baby."

She grabbed his jaw and kissed him. Whispered on his lips, "Always."

And in their little bubble of ecstasy, they pressed their foreheads together as Violet scrunched her face through another peak, her entire body tightening. Jack followed right after her. She clung to him. His nails raked down her back. One last grind and she shuddered, collapsing into his arms.

Once she caught her breath, Violet pulled back and looked at him. "What the fuck?"

A dimpled smile split his face. He brushed away her sweat-matted hair. "I think we sinned pretty well."

She laughed, bright and warm. He chuckled along, and together they fell into the bed, wrapped into each other, until her eyes drifted shut and sleep murmured her name.

He pulled out, but his warm body drew her into his chest, strong arms wrapping her middle, and her half-thought was what in the worlds had she done to deserve this.

A kiss burned her forehead.

By the skies, did she sleep.

And it was dreamless.

54

TWINS

"HERE IS YOUR DRINK. THAT is two *havs.*"

Violet held up the portable scanner and the customer tapped their identification card on it. Five havs came back as a tip.

They took the bubbly purple concoction with a smile.

She smiled back.

"You're good at this, darling."

Madam Zona, the Quinam owner, bumped her hip with Violet's, nearly sending Violet into the dishwasher.

"I grew up doing my homework while my guardian bartended." She wiped the counter and slid a look to Jack, who leaned over the bar and grinned at three female Lovuphal patrons. He dropped small fruits into their drinks and gave them with a wink. They giggled back.

"He makes more tips than you," Zona said.

"I'm not surprised." Violet scowled.

It was nearing the second week of working the bar and staying in the candidate's house. Anaya was a shot girl, Rio a busser, and Jack and Violet were bartenders. As long as they worked five night shifts a week, they had their amenities and bedroom, along with using their tips for drinks and food.

Madam Zona's, the bar itself, was known for its red-light ambience and casual atmosphere. Here there didn't need to be heels and dresses, but more eclectic tastes or whatever wanted to walk through the door. Violet's color-blocked crop top and leggings, hair half-tied into two ponytails atop her head, glitter-dusted skin, and the winged liner was the most comfortable and free she felt in a long while. The Bottom was the place to express oneself, and there were the regulars who came in nightly, whether they wanted to sport dresses as males or suits as females or a mix of everything in between, or no label at all. Madam Zona welcomed everyone with two rules: be kind to her workers and no weapons.

"Two blue elisians to the back corner booth," said Adrian as he hurried past the bar to deliver another round of shots. The night was young, but bodies already bopped to the deep-bass music on the dance floor and there was already a line out of the door. "Can you take it to them?"

Violet nodded and poured the drinks. She wove through the back of the bar when a hand stopped her. Lips met her ear; "I like your outfit tonight."

A shiver ran down her spine and she turned her head to Jack. His curls were held back in a bun, his shirt simply black but ripped in a couple of places, followed by tight pants.

"Have fun staring at it," she teased back.

His breath tickled her neck. "I can't take it off of you?"

Lust purred within her as she said, "Do you ask that of all people who've given you their numbers?"

"You know that's just for the tips." His finger dragged down her back. His voice was dark, husky, as he said, "What can I do to make you moan my name tonight?"

Heat crept to her cheeks. "I need to bring these to my table," she said quickly.

She hurried to the back corner booth where two men lounged. Long coats fitted their broad shoulders. There was a similarity between them. Twins, was her first thought, and as she drew closer, she guessed at least that. Or very similar-looking brothers.

Light mixed skin of russet, tall, early or late fifties, and human. One laughed as the other mumbled something, and when Violet drew closer, only one pair of eyes lifted to her. The other was wholly unbothered and uninterested.

Deep umber eyes, full lips, straight nose, wide nostrils. Their eyes were very cat-like, piercing, slanted, and a hint of something otherworldly beneath.

Long locs fell down one's back, half of it piled atop his head and beaded with silver. His mouth curled in a friendly, closed-lip smile. "You're a doll, thank you." His gaze dipped to her hand. "I'm assuming there is a bloodsworn scar there?"

Violet placed their drinks on the table and flashed her palms. "Take a guess."

His eyes dipped between both, and an air of surprise came about him. "That's very interesting."

He flashed his bloodsworn scar. "Seven years ago, along with my brother. I'm Jodin." He nudged the other who kept his gaze on his drink. "This is Yarrow."

"Violet," she said. "Just came in this year."

The other's gaze snapped up. A confused look passed on his face before he gruffed, "You're awfully young."

"Nineteen." She shrugged. "Maybe twenty at this time. Not sure. My birthday is mid-autumn."

"Twenty years…" Yarrow mused. He knocked a knuckle on his temple. "I can't remember that far. But you look familiar."

"Maybe you knew my mother." Violet shrugged. "I'm told I look exactly like her."

"Your mother happy you're in the Sins?" asked Jodin.

"She's dead, so I haven't been able to ask her yet."

Jodin chuckled. "That kind of attitude makes a survivor of the Sins."

Violet nodded awkwardly. "Is there anything else I can get you?"

"Just another round of drinks when these are near empty," said Yarrow. He took a long gulp, and before Violet turned away, she caught the odd filigree lines swirling over his hands, as if light glowed so brightly it had bleached it.

Filigree like…

Violet whirled back toward the bar. Attempted to relax her posture and not bring any attention. She squeezed her eyes shut. She imagined it. There was... *he* was not the Worldbreaker. The Worldbreaker's skin was pure, pale white. But those lines... glowing lines she'd glimpsed in those last moments.

A coincidence.

But there never seemed to be coincidences in the Sins.

By the time she sidled up next to Madam Zona and was given a list of drinks to make for the next orders, the interaction was in the back of her mind. For once her friends had regular smiles on their faces, happiness not a teasing hope that they could never reach.

After she slid another drink across the bar, an arm slung around her shoulders, and a gleaming, silver object was thrust in her face.

"I hate this sin," grumbled Rio.

Violet pushed the Iris out of sight. "Good on you for getting it."

"Casual sex is not my thing," was all Rio said before he shoved it into his belt loop and piled the dirty dishes into the bus bin. "Believe me, the women here are beautiful, but it's like...a few words, and their hands are at my pants. And I just... can't stand the voice pushing me in my head. I'm not about it."

Violet frowned. "Do you want me to take over for you?"

Rio shook his head. "I'm good. Madam Zona kicked the female out."

She turned her head toward the front doors, and just like Rio said, Madam Zona had her green hand wrapped around an Aurien's upper arm and shoved her outside. A slew of Carcadian curses passed through the door before it slid shut and silenced the rest of Zona's yells. The Aurien shook her head, dazed, before hurrying off down the street.

Madam Zona returned inside, but before the doors could slide shut, a dark figure prowled in. Tall, lanky, but lean. A white-skinned hand grasped the lip of their hood and pulled back.

A man. A non-human aura. Violet froze in her spot as some dark lightning crackled around his fingertips and then disappeared. Long legs paused. His puffy lips pouted as his single-lid eyes took in the bar. Pitch-black hair fell straight behind his ears, meeting the curve of his neck.

He didn't look... real. Violet blinked, convinced he was a figment of her imagination, but when she opened her eyes, he was staring at her, lips quivering into a smile.

"You."

She opened her mouth, hand already on the plasblade underneath the bar, when one of the twins—Jodin by his long locs—appeared and wrapped a hand around the new arrival's shoulder. Despite Jodin's smile, his face was tight.

"Zavar, you devil." Devil seemed not to be a term of endearment. "What are you doing here?"

"I thought I'd pay a visit." He shrugged. "I've missed you two. You know how much I love this world."

Jodin seemed to notice that Violet was watching the interaction, so he pushed Zavar out the doors. Zavar lifted his eyes and waved at her, that black lightning crinkling atop his skin.

The moment the door slid shut, she rushed out of the bar and tracked down Adrian in the kitchens. "Where's the portal to the next world?"

He balked at her. "You're going?"

"Can you sneak us out?"

Adrian swallowed, disappointed, but nodded. "The portal is at the center temple gardens, where the Qors meet. It's hard to miss. I can call you a taxi—"

"Call three of them," she said. "We need to leave."

"You're in trouble?"

"By the one and only," she mumbled.

Adrian's eyes widened. "Gather your stuff and meet at the backdoor. I will grab the others."

"Don't raise alarm."

"I'm a Souther, baby, there's never any alarm." He winked and then slapped his hand on the kitchen table. "Turn the music up; it's a rager now!"

A worker rushed out and the music volume blared louder. The

crowd roared in excitement.

Violet rushed to their rooms and shoved whatever she could in their bags. Plasblade hilts went to her belt, Gwen's dagger in the leather sheath. She just prayed Rio didn't lose his Iris.

By the time she ran back to the chaotic kitchen, her three friends were there. They each took their bag and Rio breathed out, "It really couldn't last longer, could it?"

"There are three men here who acted strange. The last one just entered and looked...well he said something along the lines of liking this world, as if he routinely visited and I...." Violet ran a hand through her hair. "I hate it as much as you all do."

"Well, we destroyed the Farm and his little robotic factory so..." said Rio. He lifted his shirt and revealed the Iris tucked in his belt loop. "I'm surprised we made it this long."

"Don't count our luck just yet." Jack smacked Rio on the shoulder.

Anaya frowned.

"You can stay," blurted Violet. "I wouldn't blame you but—"

"My place is with you three." The Endolier lifted her chin. "It wouldn't be the same without you."

"Endearing," said Jack. "Let's save the appreciative comments for the next world. I'm sure those guys are prowling the bar for us as we speak."

55

BURNING

JELAN

WITHIN A WEEK, JELAN HAD the plashield prototype outside of the neutralizing table. It took a while of fussing with the bracelet so the plasma slowed to the point she wanted the shield to end, but after numerous experiments and many different things hauled at it, Jelan was beyond herself that it worked.

Truly worked.

But despite the wonderful success of her shield, outside of the apartment, things were dark.

Jelan stepped into the kitchen, ready for another cup of coffee, when she spotted Lucien poring over the stolen blueprints, rings under his eyes.

"There's nothing to figure out," mumbled Jelan.

Lucien flinched, looking up from his seat at the counter. He forced a smile. Rubbed his face. "I didn't hear you come in."

"Based on the reports you debriefed me on, and the fact that four more bodies have shown up, focusing on this won't do any good." She frowned. "If aether means more arches or portals—what does he want to do? Start another game like the Sins?"

"Arvalo doesn't have that kind of power," said Lucien. "However those games were started, perhaps Arvalo wants to achieve that kind of lasting greatness. But that would mean he has to be a god, control the elements, put a curse, and then what? A seven-world game? Arvalo can create plasweapon after plasweapon, but he is not a god. He is not whoever made the curse."

"Maybe that is how he wants to get the city to its knees."

"He'd look to Emperor for that. It's as close to power as he'd get." Lucien pushed a hand through his hair. "I just wish...I wish my brother were here."

Jelan's heart sank. She took a step forward, then another, until she was next to him as his body hunched on the barstool. She wished her plashield would be big enough, strong enough, to shield him from these emotions and the world outside of these penthouse walls.

She lifted her hand, let it still in the air. Lucien picked his head up and looked at that scarred mess with saddened eyes.

"Don't," said Jelan. "Don't look at my hands like that."

"They're beautiful," he breathed. "I never thought otherwise. I hate that you can't see it."

Her heart raced in her chest as his hand met hers, brushed that mangled skin with the gentlest of touches until his fingers clasped atop and he thumbed her palm.

She wasn't breathing. She'd never...never let anyone touch them like that.

And then he did the most boggling thing.

He brought her hand to his mouth and kissed it. Each ugly fingertip. Her palm.

"The most beautiful thing that these hands did was that they didn't create a weapon. They created defense. They created protection from plasbullets and plasblades. They created hope."

"Create is not the word I'd use."

"Give yourself credit, Jelan. They *also* belong to a very beautiful human being," he said. "That the skies took their time in creating."

She took a step forward, and he lifted his head.

"Your Marin charm is like a bug I need to swat away," she said.

He chuckled. "I know. I'll buy you a fly swatter and permit you to smack me anytime I use it."

"That's all the time."

His eyes darkened. "Around you, yes."

Her stomach fluttered. He leaned in—

"Man, I need a fat-ass breakfast after the amount of shiva Kole and I drank last night."

Jelan jumped away, pulling her hand with her, as Hira strutted into the kitchen, rubbing at her eyes.

Lucien winked at Jelan, then turned back to the blueprints. "Help yourself."

Hira paused, giving Jelan and Lucien a look over, before smirking. "Aw, did I cockblock?"

A blush crept to Jelan's cheeks. "No, Lucien was just confiding in me about how to ask you for the penile enlargement serums."

Hira snorted. Lucien turned to her, a surprised, joyous look on his face.

Jelan surprised herself at that joke.

"I do not need that," grumbled Lucien.

"Sure, baby." Hira opened the pantry and piled all sorts of food into her hands. "I'm going to make enough for the whole penthouse. What do you want?"

"Pancakes," said Jelan. "With chocolate."

"Done." Hira smiled.

Jelan grabbed her cup of coffee and sat at the small table, gazing out through the expansive windows unto the city. The South and the Mid sprawled in the distance, hazed by the morning sun.

"Where's Meema?" asked Jelan. The woman had been spending time figuring out the plasphones—the tablet Lyla used—to call the servants in the house whenever she needed something. Most of the time she was yelling at the home screen and sending Hira—her top-listed contact with a heart—a mix of icons and letters when she couldn't figure it out.

Hira laughed every time.

"I think she's bothering poor Henry about redecorating her room. She doesn't want to look at the stupid Elite towers. She's sent numerous calls to Jenkins asking him to bring her everything she loves in the South—whatever pops into her head at the moment, really. I think Jenkins is ready to break her phone."

"She's actually yelling at her physical therapist right now," said Kole as he walked in, clearly hungover. "Like clockwork—it's my alarm at this point."

"That's nice," mumbled Jelan as she gazed out at the city again, eyes crawling along the horizon of the South. The smoke, the—

The smoke?

Rising like a beacon, black like the night.

Jelan stood. "It's burning."

"I cook my pancakes just fine, but thanks for the vote of confidence—"

"No," said Jelan. "The South is burning."

Silence descended over the room as all eyes turned to the windows. Like beams, smoke started to trail from the South and into the Mid, burning pyres atop roofs. A signal? A—

"Bronto! Get me Lyla and Cairo. Figure out what is going on *now*. Ashan, send groups to secure the South." Lucien stood from his chair. "Call the other Commanders—I want the city on lockdown!"

"Yes, sir!" Bronto and Ashan responded.

"What's going on?" Kole asked.

But the elevator dinged, and Lyla rushed into the kitchen.

"Arvalo is at the Emperor's Circle." A horrified glaze appeared in Lyla's wise eyes. "He's to fight Neuven within the hour."

"Well, fuck," mumbled Hira. Pancakes forgotten on the stove. Burning.

❋❋❋

When someone challenges the Emperor for the throne, all members of the government have to be in attendance and declare the winner when the fight is over. In Veceras's history, sometimes the fight had lasted seconds, sometimes hours, and even, one time, a full three days.

The Emperor's Circle was where that challenge happened. Across the Trollova Bridge, in the government sector. It was normally so heavily manned that two years ago, when Jack Marin planned to storm the bridge and fight his way to the Circle, Arvalo had stopped him by threatening the city he fought for.

Once the current Emperor and the opponent entered the Circle, they could not leave until the other was dead.

Hira, Jelan, and Kole remained at the penthouse under strict orders by Lucien. They were not to leave, not to make any contact with anyone.

"I will sort this out," he had said, gripping her hand and squeezing it.

Sort it out? she wanted to blurt. *Arvalo going after the government is something to sort out?*

Jelan was left in the kitchen, eyes running over the little plans while the South continued to burn in the distance. A plasbomb went off in Souther's Square—a distraction, Lyla had said. Fourteen casualties so far. A large gardia team of Lucien's was sent to evacuate and comb the area of other potential bombs. Alexia Javez had sent a team of medics there, too.

Jelan's gut hadn't stopped turning the whole time.

"This isn't the only thing going on today," mumbled Jelan.

Hira stabbed her burnt pancakes and ate them deliberately. "A bomb in the South turns eyes from the bridge. It was what Arvalo wanted to do all that time ago when he thwarted Jack."

A plascreen played video of Arvalo waltzing down the bridge with thick armor, his gardia surrounding him, plasguns raised at every Redder who merely stood there. Unmoving.

"They have something else," Jelan said. She turned to Kole who had his head buried in a coffee cup. "What else is there?"

"My father," Kole mumbled.

"Plasma runs like oil within our land. It is mined far from the city because mishandling can be...dangerous." Jelan scratched her chin. "So these points on Calesal's map could easily be accessible plasma points. But if they are tapped, it could destroy the city."

"That would ruin Arvalo's whole stint for Emperor. If we all just died, what would be left to rule?" said Hira. "The stupid fucking arches?"

Kole sat up, hand on his head. "They also talked about those."

"The arches?" asked Jelan.

"And whatever aether is. The thing written all over the map. They couldn't figure it out, but they could measure it. In like... the tiniest degrees, but it's all written there so it's stuff you already knew."

"So these points aren't plasma—" Hira walked around the kitchen island.

"No, they are," said Jelan. "Arvalo has some threat that is allowing him to cross that damned bridge with no challenge." And then Jenkins's words from that car ride so long ago came back to her. *"It is when the Empire reminds us that ultimately, they have the power. They cage us in a wall and submit to the curse."*

"What is that nonsense?" Hira said.

Kole's eyes widened. "They are at the Aariva."

"The only thing the Empire has control over are the Sins, the wall, and everything outside of the wall. But what if one of those things were taken hostage? By using these points?" said Jelan.

"One or two plaspoints might just be big enough to threaten the Aariva," said Kole. "I mean, didn't Lucien say plans were stolen after Jack Marin went in? I'm willing to bet these are the plans because the Empire would not want these dangerous plasma locations to be public knowledge, not with the gardia wars, or with any citizen."

"Someone could stop the whole Sins with this threat," said Hira. "If they bombed the arches and succeeded, Violet and Jack would never be able to return."

"And a good threat to venture off and fight the Emperor."

Little shuffles scuffed the floor. Meema appeared, hair unruly and eyes narrowed in her permanent scowl. "You little shits are real annoying with all your talking."

"Meema, you're pretty archaic." Hira smirked. "Have the arches ever been bombed before?"

"You're asking someone recovering from memory issues?" Kole

said.

"Skiv off," said Meema. "I'm not archaic, you shit. And the answer is yes. They've been bombed before. Shut down a portion of the city to see if they could be destroyed. I remember being at home for a long week while the ground shook." Meema frowned. "But the arches still stood, although they did have scratches on them."

"So they can be destroyed," said Hira.

"With really intense plaspoints. Perhaps enough where the Mid and a portion of the South is gone."

Jelan turned back to the burning. "Arvalo would not be the kind of person to want to submit to the Sins. He would do it. He would be willing to destroy it if it means the Emperor's power."

"My father would too," Kole said softly.

"We need to go. We need to find these points and secure them." Jelan stood, gathering the map.

"We can't leave," said Kole.

"You fucking Northers," Hira said as she wrapped her hair back into a bun. "Don't you know the rest of us don't play by the rules?"

Jelan turned to Meema. "Can you...make a distraction?"

"I'm not as flexible as I used to be, but I'm sure I can still seduce—"

"No, Meema, sweetie, like... medically." Hira placed her hands on Meema's shoulders. "Faint or something."

"Do you see how many guards are at the door?" Kole said, lowering his voice. "Like nine. They are not all going to react."

Jelan stood up and went over to the plascreen on the wall. She tapped a few buttons until she found the number.

"We are not supposed to contact—"

"Kole, we don't play by the fucking rules," snapped Jelan.

Hira patted the man's head. "Sit tight, sweetie. Go massage Meema's feet."

Meema was already grabbing her coffee and shuffling out of the room. "I have some nice lotion, darling."

Kole grimaced.

Jelan tapped the number and it began dialing. The familiar voice came on the second ring. "Lucien, aren't you supposed to be stopping the damned Arvalo by now?"

"Hi, Jenkins."

"Oh, scarred one." There was a rustling. "You need something."

"You have seniority, right?"

"People listen to me, yes."

"Call off the guards at the penthouse and get your bug eyes on these locations." Jelan listed off the coordinates and Jenkins grunted at each one. "I need to get plashields at each one. You have a team, right?"

"Of course."

"Get them here, I'll teach them how to install the shields. These places need to be protected, no matter what."

"You think you can boss me around now?"

"I think you do love this city more than you say, and I think this is Arvalo's next plan."

Jenkins was silent before he sighed. "You've grown, scarred one. I like it. I'll have teams to your places within the next twenty minutes."

"Fast fucking car," muttered Hira.

"The streets are shut down, poisonist."

And with that, Jenkins hung up.

56

RACE

THEY TOOK SEPARATE TAXIS. VIOLET reluctantly separated from Jack, who gave her an eye roll and pulled her back for a swift kiss before departing for his vehicle.

Anaya looked her up and down and said, "Not doing that again."

"I don't blame you," deadpanned Violet.

Anaya headed to her taxi.

Violet and Rio took the last. She readied the hilt of her plasblade as the car zoomed into the air, fear and resentment swarming in her blood. Rio looked back at her, eyes wide.

"Just hold on to that Iris," she muttered. The life of Lust carried on as the night met its peak. Traffic flew through the buildings, big cars sporting parties, everyone else oblivious to the overarching danger of the Worldbreaker.

The looming presence sent a shiver down her bones. Zavar's delighted smile replayed in her head.

"See anything?" Rio asked. He glanced at the robot driver, then back to the landscape as they passed around a large skyrise.

Violet leaned out of the car to glimpse the air below them, the ground a blur in the distance. The taxi lifted, swirled around another building, but nothing was out of the ordinary.

She clutched the plasblade.

Another turn.

Rio gasped.

The Center Temple rose in the nocturnal haze. The epicenter of the vast, endless city grew busier with traffic. The car stopped, floated, and with Rio's frantic pleas, they moved along. Violet had lost track of Jack and Anaya's cars, praying that there wasn't an ambush waiting for them. The men at the bar hadn't looked ready to fight, but she knew her group was their target, and the night wouldn't have ended with any of them alive. Or in this world.

Violet's heart thumped in her ears as she gazed around, hoping to catch them.

A clap of thunder roared through the city. Lightning flashed, and one by one, lights flickered out atop the massive towers, all the way to the bottom. She put the pieces together; the same non-storm that happened during the Bloodswearing Ceremony, and the same entrance when the Worldbreaker appeared in Envy.

"He's coming," she muttered. A tingle spiraled up her arms, static raising hairs. Beneath the car, the city turned black. Screams echoed around. Silhouettes pointed to the sky. Figures ran indoors. Thick droplets of rain splattered her face.

Violet thumbed the plasblade, and bright yellow plasma lined it.

The hover taxi quaked. Jerked forward. Violet careened into the front passenger seat, slamming her temple.

"What's going on?" Rio asked the driver.

"I—I—*malfunction*." The driver sputtered in Carcadian and glitched, then fell against the steering wheel. The car blinked, its purring dimmed, and it began to descend.

"Shit! Move him!" Violet lurched forward while Rio shoved the driver out of the seat and over the lip of the car.

They plummeted, hair blowing back and stomachs dropping. Rio screamed and Violet yanked herself in the seat, pulling on the wheel while pressing the pedal underneath. The taxi groaned but righted before they crashed into another car.

"It's there!" Rio cried, pointing ahead. "Hurry!"

Another streak of lightning lit up the temple. Thunder shook her fingers as she gritted through the velocity and jerked the wheel.

The car drove forward, up and up, hot fuel bursting from the back. Screams echoed from the vehicles around them. Fingers pointed upward.

Shadows flocked the sky.

Not the sky.

"There are things on the buildings." Rio trembled.

"Do *not* let go of that Iris." Violet jammed on the gas and aimed for the temple ahead, a jutting veranda her target. She wove around the idle cars and terrified cries of Carcadians, pushed the accelerator harder—

A bang hit the back of their car and Violet stopped herself before her head slammed into the wheel. Rio grunted as his arm shot out, halting him.

She grabbed her plasblade. "Get in the seat."

Rio obeyed, switching places as she stood in the car and turned. A taxi followed them, headlights gleaming, but Violet knew the two figures. Billowing coats, twins. Jodin stood on the hood, plasgun raised, while his brother drove, the long end of an arrow sticking out of his back. They swerved in the incoming traffic.

"Skivvin' shit," cursed Violet as another shot nearly missed her head. She waved the plasblade again, catching the bullet with the weapon so it sputtered out in a flay of sparks. "Drive, Rio!"

"I never got my license!"

"Does it matter? I didn't either!"

"What?"

"What?" snarled Violet as she blocked another plasgun shot. The back of their car smoked from the first hit, a petrol smell filling the air. It crackled and burst. Jerked the car forward.

Rio slammed his foot on the accelerator over and over. "It isn't moving!"

"Aim for the temple!"

She looked back at their pursuers, and to her bewilderment, she watched Jodin's arms and hands ignite with those twisting lines. He disappeared.

Burst into thin air at the back of the car.

Teleported.

Violet choked on her breath.

"Hello, little one." Jodin grinned, plasgun in his hand. "You're coming with me."

"Violet!" cried Rio.

Jodin's arms lit up, along with two slits underneath his eyes. He reached for her, wrapped his hand around her arm—

Violet jerked into a world filled with tethers. Ribbons. Lust was a translucent haze around her. The wind slowed, her hair settled, but ribbons of twisting blues, greens, purples and whites appeared, shooting up into the sky without an ending, and then down into the depths of dimension below.

Her arms lit with the same lines.

An overwhelming jolt tugged at her core. Something more tangible, more aggressive than the tug she'd felt every time she transferred between worlds. Her blood burned beneath, and within her chest, something beat.

Like a new breath, a new soul, a new being gasped for life.

Jodin pulled her. Reached for one of those tethers and Violet glimpsed within it. A different world shimmered: a volcano, two giant cities, a grand fortress of gray stone and black turrets.

She gasped. Yanked back. Jodin whirled on her, and when his eyes glimpsed her arms, horror flooded his face.

"Vanisher," he said.

Violet used her free hand to grab Gwen's dagger and stabbed it into his forearm.

The tethers vanished. Jodin cried in pain, letting go of Violet's arm. She kicked him. He went flying out of the seat and into the Carcadian abyss.

"Duck!" Rio yelled.

She burrowed into the passenger seat as they plummeted at an angle, the wide veranda of the Center Temple closing in.

They crashed on the marble and slid straight into a towering column. The column didn't budge, but the car was trashed, the entire front caved in. Rio heaved a breath, lifting his head—

"Don't," warned Violet.

A giant prong of metal poked through the window shield, right where Rio's head would have been.

Violet pulled Rio out of his seat, exited the totaled car, and checked his body. Other than shaking and minor scratches, he seemed okay.

Blood warmed her head and she reached up, touching the slight gash to her temple.

"It's superficial," said Rio as he examined it.

A clap of thunder smashed overhead. Her plasblade sang with the next flare of lightning.

Rio grabbed her hand and dragged her toward the wide marble doors. "Is this him? Vi?"

She was staring up into the stormy sky. Rain dripped onto her face as she searched the cityscape for signs of the twin assassins, but they had disappeared.

Ice crested her spine. Teleporting was beyond her comprehension when it came to the Sins…so what else was there? The Iris and the portal made a pathway between two worlds, but what Jodin just did…

Rio tugged her into the temple.

The Center Temple boasted marble halls, gilded sconces twisting with different shades of fire, and looming columns wrapped with vines and blooming elisian flowers. It would have been a grand place to host a decadent party filled with drinks and dancing. Now, it was cold and empty, smelling like wet stone and tasting like blood.

The rain pounded the roof above, muffling their footsteps.

"Where to, Rio?"

"I—Well…" Rio turned, then looked to the rectangular atrium at the far end of the gaping entrance hall. "I think it's past there. I can't see the beacon anymore."

Marble slammed, like boulders crashing against each other. They whirled to the main doors. Shut. A click echoed and a lock slid into place.

"We have to find the others," said Violet.

"No, we need to *go*. We can…reunite in the next world." Rio grabbed her hand, eyes darting.

She pulled out of his grip. "What makes you say something like that? You wouldn't abandon them. I won't."

Rio shook his head. "He told me…."

"Jack?" she uttered. "He told you what?"

"That if we made it to the Center Temple and they hadn't arrived, we should go on without them."

Violet's chest constricted. "No."

"He said—"

"He says a lot of shit, but that's about the dumbest thing to come out of his mouth," she said. "I'm not leaving them. Not after we got Anaya out of her world, not with the Worldbreaker coming, not when…"

Rio cringed. "I have the Iris. You…Anaya said she and Jack would be all right. He made me promise that I would keep you safe—"

"I'm *not* leaving them."

Rio jerked forward to grab her arm. "We don't have a choice."

She watched his movements, the spell cast around them, the dilation in his eyes. She backed up, shaking her head. "He didn't."

Rio's expression saddened. "You know I would help you. Just like I know you'd do the same for me."

"Why?" pleaded Violet.

"He said death follows him," breathed Rio. "And he didn't want you to follow death."

The fresh bloodbond mark on Rio's hand spoke of that. When she looked at her own, Jack's bond mark was still there. "When did this happen?"

"Yesterday." Rio scratched his head. "You were asleep, according to him. He dragged me out of my slumber."

The tenseness in Rio's body displayed his bond, forcing him to lug her to the portal and whisk her away to the next world. But without Anaya…without Jack…

She lifted the plasblade. "I'll knock you out, Rio."

"Yeah," he smiled sheepishly, "He knew you'd threaten me."

Rio turned and continued walking down the hallway, unbothered by the humming blade.

Violet cocked her head. "What—where are you going?"

"He knew you wouldn't *actually* knock me out, Vi," Rio said as he passed between the gaping archway and into the atrium. "Put the plasblade away. I'll walk as slowly as possible."

Violet scowled, stomped her foot in frustration, but stalked after Rio. "So what does this bloodbond mean? That you'll drag me through the portal?"

"Wow, look at this place," Rio said.

"*Rio.*"

"I can't hear you! Let's go!"

Violet hurried into the atrium. The gaping windows around pushed rain in. Lightning flashed and brightened the room for a second. If it were a normal night in Lust, it might have been beautiful with the crawling gold vines filled with glowing, purple elisian flowers, the fountains, and waterfalls, but amidst the doom, it drew a shiver down Violet's spine.

"It's this way," said Rio.

They hurried through the atrium and down another hallway that extended into a throne room—similar in décor, but with tall-backed chairs along the walls that held a seat for each Qor.

The portal stood on a dais at the far end of the room. It winked in the lightning, potential safety a call behind it.

Violet stalled. Took a step back. Rio whirled and jerked forward. He gritted his teeth. "I have to take you."

"No," she seethed.

He lunged for her arm, movements unnatural. Violet ducked, twisted out of the way, but Rio, despite him not being a fighter, was agile and fast.

"Stop it!" she cried.

"I can't." He reached out for her, swung at her. She ducked, dodged his hand. "Please, let's go."

"I'm not leaving them!"

"*Violet*," he pleaded, reaching for her.

She dove out of the way. "*I'm not leaving them—*"

A feral snarl ripped through their struggling. A black shape pounded across the room. Wisps of smoke carried from the massive dog, teeth slick with saliva, and that shimmering nostor metal gleamed along its spine.

"Rio!" Violet called.

An arrow flew through its head, and the demon-dog burst with ichor as it fell limp before Rio, large, sharp teeth inches from his calf.

Rio hurried out of the way. Their heads whipped.

Anaya stepped into the room from the back, a bruise on her cheek, scales rippling to match her skin and not the dim room.

"Thank the skies," breathed Rio.

He lunged again at Violet.

She dodged. "Stop this!"

"I can't, Vi—"

Another hound burst through the window, followed by a third. They scaled down the wall, teeth snapping. Violet readied her plasblade, slicing when one lunged for her. Anaya strung another arrow and shot the other.

Anaya hurried over to them, readying her bow again. "Twats got my car and I had to jump out into some other damn taxi before they vanished, realizing it wasn't you." Her gaze flicked to Violet with a smirk. "I landed a nice arrow on one's shoulder."

"Where's Jack?" asked Violet.

Anaya frowned.

Shadows burst through the windows. More of the robotic hounds. Anger rippled through Violet at the damn interruptions. She dodged the long teeth, jammed her plasblade into the belly of one, whirled to the next that jumped for her, and arced the blade, severing its head. Black blood sprayed across her face. "Where is *Jack?*"

"I saw his car take another way. But then they—" Anaya shot another down. "The twins—were shooting at it." She abandoned her bow as one hound flew past it, plasblade out and rung with green. "It was still flying when it rounded a building. I lost track of it, but soon the twins were on top of my car—*twat, get back*—so I don't know what happened to Jack."

Violet slashed through the sleek, shadowed fur, fear and fury burrowing in her gut. She twisted and cut again down its spine. The hound fell.

"Fucking idiot," snarled Violet as Anaya flung a dagger over her shoulder and caught another hound.

Violet felled the final one.

"What's with the dramatic entrance?" Rio started.

"He's testing us," growled Violet. "The fucking Worldbreaker wants us weak before we meet him."

A horrid growl sounded behind Violet. She whirled too late, plasblade missing the last hound—

A dagger came whipping from the hall, jamming into the eye of the hound with a sickening squelch. It roared feebly but fell at Violet's feet. She brushed the light teeth marks on her arm, no cut made.

She spun.

Jack strutted down the hallway like a god risen from the dead. Black blood covered him, an icy look on his face. He opened his mouth.

"*You*," Violet said nastily, raising her plasblade.

Jack's gaze was challenging, furious. "Are you hurt?"

"Fuck off. You don't get to make bloodbonds with Rio to leave you and go to the next world." She stepped up to meet him, hand twitching, wanting to punch his stupid, bloody handsome face. "You don't get to make my choices, you damn stupid man—"

Jack grabbed her hips, pulled her into his body, and collided his lips with hers.

Rio whistled behind them. Anaya scoffed.

His mouth was warm, and he kissed with a passion that told her he didn't give a shit about what she thought. Didn't care she was mad. He'd let her be mad and blow into the fireball that she was, and he'd still kiss her. Burn with her.

She kissed back with enough ferocity that she bit his lip, and he laughed in her mouth, pulling back to breathe, "How much do you hate me right now?"

"With my entire being," she gritted.

"Good," he said, dragging a hand down her face, eyes darkening as he caught the gash along her head. "How many did you kill?"

"Lost count after seven."

"Hah, I got fifteen. I beat you."

She shoved him away and he laughed as she stalked back, motioning to the portal. "Let's get the skiv out of this world."

Two flashes of light appeared before the portal. Jodin and Yarrow. Their plasblades ignited. A third figure stepped up between them, black lightning crackling at his fingers.

"I heard we have someone special in the room." Zavar smiled, cool, excited. "I knew the trip would be fun."

"Put the lightning away, Zavar," grunted Jodin as he held his arm to his chest. "You will kill them."

Zavar frowned. "One little shock won't kill them."

"Yes, it does," warned Yarrow. Blood leaked down his sleeve from his back.

Guards poured in from every exit; rapiers, katanas, all lined with plasma, bursting and whirling with color, more advanced than Violet had ever seen. They were armed for battle, and the four backed up again to the middle of the room, pressed together. Their faces were half-covered by a black mesh, and they wore short capes. The same fabric molded with the plates of metal and leather armor. Silver—a twisting, glimmering silver so like the material of the Iris— shined against the outlines of their armor.

There was a great flash of light as if a bolt had struck the center of the room. The same she saw in those final moments of Envy.

The same twisting lines like Jodin and Yarrow. The same smile as the bright gleam faded. A man stepped out, clapping.

"No," Rio breathed.

The Worldbreaker.

57

THE WORLDBREAKER

HE WAS PALE. SO EXTREMELY pallid that Violet had a hard time believing blood ran beneath his skin. Limestone-white hair neatly styled, a crisp suit marked his physique, and polished boots snuffed the ground in tufts of smoke.

He had just…appeared. Teleported like the twins and Zavar. Whatever power, or magic, existed in this universe that enabled them to portal between worlds came from this man before them. Man? Human? Violet didn't know. He reeked of difference. Alien. Something so otherworldly and something not entirely there. Scars crawled at his neck, mangled burns lined his knuckles and palms. His dark eyes, crinkled in amusement, took them all in.

"That was fantastic." It was a cold, soulless voice. Bumps rose on her skin. "Four Sins," the Worldbreaker mused. "Did you enjoy the journey?"

As his eyes raked over her friends and then landed on her, studying her, tilting his head just a notch to the side as she became a real, present thing in his game, she felt *drawn* to him. Her blood sang. It hummed and electrified underneath his gaze.

Jack was as calm as death, while Rio shifted next to him. His face revealed a fight in his mind; one of surrender or…whatever other option there might be.

"Now, I know the first three worlds aren't easy. I built them myself, you see. I wanted to ensure that only the best reached my world—to ensure that I had warriors for my fight. These are the ones who succeeded." He motioned to the guards lining the walls, the masked Captains of the Fringe at his back. "But you four have caused quite the disruption within my worlds—"

"They aren't yours," snarled Anaya. "You took them and then ruined them."

Rio stepped toward her.

The Worldbreaker smiled, and it was a savage thing to look at it. "Or they were never something to begin with, and I made them better. Grander, and in the end, *worth* something." His eyes roamed her. "Little Endolier...although, not fully Endolier, are we?"

Anaya clenched her fist around her bow but said nothing.

The Worldbreaker walked forward. Something about the way he moved was *off*. It was as if the world around didn't touch; as if he wasn't wholly there. He stalked, hands behind his back, into the small pools of hound blood at his feet. If a drop touched his shoes, it was swallowed within, as if no blemish would ever exist. The light wind that curved through the verandas shifted the black cloaks of his guard, but not his. The lightning flashed and broke against the stone, but *not him*. The elements didn't touch him.

"The rest of you are from the Original City?" he asked, stopping a healthy distance away.

Again, no one said a word.

"Surely you will tell me something." He held his scarred hands out, as if he meant no harm. "I will give you my name, if you give me yours."

"It seems, Master, that they might be deaf." Zavar strolled from the dais, around their group, and stood by his master.

Jack finally shifted. "That or mute."

"Oh, the pretty one speaks, then," said Zavar.

"Settle, Captain Zavar," said the Worldbreaker. "They are still so innocent."

Zavar sauntered, a casual, feline grace to his movements. He struck her like a child who was never allowed to play, and then when he was finally let out of his cage, it was pain that called to him. "The Master asked you your name. It would be in your best interests to answer."

"I'll skip the introductions," Jack said.

In a blur, Zavar's plasblade was out, whipping to Jack's neck. Violet lurched her weapon, colliding with Zavar's in a clash of sparks. "Back." She pushed her blade and heat drew from the plasma. "*Off.*"

"You have a feisty one at your hip." Zavar pushed in with ease, and Violet struggled. "They are the most fun to break."

Then, like nothing, Jack's plasblade slipped in between theirs and pointed at Zavar's neck. His face betrayed no emotion, unlike Violet's actions. There was a clench of jaw, a blaze behind those green eyes. Commander Marin had arrived.

"I suggest, Zavan—"

"*Zavar.*"

"I suggest that you take your little leash and go back to your Master," Jack said coldly. The plasblade pressed and skin sizzled. A leer rose on Jack's face. "Or your mother. A pup need not stray far from its bitch."

"How dare—" But Jack pressed on his blade and Zavar backed off. Violet retreated. Anaya lifted her weapon, snarling at the rest of the guards.

"Go back to him, Zavian," taunted Jack.

The Worldbreaker stood smug, if not a bit surprised. He watched as Zavar retreated. Something told Violet it wasn't because of Jack's domineering, but rather some unspoken conversation between the master and pup.

"Power recognizes power, and you have it," the Worldbreaker said. Zavar scowled behind him. "I feel my guards… there's a tension in them when they look at you. At least some. They are not happy that you're here. What is your name?"

Jack carefully looked around the room. A strange position to be in, but the slight smirk on his face never left. He would never let them see if he was afraid. As his eyes drifted, they brightened on some figures. Maybe it was in the way they held themselves, or a permanent mark that sparked familiarity.

"I'm sure many of them have a lot to say about me," he said.

"Jack Marin," snarled a Fringe Captain.

"Ah, I do know you. Gave the Original City quite the scare for some years...You may call me Cyran."

"Master," hissed Zavar.

"He has striking potential. But he has...a tether. And those become distractions to full potential." Cyran's eyes turned to Violet. "Who are you?"

Violet kept her mouth shut.

Jodin spoke for her, "She is...."

Cyran's pale brows furrowed. His gaze snagged on Jodin and then landed back on Violet. "It is her?"

She could feel Jack's stare. Anaya's confusion. Rio's frown.

Fury poured through the room. Cyran's fists shook. "Her? *Her?*" He took a step forward. "Show me your hands."

"No," Violet breathed.

"If you are what they say you are, girl, understand that you are more a danger to those around you than I am to you." Cyran circled her. "It also means you have a place with my Captains—those who can freely travel between worlds."

The world stopped and blurred, and a few things happened at once: Cyran's eyes flashed with an iridescent light. He twisted his hand and two screams seared the air. Rio and Jack dropped, convulsing in agony. Blood rushed underneath their skin, as if it... bubbled. Cyran lifted his other hand and called the storm outside. The wind ravaged, lightning streaked again, and the ground quaked.

Control. Control. Control.

Anaya whipped out a dagger and flung it at the Cyran, but an arrow shot from the guards and jammed it away before he could blink.

Violet was shoved to her knees and the top of her shirt was ripped. Zavar bent over her, finger grazing her collarbone—

"Awaken her, Master."

Black lightning tickled her skin, and a metallic taste soared up her throat. Violet coughed, crimson blood splattering on the ground before her. Pain flared from her chest. Her vision blackened and her heart beat fast, too fast that she couldn't grasp a breath. Blood pooled from the edges of her mouth—

Cyran flicked his wrist and Zavar went flying. He crashed into the marble floor. It caved beneath the impact, cracks fissuring. Zavar groaned and pushed the marble debris off of him. Dust covered his black ensemble.

"We do not harm other Vanishers," was all Cyran said.

Violet was on her hands and knees. Her body trembled, both in fear and relief from that terrible lightning. Death lightning.

One shock and she'd be done.

Her gaze lifted, past Cyran to the Fringe where she desperately searched.

Be here, be here.

A tug at her gut had her eyes flashing to the farthest figure on the left. Her shoulders sagged. A tear slipped down her cheek. Blue eyes were wide as they looked down at her.

But Reed didn't move.

Didn't blink.

Only stood there as his little sister coughed blood onto the foreign floor of a foreign world in a universe she didn't understand.

❀❀❀

Rio and Jack lay still in the pools of hounds' blood, mouths open and eyes blinking up at the ceiling. Anaya had picked up Jack's blade and held it out to guards who slowly advanced on her. She twisted and turned it masterfully, baiting anyone who dared challenge her.

Violet could not take her eyes off Reed. He was here—yet *there*. Dressed in that black mesh and a part of Cyran's guard. Not even just the guard—the Fringe. His inner circle. Some fucking stranger. *Vanisher.*

Betrayer, her mind hissed. *Traitor.*

He mouthed her name. *Violet.*

"No," she breathed. The world still blurred and Anaya's cries to her went unnoticed. Violet spit out more blood.

Anaya was on her, calling her name from so far away.

Violet—Violet—Violet!

Zavar stepped into her vision, shaking the dust out of his hair.

Anaya dragged her out, yanking painfully on her ear in the process.

"*Violet!*"

Fingers touched and she looked down, numbly, to Jack sprawled and reaching for her. Blood. Oh skies, there was so much blood—he was so pale.

Her eyes flicked just once to Reed.

Anaya cradled her face. "Violet, come back to me. Come back."

Violet desperately grappled for Anaya's wrist and she let the girl haul her to her feet. She pretended to fall into her arms to whisper. "He's here."

Anaya, beautiful, strong Anaya, didn't react, but she understood.

"*Violet,*" said Cyran. "The little wildflower."

He trailed around, frowning at Jack and Rio as they struggled to rouse. Any amusement, any playfulness he had was chewed and spat away. Before them, a truly different monster unraveled. Violet noticed he appeared more...solid. His scars writhed and contracted as his jaw clenched. Scars that should have killed any man. Human.

The heat of plasma met her cheek. Zavar held his blade. Another guard slithered to Anaya and did the same.

"I can't control you," said Cyran.

"What do you mean?" Violet gasped as Zavar drew closer, the blade falling to her neck.

Cyran lifted his hand and twisted. Two small, wicked cracks echoed. Rio moaned in pain while Jack bit his mouth, his face twisting as his…his left wrist bent awkwardly to the side.

Rio cried out louder and Violet lunged, only to be caught by Zavar and held firmly against his chest.

"I can control them. I can break their bones, I can stop the flow of their blood, I can squash their hearts. I can make them kill the person they love the most, but you two—" Cyran's eyes blazed between Violet and Anaya. "Do not feel anything."

Cyran frowned at Anaya. "You're spoken for, since you never swore yourself to the Sins, little mutt. But you…"

Zavar overturned her palms. Both scars showed.

"…get more confusing," the Worldbreaker continued. "Perhaps they are fakes."

Rio shrieked. His agony made Violet lunge, but Zavar held firm. "No, no, stop!"

"*Please! Please!*" cried Rio.

"*Stop it!*" Violet screamed.

Rio begged and begged, his other arm fractured, blood pouring out of his mouth.

"Are they fakes?" Cyran asked calmly.

"No!" She shook her head and held her left hand up. "I bloodswore myself to your game. Please, stop hurting them, you skiv."

Cyran waved his hand and Rio fell silent. His lips bubbled with blood, little whimpers echoing around the room.

"A Calesal native, like most of those who serve me now." His brow twitched. "I do not feel your blood, girl. Who are you?"

"Feel fucking harder then," she growled. "Why does it matter?"

Cyran's jaw clenched. "Does anyone here know who this is?"

She became hyper-aware of Reed: If Cyran could control him, he would be forced to say it. All around the room, like a ripple in water, each guard jerked and fell to a knee, muttering, "No, my Master." In her peripheral vision, she noticed Reed do the same.

But if Cyran had some blood control on everyone, Reed's actions would have been impossible.

Cyran turned back and gripped her chin. Violet's knees trembled at the contact. His touch was vile, unnatural, something that should not exist in any of these worlds. But what came with it was that flash of tethers, a different plane that was both here and not. Ribbons and spiraling ropes of white, purple, gold, blue, all reachable and yet so far away. The energy it took to look upon them drained her so much that her legs buckled and she fell out of his grip. Cyran and Zavar let her drop to the floor. At the loss of contact, that unearthly plane vanished.

"You know what this means, Master." Zavar grabbed her hair and yanked. The plasblade was on her throat.

"I thought I would save any more ravaging of my worlds by killing you four." Cyran straightened his jacket. "Then I hear, before I arrived, that my assassins found a new Vanisher, so of course I thought 'I should add them to my liege. Build my rule with another under my reign,' but if I cannot control you, then it is a waste."

Anaya snarled against her guard and Jack moaned from the ground, his eyes finding hers, pleading, and telling her something she couldn't figure out.

"What threat am I?" Violet blanched. "I mean, look at me."

And Cyran did. Under his cool stare, she wavered. Her blood iced. "I cannot allow strays in my game." He stroked her cheek. "My dear, you are a fighter, but mistakes must be put down."

A choked sob left her throat.

Mistake.

Mistake.

Mistake.

Cyran brushed her lone tear away. Caressed her face. "Thank you for playing my game, young wildflower."

"No!" Anaya called. "No!"

Her eyes flicked to the Fringe line. Her brother's knees quivered. His hand rested on his weapon. Eyes glistened.

"So believe me when I tell you this: I will always be on your side and stand with you through stupid decisions. I won't leave you."

At that moment, as she stared at her brother, Violet accepted her end. The box of her emotions lay open to these worlds, clawed and ripped apart from all the times she screamed and cried and bled and begged for it to stop. She nodded to her brother.

A tremor ran through him, but he nodded back.

Jack writhed next to her. Cyran's arm stood out, hand pointed at Jack, as he directed Jack to stand. Jack's wrist snapped back into place. The blood disappeared from around his mouth.

And that beautiful, freedom green faced her.

"I love the theatre, but I love a lovers' quarrel even more." Cyran slapped a hand on Jack. "Kill her."

Jack blinked. His eyes turned black, dilating like the sin had taken him. His voice was cold as he said, "Yes, Master."

Zavar let her go.

Jack lunged and she whirled to the right, slipping on the blood. He tackled her. They slid back and he flipped her around. Tears blurred her vision. She shrieked, "Jack, stop! *Stop!*"

He pinned her down. Face hard. Lethal. Terrifying. The same face that sent Calesal into fear for five years. A flash of metal. Gwen's dagger was in his hand, and he drew it up.

She screamed. "No! No!"

"Violet!" Anaya cried.

Jack brought the dagger down.

It slammed into a wall of air with a crack, a breath from her chest. The tip bent into itself. His dark eyes flashed in confusion.

The bloodbond.

He lifted it again while she cried, screamed his name, and that mangled tip came down toward her chest, only to meet that wall of air. She breathed, her chest rose, and the dagger rose with it. Jack's white-knuckle grip tightened and he growled in frustration.

Again, he raised it. Again, he slammed it down.

And again, he met that air.

She cried against his grip, eyes on the dagger as it split down the middle, and that beautiful turquoise blade fell into pieces.

He tossed the hilt away and reached for her throat, but his hands wrapped air, and he tried to squeeze while she sobbed underneath him. "No, no—stop, Jack."

He was too strong for her to fight, not with all his weight and Cyran's control pressing into her.

"Enough!" Cyran called. Jack went rigid, blinking in that dark haze, and climbed off her.

"A bloodbond." Cyran smiled. "How sweet."

She hated him, hated the way those eyes crawled into her mind and wanted to control her body. She hated the way Jack stepped back obediently, *smiling* at her demise. Her hands shook. She grabbed one of the shards and reeled back to throw it at him—

But Yarrow was there, grunting in her ear as his palm lit up and he pressed to her chest.

A booming cry filled the void. Wind lashed, rain poured through the windows, plasblades sang, and the room erupted. Violet dropped the shard as beaming, iridescent light overwhelmed her. She opened her mouth, wanting to scream, but also wanting to laugh, to cry, to dance, to—

"Awaken," commanded Yarrow with a gentle voice.

Fire and light bloomed through Violet. Her breath left. Those tethers extended up and down, twisting and forming. Millions stretched before her—different worlds, different dimensions. She yearned to reach them, watch as they wove between her fingers. She craved the adventure, the landscapes that flashed. A grateful sob bubbled out.

"I remember," Yarrow whispered. "You cannot kill him. He holds all seven worlds. So if he dies, each of those seven worlds perishes."

Violet's eyes moved too fast at the transformation before her. Endless worlds. Endless possibilities. Her senses cracked open, and she smelled sweet, sticky honey, then charred rock. Heard high-pitched laughter, the crashing of water, and the woosh of wind through grass. Her hands lit up; heat seared the bottoms of her feet. Pain laced in small strips beneath her eyes.

"It is beautiful, isn't it?" said Yarrow with awe.

"Can I go?" she breathed.

"Later, young wildflower."

Visions slammed into her. She buckled. Yarrow held her up.

She was a mistake! I have to watch her live, only to die?

It's okay, Vi. Just let it out.

Whoever gives you a bad day, you tell 'em to fuck off. No matter what, you keep going, baby girl.

Only the sin wins. If you give into it.

Win, agia.

Win.

The room exploded. Yarrow evaporated. Violet snapped back to reality. She was soaring through the air. The tethers disappeared and her light was gone.

"Get *off* of me." Anaya waved her plasblade at another guard. "Violet!"

Violet landed on her rear, but was on her feet in the next instant, bursting with energy. She gathered the shards of Gwen's dagger and the hilt of her discarded plasblade. When it ignited, she turned onto a guard and slashed.

The lightning disappeared, sending the room into pitch black.

"We have to get to the portal!" Anaya's voice rang, and a small hand wrapped around Violet's arm. Violet had never been more relieved by Anaya's night vision than now. Plasblades illuminated the area. One swiped at her, but another shot forward and Rio was there, gritting his teeth as he held the weapon with his good arm. He grabbed Violet and dragged her forward to the dais.

"Obey me!" Cyran cried. "Listen to me. Kill her! *Kill her!*"

"Violet—"

She whirled to her brother. His plasblade lit up his face, and a grin peeked beneath that mask. "You're one of—"

A figure burst into their circle and tackled Reed to the ground. Jack pinned Reed with a smirk. "Oh, I've been *waiting* to get my hands on you."

"Stop it!" Violet ran forward, but Rio held on tight.

Jack raised his fist and slammed it into Reed's cheek. Reed

sputtered underneath the impact, but still called to her, "You have to go, Vi. He's gone. Go—now!" An urging gaze. "*Go!* I will take care of him."

Lightning cracked through the room. Cyran locked eyes with her. Rio wrapped her middle with his good arm and dragged her up the dais.

Every dagger, every bow pointed her way. Jack and Reed still brawled on the floor, before Jack blinked and charged after her.

"No! Stop!" But Rio's grip was relentless.

"I can't," said Rio defeatedly, under the control of his bloodbond. "We will find him again."

They reached the portal. Rio yanked the Iris out of his belt and held it aloft.

"Stop her!" cried Cyran.

She turned to Jack, who stumbled before the dais. His black eyes flickered with the hint of green. "Go, Vi!" he pleaded, fighting the control.

A flash of metal.

A dagger plunged into his back. Through his chest.

"*No!*" The scream tore out of her.

Blood seeped from the wound, and Jack collapsed to his knees. Those green eyes faded, glazed. His mouth dribbled with crimson, and the slightest smile overcame his face before it fell limp.

His body crumpled to the floor.

The world flashed a bright light. Her navel yanked. Black consumed her.

58

PLASHIELD
JELAN

JELAN KNEW SHE WOULDN'T BE able to ever wrap her head around how many gardia members Lucien, and previously Jack, were responsible for.

Two teams of five, dressed in black with plasguns at their hips and the new plasblades across their backs, stood silent as she explained how to activate the plashields. They were to meet with more of their members at each location. A hundred members in total, Jenkins had said.

"These plasma points are mined deep underground, and plasma can only exist in a tiny tube, so the hole won't be big. Once activated, only this..." Jelan held up her remote. "Can deactivate it. You better get it right, because the remote is staying with me.

"You will have two seconds after pressing the final button to remove your hands from the vicinity, or else the burning plasma will sever them. So be quick. Any other questions?"

"Arvalo's guards?" asked one.

Jenkins stepped up, hands behind his back. "Well, you know the answer to that. Kill them. Defend each point. The survival of our city relies on you."

"Yes, sir."

"You are dismissed. Take the back exit and be discreet in everything that you can. Lyla trained you herself, so don't disappoint her."

That struck a chord. Each member bowed in acknowledgment, and they filed into the elevator in groups.

"Just for your info, everyone is blindfolded before they come into this penthouse. So no worries about anyone knowing this place. They are loyal, too." Jenkins looked at her knowingly. "Now, where are *we* going?"

Jelan glanced at her new outfit—gardia member leathers with a plasgun strapped to her hip. Her heart beat fretfully in her chest, but she took a deep breath. "To the Aariva."

Hira stepped out of the hallway, adjusting her outfit. "I just have a question, which side does my plasgun look better on? I want to accentuate my ass in case there is good video footage of us saving the city."

Jenkins rolled his eyes. "Get in the car."

❈❈❈

Jelan flinched at each body drop.

One by one they collapsed from the snipers on the rooftops. Guns waved, they tried to locate the attack, but a silent bullet would go through their head, and another body thumped the pavement.

The Aariva stood bleak and bare, giant black towers unlit. It was a cloudy day, and just as she had suspected, the arena had been littered with guards until Jenkins laid back in their bullet-proof car and had given the order to clean up the place.

"Brings me back to the old days." He smiled.

Jelan and Hira exchanged a bewildered look.

Jenkins lifted his radio. "Secure the Aariva."

"*Sir, Plastech Akard is here. There is a line of wires...oh skies, oh no*—*" Gunfire sounded through the static, and then all went silent.

Jenkins frowned and changed the channel. "I want an update on the plaspoints. How many are secure?"

"Three so far, sir. But there is a long wire extending from one, and it is heavily guarded. Arvalo's captains are there, barricaded behind walls. It is difficult to reach."

"Keep your eyes on the scene," ordered Jenkins. "Don't stop trying. This could get very bad if we fail."

"Comforting words, Captain," mumbled Hira.

"If we can stop or dismantle the device that would take down the arches, that should be enough. We'd deal with a small explosion from the loose plasma but...." Jelan strapped her shield device to her wrist. "It should be enough."

"You sure about this?" Jenkins asked.

She nodded. "Cover me. I can do it."

Hira nudged her shoulder. "I'll be right by your side."

Jelan sucked a deep breath as Jenkins took his radio and directed all extra troops to storm the Aariva. Shots littered the place, the bleak day a transfer back to the gardia wars that had old bloodstains on the streets in the South. She'd pass by them on her way to school every morning, and now she was at the center of it, hating how so much bloodshed needed to happen.

But the price felt little compared to letting this bomb go off.

Her anxiety rose. Jelan squeezed her eyes shut. She'd recounted her studies in her lab on bombs, the place of the wires and the cohesive structure of the most advanced plasbombs that Arvalo would have access to. She took a breath, knowing how wrong this could go if she... failed.

"I'll be right there with you," Hira said again, this time softly. "Then we will have drinks after all this is over.

If we don't blow up, was what Jelan wanted to say, but she merely gave the girl a tight smile.

"Aariva is semi-secure. Plastechs setting up a device between the arches. Chun Akard is with them. How do you want us to proceed?"

"Kill the other techs," said Jenkins casually. "I want Chun Akard alive."

Jenkins sat up and waved his finger out the window. Guards poured out of the cars surrounding them. He turned to the girls. "No heads blowing off, got it?" He glared at Jelan over his spectacles. "Let's see those scarred hands work some magic."

Jelan lifted her chin and nodded.

They exited the car. Two formations of guards surrounded them. They walked their way in and Jelan kept her head up, close to Hira, refusing to glance at Arvalo's dead guards that littered the ground. Jenkins's team cleared the way, and soon enough they passed underneath the massive columns to enter the Aariva.

Jelan loosed a breath at the empty place, only months since Violet had been here and swore herself. A long tube extended from a hole in the side of the Aariva, directly to the location of the last barricaded plaspoint on the map. It trailed the entire length to the stage.

Atop the stage where the two arches stood, that alien, swirling mist within them, Chun Akard held his hands up as guards ordered him to get down, to stop what he was doing. He quivered, then gritted his teeth and yelled in frustration.

"Put down the radio!" one guard cried. "You're surrounded. Call off your captain *now*."

"You don't know what Arvalo will do if we fail! Didn't you hear? He's Emperor! He's going to destroy all of you—" Akard clutched the radio, shaking his head. "You don't know what he's doing this for."

"Put it down, Akard, it's over." Jenkins strolled up, hands in his pockets. "We'll protect you from Arvalo's wrath."

"You?" A crazed laugh. "The Marin gardia? You're the first to go."

Jenkins shrugged. "Okay, fine—"

Akard pulled out the plasgun behind his back and held it at Jenkins. "I'll kill you, and then precious Lucien will lose another thing close to him."

"Well, if you want to hit Lucien where it hurts, shoot me then." Hira waved with a smile. "I'm his mistress!"

Akard furrowed his brows. The gun wavered to her. His gaze flicked to Jelan and the confusion deepened. "You look familiar."

"Well, you spent a long night flirting with me, and then I stole your plans, so…"

Akard blinked, shook his head. "You?"

Jelan smiled. "Me."

He turned the gun toward her and fired.

She flicked her ring finger with her thumb.

And the plashield ignited in a perfect circle before her.

The plasbullet cracked into the shield and the energy absorbed within it, rippling across the pretty purple.

Akard gaped. "What the—"

"Oh, shut up," said Hira.

A dart landed in his neck. He stalled, reached a hand up to the little feather-and-glitter capsule before he paled. His eyes rolled back and Akard dropped to the ground.

"You didn't need to kill him," said Jelan.

Hira blew the smoke off the tip of her gun in a dramatic fashion. "It was one of my sleeping potions."

"Aariva is secure, sir, but the barricade—there's no way to get through. We will make an ambush and—Reno, stop him! Stop him!"

A loud crack cleaved through the radio and then resounded within the Aariva. Great rainbow fire burst a mile away.

"They lit the fuse!"

Jelan's heart dropped. She turned toward the wall of the Aariva where that tube started and, within a blink, hot, untamed plasma rushed through. It sparked. Burst through its confinements as it followed the line to the bomb wrapping the middle of the arches.

Time slowed. Her lungs already began to panic. An old part of her would let it go, turn her back and act like it was never her problem, even as they all blew to pieces and ruined any chance of a candidate coming home.

But Jelan had not built this shield to turn her back on her city.

She ran after that spark. Sprinted like her breathing specialist made her do on the treadmill, even when pain flayed her chest. She jumped the stage and slid, gritting her teeth to Hira's cries as she activated the plashield on her wrist and lunged.

She angled the shield down. Gravity dragged the plasma into an umbrella shape. She planted it over the plasbomb, and just as the spark reached it—

The explosion rocked the earth. Blinding light and colorful flame flared but met the plashield. It screeched, whining. Jelan planted her feet on either side and pushed with all her might. When plasma met plasma, two things could happen: depending on how tame it was, it either diminished its worth, like how a bullet to her shield evaporated, or it enhanced.

This diminished. No pushback from the force, only sponging up into her shield. If she had been just one second late...air would have grabbed it, and she'd been sky-high saying her last prayers before death.

Tears in her eyes from the burning heat, Jelan willed all her work and experiments to hold her little shield together. Some purple plasma splattered out of its confinement, catching bits of her armor and even landing on her neck, but she held on as that familiar burn met her skin.

"Jelan!" Hira screamed.

"Protect her!" cried Jenkins.

Guards barricaded around her. The explosion went on and on, encapsulated, destroying only the air and the materials within. Her lungs begged for fresh breath, her hands trembled from the proximity of the plasma, but Jelan withstood the torture and pushed every ounce of strength into her work. Her dream.

And like it had started, it snuffed out. Thick smoke clouded within. Her shield hummed fretfully, but it held.

She let out a slow breath. Gunshots went off behind her, but she only stared at her precious little thing. A smile jolted her lips.

Jelan held the shield until her back ached from the position. When there was no tremor, she gently peeled it away. A woosh of air and smoke whipped out, covering the Aariva stage, nearly shadowing the entire arena. But no explosion, no broken arches, no catastrophic decimation to her city.

She lifted the entire thing. The materials for the bomb had burned up. She flicked her thumb against her ring finger once more, and her shield dissipated into her wrist mechanic with a whine.

Through the smoke, the arches stood with their magical might.

"You better come home, you bitch," Jelan said to the exit arch. To Violet.

By the time the smoke had cleared, all of Arvalo's guards had been dealt with. Bodies were moved to the side to be identified while one of Arvalo's captains was taken into cuffs, blood oozing from his leg.

Chun Akard's unconscious body was wrapped in restraints and transported to a car to be taken to an undisclosed location.

Jelan jumped to the bottom floor and was assaulted with a hug. Hira's vanilla scent flew up her nose. Tears met her neck as Hira buried her head into it.

"Oh skies! I thought you were going to die. I'm so, so happy you're not dead." She pulled back and cradled Jelan's face. "You just saved the fucking city."

Jelan merely said, "I think I need a drink after this."

Hira laughed. "We will get you that drink. Don't you worry, baby."

Jelan's hands trembled as Hira wrapped an arm around her and escorted her out of the Aariva. Jenkins bossed his members and yelled at the girls, "Straight back to the penthouse! I'm going to be flayed by Lucien for this, but...." He rolled his eyes. "Jelan, Hira, you did good."

And that was the best compliment she'd ever get from him.

※ ※ ※

By the time they arrived back at the penthouse, Meema was in hysterics.

"Oh, Violet. My baby flower. She's in the Sins? Oh no no no no

no—"

"She goes through remembering that a lot." Hira frowned.

"Fight through it! You better fight through it, you skiv!"

Jelan's heart dropped and she rushed into the sitting room. Meema sat before a plascreen, tears streaming down her face as she watched Violet's tracker blink red in the fourth world. Jelan fell to her knees before the screen, shaking her head. "Please no, please no."

"Come on, Violet! You...you...you skiv!" Kole shouted. "Don't you give up now!"

"Look at Jack, too." Hira's jaw slacked open. "He's blinking. Where is Lucien? Does he know?"

The elevator doors beeped open, and a moment later Lucien stomped in, a furious look on his face with an even angrier Lyla behind him.

His gaze landed on Jelan. "What the *fuck* were you thinking?"

"I...I had to." She peeled herself from the carpet, eyes wide.

"You could have blown up! All of you! I thought you listened." He ran a frustrated hand in his hair. "I thought—"

"They were going to blow up the arches, and if you want any chance of your brother coming back, then Jelan saved that chance." Hira lifted her chin to Lucien. "Go cry about it later. Jenkins helped us, and Jelan stopped a chunk of the city from being bombed. We *knew* there was a chance of dying, so don't go thinking we skipped around and did lines of shiva shots on the Bloodswearing stage."

Jelan's eyes widened at Hira's clap back. Lucien even looked stunned, and Lyla rolled her eyes. She stormed around Lucien and Hira and grabbed the remote, flicking the channel to the news. "Now watch."

Jelan turned to the plascreen. Her stomach flipped at the images.

On it, a video played. Over and over. Like a loop. Arvalo before Emperor Neuven.

Emperor Neuven dead, bloodied, head blown in by fists.

And Arvalo crowned Emperor.

The room was silent. A defeated sob erupted out of Kole. Even Meema looked downcast before she said, "When one good thing happens, a bad usually follows."

"Put it back on the trackers," breathed Jelan. "Jack and Violet are in danger."

Lucien paled but nodded to Lyla, who flipped the channel to the tracker updates.

For a moment, their trackers beat like the rapid thump of Jelan's pulse. A pause. A breath later, and Violet's name disappeared, along with Rio Gaverra's...

...and appeared in the fifth world.

Cheers erupted in the room. Meema howled, holding her tumbler of shiva aloft. Kole reached in to hug her, but with a stern look from the woman, he grimaced and backed off. Hira shook Jelan's shoulders in excitement. "See, she did it!"

"No," breathed Lucien.

"Yes, she did it! She is in the fifth world! Although, Jack didn't...." Hira trailed, voice going soft. "Oh, no."

Jelan switched her gaze back to the fourth world. Found Jack Marin's name and the dot next to it.

A solid red dot.

Dead.

Everything went silent. Tears sprung in Lucien's eyes and Jelan's heart tugged so fiercely that she rose, ready to comfort him. His brother, his family, gone. Suddenly the penthouse had a haunting feeling to it; Jack's home, the one he walked through the halls, felt safety in.

A home, with its soul now gone.

A great roar exploded from outside. Heads swiveled to the veranda. Jelan found herself walking toward it, opening the door, and stepping out.

All around the North, people exited onto their balconies and screamed. Cried. They rose and rose like a cacophony of agony, mourning their lost leader. It grew in number, the sound so loud and overwhelming that Jelan's hands twitched to cover her ears.

"It's all over the news," mumbled Lyla. "Jack Marin is dead. Arvalo crowned Emperor."

Jelan turned, tears burning her eyes. The wind whipped and the North continued to cry. She didn't know what to say.

"There's a riot in the South." Hira poked her head out. "Word's gotten out that Arvalo bombed Souther's Square. It is…it is chaos."

Jelan turned her gaze back to her city. She stared at the South where smoke rose from rooftops, fires burning and the screams all around echoed the pain of the Southers from far away.

"Arvalo's only enemy is dead." Hira stepped up next to her. "He can do whatever he wants."

Jelan clenched her scarred fists, no waver in her voice. "Not to those who don't play by the rules."

59

The Fifth Sin

VIOLET SLAMMED INTO FLUFFY GRASS and warm soil. Petals assaulted her. The smell of salt and water hit her nostrils. The wind peacefully blew through the long stems of wildflowers while the sun cast buttery light all around.

Violet stood and blinked. Someone was coughing near her—Anaya.

"I think I inhaled all of this damned soil."

"Jack," Violet whispered. She shook her head, unbelieving. She replayed the last moment, over and over, but she had seen him—"No, no, no...." She yanked at her hair, scrubbed at the blood on her skin. "Oh skies." Tears tore out of her. A sob escaped. "He's dead. Jack's dead."

Anaya crawled up, placed her small hands on Violet's knees. "It's okay. It's okay, Vi."

She clutched at her chest. "No, no, he can't be dead."

"It will be okay."

"He can't be dead, but the dagger, the blade, everything...there was so much blood and no, he can't be dead—Anaya, he can't be dead!"

A hand slapped across her cheek. Violet's tears flew off her face. Anaya's hardened expression filled her vision, and the beautiful world beyond it.

"I know, Vi. But…" Anaya's tears spilled. The first time Violet had ever seen the Endolier cry. "We need to move. We can't stay here."

"He's dead," Violet whispered.

Anaya nodded and a sob broke through her. She pulled Violet into a hug. "It's okay. It's okay."

Over Anaya's shoulder, Violet looked unto the new world with growing numbness.

They were on a hilltop of fluffy, soft pale grass. Around them poked flowers she didn't have names for; large, opulent, with bright and cheery colors. Trees spread like a field toward the west; their trunks a barky white, and branches that rained down with yellow leaves. Over to the east, waves from a vibrant, blue sea rocked the shore of yellow sand—a beach. An ocean. The expanse of it continued until the horizon was but a solid blue line.

When she was younger, she thought she might have a home somewhere like that. When agony and despair had yet to touch her heart. When her ignorant soul believed that love always flourished and pain was only temporary.

She steadied her breathing. Looked inward. Her chest hurt. Her stomach nauseous. All she could see was the blood spilling from his heart, that terrified, wild look in his eyes as Cyran's control escaped in those last moments.

"We have to go—"

"There's no *we*." Violet let out a soft snarl and pulled away from Anaya. She clenched her hands. "There cannot be we. He is after me—he wants *me* dead. He doesn't care about you or Rio. You guys can move on, go far away, and forget about all of this and live a peaceful life. There's no we. Not anymore."

She rubbed at her chest. It hummed with low vibration. She squeezed her eyes shut against this peaceful world. Whatever Yarrow did, whatever had happened, her entire body felt different.

Wind brushed her ear, and a soft voice whispered, *Why do you suffer? There is no need to suffer.*

"I'm going to stop you before you continue with that nonsense," Anaya snarled back. "I didn't realize how deep in shit this whole game was, but I can see there is no escaping it. So don't be some martyr thinking you have to go off and die because that ugly, scarred man demands it."

"I'm not—" Violet started.

"Yes, you are," Anaya said. "And Rio and I can take care of ourselves. We want to—"

"I'm not letting you die!" Violet snapped. "Did you see what that was? What that man was? We, the three of us, *cannot fight that!* Even if he can't control you and me, we cannot stand up against that."

Anaya looked at her solemnly. Her mouth parted and then closed.

Violet continued, "The Sins are done. Over. It was a silly game to begin with—all to mask *him*. The Worldbreaker. Why do you think everyone calls him that? Because he breaks these worlds apart. It is all for him. He tears them to pieces and reaps all of the rewards. Not only that, but he *controls* it. Do you know how much power that means? We were lucky to get out of there alive, and that's all it is. Luck. It won't be long before some hunting party is sent for me, and if you and Rio decide to stick by me, then you die too. Do you understand that?"

Violet's hand clenched at the middle of her chest, fisting into the fabric of her shirt. Over and over, she heard the squelch of the dagger going into Jack's back. She saw the last glimmer of life in those eyes. Her freedom—was freedom even fathomable now?

Anaya glared at her and harshly wiped her own tears. "I'm not leaving, you idiot."

"You'll die."

"I *was* going to die!" Anaya's hair shook with her rage. "My world was turned to shit, and I was eventually going to go down with it! Don't you see my hope?"

Violet got into her face. "Of course, I see your hope! And I want you to keep having that *fucking* hope."

"Well, I want to stay here! That's what I want."

"You *will* die!"

"Fine! I'll die if it means handing you the dagger to kill that twat man." Anaya pushed at Violet's shoulders. "I'm not leaving you. I'm not walking away when shit gets bad. I don't do that."

"I second the small one," a voice croaked.

Rio limped up the hill, dirt plastered to his cheek and a wildflower sticking out of his hair. He held his broken wrist to his chest.

"Jack didn't deserve that." Rio sucked in a breath, holding his tears back. "At this point, I should have died like…forty million times, so if I'm to die again, I hope it is while I stab twat man." Blazing fire, the same as Anaya's, the same Violet felt in her chest, reached Rio's eyes. "We will avenge him. I owe Jack my life." His gaze turned to Violet. "And I owe you my hope."

A silent moment passed before she found her voice. "We need a plan, and a good one."

Anaya's hand came to rest on the hilt of her blade. "Well, the next world is the Worldbreaker's. So one more Sin and then we can infiltrate his." She frowned. "He was awfully mad about us escaping—do you think this world sucks for him?"

"It's Sloth," said Rio. "It is why it took me so long to get up. The sin told me to stay, ignore it all."

"It's peaceful," whispered Violet.

"What a welcoming surprise," Rio said.

Another burst of life, of energy, of hope ran through Violet as she looked at her two friends—her dear, loved friends—and prayed for a future together. For all, or even just them, to find some peace in these worlds or in her own, and hope that after this fight, after this challenge, that they would breathe easy. Finally.

"So, what kind of hell are we bringing?" Anaya's voice was level, her mouth twitching.

They all looked toward each other.

Violet's voice was steady, and in her heart, a piece was picked up and stitched together.

"A wild one."

ACKNOWLEDGEMENTS

Oh my fucking stars.

I can't believe I just did that.

Four years ago I was a lonely girl, in a lonely world, with a lonely, sad little mind, and this story bloomed from all of that. From pain, anxiety, and the basic yearning for adventure. Something that I could escape to amidst the shrouding darkness that surrounded me. Not to be like…deep or anything, but I want to, right here and right now, tell that girl who first had that epiphany of *another* girl waking up in a world that wasn't her own, that we did it. We fucking did it. I'm so damn proud of you, my wonderful, persevering self, for pushing through every word, every rewrite of this story. Look at us. Being all official and shit now.

I first want to thank my incredible friend Alexis. This book would not be in your hands without her. I'm so thankful that you, Alexis, found my little post in a forum and asked to beta read for me, on my first draft at that, and said 'not to brown nose, but this was fire.' That little line, that little sentence, pushed me to where I am right now. Writing the acknowledgements on my debut novel. Alexis, this whole book is really dedicated to you, because you taught me everything I know about self-publishing and on top of that, you gave me the confidence to do it. This process is *hard*. It is exhausting to do it all yourself, but the reward is incredibly worth it. Thank you for believing in me and my story. Thank you for always answering my random texts, for laughing with me about cringe-worthy sexy scenes (I know you're a prude, I won't go into detail) and holding my hand throughout this journey. I owe it all to you. I hope you enjoy the thousands of edible arrangements that are coming your way. (Do you like fun-shaped fruit? I'll text you right now and see.)

I'd like to thank my wonderful editor, Nick Hodgson, for her incredible input and helping me transform it into this. You have been so patient and supportive with me, and this truly manifested into a wonderful story because of you.

Thank you to Nat, the most amazing book cover designer, for being so gracious and excited to work on this little project. I wanted to go for the fall-off-a-bookshelf-and-hit-me-in-the-face cover, and you delivered.

Thank you to my betas: Inyene, Anna, Trinity, and my science fiction & fantasy group. You guys gave me the confidence to keep going, and I am forever grateful.

To Jessica, my proofreader, thank you for your kind words and feedback. It really made this last stretch of writing all the more worth it. I'm sorry that you had to emotionally recover (not, sorry because I high-fived my dad after I read that).

I'm a little looped up on wine right now, but big thank you to all of these guys: CJ, Caitlyn, Tommy, Kirenjot, Jessi, Brian, Maya, Emma, Darnelle, and all the other family 'n friends whom I might be missing (lol). Always my biggest supporters, and those who have been along the ride with me for a while!

To my GE family, you guys have heard me ramble on every morning about my writing when I walked in late with my coffee, and I thank you for letting me ramble, because it gets exhausting when you are talking to yourself like ninety percent of the time.

To my bruhs, Ashton, Ashley, Josie, Shelbylin, Melissa, and of course, Suitcase. You have been the best cheerleaders. I will purchase matching uniforms when I'm a trillionaire.

To the early birds: Lili, Anabela, Finn, and Karin.

Lili, my wonderful Danish soulmate and fish, I fucking love you so much, and I will scream it from any rooftop I find myself on. I'm so thankful for you. You have helped me through so much anxiety, panic attacks, and other shit that I couldn't be more grateful for. I'm so happy we found each other outside Selina's in

Costa Rica, sipping beer and rolling from basic conversation to our deepest traumas within the first fifteen minutes of knowing each other.

Anabela, my Portuguese lover, I can't wait to ride more camels, get lost in medinas, and be horribly sick next to each other again. Cheers to our bad luck with men, and to more alcohol when they talk to us.

Finn, my darling Irishman, you have supported me since I first mentioned I was even working on a book. You ran back to your hostel, no shoes, and hopped straight on a computer to read an excerpt I'd literally sent you twenty minutes before. That right there told me that people care, deeply, even though we might have been tipsy off mid-day mojitos, and are excited to see whatever else I might write. You are golden, my love. I can't wait to crash a stick shift next time I'm in Ireland.

Karin. My Swedish mother. I think you're the only person I've legitimately peed my pants around. After parting the sea of my thoughts and finding a true path with this book, I still never forgot when we were bobbing on our surfboards under the strong Costa Rican sun, and you turned to me, saying, 'Rach, you're a fucking genius.' Because the way you said it, and how much I trust you, made me believe it. I'm here because of that. Because of you. Please send me meatballs from across the sea.

To Meghan—you are my sunshine. I have never been more grateful for spilling out ideas to you and you sitting there, asking me, 'why?' The 'why' enabled me to deepen this story and pave the path for the other books. You are so incredibly intelligent and beautiful, I really wish we were attracted to each other because I think we would make a great power couple. Oh, well. Also, Beau, your godmother loves you so much. I miss your furry cuddles.

Kelsea, my beautiful cousin. I love you. So much. Especially when you figured out how to make my first draft basically an audio book. I should have kept my in-writing notes just for you. Thank you for always texting me in all caps to support me when I was down. I can't wait to move (somewhere) with you.

To my fantastic family; Mom, Dad, and Justin. You guys knew I was straight up weird from the start, and now look how that turned out! Dad—your copy will have all sexy scenes blacked out. Don't worry. Thank you for always supporting me in my wildest dreams, but even more, Dad, thank you for telling me to DO. When I wanted to travel? You held me while I cried, scared to go across the world alone, but told me I needed to DO it. When I wanted to write a book? Your voice was always there, telling me to stop dreaming and DO. Before the first word of this book was written, you inspired me to chase my dreams and you, Mom, told me to never apologize for that. To run wild and carve my own path in this life. I can't wait for all your Facebook friends to read my book. The reactions can go two ways, and I'm ecstatic for both of them.

Damn, this is long. But we have the last one. To my therapist, Susan. You saw me during my lows. You were there during my highs. You have been my rock for so long, and you were the first person I could talk to about all these ideas in my head without feeling judged because, as you know, it took me a very long time to even mention to others that I was writing a book. I'm so grateful to have you in my life, and I can't wait for our next session so I can tell you about all the shit I made my characters do.

Lastly, this is for future me. I hope this book helps pave the way toward a life we've dreamed of. Also, to my future dog, you best believe I'm writing all of this to eventually purchase a giant backyard filled with toys.

And to you, my readers. Thank YOU for picking up this book. For an indie author, it means a lot. I hope you enjoyed the journey, and I'm sorry about the cliffhanger.

Okay, I'm going to start crying now. BYE. See you for the next book. ;)

Milton Keynes UK
Ingram Content Group UK Ltd.
UKHW011808190923
428965UK00004B/479